PRAISE FOR THE AUTHORS
SINFUL AND THEIR NOVELS

New York Times **bestselling author**
LORI FOSTER

"Thoroughly enjoyable . . . fast-paced, and sexy."
—Linda Howard

"Lori Foster writes about real people you fall in love with."
—Stella Cameron

New York Times **bestselling author**
MAGGIE SHAYNE

"Hauntingly beautiful."—Kay Hooper

"Rich, sensual, and bewitching."—*Publishers Weekly*

New York Times **bestselling author**
SUZANNE FORSTER

"A wild, dangerous, erotic thrill ride."—Jayne Ann Krentz

"A stylist who translates sexual tension into sizzle and burn."
—*Los Angeles Times*

KIMBERLY RAYE

"Witty, sexy, and, most importantly, leaves the reader
with a smile . . . Sweetly poignant."
—*The Romance Reader*

Sinful

LORI FOSTER
MAGGIE SHAYNE
SUZANNE FORSTER
KIMBERLY RAYE

BERKLEY SENSATION, NEW YORK

THE BERKLEY PUBLISHING GROUP
Published by the Penguin Group
Penguin Group (USA) Inc.
375 Hudson Street, New York, New York 10014, USA
Penguin Group (Canada), 90 Eglinton Avenue East, Suite 700, Toronto, Ontario M4P 2Y3, Canada
(a division of Pearson Penguin Canada Inc.)
Penguin Books Ltd., 80 Strand, London WC2R 0RL, England
Penguin Group Ireland, 25 St. Stephen's Green, Dublin 2, Ireland (a division of Penguin Books Ltd.)
Penguin Group (Australia), 250 Camberwell Road, Camberwell, Victoria 3124, Australia
(a division of Pearson Australia Group Pty. Ltd.)
Penguin Books India Pvt. Ltd., 11 Community Centre, Panchsheel Park, New Delhi—110 017, India
Penguin Group (NZ), 67 Apollo Drive, Rosedale, North Shore 0632, New Zealand
(a division of Pearson New Zealand Ltd.)
Penguin Books (South Africa) (Pty.) Ltd., 24 Sturdee Avenue, Rosebank, Johannesburg 2196,
South Africa

Penguin Books Ltd., Registered Offices: 80 Strand, London WC2R 0RL, England

Cover photo by Getty Photodisc Royalty-Free Luis Alvarez.
Cover design by George Long.

PRINTING HISTORY
Jove mass-market edition / January 2000
Berkley Sensation trade paperback edition / July 2009

Berkley Sensation trade paperback ISBN: 978-0-425-22668-1

The Library of Congress has cataloged a prior edition under LCCN: 2002559873

PRINTED IN THE UNITED STATES OF AMERICA

10 9 8 7 6 5 4 3 2 1

Contents

Unbuttoning Emmalina

Suzanne Forster

One

Jeff Weston dropped his shorts, stepped out of them, and walked naked and proud to the stack of plush green spa towels. He was just over six feet, reasonably athletic at forty, about twice as broad at the shoulders as the hips, and his butt was still right where it belonged. Behind him. He knew this because he could see his reflection in the mirrors that lined the walls of the Marina Athletic Club locker room. In fact, he could see himself from just about every angle known to physics. Thank God they hadn't put mirrors in the floor yet.

No one would have known by looking at him that he hurt like hell. At least, Jeff liked to think they wouldn't have. He'd wrenched his knee, jammed his shoulder, and had a racketball drilled into the back of his thigh. Excruciating agony was a small price to pay, though. He'd wiped up the court with his friendly rival, Max Gallagher—14–7, 18–3, and 21–0. Life was good.

Jeff grabbed a towel from the stack and knotted it around his waist. "Bring on the steam," he said, grimacing as he forgot and nudged the door open with his bad shoulder.

The wet heat hit him like a tropical storm when he entered the club's labyrinthine steam room. The fog was so thick he couldn't see his own knees. Moments later, having felt his way along the tile wall, stepped on some toes, and probably touched a few things he shouldn't have, Jeff found what he hoped was an isolated alcove and took possession.

He unknotted the towel, snapped it, laid it on the bench, and arranged himself on it like a sacrificial offering. The Warrior's Rest, he thought. This was the way it was supposed to be—the man in his cave, restoring himself for life's battles, isolated from anything that could possibly sap his strength and divert his purpose, like women and—

"Crawled off to lick your wounds, Weston?"

Like women and smart-ass *friends*. Unless Jeff was delirious from the pain, that was Max Gallagher's voice coming from the other bench in the alcove. He should have known Gallagher would find him like this, flaked out and in need of an emergency room trauma team. They'd been fierce competitors since college, when Max had walked away with the senior varsity wrestling trophy. Jeff swore Max rigged the match by bribing the officials with hot stock tips. A high-stakes poker game had put the trophy back on Jeff's mantel—where it belonged—but they'd been wagering hotly on the thing ever since.

Max had it now, under guard, probably. They'd bet on whether or not Max would find the perfect wife by his goal age of forty, and Jeff had smelled the brass being polished. Max was a financial wizard. The guy could make money in his sleep, but he was clueless about women.

As it turned out, they'd both been clueless about Abigail Hastings, Max's shy, devoted secretary. Max had made the mistake of assigning timid little Abbie to find him a wife, and before she was done, she'd seduced him with a striptease, taken advantage of him with a love potion, and bagged him for herself.

Max hadn't been the same since. Lucky stiff.

Except that he still had the damn trophy.

"I was playing with blisters," Max claimed.

"Yeah, right, and I had my eyes closed."

"Try that on the freeway and let me know how it works."

"Accept defeat gracefully and *slink away*."

But Jeff heard a towel snap and knew Max was there to stay. His friend gave out a grunt of pain as he sat down, and Jeff smiled. Life was still good. He closed his eyes, concentrating on the Warrior's Rest until Max rudely interrupted him again.

"Tell me about the woman," he said.

"Which woman?" Jeff had so many of them in his life he couldn't keep track. There was Gretchen, his ex-showgirl assistant, whom he had hired for her incisive mind, although no one believed that. There was Pamela, the supermodel, and Gloria, the architect, both of whom he was dating. There was his mother, Beverly, who was in Palm Beach this time of year, he imagined, or possibly Switzerland, at some rejuvenation clinic.

And of course his great-aunt Hilary, the sharpest old bird he'd ever known, and the only one with the power to zap his forty-year-old, still firm butt. And who undoubtedly would have done so, if she could have hurled lightning bolts from heaven. A lingering illness had claimed her recently, but Jeff still couldn't imagine her gone.

He had a little trouble with the next breath he took. It hurt. And it wasn't the steam heat or the shoulder he'd hit. He didn't like thinking about what had happened to possibly the only human being he'd ever really respected. He'd done good things with Advan Diversified, his great-aunt's holding company, since he took it over a few years ago, although she probably wouldn't have approved of his tactics.

Whereas Max had an instinct for investing, Jeff had an instinct for brokering deals. He lived for that, fed his soul on knowing precisely when to go in for the kill. So Advan was a big holding company now, worth a billion-plus, but Jeff would have given it all up to have his great-aunt back, chewing him out on a regular basis for his "finagling," as she used to call it.

"The *woman*," Max intoned. "The mental case."

"Damn—" Jeff sat up too quickly and touched his forehead. So much for the Warrior's Rest. It felt like he'd been shot between the eyes.

"Something wrong?" Max asked innocently.

"Headaches. Nothing helps anymore."

"You're getting migraines at the mere mention of this woman?"

"They're not migraines. Men don't get migraines. And they have nothing to do with *her*." Jeff had actually managed to get Emmalina Price out of his head for about two seconds, he realized. That was progress.

"Finally met the Immovable Object, Jeff?"

"Let it go." Jeff growled with what he hoped was the menace of a pit bull. If his head hadn't been about to fall off, he would have been nose to nose with Max Gallagher. And if it did fall off, he'd throw it at the bastard.

"I haven't even tried to move her yet," Jeff pointed out. "And when I do, she'll know she's been moved. Trust me. She won't *stop* moving for a month."

He'd been letting his people handle the situation up to now. That was what they got paid the big bucks for. But clearly Jeff had to step in now, and that didn't make him happy.

Max gave another chuckle, obviously loving it that some green-as-grass shopkeeper in Portland, Oregon, had his friend by the cajones. Maybe Max thought it was karma or something, since Jeff had always been the lucky one with women.

Yeah, that's what it was. Max was jealous.

"I hear you've sicced everyone on her but the NATO forces," Max crowed. "I also hear all your emissaries have struck out and even your lawyers can't budge her. Want my advice, Jeffster? Give up. You've met your match."

"Did you happen to hear the woman's a *crackpot*?" Jeff whipped the towel around him and knotted it.

"She puts out a newsletter called 'Modesty Manifesto,'" he informed Max, "and she's threatening to host a radio talk show on old-fashioned virtues. She's single-handedly trying to stamp out sex, for God's sake. She wants to bring back Victorian morals!"

But the real problem was that Emmalina Price was sitting on a parcel of land that Jeff had already promised to a developer. She ran a frilly little gift shop called Priceless from the parlor of the Victorian home where she lived, and she insisted not only that she held the title to the place but that it was originally signed over to her grandmother by Jeff's great-aunt.

Jeff's lawyers had paid her a visit, reviewed the document, and informed her that they believed it to be worthless. They also suggested her shop was in violation of some zoning ordinances. In other words, they put the squeeze on her. Her reaction was to politely invite them to join her for tea, after which she politely sent them on their way. Every team Jeff had dispatched had come back full of tea and cookies, but empty-handed.

Nothing had worked. But Jeff had only begun. There were ways to deal with reluctant parties. Since he was still functioning as landlord until the title dispute was resolved, he could raise the price on Ms. Priceless. *And* alert the building codes people. *Or* the board of health. She was probably serving food without a restaurant license. But Jeff had something else in mind for Ms. Price, who had not yet been exposed to the well-documented Weston charm. Oh, yeah, he had plans for her.

"I'll have her out of there before the dust settles," he muttered, aware that his voice was still doing the pit bull thing. He couldn't even talk right.

"Want to bet?"

Jeff peered through the clouds of steam, searching for the evil gleam in his friend's eye. "How much?"

"You get the Immovable Object to move by, say . . . the end of the month, and I will humbly relinquish the trophy."

"Humbly? How humbly?"

"I'll do a backbend and present it to you with my teeth."

"You're on, Gallagher."

"Good luck," Max said ominously.

"It's a slam dunk," Jeff assured him. "I'll have her out of there *before* the month is over. And who knows, maybe I'll have her out of those Victorian bloomers too."

"That would give her something to write about in her newsletter."

Jeff didn't like the sarcasm in Max's tone. It couldn't be that his friend knew something he didn't, could it?

A telephone shrilled somewhere in the wet steam, and Jeff reached down reflexively, as if he had a pocket. All he got for his trouble was a handful of towel. His life was phones, faxes, pagers, call forwarding, e-mail, and voice mail. He'd never thought to bring a cell phone into the steam room, but apparently someone had found a way to strap one to his bare behind. Jeff would have to look into that. Right after he'd dealt with the mental case.

Two

Jeff wheeled his rental Ferrari Testarossa up in front of the stately old Queen Anne Victorian and ducked down to get a look at the house number. The engine idled at a roar, probably alerting the enemy to his presence, but Jeff had a different concern. He couldn't see around the platinum-blond bombshell in the passenger seat.

"Gretchen, take a deep breath and hold it a minute, would you?" The bombshell was his assistant, and she was busily putting together a prospectus for him on a merger he had in the works.

"This is the right place," she informed him without taking her eyes off the palm-top computer on which she was crunching numbers in the eight figures.

"How do you know?" Jeff wasn't Italian, but he wanted to kiss his fingers to her astonishing efficiency. The woman had a Pentium chip for a brain.

"Number's on the curb. Couldn't miss it as we drove up."

That isn't hair, he decided, studying the blond tendrils that wisped around his assistant's face. Each strand was an antenna, and she was from outer space. Finally he understood. She wasn't one of them. At night she lived in libraries, memorizing the encyclopedias in preparation for taking over the world.

Jeff smiled, turned off the engine, and left the brilliant, bodacious Gretchen to her calculations. He wouldn't have dreamed of messing with that one, no matter what anybody thought. She was *way* indispensable.

He let himself out of the car and took a moment to scan the neighborhood, which no longer bore any resemblance to the family compound where he'd spent summers with his great-aunt Hilly. Now paved streets and a string of mostly abandoned strip malls stood where there'd once been wooded hills, a willow grove, a duck pond, and two nearly identical Queen Anne Victorian houses.

Hilly's passion for all things Queen Anne had inspired her to have a second house built on the land in hopes that her only family, a niece who was Jeff's mother, would spend summers there. But Beverly Chase-Weston couldn't seem to fit Hilly into her busy social schedule, though she'd been more than happy to send her young son to keep his great-aunt company.

Jeff's parents had always lived a jet-set lifestyle. His father was an international financier, and the couple's summers were spent on the Gold Coasts of France and Spain, in the mountain spas of Eastern Europe, the turquoise waters of the tropics, or whatever new playground called to them.

Jeff had always sensed he was being shipped off to Hilly's in much the same way that the family pets were boarded. He only hoped the pets were as happy as he was. He'd loved those summers, and yet one of the first things he'd done after Hilly's death was put her beloved Victorian up for sale. The other house would have been gone too if it weren't for the title dispute. Maybe he thought it would ease his sense of loss to get rid of the property. At any rate, he wanted no reminders.

Even now there was such a heaviness in his chest that he found it hard to breathe. He'd come to hate the feeling, which was why he hadn't been near the compound since Hilly fell ill with a respiratory condition all those years ago and moved to the desert. It was also why he'd turned the property over to one of his people for handling.

Squinting at the brightness, he settled his sunglasses in a mop of chestnut hair that had gone bronze from the sun. He was looking at several city blocks of deserted storefronts, sprinkled among businesses gone to seed. On the side where he'd parked was a hair salon, a chain clothing store, a French cupcake bakery with windows so grimy you couldn't see the goods, and an adult video store. There was also a convenience store on the corner, with some unsavory types loitering about.

Stranded in the midst of it all, protected only by a white picket fence, the other Victorian looked like a dowager in family pearls who'd wandered into a pool hall by mistake. And entrenched inside the green-and-white clapboard was the infidel herself, Miss Emmalina Price, who had to be made to understand that her clock was running a little behind—like a hundred years. This was the turn of the twenty-first century, not the twentieth.

"Gretchen?" He bent over to look in the car, where his assistant was still busily crunching. "Let's go kick some Victorian butt and close this deal. And bring the laptop, would you? Legal will be faxing a contract for Miss Price to sign, and meanwhile I need you to stay on top of Wizard Technologies. Max predicts it will bottom out around sixty, and I want to buy big when it hits."

Jeff had fired his broker, who was constantly churning Jeff's personal portfolio, piling up fees and padding his wallet. So far, Gretchen had proved to be a whiz at online trading, where killer commissions were a thing of the past.

By the time Jeff got around to her side of the car, she was already out, juggling a computer case, cell phone, and the palm-top—plus she had an update for him on the stock. Why did that not surprise him?

Jeff relieved her of the computer case and led the way. He knew you weren't supposed to do that. Most of the women who worked for him wanted it known they could carry their own weight, even when it came to briefcases. But if his load was lighter, why not share hers? He would have done it for a guy.

The house had a great old covered porch, rambling and creaky, with a patch or two of peeling paint, but otherwise it looked well maintained. There were hanging plants everywhere, dripping with vines and flowers. And the window boxes were crammed with crimson begonias and bordered with delicate little blue-and-white clusters.

A sign hanging on the screen door knob said they were open for business, so Jeff let himself and Gretchen in. He wasn't sure what he expected, or if he'd even thought about it, but nothing could have prepared him for the weird fairy-tale charm of the shop. Or for Gretchen's squeal of delight. He wouldn't have thought her capable of a noise like that. She mostly sounded like a recorded message, polite but uninvolved.

"Jeff, just look at this place! It's darling!" She twirled around as if trying to take in everything at once—the white wicker furniture, the antique dolls and flowery tea things. There were filigreed trees of lacy valentines and ribboned picture frames and shoe-shaped carved boxes for holding candy.

A breeze carried the scent of lilacs, and harpsichord music wafted from an old phonograph. But what caught Gretchen's eye was a crystal conservatory the size of a doll house. Despite her spike heels, she was down on her knees, peeking inside at the jungle of greenery. A moment later she rose to her feet and discovered a chiffonier with a drawerful of sheer cuffed gloves and, next to it, a rack of antique dresses.

"I can't believe this shop!" she exclaimed to Jeff. "Isn't it just precious?"

Precious? It looked to him like someone had bombed a chintz

factory. Or maybe a lace factory. Or maybe a pink-satin-heart factory. Guinness, break out your record books, he thought. He wouldn't have bet it was possible to get this much froufrou into a few hundred square feet.

He was certain it wasn't healthy. He'd heard of prison experiments where they assigned violent inmates to pink rooms, which induced calming brain-wave activity but ultimately shriveled their private parts. Jeff clenched a fist, testing his grip strength. Where the hell was Gretchen? He could hear her oohing and aahing, but he'd lost sight of her. He wanted her to remind him to have his testosterone checked when he got back.

Meanwhile, where *was* Miss Price? Where was anyone?

He ventured farther into the room and ducked to avoid a low-hanging birdcage. There weren't any signs of human life in the place. *But somebody had to be taking care of all these birds*. There were wrought iron cages on the floor, hanging from the ceiling, perched on the fireplace mantel. They were everywhere. They were frilly. And they were full of chirping birds.

God help his migraines.

He spotted a countertop with an old-fashioned cash register and a silver desk bell. There were also some postcards on display that looked like early photographs of the house in its original state, before they drained the duck pond and turned the area into the mess it was now.

He picked up a card and studied it. There was a burning sensation in the back of his throat as he returned it to the holder, then reconsidered and stuffed it in his pocket. He hit the silver bell several times, but his *dings* went unanswered. And by that time he'd noticed French doors that revealed what seemed to be a patio. At that moment no one was more desperately in need of fresh air than Jeff Weston.

The patio had the same quirky charm as the parlor. It was done up like a gazebo, but it wasn't pink and she'd gone easy on the frills.

This could work, he thought. There was a redwood patio set where they could talk and—more important—where she would sign the contract.

Meanwhile, he could detox. He'd been exposed to far too much femininity.

He was standing by a trellis of climbing roses, cleansing himself with a deep draught of fresh air, when a woman bustled out to the patio with a large tray of tea things. She'd come out the same door he had, but she obviously knew her way around, and from the way she was dressed, he figured this was the infidel.

He watched her shake out an embroidered white cloth and cover the table, then place a vase of flowers in the center and arrange the place settings. The pot of tea she set out was so fragrant with Ceylonese ginger and apricots that he could taste the flavors from where he stood. One of his holding company's ventures was a tea import business.

I'll have a crate flown in from the Covina Warehouse and delivered while we're here, he thought, looking around for Gretchen. In the year since he'd hired her, he couldn't remember seeing his assistant distracted like this for more than—well, he'd *never* seen her distracted like this. Someone must have kidnapped her.

Perplexed, he turned his attention back to his objective.

The very proper Miss Price had a great lush head of russet hair, done up in one of those hairdos no one wore anymore. A chignon, if he remembered right, and her dress was a sheer, layered thing that fell to her ankles. It buttoned up here and buttoned down there, pretty much everywhere. And it screamed of modesty and old-fashioned virtue.

Pink, of course.

He couldn't see her face, but he already knew the type. She wasn't yet thirty, according to his people, but he'd be surprised if she wasn't old before her time—narrow-lipped, a little pinched around the eyes, and faintly disapproving of anything that didn't meet her vaunted standards. Haughty. Superior. Yeah, he knew the type. They barely tolerated men like him. If Barbara Walters were to ask what kind of fruit Emmalina Price was, he knew what his answer would have been. A prune.

He straightened the hang of his blazer jacket and adjusted his open shirt collar. Short of a morning coat, he probably wouldn't be dressed formally enough to suit her. But the black blazer, snow-white dress shirt, and denim jeans were Jeff Weston's look. Other than the occasional double-breasted pinstripe or tuxedo, he lived in blazers and jeans.

Gretchen had set up the appointment, which meant his objective was expecting him. And since he had to be in and out of here in an hour, he saw no reason not to introduce himself to Miss Price and get the formalities out of the way. What he didn't see was the watering can near his foot. The noise it made when he kicked it sounded like a gunshot.

She whirled and caught herself as she saw the stranger on the patio. Her delicate shoulders bowed inward, and her lips parted with a soundless gasp.

God, she was stunning, he realized. A startled doe. Those huge brown eyes drank him in, made him want to do anything in his power to calm her and make her feel safe. He couldn't see a trace of haughtiness in that sweet face. All he could see was liquid shock. And something told him this wasn't the first time she'd been frightened half out of her wits by a man.

He held up his hands to show her he wasn't hiding anything, that there were no weapons. "I'm sorry," he called to her across the space. "I didn't mean to frighten you." He hoped she could hear his total sincerity. It was the last thing he'd meant to do.

"Who are you?" she asked faintly.

Instead of answering, he cautiously approached the table and pulled out a chair. He'd shocked her badly, and he didn't want their meeting to start this way, on a note of suspicion or distrust.

"Why don't you sit down and catch your breath? Let me pour you some tea," he offered.

She gripped the back of the chair to steady herself—and held her ground. "Please, sir, may I know who you are?"

"Jeff," he said. "I'm Jeff Weston, from Advan Diversified."

"Mr. Weston. Of course." She drew a breath and managed an unsteady smile, but her eyes had changed. They were narrowing.

"I'm here to discuss—" he began.

"I know what you're here for, Mr. Weston. And in that case, perhaps we should *both* sit down and have some tea."

With an elegant sweep of her hand, she presented the table, his chair, and then nodded at him graciously. When he didn't respond, she repeated the entire gesture, even more extravagantly, and this time a dark tendril fell from the magnificent pile of hair into her eyes.

Sit down, you silly fool, she seemed to be saying. I've prepared all this for you.

She was making a miraculous recovery, Jeff noted. And she was all those things he expected—except older than her time and pinched. She was haughty, superior, faintly disapproving, and probably the most strangely enticing creature who'd ever invited him to tea, or just about anything else.

But this was business. He wasn't going home with empty hands and a belly full of tea and cookies.

"I can see that you've gone to a great deal of trouble," he assured her, "and don't think for a moment that I don't appreciate it. But perhaps we could dispense with the tea? Time is limited, and we have things of importance to discuss, don't you agree?"

He was starting to sound like Daniel Day-Lewis in *The Age of Innocence*. Thank God, he didn't look like him, all prissy and waistcoated, although she probably liked that type, a man she could wind around her dainty little pinky.

"I do agree," she said, "which is all the more reason to have some tea and reclaim our composure. Really, Mr. Weston, how can one discuss business otherwise? It's not very civilized, is it?"

She can't be for real, Jeff thought. Who talked that way? He wanted to tell her to take a blue pill, but he understood all too well the implicit rules of negotiating with foreign cultures, and she might as well have been one. You *always* deferred to their social customs.

"After you, Miss Price."

The birds were chirping like a church choir, the flowers were closing in on him, and he was being subliminally emasculated by her pink chiffon dress, but no one could accuse Jeff Weston of not playing the game.

Once they were seated, she poured tea and forced macaroons on him, which he was careful not to eat. After an obligatory sip of the tea, he gently opened the topic of discussion.

"Miss Price, can I be candid with you?"

She very delicately settled her bone china cup in its saucer. "*Can* you? That remains to be seen, Mr. Weston."

Was she correcting his grammar or his morals? A retort burned on the tip of his tongue, but he didn't have time for any more of this polite fencing. He had a private jet waiting for him at the airport and a conference room full of people back in L.A. He needed to wrap up the Raycon merger. Today.

Where the hell was Gretchen?!

"I'm not sure I understand your position," he said, "and I most urgently want to. Since the decision on how to proceed rests with me, it's important that I know exactly what it is you want."

She blinked at him with russet eyelashes long enough to dust furniture, and then she moistened her perfect heart-shaped lips. I'm having tea with a Gibson girl, Jeff thought.

"It's quite simple, Mr. Weston. I want to stay in my home."

He knew better than to follow her down that crooked path and end up the evil landlord. Instead he politely pointed out the obvious. "I couldn't help noticing the neighborhood. It must be tough to run a business of this sort here."

"I manage," she said.

"You don't worry about your safety? It wouldn't surprise me if there were gangs in the area."

Sirens. Jeff could hear sirens outside. With any luck there'd been a robbery at the mini-mart. God must be smiling on Jeff Weston today.

"Mr. Weston, where have you been?" She blinked again, in surprise. "Most certainly there are gangs. My assistant was a gang member, and I'm quite proud of him. He's started going back to school nights since he came to work here."

She hired gang members? Jeff tried another tack.

"Miss Price, trust me, I wouldn't be here, I wouldn't be persisting in any of this, if I didn't believe that everybody wins if this deal goes through. The developer has his industrial park, the city has its greenbelt, and you—"

He paused for effect. "You have a thriving business . . . *somewhere else*. Anywhere else," he said pointedly. "Isn't there somewhere you've dreamed of carrying out your life's work? San Francisco? Manhattan? Beverly Hills, maybe a 90210 zip code?"

"Are you offering to relocate my shop, Mr. Weston?"

He nodded. "I'm offering that. I'm also offering to double whatever sum my lawyers mentioned, to throw a grand opening party, and to introduce you to the cream of L.A., or wherever you choose to go. We want you to be happy, Miss Price."

"But I am happy, Mr. Weston. Right here. I also fail to see why the industrial park, the greenbelt, *and* my shop can't all peacefully coexist?"

Jeff drew a long, hot breath. "The developer doesn't want you to peacefully coexist within his industrial park. It's going to be steel, glass, and concrete. Mostly steel. And this place is . . . frilly."

"Where did this developer of yours get the idea that everything has to look alike, I wonder? And if he's truly concerned, perhaps he could sprinkle a little wrought iron about. That's quite frilly, isn't it?"

She graced him with a superior smile and delicately adjusted the sleeves of her dress. Everything she did was delicate, except when she shredded you to coleslaw with that rapier tongue of hers.

Jeff was about to abandon the sensitive approach in favor of the evil landlord when his assistant's head popped in the doorway.

"Oh, there you are," Gretchen said with a brilliant smile.

"Where have you been?" he asked, careful to keep any hint of annoyance out of his voice. There was a needlepoint pillow in the chair next to him that said, GOOD MANNERS AVOID NEEDLESS VEXATION.

"Sorry!" Gretchen shrugged apologetically. "It's just that I found the sweetest outfit, and I had to try it on."

"Sweetest outfit?"

"Yes! They sell clothes here, too," she reminded him. "Want to see what I found?"

"Most assuredly," he said dryly.

Gretchen danced into the doorway, and Jeff groaned inwardly. She was wearing a corset that Victoria's Secret wouldn't have allowed in its catalog. It was whorehouse red and cranked so tight at the waist that Gretchen could have done a Dolly Parton imitation. There was way too much girl or way too little corset. Probably both.

"Isn't it just adorable?" she wanted to know. "I could wear it with my black pinstripe jacket, although not to the office, of course."

He thought he heard a haughty sniff, but the proper Miss Price seemed more amused than anything else.

"At least your assistant appreciates what I'm doing here," she pointed out. "Although I can't imagine that Queen Victoria intended for her corsets to be worn as bustiers."

Gretchen dashed off to put her clothes back on, while Jeff made a halfhearted attempt to explain her behavior. "My assistant probably works too hard," he said. "She's never like this. She's very efficient."

"I'm sure you work her very hard. Quite the slave driver, I would expect."

His hostess had taken it upon herself to settle back and scrutinize him, but her chilly grace didn't completely conceal the dry tone or the innuendo in her expression.

The very proper Miss Price was not talking about the same kind of work he was, Jeff realized. Now there was an idea with possibilities he would love to explore. Was there a hint of vixen lurking beneath that virtuous exterior?

His eyes brushed over her prim pose, then collided with her curious gaze. Jeff felt a stirring inside that told him his jeans were in danger of getting crowded. Prim or not, she could hold her own in a staredown.

"A man likes initiative in his slaves," he murmured.

"And good teeth?" Was her quick rejoinder.

They were just getting back to business when a giant shaggy dog of a kid shambled onto the patio. His hair was cropped short, but his jeans and T-shirt were big enough for the whole gang he probably belonged to. This must be the assistant, Jeff thought.

His hostess had already risen to introduce their visitor.

"Mr. Weston, I'd like you to meet Spike," she said. "He helps in the shop, but I may have neglected to mention that he's also my foster son. Spike is a wonderful young man."

Jeff nodded in response to the wonderful young man's mumbled greeting. She *adopted* gang members?

No sooner had Spike shambled out to man the cash register than Gretchen reappeared. She was dressed this time, but she had a couple of slender leather-bound books in her hand.

"Look what else I found," she said. "It's Victorian erotica! There's a whole collection of it inside—*My Secret Life, Birch in the Boudoir*. This one's called *A Man with a Maid*.

"Do you want to hear a passage?" she asked with a grin looking at him innocently.

Jeff gave her a quick headshake no, definitely not, and glanced at Miss Price. But if he'd expected flustered, he was in for a surprise. There wasn't a hint of embarrassment in her cool, limpid gaze. Maybe her eyelashes drooped just a tiny bit as she returned his inquiring look.

"The collection is merely an attempt to be true to the period," she informed him. "The books are antiques, as is much of the furniture, china, and glassware in my shop."

Now Jeff found himself studying her, wondering about the body hidden under all that pink fluff, and whether it had ever strained under a skilled touch or tightened and trembled with passion. He dismissed the idea as impossible. There must be a hundred buttons on that dress of hers. What man had that kind of time?

Speaking of which. He checked his watch and rose from the chair. "Gretchen, did the fax from Legal ever come in? I'd like Miss Price to have a look at it."

Fortunately Gretchen had the document ready and marked with an *X* where the signature went. She was coming to her senses, Jeff thought. Maybe it was the fresh air on the patio. That seemed to have helped him too.

Jeff put the document in front of his hostess, supplied her with a pen, and showed her exactly where to sign.

"Something wrong?" he asked when she hesitated.

She took a deep breath and looked up at him, her dark eyes troubled and stormy. "Yes, there is something wrong. It's all wrong."

"What's all wrong? You don't like the deal?"

"Mr. Weston, may I be candid with you?" She sat forward, barely waiting for him to nod before she proceeded to be candid. Brutally candid.

"I have no intention of making a deal with Advan Diversified—today, tomorrow, *ever*. I would sooner eat my own young, sir."

It was a defining moment for Jeff Weston. He prided himself on having no outward reaction. He didn't flinch, didn't wince, jerk, or twitch. His jaw didn't lock and grind itself into dust, and no smoke steamed out of his ears. But inside he was a pinball machine of reactions. The little silver ball that was his pulse was wildly banging against everything it hit.

He had just been politely kicked where it hurt the most. He should have been gasping, but his strongest impulse was to laugh. Not at her but at himself, at the situation and how drastically he'd underestimated it. The only other errant thought that hit him as he stood there immobilized and pinging inside was that he no longer had a headache. Despite chirruping birds, harpsichord music, and drugged tea, despite everything, the claw hammers that were constantly trying to remodel his brain were gone.

Three

Emmalina Price dutifully went from window to window, pulling down the tasseled silk shades. Outside, the roseate sunset was deepening to purple. Night was falling, and her childhood fears of the dark were beginning to stir. They'd left her at peace for years, but now that she was faced with the prospect of losing her home—her haven—they'd awakened again, gasping, like a child with night terrors.

This beautiful old Victorian relic was the only place she'd ever felt safe. Much of her early childhood had been spent on the run, one step ahead of the danger that lived mostly in the mind of her mentally disturbed mother. Emmalina was six before her grandmother finally tracked down her daughter, had her confined for treatment, and brought her only grandchild back here. Six years old before Emmalina knew what safety felt like. What love felt like.

And tonight, once she had the shades down and the house secured, she would feel that way again. It had become a ritual, like afternoon tea or a musical interlude after dinner. Very shortly the back parlor, which she preferred to call the Music Room, would be warmed and softened by the light of the fireplace, and she would be sitting at the piano, playing a piece that would elevate and soothe the spirit at the same time . . . perhaps a Schubert concerto tonight.

"Yo, Emmalina!"

"Easy, Spike," she cautioned as he loped into the room from the kitchen, where he'd been cleaning up after dinner. It was one of the chores he was responsible for, along with helping out in the shop.

"I didn't break anything tonight," he said, grinning.

Emmalina drew the last shade and smiled at her charge. "The china must be celebrating."

He gave her a thumbs-up, and the silver ring that pierced his eyebrow nodded at her. She wondered what Jeff Weston had thought of her young work-in-progress, given the partially shaved head and the baggy, low-rider jeans that Spike lived in. Weston was probably questioning the propriety of the situation, just as she'd questioned his with Gretchen, although it was hardly the same thing.

Emmalina had broken up a street fight in front of her shop four years ago. Spike had been a scrawny, scratchy-voiced adolescent then, and he'd been attacked by a group of bullies. She'd run them off with the hose and some impressive bellowing, telling herself it was perfectly proper for a lady to bellow when someone was in danger.

Spike had turned out to be a runaway whose parents didn't want him, and Emmalina had not only taken him in, she'd gone through the steps to become a foster parent. She was actually closer to his age than she would have been to his mother's, but she felt a tremendous pride in the way he'd turned out. He was now a strapping six three, and still growing. Naturally the bullies gave him a wide berth these days.

"I was just about to play something." She walked to the old spinet upright and took off one of her prize possessions, an antique piano cover in alabaster sateen with macrame lace around the edges.

"Cool," Spike said. "I could go for some Mozart."

Laughter bubbled out of her. Spike had that effect. Like no one else, he could make her forget her rather rigid ways and just laugh out loud. It was as if he knew the real Emmalina, the frightened child who'd embraced another era's rules and traditions because they gave her safety and structure, as well as something to believe in.

"*A Little Night Music*?" she suggested, knowing he liked it.

"Rock me, shock me," he said.

Emmalina sat down and made quite a show of flexing her fingers. It was hard to shock Spike, but she was in a rare mood this evening, probably as a result of speaking her mind. It might all come crashing down tomorrow, but for the moment she felt strangely empowered, and as she started to play, the energy seemed to flow out her hands. Her fingers were unusually nimble, seeking the distraction of the challenging runs and chording.

Spike flashed her another thumbs-up as she finished. She smiled and rose from the bench, pretending to curtsy. But something other than Mozart had crept into her thoughts as she played.

"What did you think?" she asked him.

"Of the music?"

"No, of our visitor today—Mr. Weston."

Spike shrugged his shoulders. "That's easy. I think he's got the hots for you."

"Heavens to mercy, why? You think he's attracted to women who reject him and everything he stands for?"

"No, because of the way he was looking at you, like he wanted to run amuck in your buttons."

"My . . . buttons?" Emmalina fingered the ones at her throat nervously. She had been asking how Spike had sized Weston up as an adversary, and what reprehensible thing he thought Weston might try next. But Spike was suggesting that her mortal enemy wanted to run amuck in something besides her real estate!

The mother-of-pearl buttons felt cool and slick and decidedly round to the touch, she realized. She wouldn't have described them as sensuous exactly, but—. No, that was silly. What Spike was suggesting wasn't possible. Emmalina had seen no signs of any such thing. Weston was there to get his deal signed. If he'd been curious about her buttons, it was probably because he was wondering if they could be made tight enough to strangle her.

"He could never be attracted to someone like me," she said. *And she would certainly never be attracted to someone like him.* He was all surface and no depth. A wading pool. One had only to consider his bombshell assistant, his Chicklet-size cell phone, and his red phallic symbol of a car to know that.

No, they were Tweety and Sylvester, she and Mr. Weston. They could never be attracted to each other. It was biologically impossible. Against the laws of nature.

Having assured herself of that, she felt better. But for some reason she had a little difficulty getting the piano cover back where it should be, on the piano. It kept sliding every which way. Finally Spike came to her rescue, holding one side while she arranged the other. But the knowing smirk on his face annoyed her.

"He does not have the hots for me." She dismissed the idea with a toss of her head. "And even if he did, he had better smolder from a safe distance, because if he darkens my doorstep again, I'll—"

Actually, there were many things she would like to do to Mr. Weston, but nothing that could be mentioned in the presence of a young and impressionable person like her charge.

"You could always hose him down," Spike suggested with a hopeful grin.

"I've got her," Jeff whispered, hardly able to believe his good luck. "Damn, have I got her! She's *mine.*"

His hoot of laughter broke the solemn quiet of the county

courthouse records room. Jeff pushed back the chair and stood up so suddenly it nearly toppled over. One of the clerks shushed him before he realized he was causing a disturbance. But he really couldn't believe his eyes—or this incredible stroke of luck.

If you want something done right, *do it yourself*, he thought. That ought to be the Fifteenth Amendment to the Constitution. Delegating had gotten him into this mess. His staff had blown it, and now even Gretchen couldn't be trusted with anything but the simplest tasks. Either she'd overexposed herself to girlie pink stuff in the shop, or she'd cut off her circulation with that corset because there appeared to be some brain damage.

At any rate, Jeff had been forced to push back the Raycon deal and spend the morning in the courthouse, conducting his own personal title search. Just seconds ago he'd hit pay dirt.

Emmalina Price had sequestered herself in the wrong house. Based on the description in the document he was looking at, her grandmother had been given legal title to the second house that Hilly had built on the property, the Victorian in the willow grove. But Emmalina was in his great-aunt's house, the Queen Anne that Hilly had built for herself, the one by the duck pond.

Even Jeff hadn't realized that the embattled house he was looking at yesterday was actually Hilly's place. It had been almost thirty years since he'd been there, and without the distinguishing landmarks, the two places might as well have been identical twins. The confusion was complicated by the fact that the second Victorian was now gone. It had been sold as Hilly's house by mistake, and since torn down to make way for the new industrial park.

It was the permanently affixed porch swing that had given Jeff the clue. He'd vaguely remembered that the second Victorian didn't have a swing. His other vague memory was of the caretaker his great-aunt had hired all those years ago, a Mrs. Dorothea Price. He'd seen the woman once or twice before he'd been sent off to boarding school in Europe, ending his summers with Hilly, but he knew nothing about Hilly having given her any property or how the switch in residences had been made. If it had occurred after Hilly's move to the desert and before the current Miss Price came to live there, then there was a possibility she didn't know anything about it either.

Jeff wasn't really surprised that none of his people had caught the discrepancy. He'd only caught it himself because he was intimately familiar with the property. But the fact remained that Miss Emmalina Price did not own the house she was in, and the house she did own was long gone.

A short time later he was in the Ferrari, on his way back to the motel. He'd just spoken with his legal team, who already had copies of the title documents, and who'd promised to scour the real estate codes and get back to him. No matter who had made the mistake, Miss Price would have to be compensated for the house that was sold, they'd informed him, but they didn't believe she had any legal claim to the one she was in.

Immovable Object? Jeff snorted. Her pink butt was outta there. It was only a question of how much time he was willing to give her and how magnanimous he was feeling at the moment of reckoning. Twenty-four hours? Twelve? Before the ink dried?

He spanked the dashboard with a crack of his palm. It was good to win, especially against someone who loathed the very ground you walked on. She'd rather eat her own young?

She would be eating something, he vowed as he wheeled into the gravel lot of the motel and pulled up to his unit. If he'd known they were going to be staying more than a day, he would have had Gretchen get them a hotel with room service, but this place had been close, and therefore convenient.

Jeff was barely settled in his room before Gretchen tapped on the door and popped her head in. She wasn't grinning, squealing, *or* wearing a corset, which encouraged him. In fact, her soft-gray sweater set and skirt looked like the pre–Priceless boutique Gretchen. And when he'd left this morning, she'd been quietly at work on something in her room—with luck it was the prospectus he was waiting for.

"How'd it go?" she asked.

"She's mine, Gretchen," he said with a perfect poker face. "Mine to do with as I wish. I hold in my possession the straw that will break Miss Price's back."

Gretchen raised an eyebrow, back to her old cool self. "And how did that happen?" she asked, letting herself into the room.

He tilted back in the chair and put his feet up on the table, then shook down the legs of his jeans. After explaining what he'd discovered and the legal team's reaction to it, he asked Gretchen to have a seat while he dictated some changes to the agreement Miss Price would be signing.

"Strike any reference to relocating her shop to the dream city of her choice," he said. "That's not going to happen. And there won't be any A-list grand opening parties, either. She gets the money, but that's it."

"I'll take care of it," Gretchen said when he'd finished. She tucked her pen behind her ear and closed the notebook with a flick of her finger. "Should I make you an appointment with her for this afternoon? Or are you going to let Legal handle it?"

"Nobody gets to *handle* Emmalina Price but Jeff Weston."

Jeff's voice had dropped to a predatory growl. He was looking forward to this. He couldn't imagine anybody looking forward to a confrontation more. Except maybe Gretchen, who'd brightened visibly at his declaration of war.

"Great," she said. "When do we go? I've been wanting to check out those cute little crocheted doilies—you know, the handmade ones that look like coasters? I was thinking how adorable they'd be as brassiere cups. All you'd have to do is attach some string. And now that I'm thinking about it, sew a couple of doilies together and you've got your matching panties, too! I probably ought to buy a crate of them."

A relapse, Jeff decided. He had to get her back to L.A., and meanwhile, he couldn't let her near the shop.

"Gretchen, I need you on other things," he told her firmly. "Like tracking the stocks we talked about and finishing up that prospectus. You remember the merger? I'm down to the wire on that one."

There must be something wrong with me, Jeff thought. There's a beautiful woman in my motel room, talking about underwear made out of lace doilies, and I wish she would go away and return my coolly efficient assistant to me.

The chair tilted precariously, straining to hold him as he tipped back and stared at the stucco ceiling. But the answers weren't up there, hiding among the bubbly white cracks, and as he rubbed his forehead, he realized something even more suspicious. He was still headache-free. He hadn't had a migraine since he left L.A. This must be some kind of record.

Emmalina Price stood proudly defiant in her white-linen duster and her straw sunbonnet, a fat green garden hose at the ready.

"Whatever are you doing here, Mr. Weston?" she queried from the safety of a flower-covered arbor, where she was surrounded by the fruits of her labor—bowers of ruffly pink camellias, newly budding lilacs, and a dangerous array of gardening tools.

"I need to talk to you," Jeff called back. He was outside the white picket fence that bordered the house. It seemed the safest course, since he wasn't sure what she intended to do with the hose that was strangling in her delicate grip.

"I said everything I had to say yesterday."

"But I didn't. We have to talk."

"Have you changed your mind about forcing me from my home?"

"No, Miss Price, I haven't."

"Then you leave me no choice, sir, but to resort to force as well!" She stomped to the porch, dragging the hose with her, and cranked the spigot on full force.

"Leave my property immediately!" she warned.

"It's not your property—" Jeff dodged one blast of water after another as he searched for the legal documents in his briefcase. "I have proof!"

He brandished a copy of the title, only to see it get drilled with water. His head got soaked next, while he was bent over, shoving the precious paper into the safety of his jacket. Miss Price was starting to vex him.

"Turn the damn thing off!" he shouted.

Hunkering down like a commando, he tossed his briefcase over the fence, vaulted the barrier himself, and ducked the stinging spray until he got to her.

"Give that to me." He yanked the hose from her and flung it away, swearing under his breath with every twist of the spigot as he shut the water off. To her credit, she didn't run screaming. But maybe she should have. He'd never wanted to shake anybody's teeth loose so badly in his life.

Instead he shook the water from his hair.

"Come here," he said, giving her linen duster a tug. He wanted her out of range of the gardening tools. When she tugged back, he clamped his hands on her arms and hauled her off into the bright sunshine. The evil landlord wasn't going to catch pneumonia while he evicted the trembling tenant, thank you.

"You're in the *wrong* house, Miss Price."

The tone of his voice made her look up at him.

"What do you mean?"

He ripped the sopping document out of his jacket pocket and handed it to her. "Read the description, where it says the house is a 'three-bedroom Queen Anne Victorian, situated in a grove of willow trees.' Read it and weep, as they say. There isn't—and has never been—a willow tree anywhere near this place."

She was reading, but her hands weren't trembling yet, he noticed. God, how he wanted the satisfaction of seeing her unravel before his eyes, inside and out. He wanted her gasping in shock and overcome by her emotions just like a character in one of the Victorian erotic novels Gretchen had found. He'd never wanted that before like he wanted it now. Never wanted it from anyone like he did from her.

"Start packing, Miss Price," he said quietly. "My attorneys will be in touch with you."

When she looked up at him, her face was shock-white, and the second of pleasure he took from it evaporated like steam.

She held out the title, but nothing came past her quavering lips. She couldn't speak, and finally she couldn't look at him any longer. He imagined her crumbling inside, but somehow she still managed to keep her hand steady.

"You can keep that," he said. "I have copies."

She nodded, defeat written into her heavy response, and Jeff felt an instant pang. There was nothing more to be done here, he realized. He'd given her the bad news, and she'd accepted it with more grace than he would have expected. He wondered if she had known this was the wrong house. Maybe that made him feel a little less guilty, but not much.

He would forgo giving her the revised agreement now. There was no point in salting the wound—his attorneys could take care of the details, including the necessary signatures.

"We're done, then," he said, "unless there's something you want to say." But she'd already turned away and was walking back toward the arbor.

He did the same, heading for his car.

Ironically, he pulled out a postcard instead of car keys when he reached into his pants pocket. Bright sunlight glinted off the glossy finish, creating a strange illusion. As he stopped and stared at the proud old house with its miles of covered porch, he could almost see a small mop-haired boy in the porch swing, huddled next to an older woman in a linen duster, not unlike the one Emmalina Price was wearing today. The woman was consoling him as he tremulously told her the saga of how Gingerbread, the cat, had scratched him.

The sweet pain of that memory made Jeff want to crumple the card and toss it away. It was a different porch he'd sat on when he was five years old and he and his beloved great-aunt Hilly had swung away his childhood wounds, but the postcard made him realize that, one by one, he was cutting off all links to his past. The house in the postcard was already gone. The one behind him soon would be. How long before there was nothing left?

He turned and saw her clutching at the arbor, which was almost as fragile as she was.

"Miss Price—"

"Please go," she whispered. "Please."

Jeff's heart twisted. This was the devastation he'd wanted to see, and now, God, he couldn't imagine why. Worse, he'd brought it about, and there was nothing he could do. He knew she didn't want him seeing her like this, and he hated the idea of humiliating her any further. All he'd wanted was to walk away from this, but he didn't know how to do that now.

"If there's anything I can—"

"Nothing," she assured him, struggling to gather herself together. "I'll be gone tomorrow."

"Gone where?"

Her straw hat had fallen to the ground, and when she shook her head, dark curls came loose. "Just give me until then, please. There's a lot to pack, and I have no idea where I'm going yet."

As Jeff stared at this sad, charming postcard of a woman crumpled against an arbor, already grieving, he was beginning to understand what had to be done. The notion was too vague to put into words at this point, and he had no clear sense of whether she would approve, but fortunately he had all the bargaining power.

"I can't give you until tomorrow, Miss Price," he said. "You have to be out tonight. And I know exactly where you're going."

Four

It was another *Ripley's Believe It or Not* moment for Jeff Weston. Emmalina Price was sitting next to him in the first-class section of the Boeing 757, dressed like a Gibson girl and crocheting doilies. He would never have believed she actually wore—or did—that stuff in public if he hadn't seen it for himself.

His jaw had dropped when she'd emerged with her entourage of one from the limo Jeff had sent for her. She'd insisted on bringing Spike, the Pierced One, along on the trip to L.A., and Jeff had instantly agreed. He would have agreed to bringing the birds to get her out of the Victorian and into the real world. He'd even sent his plane back so that he could personally escort her on the flight, and he'd promised if she didn't like the "angels" in his city, he would do everything he could to salvage her precious house.

That had seemed to satisfy her. And left him wondering what in the *hell* he was doing. He never made such concessions for a deal, especially when he didn't have to. Her house was already his. And she was too.

He owned the woman and her busy little hands.

She'd been crocheting since the plane took off. Jeff didn't know any women who crocheted. They went to day spas, ate lunch, shopped, and/or had big careers. This one next to him had slowed her flashing needles only long enough to make sure Spike and Gretchen were comfortable in the row behind them. Poor Spike, Jeff thought. But then, who wouldn't have looked dazed and confused sitting next to Gretchen?

Or Jeff Weston, sitting next to Hello, Dolly herself.

Now, however, Emmalina deigned to put her handiwork down and look over at him. Her brown eyes were so wide with wonder that they made him question whether she'd ever been on an airplane before. He didn't inquire, however. She'd already put him on notice that it was bad manners to inquire *unnecessarily* into the private lives of others.

"What exactly is it we're doing on this plane, Mr. Weston?"

It was time to explain his mission of mercy, and he didn't know how, even to himself. There was no evidence that Jeff had ever had an altruistic bone in his body, but he'd decided to save Miss Emmalina Price from her self-imposed exile whether she wanted saving or not. Of course, it couldn't hurt his deal with the developer to get her out of there, either. And it was a well-known fact that he'd do just about anything to win a bet with Max. Maybe that explained it—the bet with Max.

"Have you ever heard of English-immersion classes?" he asked her. "And now that we're traveling together, don't you think we could use first names?"

She ignored the last reference. "I'm not entirely cut off from modern civilization, *Mr.* Weston. Of course, I know what English immersion is, although I'm not certain I approve of it. Non-English-speaking students are placed in classes where only English is spoken, yes?"

"Bingo," he said with a weary smile. God, he did have his work cut out for him. Even basic communication with this woman was like climbing Everest.

"And what does that have to do with me?" she asked.

"Everything, *Emmalina*. You can consider this trip a reality-immersion class. Your own personal reality-immersion class. And lesson number one? In the real world people call each other by their first names. Mine's Jeff. Say it, Emmalina. Say 'Jeff.'"

She shuddered as if he'd asked her to run naked up and down the aisles. And he might. He just might.

"Jeff," she bit out softly, then touched her mouth in surprise.

"There. Didn't kill you, did it?"

"I'm not at all sure I can do it again."

"You'll do it again," he said. "It'll be rolling off your tongue like butter. Jeff, Jeff, Jeff."

"Oh, I hope not," she whispered.

His smile was quickly disguised as a yawn. She was so damn serious about everything. And those ironclad opinions of hers. She had a rule for everything in life, including how to breathe. "One breathes from the diaphragm, with regularity and ease. You're breathing from your shoulders, Mr. Weston."

He didn't know where he was breathing from now. It felt like a certain sphincter musc—

"Champagne?" A flight attendant hovered with a trayful of flutes. Jeff took two of them, and to his surprise Emmalina thanked him for hers and downed a good bit of it in one slug. Didn't seem to be any rules for swigging champagne.

"I think I might be a nervous flyer," she explained. "The crocheting helps, too."

She'd picked up her needles again. He couldn't tell what she was working on, but it didn't look like a bra cup. Too bad, he thought, trying to imagine white lace doilies hugging the various parts of a body that appeared to be made of some rather supple curves.

She was wearing a fitted jacket that buttoned up the front, cinched tight at the waist, and flared slightly over a long, straight skirt. It was the color of wine, a deep, saturated claret that made her skin look like milk and set her dark hair aflame. It was a striking outfit that was designed to reveal inviting feminine contours to the wandering male eye, whether she knew it or not.

If he didn't stop his eye from wandering, he was going to need vision correction. He'd told himself his goal was to save her, but that didn't explain his abject fascination with her strange little ways. He couldn't remember being this fixated on anything, including a mega deal. God knew, he kept forgetting about the Raycon merger.

Emmalina Price was a mystery and he wanted to solve her.

As he watched her fingers deftly turn white yarn into snowflakes, he was revisited by the thought of seeing those same fingers tremble and lose control. What it did to his stomach, that thought—there wasn't a roller-coaster ride that could compare.

But it was not to be. Gretchen's voice rang out from behind him.

"Jeff! Wizard Technologies just dropped to the mid-sixties."

Jeff grabbed a pencil and began to make some calculations. "Okay, let's buy," he said. He was about to tell her how much when Emmalina's hand touched his arm. She shook her head.

"Something wrong?" he asked.

"It hasn't hit bottom yet."

"Wizard? How do you know?"

"I just happen to belong to a small investors' group that meets once a week. Over tea, of course," she said with a smart little smile—and then went on to give him the benefit of her unsolicited investment advice.

"We like Wizard's double-digit profit margins, but we're not impressed with the prospects for growth in the microprocessor industry, especially with the boom of low-cost PCs, which has created a market for cloned chips, you know. And then there's the excess chip inventory.

"We do a lot of dollar-cost averaging," she informed him, "and don't mind a shaky market at all, as a matter of fact. But this would not be a good time to buy Wizard Technologies."

Jeff gazed into her somber eyes, searched her luminous features, and couldn't believe what he was hearing. Max had said she was a mental case. He'd also said that the microprocessor giant would rebound like Dennis Rodman in his prime.

"We're going to *buy*, Gretchen," he called back. "We're going to buy big."

Emmalina simply shrugged and resumed her crocheting.

Once Jeff had finished his business with Gretchen, he flagged down the attendant for more champagne. "Just leave us the bottle," he told her. The roller-coaster sensation in his stomach had turned serious. Maybe he was a nervous flyer too.

The champagne didn't help all that much, and as he glanced over at Emmalina, absorbed in her task, he marveled at the woman's composure. He refused to take up crocheting, though.

He shifted to stretch his legs, and his foot hit something that reminded him this poker game was rigged. Rigged, and he held all the aces. He smiled. It was good to win.

"Tell me about your erotica collection," he said.

She didn't miss a stitch. "It's not *my* collection. It's an important part of the Victorian era, particularly in how it illuminates the repression of the times. We pride ourselves on authenticity at Priceless."

"We do?" he echoed sardonically.

He bent and drew a book from his briefcase, which was still drying out from yesterday's soaking.

"Interesting title," he said. "*Eveline: The Adventures of a Young Lady of Quality Who Was Never Found Out*. Also interesting that the book has a stamp that says it's from the personal library of Emmalina Price, and a *current* copyright date. Doesn't sound like an antique to me."

Emmalina didn't have to look at the copyright. She knew what it was. The book was originally released in 1904, and this was a reissue by a publisher of classic erotic literature. No, it wasn't an antique. And yes, it was hers.

"And where did you get that?" she asked, all very cool about it, when in fact she wanted to die.

"Gretchen bought several books along with the corset, remember? This one must be pretty good. Every other page is dog-eared, and she wants it back when I'm done with it."

He began to leaf through it, and Emmalina prayed he wasn't going to start reading aloud. Eveline was a precocious young woman who dreamed of erotic adventures and unbridled passion, but once awakened to her innermost desires, she lost all control. What she desired more than life, poor thing, was the handsome devil of an insufferable cad who'd awakened her.

No, she couldn't let him read that. He would think—

He bent toward her, lowered his voice, and began to read a passage. "'As for me, I dreamed simply of a dark-haired man bending over me to brush my lips with his burning red mouth, and I woke up overwhelmed, palpitating and happier than I had ever imagined I could possibly be.'"

She blinked at him in flushed confusion. "Why, that isn't Eveline at all. That's *Leila*, by George Sand."

"You *do* know your erotica, Miss Price." He showed her a bookmark with the George Sand passage, which must also have come from the store. She was going to have to inventory the stock the moment she got back.

"I thought Eveline was a little too raunchy to read in public." Grinning wickedly, he continued to leaf through the book and silently read passages. "Although I did like that part about the rocking horse that was too small for her. Oh, and the five fine-pointed feathers—remember them?"

Just when she'd begun to think he wasn't a totally reprehensible human being. The feathers were used on poor dear Eveline while she was sprawled on a red-velvet settee, quite naked and helpless against the mindless pleasure.

"None of it was meant to be read in public, Mr. Weston," she whispered.

"Jeff," he said.

She glared at him defiantly, and their eyes clashed in some resounding way that left her breathless. If the look had had a sound, it would have been a loud one, and Emmalina didn't like loud things. She didn't like the way her heart was palpitating, either. It might have made Leila happy, but it wasn't working for her.

"This is unbearable," she said under her breath. "I can't allow it."

"Maybe you should undo some of those buttons," he remarked. "It's a little warm in here."

It was—thanks to him, the insufferable cad of a bounder. She was warm and steamy all over, and her dress felt suffocatingly tight, but at least she was able to resist the urge to fan herself or pluck at her clothing. *Unbuttoning had never entered her mind.*

It was probably just the champagne, she told herself. Surely this couldn't be what Spike had meant by having the "hots," because if it was . . . then she would just as soon *never* have them again.

"My rules for living are very simple," Jeff said. "I want you to enjoy yourself while you're here, even if it kills you."

"That shouldn't be too difficult." Mesmerized by the view of the city at night, Emmalina stood at one corner of the terrace of his tower apartment. All she could see wherever she looked was twinkling lights, an ocean of them. It looked like the entire world had been decorated with strings of Christmas-tree lights.

"The enjoying part," she added.

They were on the thirtieth floor of the building, and other than the distant swish of traffic, nothing of the brilliant activity below them could be heard. It was a startlingly quiet night. Jeff had already given everyone a quick tour of the place, after which Spike had opted to play with the high-tech gadgets in Jeff's media room. And Gretchen had gone home to her own apartment.

That was when Jeff had suggested that Emmalina might like to see the view. And now he was standing away from her, at the other end of the terrace with a snifter of cognac in his hand. He'd offered her one, but she would only have spilled it. There was too much to take in.

His apartment was beautiful to behold. It was classic and elegant, with beige-and-black-striped club chairs, low tables, and luscious animal-print ottomans that served as backless benches. She'd never seen anything quite so masculine and sensuous, yet understated.

The artwork was breathtaking too. A Greek nude in black marble was placed by the fireplace, and matching Baccarat crystal candlesticks sat on the credenza behind the sofa.

He'd gone up a bit in her estimation when she'd seen his home. Not because of the money but because of the restraint.

"We play it by ear around here," he told her. "Breakfast is whenever you want it. Call down to the kitchen and have it brought up to your room if you'd like. Lunch is at one in the small dining room, then drinks at four in the library, and if anyone's still interested, dinner's around eight.

"It's all quite civilized, Miss Price," he said with an easy smile. "Except that I'm afraid you're going to have to live without afternoon tea."

"I don't think I can," she said in all seriousness.

He took a swallow of his cognac, and a hissing sound issued from his throat. "Bite the bullet," he said huskily.

"But surely you have tea bags in the kitchen. And I could whip up some scones."

"Emmalina, no tea while you're here."

"You mean that?" The hush in her voice was something close to shock.

"I do. Cold turkey."

"But I see no reason— Why?"

"It will free you from bondage."

"I don't consider tea bondage, thank you. I consider it tea."

"Then do it for me."

He was walking toward her, and Emmalina had no idea what kind of confrontation he had in mind. "All right," she said, hoping it would stop him. It didn't.

"Now, about your wardrobe," he went on. "Don't you think it's a little confining for Southern California weather?"

He pulled up short to look at her, and she wished he hadn't caught her plucking at her clothes earlier.

"Maybe you could talk to Gretchen about a shopping trip?" he suggested. "Meanwhile, I'm sure she'd be happy to lend you something of hers."

"I'm fine, Mr.—" She caught herself. "I prefer to wear my own clothes, Jeff, and if you're going to tell me I can't, well—we may have a problem on our hands."

He just smiled, and she felt a burning need to know what he was thinking.

"Remember the reality-immersion course?" he said. "Lesson number two is very easy: When in Rome—"

He apparently wanted her to fill in the blanks. "Wear fire-retardant clothing and prepare for the fall?"

"You're quick."

"So are you." Suddenly he was there, standing before her, smelling of liquor and smoldering male interest. It was low heat, but the burner was on, she realized. And she felt a strange variety of reactions, including the urge to press up against the wall behind her and touch the back of her hand to her forehead. Would that be swooning? she wondered.

And then it hit her.

She was doing the *Leila* thing.

"How about the view?" he said.

At this moment her view was him. But of course that wasn't what he meant.

"Have a look over there." He pointed in the direction of a spherical glass tower. "I'm sponsoring a charity bazaar, and I want you to stay for it. It's going to be held in the open-air ballroom on that roof, and you'll be my guest of honor. I want you to meet people, lots of them. I want you to get a feel for what life on the outside can be like—and how you might fit into it."

"I don't need parties thrown for me—"

"I've got a little field trip planned as well, to show you how the boutique business works in California."

"Why are you doing all this?"

"Because you're stuck in the past, Emmalina. You need to let go of whatever's holding you there and move on."

"Move on—as you have?"

He swirled the cognac, then swallowed it. "Yes," he said with finality. "Leave it behind. What's done is done. You can't change it, so leave the pain behind."

She was quite certain he was talking about himself and not her. She was also quite certain she wasn't going to probe any further. But she could give him a bit of advice.

"Turn your wounds into wisdom, Jeff," she said quietly.

He looked at her askance. "Who said that, Queen Victoria?"

"No. Oprah Winfrey."

She thought he was going to laugh. What he did was raise an eyebrow and give her a slightly bemused look. But it also seemed as if he were drawing back mentally in order to study her. And then, when she made it a point to look back at him, and to do it rather imperiously, he caught her gaze and held it.

"You are one perplexing woman," he said. "I can't decide

whether you're for real or this is some crazy act. Tea and doilies, Oprah Winfrey and erotica, the stock market. Are you putting me on, Emmalina? Are you putting everyone on, including yourself?"

She was too startled to answer him.

And the night went totally quiet as he moved closer.

Emmalina caught the scent of cognac, of rich, piney men's soap, of her own fear. She felt her heart pounding and wondered if it might rip through her chest. She actually felt disoriented and quickly tried to shake the sensation off. But when she came forward, he was there, and their hands caught, his right, her left. She wasn't certain who reached first, but it would have been so easy for him to pull her to him, to bend her head back and kiss her until she actually did swoon.

Instead he drew her fingers up and kissed them. Lingeringly, she thought.

"I don't have a clue who you are, Miss Price," he told her. "But if you're not for real, I will find out. You know that, don't you?"

Five

Jeff's cell phone glowed in the dark. It also fit perfectly in a pocket, the palm of his hand, or a pants cuff. As for steam rooms, maybe there he'd wear it around his neck, like soap on a rope. What he liked even better than its size was its speed and convenience. You hit a button, held it down, and it automatically dialed a preprogrammed phone number. Or you could simply say the person's name and get the same result.

In this case, the name on Jeff's lips was a friend from his men's club. A friend who was also a psychiatrist.

"Mike," he intoned, settling back in the darkness of his bedroom to watch the phone do its magic. He'd shut off the lights and stretched out on the bed, fully clothed, to ease the dull throb at the base of his skull. Interesting that he'd been playing hide-and-seek with a headache almost from the moment he got back to L.A.

Over the years he'd been subjected to some bizarre treatments to ward the skull-splitters off, like plunging his feet into an ice bath for ten-minute intervals to shunt the blood from his head and having electrodes strapped to his trigger points. Now he just toughed it out.

"H-hello?"

"Mike, it's Jeff. Did I wake you?" It was ten o'clock by the phone's digital display. Late, but Mike was an admitted insomniac, and Jeff had a particular need to talk to him tonight.

"Yeah, you did," his friend grumbled, "and I could kill you for that. I can't remember the last time I fell asleep at ten. In fact, I don't think it's ever happened."

"The Sominex is on me," Jeff said dryly.

"Dinner's on you, you shit."

Jeff smiled. "Funny you should mention that, my friend. That's what I was calling about. Let's set something up."

"You? Me? Dinner? Alone? No beautiful babe on your arm, who has a lonely, dysfunctional girlfriend with an unresolved doctor complex?"

"You're sick," Jeff informed him. He sat up and grabbed a couple of pillows for his head so Mike couldn't hear him chuckling. "Not fit to quote Freud."

"We've always known that," Mike agreed gamely.

It was an inside joke. A girlfriend of Jeff's had once set Mike up with her roommate, who'd turned out to have a full-blown doctor-patient, psychiatric-couch fantasy. Mike had fondly referred to it as the best night of his life, but he'd never dated her again. It was like skydiving, as he told it—once was enough.

Jeff rolled his neck and heard it pop. Sometimes that relieved the pressure inside his head. Hell, it was worth a try.

"When do you want to get together?" Mike asked. "And more to the point, why? It can't be because you miss my company. We played cards at the club a couple of nights ago."

"That was two weeks ago, buddy. And thanks for remembering. But no, I'm not in need of your sterling company. I'm in need of a favor."

"How do I know there's a woman involved. How do I know that, Jeff?"

"Because you're trained to be sensitive and intuitive?"

Jeff hesitated, aware that he didn't want Mike to think this was some kind of prank. He was actually counting on his friend to be sensitive and intuitive, but if he said as much, Mike would start reading things into the comment, wondering how involved he was.

"This is no normal woman, Mike. I need your professional opinion on her mental stability. But she can't know you're a psychiatrist."

"Then what am I supposed to be?"

"A stockbroker? She's into that. I'll tell her you're curious about her strategy, and trust me, she's got one."

"How involved are you with this woman?"

There it was, the involvement question "It's a business deal, okay? There's no involvement beyond that."

"Which means I should expect to be called as an expert witness in a court case at some point?"

Jeff laughed and rolled up to a sitting position. He lifted his chin and began to unbutton his shirt. "If I were looking for an expert witness, I'd get somebody good. I just want to know what makes this woman tick."

"Ah . . . *ahaa* . . . I see."

"No, you don't, Mike. You don't see. I'm trying to help her—"

"*Help* her? Hello? Is this Ming the Merciless talking? Jeff Weston, the Darth Vader of global commerce? I thought 'help' was a four-letter word to you."

"Tomorrow night, Mike. Eight o'clock at Entre Nous. If your schedule's not clear, clear it."

"Jeff, a bit of advice?"

"No, thanks, Mike."

"When a man wants to know what makes a woman tick, it's because *he's* already ticking . . . like a time bomb."

"Boom," Jeff said and hung up the phone in disgust. Why were people always wanting to give him advice these days? And what was he going to do about this headache?

As he rose to finish undressing, some gentle voice from his past intruded, speaking quietly. "Swing away your heartaches, little man. There's nothing wrong with crying honest tears."

And suddenly the throbbing inside his skull was gone. What hurt now was the hydraulic press bearing down on his heart.

There were precisely fifty-seven tiny looped buttons securely fastening the bodice of Emmalina's jacket, and depending on how tired she was, it sometimes took her all of a quarter hour to unhook them. This, of course, was not counting the rows on the sleeves, which ran from her elbows to her cuffs.

Emmalina sighed as she began the arduous process. She simply didn't want to be bothered tonight. There was too much pent-up energy inside her, too much sweet surprise. She had not expected to feel this way, this light and free. She'd always thought if she ever got this far away from her home, the fears would assail her and devour her like mad, ravaging dogs.

No, she had not expected to feel this way. But she wasn't entirely sure how she did feel. Frightened, yes. Slightly terrified, to be truthful, but shielded somehow. Protected, as if in a temporary state of grace. She could only hope it would last long enough to see her and Spike safely back home.

She stood at the open armoire door, working the delicate silver button hook as she observed herself in the mirror. She had always rather enjoyed this ritual, but tonight she felt an impulse to yank the silly buttons off.

When she was finally out of her clothes, she would let down her hair and brush it a hundred strokes. She loved that process and sometimes bent over at the waist and let all the blood rush to her head while she was doing it.

She was in the bathroom, taking the pins out of her hair a short time later when she heard a knock at the door. She rushed back into the bedroom, hurriedly slipped her robe on over her filmy nightgown, and called out for whoever it was to come in. Her breath was spent by that time, and her voice sounded funny.

"Oh, Spike." She could hardly hide the sharpness of her disappointment. She'd been about to pop with excitement when the towering teenager opened the door, and apparently she had done just that, because now she felt like a punctured tire. There was nothing left but the strange, thin sound of her voice.

Whatever had brought this on? she wondered.

"Are you okay?" he asked.

"Of course! How do you like your room? Isn't mine magnificent?"

Hers truly was. Opulent and dripping in luxury, the bed had a regal canopy headboard that rose to the ceiling and was draped with heavy folds of red-and-gold damask. It was a bed meant for royalty, Emmalina had thought the moment she'd seen it. When she was under its satin covers, cushioned by its satin pillows, she was sure she would feel like she was sleeping on a throne.

And the whole place smelled violently of roses. It was heaven.

"Mine's great, too," Spike said. "One of the walls is an aquarium with really cool stuff in it, fishes and eels and a baby squid, I think. It's got those buggy little eyes. Tomorrow Gretchen says she'll take me to the La Brea Tar Pits, where actual dinosaurs existed. You believe that?"

Her bed rocked under his weight as he flopped down on it. She wanted to caution him about his manners, but something held her back. Things were different here, and the normal rules didn't apply. There wasn't time for rituals like tea and buttons in this world, and she didn't know if that was good or bad.

It might be both.

She came to the end of the bed and smiled at Spike's ungainliness. He'd fallen back on his elbows and leaned his head back to look up at the muraled ceiling, a wreath of cornucopias spilling out fruit and flowers.

"How do you like Gretchen?" she asked. Her curiosity was more than casual. And she had a reason to be concerned, if Spike was going to be spending time with her.

"She's whacked in a way, but nice if you don't try talking to her about doilies and junk." His head popped back up, and his intensely dark eyes fastened on Emmalina. "And there's nothing going on between her and Weston, in case you were wondering. She's got the hots for a dude named Cliff, Weston's jet pilot."

Emmalina hid her interest in mock sternness. "When did you suddenly become an expert on the hots, young man?"

Spike's grin was sheepish. "It's so obvious. Something happens to people's voices. They laugh real loud, and then they get winded like they've been running. Anyway, they start talking funny, like you and Weston."

"Mr. Weston and I were *arguing*, Spike. There's a difference."

"Not on the plane today you weren't."

She still had a hairpin in her hand. Now she attempted to put it back—and wondered how she must look to her young charge. She'd always tried to be an example of correct behavior to him. No matter what anyone said, there was value in rules and traditions, value in personal standards, all of which were sorely lacking in today's society, in her opinion.

"That was a private discussion between two adults," she informed him. "You shouldn't have been eavesdropping. And just to set the record straight, it is Mr. Weston who has the hots for me, not the other way around. You yourself pointed that out."

"Okay, so he was talking funny that day in the shop. But you've been talking funny ever since."

"Me? No. My throat's scratchy, that's all. And no wonder. I haven't had a cup of tea in more than twenty-four hours."

She left him sprawled on the bed and went straight back to the armoire to stare at her reflection. Her hair was a little wild, half in and half out of the pins, but she didn't see anything else that would give away the craziness that had been going on inside her lately.

She almost wished she could talk to Spike about this. He'd been dating off and on for the last year, although they didn't call it that anymore—dating. Still, he obviously had more experience with courtship rituals than she did. In fact, what experience she did have was strictly secondhand, and gleaned mostly from hastily read snatches of Victorian erotica, she was embarrassed to admit.

She was self-taught, but the material she'd had access to obviously hadn't prepared her for the intense, dizzying emotions of a real attraction to the opposite sex. What it had done was cause her to wonder if sex was all spankings, silken bondage, and sweet torment with fine-pointed feathers. That possibility had proved a bit too much for Emmalina Price's delicate constitution—and had most likely contributed to the reason she'd remained a virgin to the ripe old age of twenty-eight.

Now she considered her dark and sparkling eyes in the mirror, her dry throat and patchy pulse. "So you think I'm actually *attracted* to him?"

"Is there water in the Pacific?"

Apparently she was hiding it from no one but herself. "And what do you think of him?" she asked Spike.

"All's I know is he's loaded, and it would be pretty cool to live in a place like this."

"Oh, Spike." She turned to him, alarmed. "We have to go back, you know that. We can't stay here. Mr. Weston never had any intention of us staying on with him, and I certainly couldn't imagine you and me alone in this city, could you?"

The thought sent a chill through her. "You'd miss your classes," she pointed out.

She'd encouraged Spike to enter a local trade college after high school, and he was taking computer technician classes and showing great promise. She had hopes that he would do well enough to apply for a scholarship to a university and pursue a computer science degree.

No, they couldn't possibly stay here. This trip was a great adventure, and perhaps she owed Jeff Weston a thank-you on that account, but she owed him nothing else. When the adventure was over, she was going to take him up on his promise to salvage the Victorian and go straight back to her home, where she would undoubtedly sit down and write a whole series of articles on courtship rituals for her modesty newsletter, starting with one on how to stay cool when you had the hots.

Six

Emmalina was in love. It came upon her at first sight and stole the very breath from her body. It was nothing like the passages of erotica she'd read, and everything like the lacy Victorian valentines she sold in her shop. Cupid had zinged her heart with his arrow the moment she set eyes on La Jolla, California. She was in love with a city.

She and Jeff had taken the coastal route down Highway 101, giving her plenty of time to soak up the sights, which were sea-swept and atmospherically blue almost everywhere she looked. She'd never ridden in a convertible before, so he put the top down on his Jaguar roadster and let the sun caress their shoulders and run in their hair.

The wind had blown nearly all the pins out of Emmalina's chignon, and she finally removed the few that were left and let the weight of her hair fall wherever it had a mind to. She was also wearing the closest thing she owned to a sundress, a flowery affair with capped sleeves, a modestly scooped neckline, and a laced bodice, rather than a buttoned one. Between her milkmaid's dress and her unfettered hair, she felt quite the bohemian.

Jeff seemed to think so, too, or at least he kept looking at her flying tresses like he wanted to touch them. Emmalina could easily have returned the compliment. His hair was ruffly and thick and gloriously saturated with golden light. He had on khakis rather than jeans, and his shirt was the dense royal purple of a fleur-de-lis. It was a striking contrast to his tanned skin, but what kept drawing her glances was his dark glasses. They made him look like a movie star.

Emmalina wanted to laugh. Her with a movie star? Then this had to be a dream sequence she was experiencing. It had felt a little like that from the moment she'd seen him on her patio. But the nervousness that stirred in her depths when he looked at her now was real enough. And may have contributed to her breathlessness when they finally reached La Jolla. Given the state of mind she was in, she was bound to fall in love with something, and the city seemed the safest bet.

Jeff had told her they were going to have lunch in a clifftop restaurant, then take a leisurely walk along Girard Avenue, where the specialty boutiques were located. But she'd convinced him to visit the shops first and have a snack there. That evening they were scheduled for dinner with one of his stockbroker friends, and she didn't want a heavy lunch anyway.

Miraculously he'd found a parking spot on the street itself, and they'd been strolling and browsing ever since.

Emmalina hadn't expected to think much of the designer boutiques and other such tony establishments, but the European-like intimacy of the narrow, curving street completely won her over. It was impossible not to be charmed by the mossy hanging baskets and Old World lampposts. And the shops turned out to be an intriguing mix. Sprinkled among the designer stores were art galleries, consignment corners bulging with wonderful old treasures, and tented bazaars with racks of antique clothing.

"Check out the clowns," Jeff said as they passed a children's apparel store. The window display was an old-time circus with stop-action clowns, whose occasional eye blinks revealed them to be real people and not mannequins. Emmalina felt Jeff's hand at the small of her back as he guided her out of the flow of sidewalk traffic.

How strange it felt to be with a man who watched out for her welfare . . . or to be with a man at all.

She shook back her hair, which she had left daringly unpinned, and felt very decadent as she helped herself to a soft pretzel from the bag he'd bought. They'd also sampled peanut butter fudge at a sweet shop and had some meltingly delicious jalapeno cheese sticks at a gourmet take-out place.

Guitar music drifted from across the street, where the champagne was flowing at the grand opening of a new Gucci outlet. Emmalina stuffed the pretzels into her bag as she and Jeff entered the brightly lit showroom. They meandered from section to section, sipping bubbly, nibbling hors d'oeuvres, and checking out the spring ready-to-wear collection.

Jeff gamely urged Emmalina to try things on, but she wouldn't hear of it. "I wear more underwear than that," she informed him when he picked out a frothy slip dress of pale-pink organdy.

"Flowers for the lady?" A vendor called out to them as they came out of the store.

Emmalina was prepared to tell him no thank you, but Jeff caught her hand and brought her with him while he bought a bunch of violets. He paid the man, then snapped off several of the fragrant purple blooms before he handed her the rest.

"Flowers for the lady's hair," he said, with the clear intention of doing the honors himself.

Emmalina felt quite conspicuously thrilled as he lifted the soft weight of her hair, combed it back, and slipped the flowers into a spot that seemed made for them, just above her ear. The vendor was watching out of the corner of his eye, and Emmalina had the sense that others were too. It flustered her considerably to be the focus of such attention, but it pleased her as well.

"Now you look like a gypsy girl," he said. "And I've always wanted my fortune told."

He pointed out a nearby outdoor cafe with tables for two and sun umbrellas. Once they were seated, he ordered them both frothy, ice-blended mochas with whipped cream on top, and Emmalina had to remind herself that they were made of espresso. Hers tasted like a chocolate shake.

Jeff nursed his drink while Emmalina studied his outstretched palm and predicted a change of course for the man in the Ray-Bans. He wanted details, but Emmalina was coy. "That's all I'm prepared to say."

He was prepared to say more. "I predict a shop called Priceless on this avenue," he told her.

"I've been trying to imagine that myself," she admitted, "but it's difficult. I could never make the rent, for one thing."

"You're underestimating the appeal of what you have to offer."

The way he looked at her, she wondered what exactly he thought she was offering. Quite abruptly he took her hands, coaxing her fingers into the lacery of his and nearly startling an inappropriate sound out of her.

"I wish we were having dinner alone tonight," he said.

It had been an enchanted afternoon, and all she could safely manage was a nod. She wished that too. At this moment she wished it with all her heart.

But neither of their wishes was to be granted that night, as it turned out, and it was Jeff who regretted that most. Five minutes into their evening with Mike, "the stockbroker," Jeff was wishing the floor would open up underneath his lanky friend and he would fall through the earth to China.

Jeff had picked the restaurant for its quiet elegance. He wanted a place where Emmalina would feel at ease and open up in Mike's presence. He needn't have worried. Emmalina opened up like a box of Crackerjacks, and Mike dove in like an eager ten-year-old searching for the prize.

"Jeff tells me you're quite the Victorian scholar," was Mike's opening line. "A relative left me a signed collection of Proust, and I've been wondering if it's authentic."

"All seven volumes?" she exclaimed. "How marvelous! I could help you with the names of some rare-book collectors. But I'm dying to know how you enjoyed it. Tell the truth, did you find Proust as fatiguing as I did?"

Mike laughed and pushed his big square tortoiseshells up on his nose, then planted his elbows on the table. Now he was swaying toward her as if magnetized.

Emmalina smiled, fluttering those thick velvety eyelashes.

Why wasn't Mike getting scolded for his table manners? Jeff wondered petulantly. That was Jeff's first clue that the evening was a lost cause, but not his last. Once the stockbroker and the Victorian scholar got hot and heavy into Proust, it became obvious that Mike was entranced by her, so much so that Jeff wondered why he'd bothered to order dinner, the way Mike was devouring Emmalina with his beady, nearsighted eyes.

She did look delectable, Jeff had to admit. She'd changed into a white silk blouse with a frilly lace jabot that hid the multitude of buttons he knew were lurking underneath. And her gored skirt rode the curves of her hips like a soft napa leather glove, then flared at the hem, flirting with her ankles.

Well-turned, he supposed they would have been called.

After their walk this afternoon, he'd taken her to his weekend place in the La Jolla shores area, where'd he'd done some business on the phone and Emmalina had rested until it was time to change for dinner. His beach house had two stories and a loft, and he'd put the entire place at her disposal. He'd even given the staff the weekend off, thinking, as men will, that the two of them might return here after dinner rather than drive all the way back to L.A.

Of course, it had also occurred to him that they might make love, given the way the afternoon had gone. He'd spent several intensely pleasurable moments imagining the scene: her in one of those up-to-the-nose dresses, with him taking command of the unbuttoning process and then tormenting them both with the excruciatingly slow progress before even an inch of luscious milk-white skin would be exposed. He also imagined her dainty earlobes being hotly violated by his tongue. In fact, he imagined all of that until his pants got so crowded he had to distract himself.

That was when he'd left a message on Max Gallagher's voice mail, telling him to shine up the trophy. Jeff Weston would be coming over to get it.

Or maybe not, Jeff thought now, with an inner sigh of frustration. Mike was monopolizing Emmalina to the point that she didn't have time to look Jeff's way. For the last fifteen minutes he'd been talking about his skydiving hobby, despite the fact that he'd done it only once.

"Isn't that quite dangerous?" she wanted to know. "You must be a thrill seeker at heart, sir," she marveled, "given your profession, which I understand is very stressful."

"You mean psy—"

"She means trading *stocks,* Mike," Jeff cut in.

Emmalina's voice had taken on an odd quality. It was much too soft to suit Jeff, and Mike was preening like a peacock. Now she was leaning toward him intently.

"Can you tell us how Wizard Technologies is doing?" she asked in a stage whisper.

Suddenly Mike had the wisdom of an oracle. "Free fall," he said somberly. "Wizard's gone into free fall."

He followed that up with a throat-cutting gesture that sent Jeff's heart into free fall. But it was the cute little "oops," that slipped out of Emmalina's mouth that sent him over the edge. That was it. He'd had all he could stomach of this dinner party.

He rose from the chair and put what he hoped was the driving force of a pneumatic drill into his polite request.

"Emmalina, you're going to have to excuse Mike and me for a minute. There's something we need to talk about."

Mike showed no signs of cooperating, so Jeff walked around and all but pulled the chair out from under him. Analyze that, Mr. Sensitive and Intuitive, he thought, as Mike stumbled to his feet.

They got to the foyer before Mike freed himself from Jeff's grip. "What's wrong with you?" Mike hissed.

"You're supposed to be evaluating her mental stability, you jerk!"

"I am evaluating her. How do you evaluate someone without talking to them?"

"You let *her* talk. You've been trying to dazzle her with your derring-do ever since we got here. You just had to tell her you went skydiving, didn't you?"

"I wanted to see her reaction. Some women are secretly drawn to men who have a death wish, which is not a good thing. Woman like that can kill you."

Jeff threw up his hands. "Okay, okay, what do you think?"

"Of Emmalina? She's charming."

"Yes, but is she crazy?"

Mike shrugged. "I'd need more time with her."

"You're not getting any more time with her!"

"Very well. If you want my first impression, and this is rough, I'd say no, she's not crazy. She's one of the sanest people I've met in a long time. But I'm a little worried about you, Jeff. Have you considered therapy?"

"Why?"

"I'd recommend anger management for starters. Then we could talk about your obsession."

If Mike only knew. Jeff *was* obsessed, and it was with bizarre things like earlobes and buttons. But then, why wouldn't he be? If he had a thing for her earlobes, it was only because that was all he'd been able to see. That explained the buttons, too. It didn't mean he was sick.

"Gentlemen?"

Emmalina had come up behind them, and she looked concerned.

"Is everything all right?" she asked. "I hate to be rude, Jeff, but I think we should probably be leaving soon. I'm a little concerned about Spike, and we have a long drive back."

"Spike?" Mike asked, clearly curious.

So much for Jeff Weston's mad evening of unbuttoning. He gave Mike a look that should have left him bleeding.

"Next time you go skydiving," he whispered to his friend as they left the restaurant moments later, "let me pack the parachute."

All she wanted was some tea. Emmalina had slipped out of bed and into the darkened kitchen, thinking the rest of Jeff's household would be sound asleep. It *was* three in the morning.

There were canisters. She could see the stainless-steel cylinders in the moonlight, but she bypassed them on the theory that a "controlled substance" would not be hidden in plain sight. Her host was more inventive than that.

She went through the cabinets and drawers first, then tried the butler's pantry, and finally the refrigerator. Naturally, the tea bags weren't in any of those places. They were in the smallest silver canister.

And not just any tea but one of her favorites, Earl Grey. She filled the pockets of her robe and had just grabbed another handful for good measure when the kitchen lights snapped on.

The brightness burned her eyes, but she could make out a silhouette in the kitchen doorway.

"Gretchen?" Emmalina hid the tea bags behind her.

The tall, ultracool blonde smiled and fairly marched into the room. After returning from dinner, Jeff had muttered something about a merger and called Gretchen to come by. They had worked so late that Gretchen had opted to stay in a guest bedroom rather than return to her own apartment. She was wearing sweats and glowing, as if she'd been working out. A headband held back the loose waves of her hair.

"I've been looking for you," she said. "We should talk about the charity event that's coming up, don't you think? You'll need something fabulous to wear, and I wanted to brief you on the people you'll be meeting."

"Now?" At three in the morning?

Gretchen walked to the refrigerator and got herself a Diet Coke, popped the top, and started drinking it from the can. A moment later she was fishing through a pullout pantry, where she found a packet of lite popcorn.

As Gretchen crisscrossed the kitchen, Emmalina scooted around, trying to figure out how to get rid of the tea. Now Gretchen was heading for the microwave.

"It's going to be a lingerie fashion show," she said, punching numbers on the stove's panel. Once she had the popcorn going, she turned to Emmalina. "Several name designers are involved, and since you're to be Jeff's special guest, I thought you should pick one of the charities. That way we can introduce you to the crowd. How does that sound?"

"That sounds lov—" Emmalina whirled as Spike appeared in the doorway next, rubbing the sleep from his eyes. He was wearing a Universal Studio's T-shirt and boxer shorts.

"What are you doing up?" Emmalina asked.

"I thought I smelled popcorn."

"I'm making some," Gretchen said. "It'll be done in a minute. Come on in."

Great, Emmalina thought, now the whole house will be up, wanting some—

"Is that popcorn?"

Emmalina backed against the counter in alarm at the sound of Jeff's voice. The kitchen was enormous, and he was at the other door. She spun around, getting dizzier by the second. *Please don't let him have seen the tea.*

"What's going on in here? Somebody got the munchies?"

He spotted Emmalina at the counter and walked over to her with a quizzical expression. "You didn't have enough junk food today?"

"Actually, I did," she said, inching away from him. "I think I'll just head back to bed."

He looked down at the floor, then up at her, and a dangerous glint of a smile lit his eyes. "You dropped something," he pointed out, suddenly the prince of helpfulness.

Emmalina's heart sank. Busted.

As she knelt to get the runaway tea bag, he did, too—and got a clear view of the contraband that filled her bulging pockets.

She dared a glance at him, hotly embarrassed, only to hear him murmur under his breath, "Maybe the proper young lady with the old-fashioned Victorian values needs some old-fashioned Victorian discipline. Think?"

Seven

Emmalina was faced with an impossible choice. She'd already made her decision about what to wear to the party that was being thrown in her honor tonight. She had the dress all picked out and hanging on the door of her armoire, but when she'd come upstairs to get ready moments ago, there'd been an elegant gift waiting on her bed.

The shiny white box was tied with a huge bow of pale pink organdy, edged in gold, and a single rose had been tucked into its loops and folds. Inside was the slip dress Jeff had urged her to try on in La Jolla. There was also a note from him explaining that he wouldn't be back from his business trip in time to escort her to the party, but he would meet her there. And he hoped she might wear the dress.

Simply that. He hoped. But it was enough to throw Emmalina into sighing conflict. Her first reaction was disappointment that they wouldn't be going together. He'd been gone for several days on urgent business, and she was surprised at how deeply she'd felt his absence. She'd kept busy sightseeing with Gretchen and Spike, and it was gratifying to see how nicely her foster son handled himself in this strange new world of malls, skyscraper parking lots, and theme everything. But at the end of the day, there was an emptiness that concerned and confused her. Given the choice, she wouldn't have wanted any man's presence in her life to have that much meaning.

As for the slip dress, it was as soft and flushed as a sunrise, but closer to the Roaring Twenties than her era. And though she was secretly delighted that Jeff had gone to the trouble, she also wondered what it said about his intentions. It was a bold thing, indeed, for a man to choose clothes for a woman. It verged on the intimate, to her way of thinking.

She touched the shivering bit of fabric and shivered herself. At the very least he must have imagined her in it, and once that door had been opened, the possibilities rushed in like air through a seal. She could hardly wear underthings with it, could she? The dress itself was an underthing, which might easily have encouraged him to wonder how the organdy would feel next to her skin . . . or what it would be like to take the dress off her.

Ridiculously easy, she realized. A strap here, a strap there, and her party gown would be on the floor in a fluttering pool. And what would he think if she actually wore it? Did he want her to be imagining all these things?

The dress she'd planned to wear hung like a coat of armor from the hook where she'd left it to air. Emmalina had always thought the floral silk crepe de chine lovely with its princess-seamed bodice and it leg-o'-mutton sleeves. But now it looked schoolmarmish.

Torn, she stared first at the schoolmarm, then at the flapper.

At least she could try the gift on.

Her hands were trembling slightly as she lifted the dress from the box and saw that there were two other gifts tucked inside. Wrapped in luminescent tissue was a dainty concoction of satin and lace that Emmalina wouldn't have recognized as panties if she hadn't held them to her hips.

She whistled softly in surprise. What had he been imagining when he bought *these*?

The other bundle of tissue contained high heels made of nothing but gossamer straps. And Emmalina simply couldn't fathom it. Any of it. This was some other woman he had in mind, some other woman he wanted to dress up. Not her.

Surely not her . . .

With shaking fingers, she began to pull the pins from her hair, unbutton her blouse, and kick off her shoes. The exchange of clothing was done in a headlong rush that barely gave her time to think about anything except not being totally naked. But when she stood in front of the mirror moments later, she was shocked. Shocked and frightened and thrilled.

She looked nothing like a flapper. With wings, she might have passed for a fairy princess at a costume ball. Without them, she was a nymph. What in the world, she thought, staring at her cascading dark tresses, her luminous eyes, and blinking, bewitching expression. The dress skimmed her slender body like icing. It hung longingly on her curves. It danced.

How could she ever wear the schoolmarm now?

Jeff straightened his wayward tuxedo tie in the mirrored panels of the express elevator as it rocketed upward. When the doors opened on the rooftop ballroom, he could tell by the noise of the crowd and the strains of the live orchestra that the party was going strong.

The bank of elevators was in a marble foyer, which took him out to a mezzanine, where Italian fountains splashed noisily and the trees were festooned with tiny sparkling lights. The "open-air" roof was actually a Plexiglas dome that could be opened to the heavens like a planetarium, weather permitting. Tonight the air was balmy and clear. A few stars could actually be seen winking in the firmament.

The sunken ballroom was just steps below, but Jeff paused, taking time to survey the crowd. The party was black tie optional, but most of the guests had gone the distance, which made an interesting contrast to the servers, who wore lingerie and loungewear, in keeping with the theme. Gretchen had told him that several new designers and a couple of big names had agreed to preview pieces from their lingerie lines, and news of the party had circulated so rapidly that the price of a ticket had escalated to a thousand dollars. She'd had to cut the guest list off at two hundred fifty.

The money was going for a good cause, in Jeff's opinion. Emmalina had requested that it be used for educational scholarships. She wanted to help underprivileged kids like Spike, who couldn't afford college or trade school without financial assistance.

And speaking of Emmalina, there was only one person Jeff was looking for. He was aware of breathing in, of anticipating what he might see as he let his gaze roam over the milling crowds, the fashion show runway, and the loaded buffet tables, where Spike could be seen standing guard over a platter of California Roll sushi. Closer to Jeff was a cluster of buzzing guests, and as he craned to look he saw the object of their attention. Miss Price, herself.

Emmalina stood by an enormous spray of flowers, smiling and greeting people as if she'd been born to it. Gretchen had organized the introductions, but Emmalina seemed to be in complete possession of herself, right down to her elegant button-up shoes. Her hair was in its usual chignon, although charmingly disarrayed, and her radiant cream-silk dress was proudly buttoned all the way to her chin. She really was the quintessential Gibson girl, as soft and alluring as she was proper.

Obviously she had not worn his gift, and maybe he was a little disappointed, but he also respected her for knowing who she was and making no apologies for it. He admired that. He admired a great deal about her. She was as strong a woman as he had ever met. He hadn't figured out yet if she was crazy, but she *was* strong.

Jeff had never been known for his patience, but he waited until the last of the adoring legions were gone before he approached her and touched the small of her back. He could almost feel her quiver as he said, "Emmalina?"

She turned to him, and their gazes connected with a swiftness that was disorienting. Their hands brushed next, in search of something tangible. There seemed to be a need to touch and make real what they were feeling.

What the hell were they feeling? he asked himself.

He didn't have a clue. There was too much going on all at once. His body felt light enough to hover, but it was heavy too, especially in the pit of his stomach. A grounding current was running the length of his legs, and he wanted to do something, but he hadn't figured out what. Or maybe he had. If it were up to him, he would have pulled her away and claimed her all to himself. He hadn't seen or spoken to her in days, and he didn't want to share her with these people.

It was you who organized this sideshow, genius.

"Are you enjoying the party?" he asked her.

"Yes, thank you, I am." She sounded a little surprised. "It's wonderful. Your friends are very nice."

Screw my friends, he thought. "You look beautiful."

"Oh, in this dress? It's not the one you—"

"I know it isn't. You look *beautiful*."

That was all he got to say before the house lights began to dim and Gretchen stepped up to the mike to announce that the fashion show was starting. As people rushed to take their seats, she introduced the emcee, an infectiously high-energy woman who hosted a local morning show. Emmalina glanced over at him, clearly expecting that they would be seated too. But Jeff whisked her with him to the back wall. He had a compelling need to be alone with her in this crowded room.

The fashion show held no interest for him, and he didn't need to watch it anyway. He could see everything that was happening in her rapt expression. She was perfectly serious, rarely breaking a smile as she observed the splashy spectacle, but she was obviously captivated by the stream of light and music and graceful bodies, by the flowing, diaphanous fabrics. And if some of the more risqué designs made her wince just a little, well, that was Emmalina.

Once the wares of the featured designers had been exhausted, the emcee announced that they had something special in the way of a grand finale.

"The show isn't over yet, folks," she told them. "Just for fun, we're going to wrap it up with a sneak peek at the work of an unknown talent, Miss Emmalina Price. It's yet another way to thank you all for your generous contributions."

Emmalina's hand did not reach her mouth in time to stifle the gasp. She obviously had no idea what was going on, and Jeff didn't either. This had to be one of Gretchen's ideas, he realized, bracing himself.

"And this will be a surprise to Emmalina, too!" The emcee pretended to search the crowd for their guest of honor.

Emmalina ducked, and Jeff found himself smiling.

Fortunately the music came up and the spotlights began to circle, catching a tall, leggy blonde as she strolled out of the wings. It was Gretchen, in the tightly laced red corset from Emmalina's shop—and damn little else except panties, garters, and hose. Jeff couldn't believe she'd done this without consulting him.

Emmalina was clearly in shock. Her hands were knotted at her throat, but she hadn't reacted, except to utter a strange little squeak of sound.

Just behind Gretchen came another blonde, this time a professional model wearing the identical corset in electric blue, and then another in black, and a fourth in polka dots. Within seconds the ramp was a parade of flashing legs and sashaying corsets.

The audience was applauding, but the emcee hushed them.

"Wait until you see what's next," she said. "Everything's coming up daisies!"

Another parade of models emerged, and this time they were wearing the doilies that Emmalina crocheted. Their bra cups were large single daisies, and their panties were a bouquet of the flowers, sewn together. Gretchen brought up the rear of this group, in more ways than one. Her panties were little more than a thong, made up of one very large daisy and ribbons of smaller ones, attached at the petal points.

The crowd clearly loved it, but Jeff wasn't applauding. He was ready to stop the show, and would have if Emmalina hadn't stopped him.

"Where are you going?" she whispered as he moved toward the stage.

"I'm not going to let them do that to your doilies."

"No! Don't make a fuss," she implored. "I was just caught off guard. I had no idea what Gretchen had planned."

"Neither did I," he assured her. "And as soon as this crowd clears, she's history."

"You'd fire her?" Emmalina gaped at him.

"You don't want me to? You're okay with this?"

"I don't know." Uncharacteristically flustered, she fingered the buttons at her throat and plucked at a wayward wisp of hair. "I mean, the doilies weren't really all that useful before, were they? More decorative than anything else, I suppose. Now they're both useful *and* decorative."

She shrugged as if to say maybe that wasn't such a bad thing.

"Emmalina?" Jeff couldn't believe what he was hearing. This throwback to the era of sexual repression was okay with her doilies being used as pasties and thongs?

"You wouldn't even wear my slip dress," he pointed out.

"True, but that doesn't mean it wouldn't be stunning on someone else."

Her eyelashes fluttered with questions as she glanced at him. "I thought you wanted me to join the real world, Jeff. It's a big planet, wouldn't you agree? There's room for different ideas, different tastes."

Jeff was speechless. He couldn't think of a thing to say, and he wouldn't have been heard anyway. The guests had begun to swarm Emmalina, flooding her with congratulations. Jeff watched them jostling each other and jockeying for position, and his first impulse was to part the Red Sea and get Emmalina out of there before she got hurt.

Instead, he reluctantly stepped back to give them room. No one had any intention of hurting her, he realized. All they wanted to do was give her their regards, and Emmalina was clearly enjoying the moment. She was laughing with delight, trying not to be thrown by it all, and graciously fielding their compliments by protesting that the lingerie was all Gretchen's idea. And if she was startled, it only made her glow more brightly. He'd never seen such vibrance.

"Jeff, Jeff! Isn't this fun?" It was Gretchen waving at him. She had one of the designers in tow, and the two of them were making their way toward Emmalina.

Jeff could have predicted what was coming next. He could barely suppress a grimace as he watched the young designer gush and make over Emmalina as if they were long-lost friends. He wanted to talk to her about a possible line with her imprint. They could call it Modesty or Unmentionables, or even Emmalina, if she preferred. Oh, he just had so many ideas. She'd inspired him to death.

Jeff backed off even further, with the bittersweet sense that he had accomplished exactly what he'd intended to with his reality-immersion classes. His Gibson girl had made her debut and she was a smash. What was more, she'd done it her way. This was pure Emmalina. Miss Price at her finest.

He had thought that bringing her into his world would change her. It had never occurred to him that she might change his world, even bring it to its knees. God, she was something! He was damn proud of her. He just wished he could be happier about all this. Happy about anything.

What was it she said? Turn your wounds into wisdom.

Emmalina had no idea that she was being watched with such a laser focus. Or that she could ever be the source of so much conflict. She was honestly quite dazzled by all the fuss being made, although she didn't understand it. She couldn't imagine why anyone cared a whit about her daisy doilies, much less wanted to plan an entire line of lingerie around them. But mostly she was feeling a twinge of that emptiness she associated with Jeff Weston's absence.

He was no longer beside her, she realized. Abruptly she turned to look for him, quite rudely ignoring the buzzing crowd. Her eyes searched the area, and she felt the twinge turning into a vast, empty chasm. Jeff was nowhere to be found.

Eight

A rare excitement had taken hold of Emmalina. The wonder and confusion of the fashion show still shimmered in her mind, but it was more than that. She was alone in her room now, getting ready for bed, and as she absently unbuttoned her dress, she had the awareness that life was a party to which she hadn't been invited before now.

Why the invitation had finally come after all this time was the mystery. Of course it was possible that it had always been there, languishing on her writing desk at home, and she hadn't bothered to RSVP. She might not have answered this one if it hadn't been for Jeff.

One-handed, she unfastened buttons down to her collarbone, opened her dress a little and tip-tilted her head, feeling her hair slide like silk across the back of her neck. It was a lovely sensation. Downy waves glided over skin that had rarely been touched in that way. It was loveliness, all of it, this mood she was in, recalling the evening, not caring if she ever got undressed . . . even hugging herself with her free hand while she rocked her head.

If only she knew why Jeff had disappeared and where he'd

gone. But perhaps it was better that she didn't, because something told her she would have gone to him tonight and not even questioned why she was doing it.

She'd come home in the limo with Gretchen and Spike, but Jeff wasn't here when they arrived. Gretchen had made cocoa in the kitchen, and the three of them had rehashed the evening in great detail. But in the back of Emmalina's mind, always, the entire time, had been the moment when she'd turned and he'd been standing there, right behind her. She had never felt like that before, suspended in time, hovering like a hummingbird. And even more remarkable, she had known he felt that way too. Known.

Yes, she would have gone to him tonight. She would have answered the invitation.

Her bedroom had a window seat and she walked to it, remembering the ocean of lights she'd seen the night she arrived. This time all she could see was her own reflection, but the detail was remarkable. Her hair shimmered richly around her face, and the flesh tones of her skin were warm and true.

The buttons of her bodice were covered in cream silk and held by loops. As she freed them, she had visions of watching her dress drop away, visions of nakedness. It was a curiously compelling idea, because she would never have considered doing anything of the kind—undress in the presence of watching eyes . . . even her own. It wasn't that she hadn't looked at her body. That would be unnecessarily modest, but she hadn't done it while in this strange mood of discovery.

The next few buttons brought her knuckles into contact with a pillowy softness that startled her. Her breasts felt like dandelion fluff, only warm. It was another surprisingly lovely sensation, like the hair against her nape, except that it reminded Emmalina of something else, of what she'd done earlier tonight. Something completely unlike her, almost unthinkable. She had not worn her usual layering of underwear.

She had worn what he sent her, and only that.

If she continued to undo buttons, the dress would drop to the ground and she would be naked, or nearly so. She was certain she could never bring herself to watch. It was too deliberate an act. But she couldn't stop imagining it either, and as the fingers in her mind kept traveling downward, plundering more buttons until her dress fell wantonly open, Emmalina averted her eyes.

It was too much. The feelings rising inside her were too bright and disturbing.

She didn't want to undress, not for herself. What she wanted, what her mind conjured up when she closed her eyes and allowed herself to dream, was the same thing that Leila had wanted in George Sand's book. *A dark-haired man bending over her to brush her lips with his burning red mouth.*

Emmalina's mouth went dry at the thought.

She'd never been able to admit it without feeling dreadfully wicked, but she had reveled in those dreams too. And much worse, in fact. Leila had wished simply to be kissed. Emmalina wanted to be bent over backward and kissed at the base of her throat. She wanted to feel her own hair sliding all the way down her naked back. And a man's hands circling her waist as he gazed upon her pale body with brutish desire.

She'd read that somewhere, the part about brutish desire. Obviously a passage from one of her books. She'd stolen more than a few guilty moments over the years to read them, determined to glean as much knowledge as she could about men and women. At first she'd told herself it was important to be educated about the period if she was going to run a Victorian shop. But the shock and disbelief she'd experienced at the physical pleasures described in the pages had been profound. That was when she'd secretly begun educating herself.

She'd rarely been able to absorb more than a few paragraphs at a time because the descriptions had had such a disturbing effect on her being. The cords of her belly behaved like corset stays gone mad. They drew spring-tight, nearly cutting off her wind, and the book's pages trembled as she turned them, poring over vignettes of swooning maidens and handsome rogues with unquenchable desires.

One of the later books, a sampler, contained excerpts from the most famous erotica of the era, and Emmalina had been astonished at the myriad ways in which a man could bend a woman over. It wasn't always backward, as she'd imagined, not in these books; nor did the men stop there, at bending and kissing. They touched and stroked, stirring the woman to such mindless excitement that she really would gasp and swoon before they finally took their pleasure.

And take pleasure they did. The atmosphere was positively orgiastic. Every perverse desire imaginable was indulged, and a few that baffled her even though they were described in detail. Those she went back to again and again, but only in an effort to understand, of course.

What astonished her most was the men's stamina and their endless fascination with naked feminine limbs, particularly if those limbs were looped with silken bonds. They seemed to prefer their women virtually helpless. And the women who found themselves the objects of such attention appeared to love it, too, despite their shrill protestations.

There was no end to the wantonness. Fortunately Emmalina had her limits, and when they'd been reached, she slapped the books shut, swearing never to read them and disturb herself like that again.

She smiled a little now, thinking about the road to hell and how it was paved. She'd always gone back, never believing she could do such things with a man, but knowing that some experience awaited her . . . some experience she urgently wanted to have, even though she hadn't actually confessed that in so many words before now, within the confines of this lush red-and-gold bedroom.

A draught of air cooled her overheated skin and made her glance back at the window, wondering if she'd opened it. That was when she realized her dress was undone all the way down to the dainty bit of lace he'd given her.

Careful to avoid her reflection, she unfastened the leg-o'-mutton sleeves and shook her arms out of them. With a roll of her shoulders, she let the silk dress fall to the carpet and stepped out of it. She'd never done anything so daring. It quite took her breath away, but at least she would know what it felt like now. There would be one less mystery to ponder as she lay in her bed at night.

The cooling air made her shiver and cover her breasts as she hurried to the armoire, where there was a full-length silk kimono in hues of peach and gold. Emmalina couldn't totally avoid the armoire's mirror, nor did she want to at that moment. She had nothing on but her shoes and the lace panties, which were as skimpy as the doilies the models had worn. But a very efficient bit of engineering, she observed. They covered what they had to.

With one finger she slid the panties down her legs, stepped out of them and dangled them a moment, wanting to laugh because it was so incongruous.

That was when she heard the chair springs groan.

That was when she saw him.

He'd been here the entire time. Jeff Weston had been sitting in the corner, lurking in the shadows, watching her.

She dropped the panties and grabbed the kimono. "What are you doing here? Why didn't you say something?"

His voice was as smoky and cinder-hot as his eyes.

"I don't know," he said. "Originally I came here to talk to you. Now I can't remember what the hell about."

Emmalina covered herself with the kimono, realizing he'd seen everything. But she hadn't really done anything, had she? It had all been in her mind. She couldn't remember either, but whatever she'd been thinking about, it must have aroused her terribly. She was flushed and steamy. There was perspiration above her lip and a line at the nape of her neck.

His gaze was hot with male curiosity as it brushed over her shock, but he made an awkward attempt to apologize. At least he'd done that much, she told herself, which meant he wasn't going to take advantage of the situation. Still, the possibility set her aflame with expectation, hopelessly aflame. She was shaking, and there didn't seem to be any way to stop it.

He saw it too.

"Kick me out of here," he said softly. "Now. Tell me to go." He shook his head and caught himself. "No, that's not your problem. I got myself here. I can get myself out."

With that he pivoted and walked to the door.

Kick him out of here, Emmalina.

Tell him to go.

"Wait," she whispered.

A question burned in his eyes as he looked over his shoulder, and Emmalina knew—they both knew—there was only one reason she could be asking him to stay. She turned away long enough to slip on the kimono, though she realized that it was rather late to be modest at this point. He had already seen her prancing around naked and dangling G-strings.

"Wait, as in . . . don't go?" he asked.

She gave a quick nod, and by that time he'd come back around to face her. He still had his tux on, she saw. The tie was undone and the collar open, but that only made him more attractive. If ever a man was born to wear a tux . . .

"You don't seem to need any help with your buttons," he observed with husky regret. "Is there anything else I can do?"

There was, yes. There was something else. Something crazy, perhaps, but Emmalina wanted one more tiny taste of reality tonight. She was finding it infinitely more risky than fantasy. It might even kill her, it was so awfully risky. But what if this was her only opportunity?

"Do you remember that passage from *Leila*?" she asked.

"The dark-haired man? The burning red mouth?"

"Yes, well . . . do you think . . . could you possibly?"

"You want me to—"

She nodded and closed her eyes, thinking that this was a terrible mess she'd brought about. She would die if he did and die if he didn't. "Could you?" she whispered. "Could you possibly bend me over backwards and kiss me?"

She didn't look up to see his reaction. There wasn't time, anyway. He was already there with her, hotly there, sliding a hand around her waist, drawing her close. And she was swallowing a little cry of surprise.

"Let your head fall back," he said into her hair. "Relax and do as I say, Emmalina."

He breathed the words over her face, her closed eyes, and she could have imagined those exact instructions being given to one of the women in her books. The trembling was in her legs now. It was wild and heavy. She couldn't have stood if he'd let go of her. It didn't seem possible to do anything except exactly what he said.

She let her head fall back, and a moment later she was arched over his arm and his lips were at her throat. Hot. Burning. She expected to carry the brand of his mouth for the rest of her life.

"Enough, Emmalina?"

No, she wanted more, the rest of it, the brutish part. She wanted that quite urgently. But he'd bent her so deeply she was spinning, and the shock of having her fantasy brought to life had left her weak. Blood was rushing to her head, and something enormous was burning itself into the flesh of her belly. She could feel every inch of its hungry length. It was as hot as his lips, but this firebrand was not soft. It was hard.

As hard as—

A ramrod, she thought, remembering that one very descriptive term from among the others she'd read in the books. And with that she went utterly limp.

"Enough," he said firmly.

He brought her up and set her on her feet, holding her steady as she swayed against him. He was searching her face, looking for evidence of something.

"Emmalina, are you all right? Have you ever done this before?"

"What? Asked a man to— Of course—"

"*Not,*" he intoned, wise to her soft indignation. "So what's the deal? Why are you doing it now?"

"Because I never have," she admitted faintly.

"I've never jumped off a cliff," he said with an impatient snort. "Never having done something isn't a reason."

Emmalina couldn't bear the thought of being patronized at this point, and frankly, she'd been embarrassed enough for one evening. It took her a moment, but when she had her balance, she stepped out of his arms and pulled the kimono around her defensively.

"Perhaps not for you, sir," she said, "but don't presume to make that decision for me."

"This isn't about making decisions," he came back. "It's about making sense."

"Well, If you must know, when a woman reaches my age, and she hasn't yet had physical congress with a man, she starts to worry that—" She heaved a sigh. "That it might never happen."

"Physical congress?"

"Yes, of course. Sex."

"You want to have sex? With me? Tonight?"

"And why not?" It was partly bravado, but Emmalina went on anyway. There was a point here somewhere, and it had begun to seem important to make it. Besides, she was desperately trying to reclaim her composure.

"I'm not completely naive, Mr. Weston."

"Are we back to *Mr.* Weston? Talking about sex makes you want to call me Mister?"

"As a matter of fact, it does."

He pulled off his tie and looked like he might be going for his coat next. "All right, Miss Price," he said, "why don't you tell me exactly what it is you have in mind? Rock me, shock me, as Spike would say."

Emmalina was only too tempted. She gathered her kimono around her in a swirl of silk and walked across the room to the window seat, glad that she hadn't taken her shoes off. She wanted to remember what it was like to stand tall for what she believed in, to be perfectly sure of herself.

The darkness helped, as did the ocean of lights.

"It's not all that complicated, really," she said, turning to him with a cool smile. "I believe you're attracted to me, if I may be so immodest. And I seem to have the 'hots' for you, since we're quoting Spike, so I thought perhaps we ought to do something about it."

"Like have tea and discuss it? Isn't that your rule?"

"You're the one who made me kick tea. Now aren't you sorry?"

Now his eyes were sparkling. Emmalina had never realized how green they were, like crème de menthe on the rocks.

"Ask me later," he said. "Right now I'm confused. What happened to your old-fashioned standards and the proper-young-lady thing?"

"It's perfectly proper to use your common sense, and that's what I'm doing. There comes a time in a woman's life when she either explores her options and makes some choices or she spends the rest of her days pondering life's mysteries. To everything there is a season, and perhaps this is mine."

"You're in season?"

"One could put it that way, I suppose. The point is, I seem to have the hots, and for better or worse, they seem to be for you. Therefore—"

She gave a little shrug. "I see no reason not to proceed."

"I'm flattered, I think."

"Don't be. It's merely common sense. A need exists to be filled, wouldn't you agree? Call it the law of supply and demand. If one has a fever, one takes an aspirin. And you, sir, are my aspirin."

Jeff stared at her, dumbstruck. He'd been called a lot of things in his life, but never aspirin. He could kiss the wrestling trophy good-bye—he was not going to bed with Emmalina Price. Maybe he did need psychiatry, but very little about any of this felt right to him. Making love to a woman ought to be motivated by more than her feeling the "need" to have that experience. That was a little too modern even for Jeff Weston. When had they traded places? he wondered. He hadn't seen it happening.

She had the kimono wrapped around her like armor, but she refused to avert her eyes. He fed on her haughty loveliness with his greedy gaze, and knew he was going to hate himself in the morning.

"Sorry, Miss Price," he said. "I don't make service calls, not even for you. I'd feel used."

He could see the shock in her eyes, but there ought to have been relief there too. She had just made a responsible man out of Jeff Weston, at least for one night.

"Betsy, how are you? It's Emmalina Price."

Emmalina stood at the window seat of her bedroom with the portable phone at her ear. The bedside clock radio had said eight when she'd opened her eyes, but the only reason she'd slept that late was because she'd been up most of the night.

"Emmalina? Is that you, dear? I was wondering what had happened to you."

Betsy Ross McCallum was one of Emmalina's investment group ladies, and she'd graciously agreed to take care of Emmalina's birds and collect her mail while she was away.

"I'm fine, thanks. I'm still in California, but I'm coming home, possibly today if I can get a flight."

Emmalina hadn't told Spike about any of that, and she didn't imagine he would be happy, but she couldn't stay here any longer, not after the fiasco last night. She had to go home and try to remember who she was, what she believed in.

"You're coming back here?" There was a shocked tone to Betsy's voice that made Emmalina uneasy.

"I didn't want to startle you by showing up unexpectedly," Emmalina explained.

"I'm afraid it's you who may be startled."

Emmalina lost a breath. "What do you mean?"

"There's nothing to come home to, dear. They've demolished your house."

Dread filled Emmalina's voice. She sank onto the cushions, her back to the windows. "What are you talking about, Betsy? What house?"

"Yours, the Victorian. It's gone. I thought you knew. I've been trying to call you for days. I even left messages for you on the number you gave me, but no one responded."

She'd given Betsy Jeff's voice mail here at the house. He'd never told her about the calls, and now she understood why he'd been so determined to get her out of town.

"You didn't know, Emmalina?"

She was holding the phone with both hands, but couldn't keep it steady. God, she was going to be violently ill. Her body was in upheaval, it was retching inwardly, like a feverish child who'd gone into convulsions. But her mind wouldn't stop, couldn't stop.

She was going home immediately. She didn't question what Betsy was telling her, but she had to see for herself. Something this unthinkable had to be seen. There was no need to tell Spike or involve anyone else. He would be fine with Gretchen while Emmalina made the quick trip. She would just slip out and fly back on her own.

Betsy was still calling out her name as Emmalina set down the phone. Her house could not be gone. That could not have happened.

Nine

"Over there, by the barricade," Emmalina told the taxi driver. She thanked him as he pulled up alongside the bright orange traffic cones, but those were the last words she uttered as she looked out the cab window. The block where she lived had been closed off to through traffic, but she could see beyond the barricade that everything was gone. The entire area had been demolished, as if it had never existed.

There were the remnants of a foundation here and there, mostly concrete blocks and lumber posts sticking up like dead tree trunks. But the rest was rubble.

And her house . . . gone.

A breathtaking pain caught her in the rib cage. It felt like she was being demolished too. Like she'd just stepped into the path of a wrecking ball.

If she stayed here, she would be hit again and again. But she couldn't leave. There was nowhere to go. This was her life in rubble, and she had to see if there was anything left. She asked the driver to wait as she got out of the cab, but she never heard his answer. It surprised her that she was steady enough to walk normally.

A cleanup crew was at work on the debris. Over their noise, she could hear her grandmother calling for eight-year-old Emma to come in out of the rain. She could smell the cinnamon cookies and hear the classical-music radio station that played in the afternoons. She could see dark-gold waves, sprinkled with gray, a smile as deeply creased as the worry lines, and she could feel her grandmother's soft bath-powder kisses on her cheek.

"How could he have done this?" she whispered.

Her home was more than a haven, it was the repository of her life's memories, of her family's memories. Without it the precious moments were sure to fade and be lost forever. Even the photo albums and scrapbooks were gone.

Shock must have buffered her from the worst of it as she picked her way through the debris. She couldn't even tell where the house had stood. It was all devastation. Everything was gone—her Victorian treasures, the antiques, the china. And the birds? What had happened to the birds?

She turned away, struggling with the grief. The tears began to flow as she searched for some way to make sense of what had happened. Not just for her own peace of mind. The Price family's modest legacy had been lost with her. How would she ever have explained that to her grandmother?

She found a chunk of curbside and sat there until the workmen shooed her away. She'd been digging through the mental rubble, remembering her desperately ill mother, who'd made the world such a frightening place.

Emmalina had no idea who her father was, and probably would never know him as anything other than some stranger who had briefly entered her mother's confused, disordered world before he'd become another one of her monsters, another reason to hide.

She'd been born while her mother was on the run from her imaginary fears, and even the FBI hadn't been able to locate them.

Emmalina was six before the detective her grandmother hired tracked the two fugitives down. By that time the tumor that had ravaged her mother's brain was inoperable, and death had come quickly and mercifully, bringing her the peace she'd never had in life.

Peace had not come as easily to Emmalina.

She was covered with dust when she let herself back into the taxi, but she barely noticed the hand- and footprints she was leaving everywhere. Naturally the driver asked where she wanted to go, but Emmalina had no idea.

"Just drive for a bit," she said.

They went down the side street where she'd learned to ride a bike, then around a couple of curves and past the grade school where she'd excelled at English and failed utterly at girls' softball. Down the road in front of them was a hilly area that wasn't yet developed. Weston property, she imagined bitterly.

The driver was about to turn off on another side street when Emmalina sat up and screamed. "No, keep going straight!"

Directly ahead of them, situated in a grove of willow trees on a sloping hill was a house that Emmalina had never seen before. No, that wasn't true. The dark-green shutters looked uncannily familiar, but she'd never seen the house sitting there. She'd never seen anything sitting on that hill.

"Stop the car!" she begged, pulling money out of her bag to pay him. "Please!"

He did stop, but not quickly enough for Emmalina. Victorian propriety forgotten, she let the car door bang open as she yanked up her long, slim skirt, scrambled out of the taxi, and trudged up the grassy incline. This *was* uncanny. Someone had built a house that looked nearly identical to hers. The gingerbread trim was the wrong color, gray instead of green, but otherwise everything was the same.

Braces shored up the foundation, which made her think the place was new and still under construction, but the porch steps groaned with age as she climbed them and the screen door was moldering around the edges. The front door was open too, she realized, but it was too dark to see inside.

Emmalina stopped short as she noticed the ceramic newspaper holder. Nestled amidst hand-painted flowers were the words VIRTUE, THOUGH IN RAGS, WILL KEEP ME WARM. She'd hammered the nails that held the holder up. And what was that noise? It sounded like chirping, trilling. Like . . . birds. There were birds singing inside the house!

The next sound made her shriek in fear.

"Welcome home, Miss Price."

A disembodied male voice had called to her from somewhere inside. Emmalina stepped back in bewilderment. She might have kept going and tumbled down the steps if Jeff Weston hadn't immediately appeared. He gently persuaded the old screen door to open and waved her inside.

"Sorry, I wasn't expecting you this soon," he said, tucking the tail of his white dress shirt into his jeans. He pulled a terry kitchen towel off his shoulder and smiled, still holding the door open. "I don't have the champagne chilled."

Somehow Emmalina made it as far as the foyer, then she had to brace herself against the wall to keep from fainting. Everything looked exactly as she'd left it. "What is this? What have you done!"

"I moved your house to a better neighborhood."

"Moved it . . . ?"

"Yes, picked it up and moved it with a Chinook helicopter. Amazing pieces of machinery, those Chinooks, they could probably move a hotel."

A little squeak of protest slipped out while she was struggling to control her indignation. "You moved my *home*? How *could* you? I've been in a terrible state. I thought you'd had those awful workmen tear it down!"

"Workmen?" He seemed genuinely confused. "Were you over at the construction site? What were you doing there?"

"I spoke with Betsy, the lady who was taking care of the house, and she told me you'd torn down the entire neighborhood. Naturally I caught the first plane."

"Oh— God, I'm *sorry*! You weren't supposed to find out, not like that. I flew in early this morning to make sure the house was ready, and I just sent the jet back for you. It was supposed to be a surprise."

He pulled a crumpled postcard out of his shirt pocket and handed it to her. "I left orders that this was what I wanted it to look like. What do you think?"

It was a picture of the Victorian in the willow grove, the one that her grandmother had had made into postcards. She'd said something once about having lived in that house briefly, but then had implied that her friend and employer, Mrs. Weston, hated to think of her own beloved Victorian languishing vacant for so many years. Maybe that was why her grandmother had switched houses, never thinking a thing about the legalities involved.

Emmalina could remember gazing at the postcard for hours on end as a child, wondering what it would have been like to play in the grove. That Victorian was gone now, but this one looked exactly the same, and now the willows were real. They were beautiful. And they were right outside her door.

She didn't know how to deal with the emotions that were welling up inside her.

"You had no right to do such a thing without telling me," she said, closing her hand over the card. Her voice was little better than a frog's croak.

"No, none at all," he readily agreed. "I should have told you, I know that. But if I had . . . would you have come with me to California?"

She shook her head, and his smile vanished. "I didn't think so. I couldn't take that chance."

"Couldn't take the chance of not getting me off the property?"

"Listen, whatever you must be thinking, this wasn't about a business deal. I wanted you to know you had options, that you have a future as well as a past."

Tears were threatening what was left of her composure. "You shouldn't have p-put me through this. I could s-sue. I may sue for emotional distress."

"Let's settle out of court," he said softly, "right now. Tell me what you want and it's yours."

She answered that with a haughty sniff. "You can't buy your way out of this, Mr. Weston."

"I don't want out of it, Emmalina. That's the last thing I want."

The conviction in his voice took her quite by surprise. There was passion in his eyes, passion in his declaration. And it confused her beyond words. Last night he'd rejected her, and now he was saying tender, sensitive things, and sounding like a man who cared about her. But even if he was sincere, she couldn't allow that. He'd run roughshod over her life and done terrible things. He was always doing terrible things.

"Stop it," she said.

"What is it that you want me to stop?"

"Being tender and sensitive. It's not you. It's not you at all." She turned away, avoiding his green-eyed intensity, but she could feel his smile. It was warm on the back of her neck.

"Maybe that's what you do to me—"

She left him clearing his voice of its huskiness and walked into the front parlor, her boutique. It was exactly the same, down to the candy boxes carved to look like women's shoes.

"You still have your home and your shop," he pointed out, following her into the room. "Plus the money coming to you for the house that should have been your grandmother's. It's several times what you'll need for Spike's college fund."

"One house is more than sufficient, and *I* can provide for Spike's college fund, as well as for myself, thank you."

"I have every confidence that you can provide for yourself financially. The Wizard Technologies fiasco was all the proof I needed. But money isn't everything. It isn't happiness. Can you provide that?"

"I'm happy," she said, wishing she could edge away from him. His breath was hot on the back of her neck.

"You don't sound happy."

"I thought you'd demolished my home, for heaven's sake."

"But I didn't and you're still not happy."

"I am. I am so!"

"Let me see, then, let me see how happy you are."

He touched her arm, and she stepped away from him. "If you were really concerned about my happiness, you would leave me in peace, Mr. Weston. You've accomplished your goal. My house and I are out of your way."

"Do you really want me to go this time? Or do you want me to go the way you wanted me to go last night?"

"I should have *let* you go last night!"

"But you didn't. You wanted a man, and you were woman enough to admit it."

Of all the arrogance! She swung around, disbelieving. "And you, sir, could hardly wait to turn me down!"

"I was an idiot. I thought I was protecting you."

"Well, *protect* me again."

Her voice crackled and so did his eyes. One brush of those fingers and the sparks would fly.

He gave her a measuring look, as if assessing his chances of charming an incipient tornado.

"You could be making a mistake here," he said, tilting his head until a shock of bronze hair tumbled forward. "You never know when you're going to get a fever and need an aspirin."

"I'm cured, thanks to you." She would rather have died than smile.

"All right, I'll go." He grabbed his blazer off the back of the couch. "But there's something I need to say first, and as long as I'm making an ass of myself, I might as well do it right."

"You already have as far as I'm—"

Emmalina stopped in midsentence, silenced by the look he'd given her. He wasn't kidding, she realized.

"As corny as this might sound," he said almost angrily, "I didn't know what beauty was until I met you. Maybe I thought it was Cindy Crawford's mouth or the way a Ferrari corners, I don't know. But you're not any of that. You radiate pride and integrity and honesty, inside and out. It's a beautiful thing you bring to this world, Emmalina. You bring yourself. Most of us don't have the guts."

She didn't dare to say a word. He was exposing too much. And he had exposed her. Even the birds in the shop had stopped singing.

"I thought all I ever wanted to do was make deals," he told her. "But there's another way to spell that word, with an *I* in front of it. I learned that from being around you."

"Ideals?" she murmured.

His voice dropped to a hard sigh of regret. "I never wanted to hurt you, Emmalina. I just wanted you to have a chance at something else."

His blazer was crumpled in his fist and his eyes were a little wild as he combed back a handful of hair with his fingers. There was more vulnerability in him now than she would ever have thought him capable of feeling, much less expressing.

"And there is something I want, too," she said stiffly.

"Yeah, I know. I'm leaving."

She didn't speak as he shook his coat out and pulled his sunglasses from the pocket. She simply began to undo her buttons, quietly, one by one. When she looked up, he was watching her through the darkened lenses, and after a moment, the quizzical expression on his face turned to one of deepening male interest.

"This could take a very long time," she told him.

"I've got nothing but time," was his choked response.

Quite an admission, she thought, remembering the day he'd taken over her boutique with his blond assistant, his cell phone, his pager, his fax, and whatever else he carried in his electronic arsenal. Maybe he had changed.

He shook his head as if he couldn't find words. The sunglasses were gone and so was the coat. "If your hands are tired, we could take turns at that," he suggested, meaning the buttons.

She dropped a quick, shy smile, and her fingers fell away. But for some reason her eyes brimmed with tears as he approached her, and when he saw it, his breath caught.

"I will never hurt you," he whispered.

"I can stand the hurt if you love me," she replied.

She hadn't known she was going to say it, or that he would react with a sharp intake of air. It was almost as if he'd suffered a blow. He caught her face in his hands and drew her close, his eyes sparkling with the sweetest kind of pain.

"And I can stand *anything* if you love me."

"We barely know each other," she said with shocked laughter.

"We know what we need to."

She blinked away tears, embarrassed at how emotional she'd become and unable to look at him for a moment. He thought her so proud, but could he accept her like this? Weeping and undignified?

"Emmalina, I *love* you, and I've never said that to a woman before. I'm not proud of it. It's just true."

He kissed her wispy bangs, urging her to look at him, and when she forced herself to, she saw that he was right about the knowing. She did. No more and no less than she needed to at that moment, but she knew.

He caught her around the waist, and the desire rising in his eyes was incendiary. It burned. It burned beautifully.

Emmalina tipped her head and felt his lips at her neck. She whispered, "First, you must free me from this dress, sir."

He started where she'd left off, with the softness under her chin. And if she thought her own knuckles had felt startling against her skin, then she didn't know what startling was.

His hands were hot and deft, but she could detect a hint of unsteadiness in them, and it unlocked something inside her. A flower opened in her depths, its iridescent petals unfurling like a water lily. The sensation shivered brightly. Too brightly. He'd barely begun and she was already wanting to whimper.

This was how *they* felt, she thought. All those sexually crazed women she'd read about. Now she understood the squealing and squirming, except that they were helpless, writhing in silken restraints, and her tormenter was doing nothing but unbuttoning her blouse. He didn't linger anywhere, even when she wished he would. Her breasts tingled with anticipation, but he only grazed them lightly in his quest to finish the task. He was approaching her waist now, but the buttons on her skirt went all the way to her knees. How would she ever last?

Emmalina was quite certain something must be wrong. And then she remembered what she'd gleaned from the books about the sorts of things that Victorian men liked.

She stopped him and held out her wrists, daintily crossed in front of her.

"What are you doing?" he asked.

"You've forgotten to bind me," she said. "Unless, of course, you'd rather that I finish undressing while you watch. I know men find that very exciting. You seemed to last night."

She colored slightly, waiting for him to do something other than stare at her with a furrowed brow.

"*Bind* you?"

"Yes, there are silk scarves in the chiffonier against the wall. Take your pick. You'll also find feathers in the vase on the whatnot, and a rocking horse in the corner. I think I have everything you'll need, unless"—she shrugged amiably—"you'd rather spank me for being rebellious."

"Spank you?" He turned in confusion and gave her parlor a quick once-over, taking in the paraphernalia she'd pointed out. "Hey, I'd love to— I mean, don't think I don't appreciate the encouragement, Emmalina, but all I really want is you."

"Me?" She beamed. "Are you sure? Because from everything I've read, men are very aroused by that sort of thing, and last night—"

"I think you read too much."

He rose to his full height and took hold of her arms, quite firmly. "I don't know what we need scarves for, because I can hold you down if that's what you want. I can hold you down just fine. You couldn't weigh more than a hundred pounds, and once I'm on top of you, once I'm inside you, you won't be going far."

"Except to heaven," she whispered.

Now she was truly flustered. Warm and dithery, her heart in a race with her mind. The men in the books hadn't talked all that much, except to give orders, and she'd had no idea how potent a little conversation could be.

Meanwhile, her tormenter's eyes had darkened dramatically. And at the moment his hands were doing the talking. They slid down her hips and pulled her close.

"Oh, my!" she gasped, as she came up against the prodigious bulge in his pants. She'd felt that before.

"What?" He searched her widening eyes.

"You." Her fingers slipped down and fluttered over the area in question. "Is this what they mean by flaming loins?"

His stifled laughter sounded like a groan. "You keep that up, and they will burst into flame."

"Does it hurt?" she asked. "I read that when a man's aroused, he actually has emissions prior to releasing." Her tongue darted out to wet her lips. "Do you think . . . ?"

"Feel free to check," he said, through clenched teeth.

"Well, if you're sure it's all right."

She reached gingerly for his belt, but he kidnapped her hand and brought it to his lips, biting down quite smartly on her knuckles. Then as if to soothe her, he turned her hand over and blew lightly into her palm, tracing wet little rings that tickled unbearably. Emmalina gasped at the deliciousness of it.

"That," he said, "is a tongue, in case you were wondering."

But Emmalina was wondering why she would ever need feathers when a man's tongue was so light and silken and quivery with sensation.

"Tongues are lovely," she breathed.

"There are other ways they can be lovely, too," he said.

"Oh, I know. I mean I've read. I believe it's named for a linguist, isn't it? A cunning linguist?"

A choking sound came out of him, and he had to stop what he was doing with her skirt at that moment, which was sliding it up her legs. "You know just enough to be dangerous," he said.

He bent toward her and tipped her chin with his fingers.

"I want to kiss this prim little mouth until it yields to me," he said. "Until it falls slack and sighing, aching to be filled—"

"With your tongue," she whispered, and then blushed as the next words rushed out. "And other things."

His eyes went black with desire. The sound in his throat was slow and primitive as he cupped her head and set about seducing her mouth. His skimming lips were lighter than feathers could ever be. Gradually he slowed to a near stop and began spreading her own warm wetness all over her, settling in to finish the job.

It was glorious. Draining. Emmalina felt as if she were being bathed in the taste of her own desire. More than her mouth had gone slack by the time he slid his tongue deeper into her mouth. She was sighing to the tips of her toes.

She whimpered as the sweetness flared, and was gone.

"Oh, look, I forgot a button," he said under his breath.

Now his hands were at her breasts, and she arched toward him quite helplessly, offering herself. Her nipples hardened under his gentle, ardent fondling, and this time she went slack deep inside. She was barely able to remain standing as he did to her breasts what he'd done to her mouth. He taught them to yield to his glorious manipulations.

Emmalina wanted more of his hot, slick lips, more of his startling teeth, but finally she could bear it no longer.

"You forgot my skirt too," she said pleadingly.

Not a moment later she was lying on the parlor sofa and he was seated by her hips, looking down at her as he drew her skirt up. She always wore old-fashioned hose with garters and when he came into contact with those, he breathed out a curse.

There wasn't time to be startled. In the space of a caught breath, Emmalina found her skirt swept up around her waist and her legs drawn up in a vee. She was still wearing panties, but she felt a bit exposed as he gazed at her inner thighs and slowly smoothed his palm over their quivering paleness.

He spurred a soft moan out of her. Everything was so sharp, so bright, down there. Petals were shivering, unfurling.

"Exquisite," was his comment as he slid aside the crotch of her panties and viewed the dark riot of curls.

He riffled them with his fingers and Emmalina moved beneath his touch. It was involuntary. She couldn't stop herself. If she'd been bound, she would have been squirming. She fully understood the necessity of squirming by this time, but she couldn't let herself. It was too wanton to even consider.

Squealing, however, she thought as his fingers parted the curls and slid along the ruffly wetness. She might squeal. She might well!

What she did do was moan—a wild, half-strangled utterance that slipped out as he gently began to stimulate her. Lord in heaven, it was lovely. Certainly the most intense physical pleasure she'd ever known. With each sliding stroke, the sensations in her belly flared so brightly she couldn't hold still any longer, despite all her efforts.

"Exquisite," he echoed as her hips began to writhe. "Just exquisite."

She saw him bend toward her and tried to imagine that first lightning bolt of sensation, but the sweetness began even before his mouth had touched her. His breath jetted hotly through her curls, fanning out over her skin in warm waves. He bathed her in the soft little puffs, and they were so soothing, she began to melt, despite the ache in her belly and legs. It was like having warm air currents flow over you. It was his word, "exquisite."

But then something changed. This new current felt more like electricity than air. It glided, swirled, and flickered lightly, *exquisitely*. But it was as sharp-edged as it was sweet. Hot. His breath had been replaced by his tongue, and when he pearled the length of her ruffles and dipped inside, she arched her back and gasped.

"Oh, you must stop," she breathed throatily. "I feel something happening."

"Let it happen, my love."

His voice was low and musical. It played echoing chords inside her. Rich, dominant chords. Her entire body was oversensitive, overstimulated. The lily had opened wide, its petals reaching and crying. They were iridescent with sensation, and the colors shimmering through them were shimmering through her too.

Afloat in that beauty, she realized that he'd moved over her and fit himself in the vee of her legs. He was braced by the strength of his arms, but she was effectively pinioned by his weight just the same.

"Once I'm inside you," he reminded her, "you won't go very far."

"Except to heaven," she whispered. A sigh quavered on her lips as he bent to kiss her. She felt him slide into her at the same time and couldn't believe what was happening. Dear Lord, was this what it felt like? Heaven could not be this wonderful. Nothing could be.

She'd never made love before, but her body was more than ready. It was eager for this experience, starved. There was very little resistance as he moved fully into her, easing his way through the fragile membrane.

She felt no pain, only shuddering pleasure as her body released itself to him completely. The first deep stroke brought her gasping upward. She flung her arms around his neck and held him.

"They call this deflowering," she told him when she could catch her breath. "But most people don't do it fully dressed."

"I know, my sweet Emmalina, I know." He laughed. "But how is a man supposed to hold off long enough to undress a woman like you?"

"At least you got me unbuttoned."

"Not quite yet," he told her.

He caught her by the hips and rocked deeply inside her, slowly, gyrating his hips and moving against her walls. He rocked until her body vibrated like a bowstring about to snap and her head dropped back with mindless pleasure.

"I'm going to break," she whispered.

"Yes, break," he said, moving up on her. "Shatter, Emmalina. Shatter for me."

He moved up on her, rode her high and hard for a moment, and Emmalina felt the sudden crashing freedom she'd read about. If he had never known what beauty was, then neither had she. There were no more images of opening flowers, just exploding stars, neon waterfalls, and clamorous noises, all the things that would have offended her sensibilities before this. Now they were beauty. Pure beauty.

It was enough to make her sob and call out the name of her

sweet tormenter. She was a virgin no longer, a proper Victorian lady no longer . . . *lonely* no longer.

They had barely stopped shuddering, barely fallen apart to lie facing each other, when Jeff laughed and made a pronouncement that left her speechless.

"God, I can't leave this place," he said.

"Because of me?"

"No, because I don't get headaches here."

"You are a cad, sir," she said and bopped him on the head. "I'll be happy to give you a headache."

He caught her hand and pulled her into the circle of his arms. "No cad has ever loved you like this one does. I've never met such a bewildering, exciting, *vexing* woman, Emmalina. I only have one question to ask you."

She thrust her chin at him. "No, I shan't marry you. You're not nearly good enough for me, and you're an incorrigible tease."

"Of course you're going to marry me, silly girl. I have ways to make you say yes, don't you forget, ways to make you writhe and pant and strain at your silken bonds. And speaking of which, what's the deal with the rocking horse?"

She stared at him and realized he had no idea. A rush of liquored giddiness made her giggle. She'd had no champagne, so she must have had too much sex, or too much Jeff Weston. She wanted to laugh, but no sound could find purchase in her slippery throat.

"Well . . . according to what I've read, a rocking horse is meant for long *bareback* rides, preferably over bumpy roads, and if the horse gets lazy, there's a little switch you can use to encourage him."

He pretended to give that great thought. "On the other hand," he said, "a rocking horse could also go in the nursery for our children."

"Even better," she told him, as close to making purring sounds as she'd ever been in her life.

He kissed her nose and played with her kiss-swollen mouth. "But meanwhile I hate to see it going to waste."

"Waste is a terrible thing."

"I like the way you think," he whispered exactly as she did, *as softly as she did*. "And everything else."

Tangled Images

Lori Foster

One

Mack Winston was minding his own business, as usual. His thoughts were focused inward, mostly on career choices and disappointments, but he whistled carelessly, unwilling to let anyone witness his concern. The day was snowy and cold, getting colder by the moment, and his nose felt frozen. He was distracted enough not to care.

But the second he entered the family-owned bar he saw them, all three of his damned older brothers and his two sexy sisters-in-law, huddled together at a single tiny table. They looked . . . conniving.

They'd been working on him lately, trying to cheer him when he didn't want them to know he needed cheering. It irritated him. He liked being known as the carefree brother, the fun brother. It suited him.

Since it was early and the bar was not yet open, they all glanced up at him when they heard the door close. Then they did a double take. The women suddenly smiled, and their smiles were enough to make the slowest man suspicious. And despite his brothers' ribbing, he wasn't slow.

Mack's whistling dwindled. He thought about making a strategic retreat, but then Zane, only three years his senior, called out,

"Ha! A lamb for the slaughter! What perfect timing you have, Mack."

Cole, the oldest brother and the most protective, shook his head, looking somewhat chagrined that Mack had shown himself at this precise moment. Chase, the second oldest and the quietest, glanced at Mack and snorted. Both their wives looked as if an enormous problem had just been solved. Whatever the problem, Mack knew he didn't want to be the solution.

Zane grinned. "I tried to save you, honestly, but I'll be out of town."

Cole rolled his eyes. "You're too damn willing, Zane. It unnerves me."

Chase merely snorted again. His wife, Allison, patted his arm. "You were never even considered, honey, so relax. There's no way I want the female masses of Thomasville ogling your perfect body. You're a married man now, and that means I'm the only one allowed to ogle."

Mack backed up two steps.

Sophie, Cole's wife, now seven months pregnant, ran over to Mack and latched on to his arm. "You understand, I couldn't let Cole do it. Not that he would have, anyway. You know how reserved he is. But my God, it would have started a riot! Can you just imagine how the women would react to Cole?"

Mack didn't know what she was rambling on about, but he almost smiled anyway. Sweet Sophie harbored this absurd notion that Cole was perfect, and that every female he met wanted him in the most lascivious manner imaginable.

Mack had to agree that in many ways, his oldest brother did border on perfection. Cole had pretty much raised him and Zane, with Chase's adolescent help, after their parents' deaths, and he'd done a great job of it. But Cole was so over the top in love with his wife that he no longer even noticed other women. They could riot all they wanted, and Cole wouldn't care.

Both Cole and Chase had only recently married, and Zane swore Mack would be next, that the Winstons had somehow been either cursed or blessed, the two remaining bachelors still uncertain which it was. Oh, their brothers felt blessed, and the sisters-in-law were wonderful. It was just that Zane didn't ever want to marry, and Mack didn't want to marry anytime soon.

He'd been very cautious around women ever since Chase had unexpectedly succumbed, proving the virus to be very real. Of course, Mack had been shunning the dating scene for other reasons as well. While he was in college, his studies had taken precedence over everything else. Well, everything except one very sexy, very enticing woman—who hadn't wanted a damn thing to do with him. There were still times when he dreamed of her, and someday he hoped to meet a woman like her, one that could turn him on with just a look. But until then . . .

Sophie's hand tightened on his arm, and Mack tried to step away. He didn't get very far. Though she looked small and delicate, Sophie had a grip like a junkyard dog hanging on to a prized bone.

Zane sauntered over, his eyes glinting with humor. "I still think I'd have been the best choice. But you know I'm going out of town for that convention, so that leaves you, little brother."

Mack swallowed, eyeing each relative in turn. "What exactly does that leave me to do?"

Sophie squeezed a little closer, and her tone became cajoling. "Why, just a little modeling."

His brows shot up. "Modeling?"

"Yes."

Chase snorted again.

"All right." Mack decided enough was enough. "Sophie, turn me loose, I promise not to bolt. Zane, I'm going to flatten you if you don't stop grinning. And no, Chase, there's no need to snort again. I already gather this isn't something I'm going to enjoy."

"Nonsense!" Allison, his other meddling sister-in-law, whom he adored to distraction, leapt to her feet to join Sophie. Mack felt sandwiched between their combined feminine resolve. He assessed their wide-eyed, innocent stares warily.

With a sigh Cole came to his feet too. "Sophie has some harebrained idea of offering a new line of male lingerie at her boutique."

Male lingerie! Mack stiffened and again tried to back up. The sisters-in-law weren't allowing it.

"It's not lingerie, Cole," Sophie insisted in a huff. Since her pregnancy had gotten under way, she huffed more often. "It's loungewear. And it's very popular."

Mack's head throbbed the tiniest bit. "Loungewear?"

"Yes, you know, like silk boxers and robes and—"

Zane leaned forward. "And thongs and lace-up leopard-print briefs and leather skivvies and—"

Allison slapped her hand over Zane's mouth. "Women appreciate those nice things on a man."

Zane, Mack, and Cole all stared at Chase, who immediately started to bluster, while frowning at his wife. "Oh, no. You can forget those thoughts right now! That's just an assumption on Allison's part. You wouldn't catch me dead in any of that goofy stuff."

Disappointed, they all returned their attention to Mack. He looked around at their expressions, which varied from amused to resigned to hopeful, and he shook his head. "Hell, no."

Sophie glared at him. "You don't even know what it is that I want yet."

"Honey, I don't need to know. If it involves this . . . this . . . *male loungewear*. I want no part of it."

Her eyes narrowed in a calculating way. "All I need you to do—"

"No."

"—is to let the photographer get a few pictures of you in the clothing to advertise it in a new catalogue."

"No!"

"Because there's no way I can afford to hire a real model, who would probably have to come all the way from New York or Chicago, and I have the feeling you'd look better anyway."

Well, that was a nice compliment, but . . . he shook his head. "No."

Zane pried Allison's hand away. "Not as good as *I'd* look, but as I said—"

Three voices yelled in unison, "Shut up, Zane!"

Zane only chuckled.

Sophie continued, her voice coercing, her eyes wide. "This is a great opportunity for me, Mack. The photographer is a friend of mine, willing to do this cheap for the exposure it'll bring the studio. I'm getting a special deal here. It'll only take two or three days—"

"*No.*"

"—so it won't really interfere with your schedule or anything—"

"Damn it, Sophie—"

"—and Valentine's Day would be the perfect time to advertise the new line!"

Mack groaned.

"So it's all set, then! And Mack, I *really* appreciate it." She gave him a sideways, very calculating glance. "You can consider this payback for all those study sessions with me for your college science classes."

He felt doomed. He could only mumble, "Unfair, Sophie."

She batted her pretty blue eyes at him and said, "You'd never have passed anatomy without me."

Cole's mouth fell open. "All those late nights she helped you study, it was for *anatomy*?"

Mack rolled his eyes. "Just female reproduction. That stuff's confusing."

Zane roared with laughter, and this time Chase and Allison

joined him. Cole, still huffing, pulled his wife possessively to his side while Mack groped for a chair and fell into it.

"Well, hell." He looked to the heavens, but all he saw was the ceiling of the bar. He supposed there was no help for it at all.

He tilted his head toward Zane. "You'd actually have done this if you weren't going out of town?"

"Are you kidding? The women will love it. You'll have so many new dates, you won't have time to be in a funk."

"I'm not in a funk."

Chase snorted.

Rubbing his brow, Mack tried to ignore them all. He knew Zane probably would like to flaunt himself a little. He was a born exhibitionist and wallowed in the female attention heaped upon him. But Mack wasn't that way—at least, not as much so as Zane. There'd been only that one woman he'd ever wanted to wallow with.

He glared at Sophie and said, "I'm not wearing anything stupid."

She glared right back. "I wouldn't carry anything stupid at my boutique!" Then she softened. "But don't worry. There'll be a selection available, and you and the photographer can decide together which things to photograph. Other than a few definites that have to be in the catalogue, you can pick and choose."

"Gee, thanks."

Sophie handed him a card that read "Wells Photography," and listed a downtown address. She gave him a huge hug and kissed his cheek. "Be there Friday at two o'clock, okay?"

At least that gave him two days to get used to the idea. Or rather, two days to dread it.

Mack parked in the small lot to the side of Wells Photography, as directed by a hanging wooden sign. He'd checked his mail before leaving his apartment, but still no word from the board of education. He'd been a good teacher, damn it. The best. The kids had loved him, the parents respected him. His class had scored much higher than past averages, much higher than expected.

But the principal still hadn't recommended him.

His hands fisted in his coat pockets as he walked across the broken-concrete lot. He stared at his feet, ignoring the blustering wind, the beginning of wet, icy snow as it pelted the back of his neck. The sky was a dark gray, matching his mood. He'd never felt so helpless in his life, and he hated it. The principal's judgment of him, as well as her decision not to recommend, were beyond unfair, but there wasn't a damn thing he could do about it.

Finally, after Mack had crossed the nearly empty lot to the front of the building, he focused his thoughts enough to realize that the studio wasn't a studio at all but rather an older home. The redbrick two-story house was stately in a sort of worn-out way. It was hemmed in by the empty lot to the right and another older home advertising apartments for rent on the left.

Squinting against the freezing January wind, Mack bounded up the salted concrete steps to the front door and knocked briskly.

A thin, freckle-faced girl of about thirteen answered. She grinned, flashing a shiny set of braces. Mack grinned back. "Hello."

"Hi."

"Ah . . . I'm looking for the photographer?"

She nodded. "Are you here for the two o'clock shoot?"

"Yep. I'm Mack Winston."

The girl opened the door and let him in. "You can follow me. My mom is just finishing up another session, so you won't need to wait long. We had two cancellations because of the storm. Our receptionist is sick, so I'm sorta filling in."

She closed the door behind Mack, then started down a short hardwood-floored hall. To the right was an open set of curtained glass doors, revealing an office of sorts inside, though the outside wall was mostly used up by an enormous fireplace. To the left of the hall was a flight of stairs leading to a closed door that separated the upper story. Mack continued to look around. "You say your mother is the photographer?"

The girl tucked long brown hair behind her ear and nodded, while stealing quick peeks at Mack. "Yeah. She's real good."

They entered a room that had a utilitarian beige couch and a single chair in it, a table full of magazines, and a coffee machine. To Mack, it looked to be converted from a kitchen, judging by the placement of the window and a few exposed pipes.

The walls were decorated with dozens of incredible photographs, ranging from babies to brides to entire families. There were outdoor scenes with animals in them, indoor scenes around a Christmas tree. Babies in booties, men in suits, children in their Sunday best.

All of the photographs were beautiful, proof of very real talent.

Another set of glass double doors, these closed with opaque curtains, apparently separated the studio. Mack shrugged off his coat, hung it on the coat tree, and then chose the chair in the far corner.

The girl smiled shyly at him. "You want some coffee or something?"

"No, thanks." He returned her smile. "What did you do? Skip school today?"

"We had a half day for teacher in-service."

"Ah. Lucky for your mom, huh? I bet she really appreciates your help with the receptionist missing." He grinned his most engaging grin. The girl blushed and again tucked her hair behind her ear.

Before she could say anything, the phone rang, and she dashed off to answer it. Mack chuckled. He just adored kids, which was one reason why he was determined to get a teaching position.

Of course, at the moment, his teaching possibilities looked grim. That thought had him scowling again, ready to sink into despair. God, he hated brooding—it didn't suit him at all.

Fortunately the photographer chose that moment to open the door. Mack heard two sets of feminine voices and his senses prickled. Something about one of those voices was familiar, sending a wave of heat up his spine. There'd been only one woman who had ever affected him that way, but it couldn't possibly be her. Still, he leaned forward to peer around the coffee machine.

A young woman holding a squirming baby faced him, while the photographer had her back to Mack, displaying a very long, very thick braid hanging all the way down to her bottom. *Oh, damn, he knew that braid!* He leaned a little more, feeling ridiculously anxious, holding his breath. Then she turned slightly, giving him her profile, and Mack felt like a mule had kicked him in the ribs.

Jessica Wells.

His heart slowed, then picked up speed. It was a reaction very familiar to him. Just like the last time he'd seen her, he felt his muscles tremble, his stomach knot, his body go simultaneously hard and hot.

He hadn't seen her since college, almost two years ago, and hadn't suffered such an extreme reaction to a woman since then. But Jessica had always been unaware of the turmoil she caused him regardless of how he'd tried his best to be friendly with her, to get her attention. She was maybe six, eight years older than he was, quiet and very serious. Even a little withdrawn. He'd always thought her adorable with her standoffish ways and reserved manner.

She had beautiful chocolate-brown eyes that made him think of soft, warm things—like the way a woman looked after making love. She had a narrow nose slightly tilted up on the end, high cheekbones, and a small, rounded chin.

She also had the most impressive breasts he'd ever laid eyes on. They made his mouth go dry and his palms sweat. Not that he was hung up on physical attributes . . . except that he'd dreamed about her at night, about getting her out of her conservative sweaters and her no doubt sturdy brassiere so he could see her naked, touch her lush flesh and taste her nipples . . .

He swallowed hard, still staring, taking advantage of the moment, since she remained unaware of him.

Mack had always felt intrigued by her. She'd been so different from the flighty girls who'd flirted with him continually. But the few times he'd tried to talk to her, she had turned her small nose up in utter disregard.

Well, she'd have to talk to him now. *Thank you, Sophie.*

Jessica spoke easily with the woman, who struggled to control the chubby baby boy dressed in a miniature suit. She smiled, and Mack felt the impact of it clear down in his gut. In the time they'd spent together in class, he didn't think she'd ever smiled, not even a glimmer of a smile. No, she was the epitome of seriousness, and it had made him nuts.

Mack was a natural smiler. He liked being happy, friendly, courteous to everyone. But trying to wheedle a smile out of Jessica had been like trying to get a fish to sing.

He still recalled the first day he'd seen her, when she'd walked into the same photo tech class, loaded down with books, looking conspicuous and nervous and uncomfortable. He'd been sitting in the front, and she'd sat as far in the back as she could get. He'd twisted all the way around to see her, but her gaze had met his only once, then skittered away.

He'd taken the photography class out of casual interest, thinking it might be a way to make some of the lessons more fun for his students. And it had. But obviously it had been much more for her.

While tickling the baby's chin, she said, "I'll call in about a week after I get the proofs together, and then we can set up an appointment for you to make your choices."

The woman sighed gratefully. "You're a saint, being so patient with him. I don't know why he was so fussy today."

Mack figured any guy stuffed into a suit had a reason to be fussy.

The baby kicked, prompting his mother to hurry along. After they'd gone, Jessica checked her watch, rubbed her brow, then headed for the coffee machine. That's when she noticed Mack.

Drawing up short, she stared, her dark eyes widening, but only for a single moment. Then, with a carefully blank expression, she stepped forward and extended her hand. "Mr. Winston?"

Mack resisted the urge to mimic Chase's snort. There was no way she didn't recognize him. *Was there?* Surely he'd made some sort of impression! But when her expression remained fixed, he started to wonder. Narrowing his eyes, he slowly stood and extended his hand. Here he was, indulging in erotic daydreams, and she didn't even remember him. "That's right," he said, keeping his voice moderate. "Actually, we met in college a few years ago."

She blinked lazily as his hand enclosed hers. He felt her tremble the tiniest bit as she summoned a look of polite confusion. "We did?"

Okay, so she'd always ignored him. She'd been as far from impressed by him as a woman could get. She'd still been aware of him, he was sure of it. And two years wasn't so long that she could have totally forgotten him.

He held her hand when she would have pulled away and tried for a cocky grin. "Yeah. We had a class together. Photo tech. Remember?"

Suddenly she smiled, a very phony smile that set his teeth on edge. "Ah, I remember now! Mack Winston. You were the class Romeo who kept all those silly coeds in a tizzy."

She tugged hard and he let her hand go. "Class Romeo? Hardly."

She waved his words away, as if he were only being modest. "Yes, yes, I remember now. All those foolish girls crowded around you. Half the time I couldn't hear the instructor for all their whispering and giggling. I think you probably dated every one of them. I was always rather amazed by your . . . stamina."

Every single word she said, though softly spoken, sounded like a veiled insult. It wasn't something Mack was used to. But of course, nothing with Jessica, including his feelings, was ever as he expected.

He rocked back on his heels and slowly looked her over, from the form-fitting jeans to the loose white sweater and braided brown hair. Physically, she hadn't changed at all. She still turned him on. Even now, he could feel his muscles tightening, the heat beneath his skin. He wanted her, and all she'd done so far was insult him.

Carefully gauging his words, he said, "I remember you being a recluse—and maybe just a little stuck up."

Her expression darkened, her brown eyes turning nearly black. "I was not stuck up! It was just that, compared to you . . . well, I was there to learn, not to socialize."

She sounded defensive, and he wondered about it. He also wondered what it would be like to kiss the mulish expression away from her lips. "This may surprise you, but I learned. I just had fun doing it."

"Now, *that* I can believe. The fun part, that is."

There was nothing distracted about Mack's brain at the moment. No, he felt razor-sharp, focused, full-witted and aroused. He prepared to coach her on his idea of fun, when the young girl suddenly raced into the room. When she saw her mother and Mack facing off, she skidded to a halt. "Uh, Mom, I don't mean to interrupt—"

With obvious relief, Jessica turned away, effectively dismissing Mack. "That's all right, honey. You're not interrupting anything . . . important."

Her choice of words made Mack feel relegated to the back burner. He almost laughed because he recognized her efforts to distance herself. Yeah, she remembered him. She could deny it all she wanted, but he wasn't buying it.

"Well . . ." The young girl played with her hair, sneaking looks between her mother and Mack. "Since you don't have any more appointments today, I was thinking of going to Jenna's. Her dad will pick me up. She . . . uh, invited a few friends over."

"Friends, as in guy-type friends?"

The girl grimaced, then leaned forward and said in an excited stage whisper, "Brian's going to be there!"

Mack watched as Jessica fought with her smile—another genuine smile this time. "Oh, well, in that case, how could I possibly refuse?" Before Trista could work up a loud squeal, she added, "I assume Jenna's parents will be there the whole time?"

"Yeah."

"All right, then. Call when you're ready to come home and I'll come get you."

Trista ran forward and hugged her mother, then with the energy exclusive to the early teens, charged out of the room.

Mack chuckled. "She's really cute."

"Thank you." Jessica said it with pride, and for the first time Mack felt her defenses were down.

"I gather Brian is a guy she likes?"

Jessica almost laughed. "My daughter is suffering her first crush. And so far, the 'totally awesome' Brian hasn't even noticed her."

"It's a tough age for kids."

"You're telling me! She went from wanting Barbie dolls to pierced ears overnight. Shopping has become an all-day expedition. And she absolutely hates her braces."

She seemed so natural, so at ease discussing her daughter, that Mack felt encouraged. He stepped a little closer, appreciating the softness in her eyes, the slight smile playing over her lips. He wanted to touch her, but of course, that would be over the line. "I didn't realize you had a daughter. Especially not one that old."

Jessica immediately stiffened. "No reason you should know."

"Are you married?"

She ignored him. "Sophie told me she was sending a male model."

"She sent me." He held his arms out to the side.

"Are you a professional?"

"Not at modeling."

She didn't take the bait. "This might be a problem. Getting just the right pose isn't easy."

"I think I can manage—with a little direction."

She continued to eye him, then shook her head. "I've known Sophie for a while, knew that she married, but I never connected the last name."

Mack followed her as she started into the studio. Her jeans did interesting things for her bottom, and hazardous things to his libido. Jessica Wells was a lushly rounded woman. "Hmm. Why would you have? You didn't even remember me, right?"

She stalled and he almost bumped into her. His hands settled on her straight shoulders, but then she hurried away. "That's right. Now, we should get started." Again she checked her watch. "We've got a lot to get done today."

Mack folded his arms over his chest. "Sophie told me it might take a couple of shoots to get everything done."

"Oh, no. With any luck, I can finish up today." She sounded nearly desperate as she said it, then rushed over to a long, narrow table and picked up a folder. "I have the catalogue layout right here. We'll need about thirty pictures. Some of them just of your . . . uh . . ."

Her gaze skimmed his lap, then darted away. "Just of the garments. Others will need all of you in them."

She seemed nervous, flitting about, grabbing up various papers and carrying them from one table to another. Mack leaned against the wall to watch her. For the first time in a long while, he felt totally absorbed in something other than worries about his future teaching position.

The room was interesting. Props occupied every corner and filled several shelving units. One entire wall was empty except for large pull-down screen devices that held various backdrops. All of the camera equipment was centered at the far end of the room.

The studio was at the back of the house and had two windows each on three walls. Dark shades kept out any sunlight, and bright lights had been turned on instead. Finally Jessica seemed to get herself organized. She began hauling a large box toward the table. Mack stepped forward to help her.

Against her protests, he picked up the box and asked, "Where do you want it?"

Resigned, she motioned toward the table. "Set it on the floor there. We have to figure out which things you'll model. There's a pretty good sampling of the, uh, briefs inside, and on the rack there's other stuff."

She wouldn't quite meet his gaze. Suspicious, Mack opened the box and peeked in. He immediately slammed the cardboard lid down again, then stared at Jessica.

"What?" She leaned toward the box, but he pulled it out of her reach.

Damn. He cleared his throat. "Let's start with some other stuff."

She looked equal parts curious, hesitant, and determined. "Why? Sophie wants at least eighteen shots of briefs, to give a good sampling of what she'll be offering. We're supposed to do nine shots to a page."

Eighteen shots of him in tiny scraps of material? When he was already half hard? Ha! "Couldn't they just be shot on a mannequin or something?"

Her efforts at indifference weren't overly effective. Her cheeks had turned a dusky-rose color and she wouldn't quite meet his gaze. "Wouldn't matter to me. But Sophie might not like it. She said she wanted her customers to see a real man wearing this stuff, to prove real men look good in it."

Mack grinned. "A real man, huh?" The color in her face intensified, and Mack totally forgot his own hesitation. He shoved the box toward her. "All right. You pick."

"Me?"

"Sure. You have a trained eye, so you should probably be able to tell what'll look best on me." Feeling a little outrageous, he stood up to tower over her. He widened his stance, spread his arms out to his sides. "You might want to, ah, *study* my form first, right? I mean, so you have a good idea of what would look most complimentary on my particular physique." She'd know he was aroused, but so what? He wanted her to know how she affected him.

He watched as stubbornness surfaced in her expression. She stared back at him, hard, her gaze never leaving his face. Then without looking away from him, she reached into the box. She felt around and finally tugged out a teeny-tiny pair of paisley-print thong briefs. She thrust them toward him like a challenge.

Mack almost laughed. With his baby finger, he accepted the briefs, which had no apparent backside and were so sheer that they weighed about as much as a hankie. Trying to sound earnest, he asked, "Do they, perhaps, come in a larger size?"

Pretending to take him seriously, Jessica searched through her papers. "Nope. One size fits all."

Mack gave the outrageous briefs a dubious inspection. "Hmmm. I must be unique, then, because there's no way these puppies are gonna fit me."

She lifted one slim brown brow. "Oh? They're too . . . big?"

Mack choked, but quickly recovered. He liked it that she now felt comfortable enough to tease. "Jessica, I don't think you actually looked at me when I told you to."

She shrugged. "I did, but then I guess my mind wandered."

"Ah. Got you thinking of *other things*, did it?"

"Actually, I forgot my glasses so I couldn't really see the insignificant things . . ."

This time Mack did laugh. She hadn't looked at his body, only his face, or she'd have seen some *very* significant things. "You're very damaging to a man's ego, you know that?"

She made a rude sound and shook her head. "As if your ego needed any help."

Just that easily, she went from playful to insulting again. He squatted down in front of her and leaned over the box to make certain he had her attention. "Why do I get the feeling you've made some assumptions about me, and none of them are particularly favorable?"

With him so close, she looked startled and breathless. She jerked way back—and toppled onto her bottom. Amused by her telltale response, Mack stood up and pulled her to her feet. She quickly shook him off, as if his touch bothered her more than it should, then took two hasty steps back.

"This is ridiculous," she protested. "I don't have all day to banter with you."

She was suddenly so flustered, he knew damn well she couldn't have been as indifferent to him as she'd claimed. Only a woman aware of a man could be so affected by a simple touch. Why did she continue to deny it?

He didn't understand her. They'd been joking like old friends, having fun, and then suddenly she'd seemed to realize it and retreated back into herself. He crossed his arms and gave her a curious stare. "If you're pressed for time, then we should probably get this cleared up right now."

She turned away and stalked to the clothes rack. She yanked down a hanger that held a black silk kimono robe with red piping and matching pull-on pajama pants. She thrust them toward him. "I have a better idea. Let's just get some photos taken, like we're supposed to."

Mack refused to take the garments. "Since you claim to barely remember me, and I know damn good and well I never did anything to make you dislike me, your animosity seems pretty strange."

"Look, Mr. Winston—"

He barely choked back his laugh of disbelief. "Mr. Winston? Get real, Jessica. At least admit you remember my damn name."

There was a second of vibrating silence, then she seemed to

explode. She tossed the clothing aside and thrust her chin toward him. "Well, with the girls all talking about you all the time, I suppose it'd be hard to forget!"

Her sudden anger inflamed him. Her dark eyes were impossibly bright, her chin firmed, her cheeks flushed. Her lush breasts rose and fell in her agitation, and she had her fists propped on her rounded hips.

He wanted to kiss her silly.

He wanted to watch all that anger and frustration turn into passion. Just the thought made him catch his breath. He wanted to howl, because she made him hotter than a sultan's harem, but she refused to let him close.

Never in his life had a woman reacted to Mack the way this woman did. She seemed more comfortable ignoring, antagonizing, or insulting him than she did just getting along with him. It didn't make sense—and for some insane reason, he felt more intrigued than ever.

Marshaling his limited control, Mack shook his head and managed a relatively calm reply. "I'm definitely missing something here, and it's not your hostility, because that's pretty damn clear. So why don't you just spell it out, Jessica? What's the problem?"

She struggled in silence, her nostrils flaring, and then, after a deep, calming breath, she nodded. "All right."

She looked so serious, Mack held his breath.

After licking her lips nervously, she said, "I resented you. Back then. Not now. As I said, I barely remember you."

Her breasts were still doing that distracting rise-and-fall thing that was making him nuts. He tried to pay attention to her words, but it wasn't easy. "Uh-huh. So why did you resent me?"

"Because I worked my behind off in college. It wasn't easy going back, being so much older than everyone else and having so many more responsibilities. And I was raising Trista alone, and half the time the class was interrupted by the instructor fawning over you, or one of the girls asking me to pass you a note, or you making eyes at the girls—"

Mack blinked at her, pleased by her admission. "If you'd been paying attention to the instructor, instead of me, you wouldn't have noticed me making eyes, now, would you?" He watched her face heat again, the color climbing from her throat all the way up to her hairline. She had very delicate skin, not overly pale, just smooth and silky-looking.

He wondered if she would flush like that during a climax.

Her eyes, clean of any makeup, almost exactly matched the golden-brown shade of her hair. And that hair . . . he'd always noticed it in college. She kept it long, but he'd never seen it out of the braid. It was so thick, the braid so heavy, he could only imagine what it'd be like loose. He used to wait to take a seat until she had, so he could occasionally sit behind her. Without her knowing it, he'd touched her braid, felt how warm and silky it was.

At least, he'd thought she didn't know—until she started sitting in the middle of a cluster of students, ensuring he couldn't get close.

He watched her now as she gathered her thoughts. Little wisps of hair escaped her braid to float around her face, teasing him. He wanted to reach out and smooth them down, to reassure her, but judging from her expression, she'd probably sock him if he tried it.

"Jessica?"

She worried her bottom lip for a moment, then finally sighed. "You're right, of course. And I did try to ignore you. But you were a terrible distraction and I suppose I resented that more than anything."

Cautiously, drawn by an inexplicable mix of emotions he'd never dealt with before, Mack stepped closer. "Why?"

She laughed. "You'll think this is nuts, but you remind me of my husband."

That wasn't at all what he'd been expecting. He stilled. She'd said that she'd raised her daughter alone, so he assumed she wasn't married. He *hoped* like hell she wasn't married. *She'd better not be* . . . "Are you widowed?"

She shook her head hard, causing her braid to fall over one shoulder and curl along her left breast. Mack gulped, forcing his gaze resolutely to her face.

"No, divorced. For quite some time now. But just as you seemed to be the life of the party, so was he. Nothing mattered to him but having a good time. Even when Trista was born, he refused to grow up and settle down, to be a husband or a father. And he was about your age when I stupidly married him."

"I see." But he didn't, not really. He wasn't a husband or a father, but he knew in his heart he'd take those responsibilities very seriously.

She smiled, and again shook her head. "I'm sorry. It's none of my business if you choose to make life fun and games. That's certainly your choice, and I had no right to sit in judgment of you. Whew. I feel better now."

She felt better? Mack clenched his jaw, he was so annoyed. He wasn't irresponsible or immature. He knew what his priorities were, and he kept them straight. No one had worked harder in college or taken his lessons more seriously than he. Yet she automatically labeled him because he'd managed to make school fun. Enjoyment was the standard he'd set for his students, his teaching method for making information stick. It was also one of the reasons the principal hadn't recommended him for the available teaching position. She and Jessica evidently had a few things in common. They were both self-righteous and far too somber.

Only the principal didn't turn him on, but Jessica most certainly did. She always had.

Mack kept his expression impassive. "So now your conscience is clear?"

"Exactly. Imagine, a woman my age reacting to a two-year-old resentment, especially toward someone so young."

"I'm twenty-four."

She nodded, as if that confirmed her suspicions. "It's ludicrous. Why, obviously your outlook would be different from my own."

"Because you're so . . . old?"

"Well, if thirty is old, which I suppose to someone your age, it is." She smiled again. "So, can you forgive my surly attitude? Do you think we can start over and go ahead with the shoot?"

He didn't want to; he wanted to keep talking to her, to get to know her better. But he had promised Sophie. And he had no doubt Zane would ride him forever if he let his reactions to this one woman keep him from getting the job done. He could console himself with the fact that she'd noticed him, she just didn't like noticing him.

When he hesitated, she sighed again. "I don't blame you, I guess. But really, I'm not one of those bitter divorcées who can't talk about anything else. I promise not to even mention it again. And to tell you the truth, I was really looking forward to this shoot. It'll be a nice opportunity for me, more than I've ever done before, since my work usually only includes portraits."

"So you want this job?"

"Yes, of course."

Mack nodded. Now he had something to work with. "I'll stay."

He saw the subtle relaxing of her shoulders, the relief she tried hard to hide. "Good."

"We only have one problem."

"Oh? And what's that?"

"You promised not to mention your husband or your divorce again."

"That's right."

Mack smiled, and he knew damn good and well his eyes were

gleaming with intent. Good. Let her know he wouldn't be brushed off. "I want to know about your husband. And your divorce. I want lots of little details. Since I remind you of the guy, it only seems fair. Don't you think?"

Two

Jessica stared at Mack Winston, caught between wanting to laugh and wanting to smack him. She was used to that particular reaction—and other, more sexual reactions as well, if she was honest with herself.

He was so incredibly gorgeous, so young and handsome and sexy. He'd whizzed through college, not caring about his grades, always joking, always having a good time, while she'd been forced to struggle to make mediocre B's.

His carefree attitude and abundant charm did remind her of her ex-husband, and that's why her attraction to him scared her so much. Why couldn't she be drawn to a staid, mature man, one that would be steady and responsible? She'd tried dating a few times a year after her divorce was finalized, but the men she wanted to be interested in didn't stir a single speck of interest in her.

And the one who did, the one who made her feel young and alive again, was exactly the type of man she knew she should stay away from.

When she'd graduated, she'd thought to never see him again. It had been both a relief, because he was a terrible temptation, and a crushing pain, because she still thought of him often, still awakened in the night after dreaming of him. And now, here he was, in the flesh, and if anything, two years had added to his appeal. *Darn Sophie Winston, anyway.*

Drawing a deep breath and dredging up another nonchalant smile, she asked, "What exactly would you like to know?" She had no intention of letting him see how uncomfortable he, and the conversation, made her feel.

Mack picked up the sexy pajamas with a smile. "How about I change while we talk? That way I won't hold you up."

He'd gotten his way, so now he'd be accommodating? She swallowed her huff of annoyance. "That's fine. You can change behind that curtain."

He gave her a smile that she was certain had melted many a female heart. When Mack Winston smiled, you saw it not only on his sexy mouth, but in his dark eyes that always glittered with humor, in the dimple in his lean cheek, in the warmth that seemed to radiate from him. She expected that nearly every female in Thomasville, Kentucky, had fantasized over him at least once.

But fantasizing was all she would ever do.

While he was occupied, Jessica rummaged through the cardboard box, looking in vain for items that wouldn't expose his body overly.

"Tell me why you divorced him."

She glanced up and saw Mack's flannel shirt get slung over the curtain rod. She gulped as a sharp twinge of excitement raced down her spine. A white T-shirt and belt quickly followed, making her imagination go wild.

"Jessica?"

"I, ah . . . I told you. He wouldn't settle down. He kept losing jobs, running through our money. Trista was not quite seven when I filed for divorce, eight before everything was finalized. I decided to go back to college so I could bone up on the newest photography techniques. It was something I'd always wanted to do, but I'd worked to get Gary through college, and then Trista was born, and, well . . . I just never got around to it. After the divorce, I needed a way to support us both—"

"Is he still around?"

His worn, faded jeans landed on top of the flannel, and her tongue stuck to the roof of her mouth. *Mack was naked behind the curtain.* "Who?"

"Your ex."

"Oh. Uh, no. Well, sometimes. He lives in Florida, and every so often he remembers Trista and sends her a card or a gift." She looked down at the pile of so-called briefs and quickly tried to decide which ones would conceal the most.

"He doesn't pay child support?"

"Ha!"

"You could sue him for it, you know."

Everything she picked up was far too scanty, too revealing, to actually suggest that he wear it. She was a thirty-year-old woman who'd been celibate for too many years to count. Her heart wouldn't take the strain. "But then I'd have to suffer his presence. This way, he's almost completely out of my life, and he's not messing with Trista's emotions."

"What have you told her about him?"

She stared at the damn briefs, imagined them filled out by his masculine flesh, and felt flustered. "Only that we didn't get along, but it had nothing to do with her. When she asks me why he doesn't come around more, I tell her that he does love her, it's just that some people have a hard time settling into domestic roles."

"That's pretty wise of you, you know. So many times, parents are bitter and they force their kids into the middle of things without even meaning to. And the only ones who get hurt by it are the kids."

"I would never tell Trista what a jerk her father is. Hopefully, by the time she gets old enough to figure things out on her own, he'll have gotten his act together."

She glanced up as Mack stepped around the curtain—and froze. He adjusted the waistband, leaving the sheer pants to hang low on his lean hips. The robe was draped over his arm. He was barefoot, his hair appealing mussed, his hairy chest wide and sexy and hard. His abdomen was sculpted with muscle, and a line of silky hair led from his navel downward. She wanted to look away, but she couldn't quite manage it. Her heart beat so hard it hurt, and her stomach did strange little jumps that felt both sweetly tantalizing and very disturbing.

Oh, Lord, it had been so long since she'd seen a mostly naked man.

And she'd *never* seen a man like Mack Winston.

He paused in the center of the floor, then simply stood there, hands on his hips, and let her look. His eyes narrowed, direct and hot and probing, and his smile tilted in a sensual, teasing way.

Finally, when it dawned on her how long they'd both been silent, she jumped to her feet. An impressive array of colorful, silky underwear fluttered off her lap and onto the floor, like a platoon of male butterflies folding ranks. She looked down, realized she'd been practically buried in the damn things, and almost groaned. She swallowed, staring at the heap on the floor. "I was . . . was looking for which ones you should pose in."

She felt more than heard him move closer. "It's not going to be an easy job."

Didn't she know it! "We'll figure out something." She cleared her throat roughly. "Now, would you like to put on the robe?" She contrived a polite smile, managed to raise her gaze to his face without lingering too long on all the exquisite male flesh in between, and then wished she hadn't bothered. He was just so handsome, he took her breath away.

"The robe is a little tight in the shoulders. I'll put it on when you're ready to take the picture."

She nodded dumbly, stared some more, then shook herself. She was not, and never had been, a giddy coed. She was a mother and an independent businesswoman. "Right. Uh, just let me get a few things ready."

It took her only seconds to arrange the set as she wanted it. She pulled down a background that looked like a kitchen, set a tall stool and a coffee mug nearby, then motioned him over. "You're going to pretend you're just out of bed, okay?"

"I'm supposed to have slept in this stuff?"

"Is that a problem?"

"I sleep naked."

Jessica faltered, verbally stumbled over a few gasps, then glared at him. "It doesn't matter what your normal sleeping habits really are. This is just to show the clothing to advantage."

"Jessica, no man in his right mind would try to sleep in this stuff. Have you felt it?" He offered his thigh for her to test the material. She backed up, feeling foolish, yet utterly appalled at the thought of actually touching that thick, hard thigh.

Mack blinked lazily at her, his look so knowing she felt another blush. "It's slippery. And there's no give to it. No man would sleep in it—"

"Then pretend you just pulled it on after you got out of bed!"

"When I'm alone? Why would I do that?"

She closed her eyes and counted to ten, doing her best not to imagine Mack traipsing around his home impressively naked. She failed. The image flashed into her mind and refused to budge.

It felt like a Bunsen burner had been turned on inside her, especially low in her belly, where the heat seemed to pulse. "Mack." She said his name through her teeth. "Just sit on the damn bar stool and sip your coffee, okay?"

He shrugged. "If you say so, but it's a dumb pose."

She gave up. "Okay, how do you suggest we set it?"

"Maybe in the evening, in front of a fire." His gaze met hers. "With company."

"Company?"

He stepped closer, and the lamplight shone on his hard shoulders, heating his skin. "Sure. This stuff is supposed to appeal to women, right? So wouldn't a guy only wear it for a woman?"

She hated to admit it, but he had a point. "All right. Let's try this." She replaced the kitchen backdrop screen with one that featured a glowing stone fireplace. With Mack's help, a plush easy chair replaced the stool. Jessica used the stool to situate a female mannequin's arm, holding a wineglass, just to the side of the chair. The arm would be visible from the elbow down, as if a woman were offering the glass to Mack.

He approved.

They got several nice shots of him lounging at his ease, smiling in the direction of the phony woman. The robe was open to show his hard belly, his sculpted pecs.

She probably took more shots than she needed, but he was such a natural, she could almost feel jealous of the damned plastic arm.

After that, they took two sets of photos of Mack in drapey silk boxers. He admitted to liking them, and she admitted, only to herself, that he'd definitely draw in the female customers, just as Sophie had expected.

Though the snow continued to fall and the temperature continued to drop, Jessica felt much too warm. She realized she was turned on just from photographing him, and prayed he'd never know.

"What now?"

"Reading the morning paper on the terrace—and no, don't tell me you wouldn't go outside in your underwear."

"Sure I would."

She almost laughed, he was so incorrigible. They arranged the set together, using a small bistro table and chair, a pot of silk flowers, and a screen showing morning sunshine and blue sky.

"Now we need to pick the underwear."

Mack glanced doubtfully at the pile she'd left on the floor. "I don't know . . ."

She hesitated as well. She didn't *want* to see him in nothing more than a strip of silk or mesh or vinyl. Her pulse raced just at the thought. The damn boxers had been difficult enough, though at least they weren't so blatantly suggestive. They hung over his masculine endowments, rather than hugging them. But the skimpy briefs . . .

She really had no choice.

And, she thought, if it was any man other than Mack Winston, it wouldn't even be an issue.

She glanced at her watch, dismayed to see that they hadn't gotten nearly enough done, then struggled to achieve a level of professionalism in her voice. "After this shot, we'll just take some of the various briefs. The photos will show only your navel to your upper thighs."

Mack blinked at her, and no wonder. Her voice had sounded like a frog being ruthlessly strangled.

She forged onward. "Would you like to choose the briefs or should I?"

Mack waved at the pile. "Be my guest."

Bound and determined to get it over with, she grabbed the pair closest to the top. "Here."

Mack frowned. "What's wrong with them? They're kind of bunched up."

She looked at the thin blue underwear carefully, then wanted to kick herself. Lifting her chin, she explained, "They have a seam down the back."

"Why?"

"It's . . . it's a . . . well, here. I'll just read the description to you."

She rushed over to the table and picked up her file. After flipping through a few pages, she found the item number. "It says, 'cheek-enhancing feature with rear seam to shape comfortably—"

"You can damn well forget that pair!"

There was no way she could look at him. "Mack . . ."

"My backside doesn't need enhancing, thank you very much."

She couldn't have agreed more. "Ah, fine. You pick. You're the one who has to wear them. But keep in mind, if you choose a thong, you'll probably have to shave."

"Why? I thought the shots were only from my navel down."

It felt like her heart lodged in her throat. "Yes, and that's where you'd have to shave. Too much body hair—"

"You can forget the damn thongs, too!"

Relief made her chatty. "All right. Good. I mean, fine. We can maybe take a shot of you hanging them on a clotheslines—"

He grunted, as if that idea didn't appeal to him at all either, but he'd accept it rather than the alternative.

"Are you almost ready?" The longer he took, the edgier she got.

"I'm looking. But I can tell you right now, no thongs, no animal prints, and no vinyl."

She peeked out of the corner of her eye, pretending to rearrange her papers, while Mack held up pair after pair, finally choosing the one with the most fabric.

"I'll be right back." He stomped off behind the curtain, and Jessica held her breath until her lungs hurt.

Ridiculous, she told herself. She was thirty years old. She'd been married and divorced. She was an independent woman. She'd more than learned her lesson about run-around, frivolous men who . . .

Mack stepped out.

Her wits scattered, every logical argument vanishing in an instant. *Impressive.* She no sooner thought it than she squeezed her eyes shut. Good grief. She was not a sex-starved woman who went about measuring men's endowments. But—well, he looked incredible. Better than incredible. Perfect. A very impressive male specimen.

He cleared his throat impatiently, and she opened her eyes again. It was an effort, but she essayed a look of outward indifference, when inside her body was dealing with numerous responses to his appeal.

Then he stepped into the harsh lamplight, and she saw that the material miraculously turned transparent. *Oh, my God.*

"Jessica, you're staring."

The black briefs now looked like a mere shadow on him, and she'd never seen anything so enticing.

"If you continue to stare, I won't be responsible for what happens."

She swallowed hard and tried to get her gaze to move, but the effort proved more than she could manage. The man was all but naked. Surely no sane woman would look away.

"It's a perfectly natural response, you understand, when a sexy woman stares at a man like she wants him."

That got her attention. Her gaze shot to his face. "Sexy woman?"

He didn't move, except to frown slightly. "You."

"I'm not—"

"Yes, you are." He sounded very positive and his eyes glowed hotly. "Very sexy. Just about as sexy as a woman can possibly get." When she gave him a blank stare, his expression turned tender. "You didn't know?"

"But . . . that's ridiculous."

"Afraid not."

"You never paid a bit of attention to me," she said in near desperation.

He started forward, prompting her to back up. But at least he was moving away from the light, and his briefs were once again opaque. The relief afforded her a modicum of sensibility.

"Mack, we were in the same class for two semesters. Other than a few smiles tossed my way, you ignored me."

"That's not the way I remember it. And I bet if you think real hard, it's not even the way you remember it." He kept moving forward until he stood a mere foot in front of her. He searched her face, his gaze lingering on her lips. "Jessica, you always fascinated me. I tried my damnedest to get your attention, but all you ever did was turn your nose up at me."

She'd backed up so far, her bottom was pressed to the edge of the table. She reached back and gripped the table for support. "You had about a million girlfriends. All young and silly and—"

"They were *friends,* honey. That's all."

She snorted as rudely as Chase ever had. "You expect me to believe that?" Before he could answer, she added, "Not that it matters, anyway! You could have slept with the instructor and I wouldn't care."

"I think you do care."

"Well, you're wrong."

"Jessica, I have a lot of friends, a lot of female friends. That doesn't mean I'm sleeping with them all. And that doesn't mean I react to them all the way I'm reacting to you, the way I've always reacted to you."

Her heart rapped up against her breastbone and she trembled. "I don't know what you're talking about."

One side of his mouth kicked up in a very boyish grin. "I have an erection, honey. In these stupid flesh-hugging briefs, it's not really something I can hide."

Of course she looked, just as he knew she would.

He chuckled softly. "Your staring is what caused that in the first place. If you hope to take any more pictures today, I think we need to cool things down a bit."

He wanted her? The truth of that hit her like a thunderclap. Her hands shook, and she curled them into fists. Her breathing became shallow, her skin too warm. She drew in a slow, uneven breath, but it didn't help.

"Then again," he said, his voice a low, rough rasp, as he watched the signs of arousal blooming in her features, "maybe not."

She felt the heat pouring off him, felt his sexual tension. She looked up, and it was her undoing. His eyes had darkened, narrowed intently. His cheekbones were flushed. He touched her chin with the edge of his hand, raising her face more. Then slowly, giving her a chance to pull away, he leaned down.

She didn't want to pull away. It had been so long since she'd been with a man, long before the divorce became final. Though she did her best to deny it, there were times when her body ached with need. But never so much as it did right now. Mack affected her in a way she hadn't even known was possible; every nerve ending felt acutely alive and needy.

His mouth barely touched hers, moved away, came back. The kiss was tentative, exploring. He skimmed her lips, teasing, moving over her jaw, the tip of her nose, her chin. She panted, following his mouth, hungry for it. She went on tiptoe to bring his mouth closer.

He only touched her with that one hand, holding her face up, keeping her expectant. Rational thought was nonexistent. She stepped away from the table to get closer to him.

Their bodies brushed together, and he groaned. "Damn, I've dreamed about this."

"Mack . . ."

He settled his mouth against hers, and she felt drowned in the moist heat, the delicious taste of him. His hand opened, his calloused fingertips sliding over her jaw and into her hair. His hand curled around her head, tilting it slightly. His mouth moved, urging her lips to part for his tongue.

Her hands were still fisted at her sides, and she realized he wouldn't come closer until she invited him to do so. In a near daze, mindless with heat and lust and desperation, she raised her arms. His shoulders were hard, his flesh incredibly hot and smooth under her palms, and she felt him, greedy for more. She stepped closer still, pressing her breasts into the hard wall of his chest. The low, harsh sound he made sent goose bumps dancing up her spine. She clutched at him, and he wrapped one muscled arm around her waist, practically lifting her off her feet.

His erection throbbed against her belly.

"Mack . . ." She pulled her mouth away, gasping.

In between kissing her throat, her shoulder, he whispered, "I love hearing you say my name." He pressed his forehead to hers and sighed. "Am I moving too fast, Jessica?"

She could only groan, which he evidently took as encouragement. Kissing her again, he slid one hand down her back to her bottom, then urged her closer, moved her against him. She felt his fingers caressing, cuddling, squeezing. His hand was so large, and she could feel the heat of his palm even through her jeans. He lightly bit her bottom lip. "God, I'm about a hair away from losing control. You feel so good, so sexy and soft."

No man had ever told her such things. Her husband had wanted her in the early part of their marriage, but he hadn't indulged in much pillow talk. And not long after they were married, he'd gotten bored and started to roam.

Remembering caused her to stiffen. Mack immediately noticed the change. Even as he continued to nuzzle her, he cradled her face in both large palms. After one more light kiss, he looked at her intently. "What is it, babe? What's wrong?"

It was so difficult to get the words out. He appeared to be consumed with tenderness, with desire. He was on the ragged edge of desire—she could feel his muscles quivering—but he was also concerned. And the dual assault of a man wanting her and caring about her made her vulnerable. She looked away from him so she could gather her wits. She absolutely could not do this. Not again. "This is insane," she whispered.

His thumb brushed her temple, and he turned her back to meet his gaze. His smile was gentle. "It doesn't feel insane to me." He searched her face. "It just feels right."

"Mack." She caught his wrists and lowered his hands, then stepped away. Her legs didn't seem too steady, so she kept one hand braced on the table. "How can it possibly be right when we barely know each other?"

"Jessica . . ."

"No! You've only been here a few hours, and we're carrying on like . . . like animals."

He gently tugged on her braid, and she knew without looking that he was smiling. "You say that like it's a bad thing."

Here she was on fire, and he found the wit to tease. It was just like him, just like the man she knew him to be, and it reinforced her impression of him. Swallowing hard, she said, "You're just out for a little fun, aren't you?"

He gave a short, incredulous laugh. "Well, hell. If it wouldn't be fun, why do it?"

She groaned and covered her face.

"Jessica?" His tone dropped, became more intimate. "You *would* have fun, sweetheart. I'd make sure of it."

Shaking her head furiously, more to convince herself than him, she said, "Is that all you think about? Having fun?"

His fingers touched her hair, trailed down the length of her braid next to her breast. "I think about you. I've always wanted you."

She wouldn't look at him, not when all he wore was a heated look and what amounted to mere decoration. She knew her own limits, and she didn't want to tempt herself. After a deep, steadying breath, she whispered, "I'm a little embarrassed, if you want the truth. You might be used to women throwing themselves at you, but I swear I'm not usually like this."

"Which only goes to show that we're both very aware of each other, because despite what you think, I'm not usually this way either."

Oh, he was good. Not that she would buy it. He was just so experienced that he knew exactly what to say and when to say it. She bit her lip, then forged onward, searching for a credible explanation, something to defuse the situation.

Nothing, not even the truth, seemed overly redeeming. "It's . . . it's just that it's been a . . . a long time for me, and I guess that's why—"

"How long, honey?" He continued to play with her hair, and it was maddening.

She wanted to step away but couldn't quite get her feet to move. That overwhelming hot need still pulsed inside her. "Since before the divorce."

He stared, leaning down to see her face. He looked shocked, but also fascinated. "You're saying . . . *years*?"

She turned her back on him. If he laughed at her, she'd . . .

He stepped closer, and she could almost feel him touching her back. All her nerve endings seemed to scream, and she wasn't sure if it was an alarm, or a plea.

"Not that you'll believe me, but it's been a damn long time for me too. Not as long as you, but . . . well, long enough. I didn't expect this any more than you did. No one in his right mind has indiscriminate sex these days." She nearly choked over that little truism, prompting him to give her a squeeze. "I know you don't think much of my morals, but I'm not an idiot."

"I never said . . . !"

"You called me the class clown, a goof-off, remember?"

She could feel her bottom lip starting to tremble, but she would have died before she'd cry in front of him. "I didn't mean to insult you."

"Well, now, I think you did. And you know why? Because we're having a little fun together, and that scares you."

"No."

"And because you want me." She could feel his breath on her nape, the touch of his warmth. "You were as aware of me two years ago as I was of you. And you didn't like it any more then than you do now."

She turned without thinking. "That's not true!"

His expression softened. He looked at her face, down the length of her body and up again. Her breasts tingled when his gaze lingered there, and she knew her nipples were stiff, pushing against the sweater. His smile seemed ruthless, when she'd never thought of Mack that way.

"You want me still," he growled. "Why don't you admit it and let's see what happens?"

She felt cornered with him standing there so tall, so strong, his body all but bare. She'd forgotten all the wonderful differences men afforded, the incredible scents, the heat. Or maybe no other man had been like this. Though she'd tried to deny it, there had always been a chemistry between them, a sexual awareness that had taken her by surprise and stormed her senses. When they'd shared the class, she'd been painfully aware of every small move he made. And he was right—that awareness frightened her.

"I think we're done for the day."

He sighed. "I'll go. But promise me you'll think about what I've said, okay?"

"There's nothing to think about."

"There's this." He bent and kissed her again, a short, quick kiss that curled her toes and made her heart leap. Then he turned and walked away, unconcerned with his near nudity, with the tempting display he made as muscles and sinew shifted under his smooth flesh.

Jessica stepped out of the studio. The room, changed over from a master bedroom and bath, had always seemed immense to her. But with Mack inside, it was almost crowded, and at the moment she needed some space.

She waited by the window in the outer room, watching the ice and sleet fall, hearing it tap against the windowpanes. Confusion swamped her, but also shame, because despite what she knew was right, she didn't want him to go.

She heard his footsteps come up behind her. As he was pulling on his coat, he asked, "When do you want me again?" She stiffened, then heard his soft laugh. "To finish the shoot, I mean."

God, she didn't know. She needed as much as wanted the job. Even with giving Sophie a deal, she'd stand to make a lot of money off this. And adding the catalogue to her portfolio would bring in other commissions, would expand her possibilities. She shook her head, unable to sort through all the ramifications. And then the phone rang.

She felt so tense and edgy, she nearly jumped out of her skin. Mack watched her as she stepped around him and hurried down the hall to the phone. He silently followed.

"Hello?"

"Mom, can you . . . can you come pick me up?"

She frowned at the strained tone of her daughter's voice. "Trista? What's wrong, honey?"

"I just wanna come home now."

"All right. Hang on, sweetie. I'll be right there."

"Thanks, Mom."

Mack looked at her as she laid the receiver back in the cradle. "What is it?"

"Trista." She headed out of the room to get her coat and keys, and Mack again followed. "Something's wrong. She sounded about ready to cry. I . . . I have to go pick her up."

Mack nodded. He didn't question her decision to walk out with things still unresolved. He just kept up with her hurried pace, even helping her to slip on her coat. "Do you think it's anything serious?"

"No." He opened the door for her and she stepped out into the biting wind. "Jenna's parents are nice people. It's probably just an argument with a friend, but . . ."

"You have to go. I understand."

"I know we have . . . unfinished business, but . . ."

"Jessica." He squeezed her shoulder. "She's your daughter. If she needs you, of course you have to go."

He sounded so sincere, she blinked up at him. "You mean that, don't you? You don't think it's silly for me to rush out to get her?"

He gave her that endearing crooked smile again. "If you say she sounded upset, then I'm sure you're right. If I had a daughter, I'd do the same thing."

And he would. Though it amazed her, she could tell he did understand, and a small knot of regret settled in her belly. Maybe she had judged him too quickly. "My husband used to say I spoiled her."

As soon as the words left her mouth, she gasped. Good grief, she hadn't meant to share that.

Mack touched her cheek. He kept touching her, as if he couldn't help himself. "You can't spoil a child with too much love."

They had circled to the side lot, and as she neared her car she looked up at him. "Thank you."

Mack stared at her car with a frown. "Don't thank me yet. I have a feeling you're going to need my help."

Confused, she followed his gaze and saw her car was literally frozen beneath a layer of ice. The old house didn't have a garage, so her car was at the mercy of the elements. And since she hadn't driven it in a couple of days, she knew it would take a while to get it ready to go.

Mack held out his arms like a sacrifice. "Behold, your white knight. Or maybe I should say your chauffeur."

She didn't want to prolong her time with him, but she was already shivering, and it didn't make sense to stand out in the cold arguing about it. Especially not when she knew Trista was upset and waiting for her.

Mack stood there, determined to come to her assistance despite what had happened between them. Unlike most men, who would have stormed away mad over being rebuffed, he wanted to play the gallant. Frost collected on his dark hair and his cheeks turned ruddy. He looked young and strong and capable; she'd almost forgotten what it was like to have a man share her burdens. She'd wanted to forget, to prove herself independent, capable of handling anything alone.

Right now she was simply relieved to have a good excuse to keep him close.

Knowing that her own nose had to be cherry-red, she lifted it anyway and said, "Fine. Let's go."

Three

Since he'd been expecting more stubbornness, Mack was nearly bowled over by her compliance. But only for a moment. He took her arm and quickly ushered her toward his truck. He held her close and said, "Be careful. The pavement's slick."

There was a coating of ice on his truck as well, but he easily forced the doors open. Once inside, Jessica huddled into a corner. Her long braid was tucked beneath her coat, and she shivered uncontrollably. He wanted to pull her close, to share his warmth, but she'd already made it clear what she thought of that idea.

It was his own fault for going too fast. Not that he could have helped himself. He'd simply wanted her for too long, dreamed about her too many times, to pass up such an opportunity. She'd looked at him with her soft doe eyes filled with lust, and he'd damn near exploded.

She'd tasted better than he'd expected, felt better than he'd imagined. All the fantasies he'd stored up hadn't prepared him for the reality. Damn, but she packed one hell of a carnal punch.

Yet for some reason she'd apparently sworn off men. He wouldn't give up on her. He wanted her too much for that.

Her breath frosted the air between them as she watched him fasten his seat belt, start the truck, and ease out onto the road. She was silent, but he could almost feel her thinking. He glanced her way as she gave him directions, and noticed how cute she looked with a red nose and rosy cheeks.

It was already dark, and the streets were in terrible shape, but they made the few blocks to where Trista was waiting in less than five minutes.

Mack sat in the truck, relieved that the thermostat was finally warming up, while Jessica climbed out to get her daughter. Trista saw her from the doorway and met her on the sidewalk, looking curiously at the truck. Mack gave her a smile of encouragement as she slid into the seat between him and Jessica.

"Can you get the seat belt okay?"

She nodded, and kept sneaking glances at him. She looked utterly morose, and Mack smiled, remembering how life-altering everything felt when you were a teenager. "You're wondering why I'm here, right?"

Her answer was a cautious look toward her mother.

"Hey, I like your mom, and she was all in a dither to get to you, and her car was completely frozen over, so I offered to drive. I hope you don't mind. Just pretend I'm not here."

Both Jessica and Trista stared at him. He chose to take it as an encouraging sign.

The silence was heavy, so he asked, "It's got to do with that Brian guy, right?"

Trista tucked in her chin, watching him warily.

"I could be a big help, you know. I mean, who better to understand the warped-guy psyche than a guy? Think of all the insight I can give you." He leaned closer and whispered, "I was thirteen once myself."

Jessica cleared her throat. "Uh, Mack . . ."

He interrupted her with a wave of his hand. "We could discuss it over hot chocolate. What do you think?"

He'd rushed the physical side of things earlier. Now that he wasn't holding Jessica, now that he was fully dressed and his body was back under control—thanks mostly to the frigid February weather—he could think more clearly. Or at least, he could think without salacious intent clouding his judgment.

He wanted her. He wanted to make love to her, to explore her body, especially those incredible breasts of hers. He wanted to taste every inch of her and listen to her moan his name. More than anything, he wanted to see her beautiful dark eyes as she climaxed with him.

But he also wanted to talk to her, to tease her and listen to her huff and watch her face when she blushed. He wanted her to share her sharp wit, the love she felt for her daughter. He wanted to know more about her work, her divorce, how she felt about things, and what her life had been like.

Despite their moment of intimacy, she was determined to push him away, hesitant to get involved on any level. But it wasn't because of lack of mutual appeal, that much was certain. He could still feel the burning touch of her stiff little nipples against his chest when she'd rubbed against him, the way her fingers had dug into his shoulders, how hot she'd tasted on his tongue. He shuddered with the memory.

All he needed to do was keep his cool, ignore her occasional insults, and figure out why she had such an aversion to men in general and him in particular. She'd said he reminded her of her ex, but it had to be more than that; he felt sure of it. She was an incredibly sensual woman, yet she'd been years without a man. The very thought boggled his mind.

Patience, that's what he needed.

Patience, and a lot of determination.

Trista tucked her hands between her knees and said to the windshield, "I don't care what Brian does. He's a jerk."

Pretending offense, Mack said, "Well, give me some credit! I already figured that out."

"You did?"

"Of course I did. You left with a smile, but came back with a frown. Only a jerk could cause that."

Trista gave him a half smile before remembering she was piqued. "He called me a dummy."

"He's a jerk. I rest my case."

"I don't do too good in science, and we're going to have a big project coming up. I thought he'd be my partner, but he asked Jenna today instead."

Jessica reached over and squeezed Trista's hand. "Let me guess. Jenna said yes?"

"She only likes him because I do."

Mack pulled into the lot behind the house, parking as close to the brick structure as he could in hopes that some of the icy wind would be deflected. "You know, I had a lot of trouble with science, too. My sister-in-law used to help me study. Sometimes all you need is a little help."

Jessica patted Trista's leg with a smile. "I can't claim to be a whiz at seventh-grade science, but I'm sure we can study up together."

Mack cleared his throat in an imperious way, and though it was sneaky, he spoke directly to Trista. "Well, now, considering I'm a bona fide teacher, and I've finally mastered science, I *can* claim to be a whiz. So whatdya say I tutor you a little? Not so you can prove anything to Brian, because what he thinks doesn't really matter, right?"

Trista grinned. "Right."

"But this way, you'll know he's wrong if he ever says anything so obnoxious again."

Trista immediately turned to her mother. "Could I?"

Mack knew he had her. He added, just for good measure, "I need to be here a couple more times anyway to get the magazine photos all taken care of. We could work on that while Trista is in school, then I could stay after and do some studying. What do you say?"

She looked like she wanted to smack him, but since Trista sat between them she held back. "If you're a teacher, won't you need to be at school?"

That stumped him. He hated to admit he hadn't landed a permanent job yet, but he really didn't see any way around it. He hedged just a bit instead. "I'm still waiting for my final placement. The school board has to go through several interviews, and until that's done, my days are free. Unless, of course, someone calls for a substitute, but that doesn't happen that often."

Trista looked excited. "Are you going to teach at my school?"

"Nope, sorry, kiddo. I've sort of specialized in inner city. That's where good teachers are needed most because the kids have so few advantages. I'm hoping for a permanent placement at Mordmont." He glanced at Jessica. "And I'm a very good teacher. That's where I did my student teaching, and I'm kinda close to the kids now, so I'd like to go back there."

"Bummer. It'd be cool to brag that we had a model for a teacher."

He could just imagine how that info would go over with the school board. Not that it would really matter to them. They'd tried using his family connection to a bar as a reason to get rid of him, but that didn't carry any weight, considering the backgrounds of some of the other teachers. Most of them were questionable old relics who wouldn't know a modern method if it bit them in the butt, and that's why they hadn't wanted him. He challenged their outdated methods, refused to conform, and any nonconformity scared them shitless, even when they could see the advantages to the students.

If worse came to worst, he'd have to go out of the area. But that would be a last resort, because in the inner city he'd felt he made a real difference, and that's what teaching was all about for him.

The truck had gotten toasty warm, but they couldn't keep sitting in it forever. He looked at Jessica and said, "About that hot chocolate . . ."

She stared him straight in the eye. "Not tonight, Mack. I'm sorry, but it's been a long day. I started early this morning and I spent all day in the studio. I still have tons of household chores to get done. And my weekend, as well as a good part of next week, is already booked. I was going to see if Thursday morning would work for you to do our next shoot. That'll still give us plenty of time to get everything together for the catalogue."

And it would give her plenty of time to forget about him. He needed to make a diplomatic withdrawal, before she could refuse him everything, but no way would he withdraw enough to let her rebuild all her defenses.

He smiled at her. "No problem. I wouldn't want to get in your way." She looked slightly dazed at his easy acceptance, and he added, "But Trista and I don't need you to help us study, anyway. Saturday I'm busy, but I could come Sunday and the rest of the week until you're ready for me."

Her eyes narrowed, and he could just imagine what she thought he'd be doing on Saturday. He had no doubt her thoughts included sexual indulgence and wouldn't be overly flattering. If only she knew what a recluse he'd become. Working at the family bar on Saturday had been the highlight of his social life lately.

Trista filled in the gap of silence. "I'll bring home the instructions for my science project on Monday. Maybe you can give me a few good ideas?"

"I'd be glad to." He turned off the motor and walked around to open Jessica's door. "Come on, ladies. I'll see you inside."

Trista giggled, but he thought he heard Jessica growl, "We don't need you to—"

Mack looped an arm through each of theirs and proceeded onward, ignoring Jessica's protest while practically gliding her across the icy ground. "Hang on tight. The walk is pretty slick."

She huffed, but had no choice except to hold on or fall. "I gather you think you're steadier than we are?"

"Sure. I've got bigger feet, don't I?" Jessica wasn't amused, but Trista chuckled.

When they reached the door, Jessica fumbled with the key while Mack turned to Trista. "I don't suppose you have your science book at home, do you? It'd help if I could see where you are in it."

"I don't have my book, but I have all my papers from last week."

"How about I take them home with me and look them over? Then we can get started right away on Sunday afternoon."

"I'll go get 'em!" She dashed inside and Jessica, still with her back to him, started to do the same.

Mack caught her arm. "Whoa. Can we talk just a second?"

Reluctantly, she turned to face him. She didn't look pleased, and the second she spoke, he knew why. "I don't like being manipulated, Mack."

Though he knew he'd do it again in a heartbeat, he did feel bad about cornering her. He wasn't in the habit of forcing his company on women. "I'm sorry."

She gaped at him. "You're not even going to deny it?"

"Why should I? I want to see you and this seemed like my only chance. You didn't really think I'd give up that easily, did you?"

She looked astounded and chagrined and, if he was reading her right, a little complimented.

"This is ridiculous—"

"You keep saying that, but damned if I see what's so ridiculous about it."

"I'm too old for you."

He laughed.

"Will you be serious!"

His smile disappeared, but she could still see the slight amusement in his eyes. "Okay, how's this for serious? If I kissed you right now, would you think about me tonight?" She drew a deep breath and he added, "Try being honest with me for once, okay?"

Her chin lifted. "All right. Yes."

"Yes, you'd think about me?" He was so pleased with her he wanted to lift her in his arms, swing her in a circle. He wanted to kiss her silly, to touch her all over. He wanted to devour her, actually, and not even the damn cold could temper his lust.

"Yes, I probably would. But you're not going to kiss me, Mack, so it's a moot admission."

There was no way he could contain his grin. "I bet you'll think about me even if I don't kiss you."

She made a disgusted sound. "Oh, for pity's sake."

"Won't you?" He ducked his head, trying to see her averted face. "Jessica? Tell me you'll think about me, because I'll damn sure be thinking about you."

"No."

"No, you won't tell me or no, you won't think about me?"

She laughed, covering her face with her gloved hands. "You're impossible!"

He pulled her hands down and kissed the end of her icy-cold nose. "I'm infatuated." She started to back up and he let her, pretending it didn't bother him. "I really will enjoy working with Trista. Don't think I'm not serious about that, because I am. Even though I used it as an excuse to spend more time around you, I do think I can help her out. I'm a good teacher." Modesty kept him from total honesty. In truth, he was an *exceptional* teacher.

"It's hard for me to imagine you at the head of a classroom."

He looked away. "Yeah, well, the principal has the same problem."

Tipping her head back to look at him, she asked, "What does that mean?"

He was saved from any morbid confessions by Trista's return. She looked embarrassed as she handed him a stack of papers. "Some of the grades on those aren't too good."

He'd seen the same uncertainty on dozens of different adolescent faces, and it always filled him with compassion. School, in his opinion, shouldn't be about failures so much as accomplishments. He neatly folded the papers in half and stuck them in his pocket. "Did you do your best?"

"Yeah."

"Good girl. No one can ask for more than that, regardless of how you scored on the paper. Let's forget about these grades and concentrate on the next ones, okay?"

"You really think I'll do better?"

"We'll both give it our best shot."

When she smiled, the streetlamp reflected off her braces. He loved making kids smile. Sticking out his hand, he said, "Trista, it was a distinct pleasure."

She shook his hand, giggling, then said a proper good night. With a quick, calculating look at her mother, she ducked back inside and pulled the door shut. She even turned off the porch light. Jessica groaned.

Without conscious thought, Mack moved closer to her, sharing his warmth. Their breath mingled. "Your daughter likes me."

"My daughter doesn't really know you."

He bridged both hands against the brick wall on either side of her head. He felt her nervousness, her excitement. "This may surprise you, but you don't really know me either."

She lifted her chin. "I know what I saw in college. There's not only a big age difference between us—"

"A few piddling years."

"—but we also have very different outlooks."

"Because I want to have fun and you don't?" He'd leaned down so close, his nose brushed her soft, cold cheek. She smelled sweet and fresh and like the brisk outdoors. He nuzzled against her, drinking in the wonderful scent.

"Mack."

It was a weak protest, and they both knew it. But he was a gentleman and he didn't want to push her. He wanted her to want him, to admit she felt the same incredible things he felt. He rested his forehead against her crown for just a moment, relishing the simple enjoyment of holding her. "If you change your mind over the weekend, call me."

"I won't change my mind."

She sounded less than certain about that, and he smiled. "Sophie has my number."

"I won't change my mind."

He leaned back to look at her. "Tonight, when you're in bed alone, think about me." Her brown eyes were huge in the darkness, and she stared at him without answering. He opened the door and gave her a small nudge in the right direction. "Sleep well, honey."

Just before she pulled the door shut, she whispered, "Mack? Be careful driving home." Stunned, Mack stood there a moment until he heard her turn the lock. Then, slowly, he started to smile. He even laughed out loud, but the sound seemed more ominous than not in the cold, quiet night.

Damn, he felt good.

And then he remembered the Winston curse.

Sophie was ringing up a customer when Mack walked in. The little bell over the door jingled, and she looked up with a smile of welcome. Three other women looked up as well, then proceeded to stare rudely, as if he'd invaded their private territory. Mack merely grinned, sauntered over to some lacy bras, and began browsing.

Allison came out of the back room and spotted him. "Hey, Mack. How did the photo shoot go?"

Why did Allison look so suspicious when she asked that? He narrowed his gaze at her, then shrugged. Maybe she was waiting for the curse to hit him. She couldn't know that he'd already resigned himself to his fate. Hell, he was half anticipating it.

"It went okay. Though some of that stuff isn't coming anywhere near my body."

"Spoilsport."

Sophie joined them, looking indignant. "Which stuff?"

"G-strings? Those filmy briefs with the see-through front? And what about those clear vinyl thingies—"

Laughing, Sophie put a finger to his lips. "Hush. Every lady in here is eavesdropping."

Allison looked at him over the rim of her round glasses. "See-through vinyl?"

"Yeah. You should get Chase a pair." He tried to hide his amusement, but it was impossible when Allison seemed to be seriously considering the idea.

Sophie took his arm and dragged him to the other side of the room, where there were fewer ears to listen in. "Some of those things are just for fun. They're not meant to be taken seriously."

"Well, I'm seriously not modeling them."

"Is that why you're here? You're not going to back out on me just because a few of the items are a bit . . . risqué, are you?"

"No, I'm not backing out."

She suddenly stiffened, then grabbed both his hands. "Oh, wait! Did you hear from the school board? Did you get the position?"

"No, I didn't hear anything yet." He almost wished she hadn't reminded him. His preoccupation with Jessica had driven away much of his frustration. Which was just as well, because he absolutely hated to sit around fretting like an old schoolmarm.

Sophie looked ready to embrace him, and he quickly sidestepped her. She had this mothering tendency that sometimes made him uncomfortable. It had been especially noticeable since she'd gotten pregnant. "I'm fine, Sophie, really. It's not a big deal."

"Baloney. I know how hard you've worked to be a great teacher."

"Yeah, well. A lot of good it's done me."

"Oh, my God. I just thought of something. What if the school board sees you in the catalogue?"

"That's not an issue. Nothing I wore is that revealing, and I seriously doubt they'd ever see it, anyway, since they're two districts away. No offense, hon, but it's not like your boutique is well known across the state."

She sniffed. "No, it's a quaint local shop."

"Very local. And the school board can't touch me on morals charges. Not when one of the teachers moonlights at a strip club and another has been picked up twice for brawling. Their big gripe is that I don't follow their procedure, even though I've proven my procedure to be more effective."

Sophie gave him a sad smile. "This matters a lot to you, doesn't it?"

Damn. How had he let the subject get so sidetracked? "It matters," he admitted, "but that's not why I'm here." He suddenly felt a little self-conscious and reached out to touch a satiny-soft camisole hanging on a rack. "I, uh, I wanted some advice."

Allison crept back over to them. "Oh, good. I love giving advice."

Mack ran a hand through his hair. "The thing is, I know Jessica."

"No!" Sophie put a hand to her chest.

Allison nudged her, then cleared her throat. She gave Mack her undivided attention. "You know her? From where?"

Something wasn't right, but damned if Mack could figure out what. He'd never understand his sisters-in-law, and he'd given up trying. "I knew her in college. We took a class together. I always liked her, but she—well, she's not too fond of me for some reason."

Sophie raised her brows in theatrical surprise. "Wait a minute! Jessica isn't the woman you always talked about when I helped you to study, is she?"

"One and the same."

Allison leaned back against a display table of panties. "Fascinating coincidence."

Frustrated, Mack paced away, then back again. "Yeah, I know. I didn't think I'd ever see her again. But now that I have seen her again, I want her."

Allison straightened at that. "Maybe I'm too young to hear this."

Sophie smothered a laugh. "I'm not. Go ahead, Mack."

He stared at both of the women, then blurted out, "Which of those goofy lingerie things do you think she'd like the most?"

They looked at each other before Sophie asked, "You want us to tell you which things will be likely to . . . uh . . ."

The women were staring at him so wide-eyed, he felt his ears turn red. He wanted to get this over with so he could get back to his planning. "To turn her on. Yeah. So what do you think?"

Sophie choked, but Allison gave it serious thought. "I like the soft cotton stuff. Cotton feels so good on men and it hugs all those sexy muscles. Chase looks just adorable in cotton boxers, especially the snug-fitting kind." She turned to Sophie. "Weren't there a few of those in the box?"

Sophie tried unsuccessfully to get rid of her grin. "Um, yes. They have little"—she gestured toward Mack's fly—"silver snaps up the front."

Allison patted his arm. "With your dark coloring, try the black ones. Or the forest green."

Sophie shook her head. "I rather like the silky ones. In white."

"So you think if I wear those for Jessica, I mean for the shoot, she'll . . . ah, enjoy the sight?"

"Most definitely."

"Absolutely."

Mack shook his head, grinning. "Why do I get the feeling you two are up to no good?"

Sophie shrugged. "You obviously have a suspicious nature."

She looked too innocent, and he didn't like it. "Where exactly did you meet Jessica?" He didn't think he had ever shared her name with Sophie, though he had described her on numerous occasions. Hell, for a while there she was all he could think of, until he'd resigned himself to never seeing her again.

"She shops here."

Mack felt like someone had doused him in fire. He looked around at all the sexy stuff on mannequins, hanging in displays, stacked softly on tables, and his heart thumped. He pictured her stretched out on a bed, *his bed*, her lush body barely covered in black satin or white lace. "She really wears this stuff?"

Allison gave him a pitying look. "What did you think she wore? Burlap?"

"No, but . . . which stuff?"

"Ah, now that would be telling, and I can't do that."

"Sophie?"

Sophie crossed her arms and lifted her chin. "Allison's right, Mack. If you want to know what kind of lingerie Jessica wears, you'll just have to find out on your own."

He damn well intended to.

A few minutes later Mack walked out the front door, thinking what lucky dogs his brothers were. He glanced back once and saw Allison and Sophie collapsed against each other, laughing hysterically. He smiled. He didn't mind their ribbing at all since they'd been totally honest with him. Poor Jessica. She didn't stand a chance.

Four

Jessica felt so confused, she didn't know what to think, or precisely how to handle her new decision.

Mack had been hanging around all week, working with Trista, laughing and joking, making his presence unmistakably known. When he was around, Jessica felt it in every pore of her body. She'd catch herself listening for his laugh, or looking to catch a glimpse of him in between appointments. He and Trista mostly worked in the office, but after the first day Trista had asked if Mack could go upstairs with her to help make lunch. The upstairs was where they lived, and Jessica didn't want him invading her home as well as her office, but she couldn't find a reasonable excuse to deny him. And after that, they often went upstairs, getting drinks or looking for books, or using the computer. Trista adored him, and already she had new confidence in her abilities at school.

Often, when Jessica's workday was over and Mack had gone home, she'd find signs of him upstairs still. Notes he'd scrawled for Trista, a hat he'd left behind, even his scent lingered. Sleeping was difficult, because no matter how she tried, she couldn't stop thinking of him and how he'd made her feel. He'd only kissed her and barely touched her, yet she'd been more aroused than she could ever remember. She wanted him, and the wanting wasn't going to go away.

He hadn't been especially familiar with her since that first day. He was, in fact, a perfect gentleman, talking politely, minding his manners, respecting her wishes to be left alone.

Though it shamed her to admit it, she hated it that he'd given up so easily. Or had he?

She hoped not, because she'd already decided she wanted, needed, to know what it was like to be with him. He looked at her and it affected her more than a physical touch. She hadn't felt like her old self since he'd first kissed her, and she saw no reason she shouldn't indulge herself for once. But just once.

Today he'd be back for the shoot, and she didn't quite know what to expect or how to make her declaration. Since that first day Trista had been close by to act as a buffer, and she supposed that could possibly account for part of Mack's restraint. When he was studying with her, his attention was undivided. But now Trista would be in school, and she and Mack would have quite a few hours alone and uninterrupted.

And Mack would be wearing those damned seductive undergarments again.

Just the thought of it made her palms sweat, her heart jumpy. She looked around the studio, making sure everything was in place. With any luck, they could finish up early and then, if Mack was still willing, use the rest of the afternoon to make love.

The doorbell rang and she jerked around, feeling guilty about her thoughts even though no one would know. She hurried out of the room, but at the door she stopped to compose herself, feeling like a foolish coed yet unable to help herself. She pasted on a smile and pulled the door open.

Mack leaned on the door frame, arms crossed over his chest, his breath frosting in front of him. At the sight of her he smiled lazily. "Hey."

Just that small smile, and her insides fluttered in anticipation. “Hello. Right on time.” She opened the door wider and he came in. Only he didn’t step to the side of her. He came right up to her. He cupped her face in his gloved hands and, casual as you please, he kissed her.

“I missed you,” he whispered against her mouth.

Flustered, she stammered, “You’ve seen me all week!”

“Hmmm. Seen you, but not been able to touch you.” He kissed her again, a light, barely there kiss, making her want more. “Did you miss me too?”

“Mack. This is—”

“Ridiculous?” He touched the tip of her nose and stepped around her, then peered into the empty office. “Where’s the receptionist?”

Swallowing nervously, Jessica tried to remind herself that she was thirty years old, an experienced woman, a divorcée who knew how to handle herself in any situation, never mind that she hadn’t been in this situation in too many years to count, and never with a man like Mack.

She laced her fingers together to keep her hands from shaking. “You’re the only appointment I have today, so there was no need for her to come in. She helps out mostly with appointments to view proofs or to pick up packages.”

Mack looked at her intently, one brow raised. “Then we’re here all alone?”

Now he would probably kiss her again. She licked her lips, anticipating his unique taste, the heat of his mouth. “Yes.”

He nodded, still looking at her. “I suppose we should get started?”

Disappointment filled her, but she hoped it didn’t show. “Yes, of course.” She didn’t understand him at all. He seemed to still want her, but if he did, then why was he waiting? She started down the hall and for the first time questioned her choice of clothes. The scoop-neck, cream-colored sweater was soft, and her plaid skirt almost reached her ankles. True, she often wore long skirts to work in because they were so comfortable, but today it had been a deliberate choice; she'd wanted to look more feminine for Mack. That decision now seemed beyond pathetic, and she had the irrational fear that he'd know it.

She cleared her throat once they were in the studio. "Sophie called and mentioned a few other things she wants you to wear."

His brow shot up a good inch. "She did?"

"Yes. There's some snap-front boxers and matching ribbed undershirts she definitely wants in the catalogue."

Mack grinned, and an unholy light entered his eyes. "I see."

Jessica handed him the first change of clothes, and Mack went behind the curtain. While he was there, she readied her camera and set up some scrims to filter the light, making the scene softer, more intimate. This particular scrim, or mesh filter, had denser spots, which provided a dappled look, like sunlight through leaves. She placed an old-fashioned quilt on the floor over artificial grass, then added some props to give it an outdoor look. She used a birdbath, a small bush, some flowers.

Mack stepped around the curtain just as she smoothed the quilt one last time. She smiled at him, barely managing to still her sigh of appreciation. The snug boxers and ribbed undershirt showed his big muscled body to perfection.

"For this shot," she said, her voice just a little husky, "it's going to look like you're resting outside, enjoying the sunshine, totally at your ease. It's to sort of show how comfortable the clothes are."

"I can buy that." He rubbed one large hand over his abdomen. "They do feel nice."

She swallowed hard, wondering how it would feel to her hand—not just the fabric but his body beneath it. With a sigh, she looked him over from his tousled dark head, his intent eyes and stubborn, clean-shaven jaw, to his broad shoulders, lean hips, and long legs, all the way down to his big feet. She couldn't imagine a man who looked more perfect or more sensually enticing than Mack Winston.

Her heart beat a little too fast, and she had trouble drawing an even breath. Mack watched her face, and after a moment, he said softly, "I like it when you look at me like that. You know, I memorized your features back in college. You'd sit there, refusing to look at me, staring at the instructor as if she spoke gospel, and I'd study you. Every little angle, the tilt of your nose, the slant of your jaw, how your lashes left shadows on your cheeks. I'd go nuts looking at the profile of your breasts."

Jessica knew that was always the first thing men noticed about her, and it annoyed her. From the time she'd hit puberty, she'd worn a C cup. It had always been more of a nuisance than anything else. "All women have breasts."

"All women aren't you." He came closer, then dropped to his knees directly in front of her. With only one hand, he touched her jaw, smoothed her hair back to her braid, then trailed his fingers down her neck to where it met her shoulder. He lifted his other hand and cradled her head, using his thumbs to stroke her jaw. Jessica felt herself trembling in anticipation, and knew he felt it too.

After a moment of heavy silence, he tilted his head to the side. "What is it about you, Jessica, that makes me feel this way?"

She stared at his collarbone, at where the low neck of the undershirt showed just a bit of hair on his chest. This close, she could smell him, the musky smell of aroused male. She swallowed hard and asked in a whisper, "What way?"

"Like I have to have you." His hands drifted down to her shoulders, then inward, his fingers spreading wide over her upper chest. "*Have* to, just like I have to breathe, or eat. It was pure torture in college, trying to concentrate when I had a hard-on all the time. And all you wanted to do was snub me."

She shook her head, unwilling to be pulled in with lies. "How could you have been thinking of me when all those skinny girls kept throwing themselves at you?"

He was looking at her breasts, and his hands skimmed over her sides to her waist. "I didn't—"

Jessica scrambled back, wrinkling the quilt. "You did. You flirted and played around, and all the girls adored you."

Mack dropped back to sit on his heels, studying her closely. "I also got straight A's. Which I earned."

"That's impossible!"

"Ah, surprised you with that one, didn't I? I guess you figured I coasted through with the lowest passable grades possible? Did you think that's why I was interested in teaching inner-city kids? Because no influential school district would have me?"

She shook her head. "I don't know." But of course she had thought it.

"You're confusing me with him," he said gently. "I'm not the one who hurt you, not the one who used you." He lifted one shoulder, and his look was sad. "Honey, having fun doesn't make you a bad person. It doesn't make you irresponsible or frivolous. It's okay to enjoy everything you do—your schoolwork, your friends, your job. Life."

It hurt her to admit he might be right, that she might have been the one with the wrong outlook. "I guess that's easier for some people than others."

"Why? Why can't you have a little fun?"

Despite herself, she smiled. "Fun, as in fooling around with you?"

"No fooling to it. Sometimes you need to take your fun very seriously."

She had no idea what to make of that. His look was direct, hot, and very sensual. She shivered, then admitted, "I . . . I want to."

His eyes gleamed, and though he didn't quite smile, she saw the dimple in his cheek. "But?"

"It's not easy to explain."

"Well, now. I can be a pretty good listener when you give me a chance."

No doubt Mack would be good at anything he did. But talking about her inhibitions, the problems that had nearly suffocated her just a few years ago, wasn't easy. Talking about them with Mack was doubly hard, because she suddenly cared what he thought. He scooted closer, crossed his legs Indian style, and gave her a look of encouragement.

He looked young and sexy and caring and considerate. His body was hard and beautiful, his smile gentle. He was a female's fantasy come to life, the epitome of temptation and magnetism. And he sat before her, waiting.

With a sigh, she gave in. "My husband and I met when I was a high school senior and he was in his second year of college. I'd always been sort of mousy, real quiet, and he was the first really popular guy to pay attention to me."

Mack picked at a loose thread in the quilt. "It's tough for me to imagine you as mousy." He glanced up and caught her gaze. "You're so damn sexy now."

She blushed. "Mack . . ."

"Go on."

He flustered her so with his compliments, it was hard for her to gather her thoughts. "He was so much . . . *fun*. I was completely overwhelmed by him, and like a dummy, I wasn't as careful as I should have been. I got pregnant."

Mack snorted. "He was older, and no doubt more experienced?"

She shrugged, a little embarrassed to have to admit it, but she did. "I was a virgin."

"So why the hell wasn't he being careful? Any man who cares about a woman protects her as well as himself. My brother pounded that into my head when I was about fifteen, long before I ever got around to even trying anything with a girl." He grinned slightly. "I guess after Zane, who's more wild than not, he wasn't going to take any chances."

"Your brother is older than you?"

"Yeah, by about fifteen years. My mom and dad died when I was young, so Cole pretty much raised the rest of us."

"Oh, Mack." Her heart swelled. She was still so close to her parents, she couldn't imagine losing them. "I'm so sorry."

He gave her that adorable boyish grin. "It's okay. It was a long time ago, and Cole made certain we had everything we needed. He was a mom and dad and big brother all in one."

Fascinated, she asked, "How many brothers do you have?"

"I'm the baby." He grinned shamelessly at that admission. "Then there's Zane, who's a complete and total hedonist, but we forgive him because he's a damn good brother too. And Chase, who's pretty quiet, except maybe not so much now that he's married to Allison. And then Cole. He's married to Sophie."

"You're all pretty close, aren't you?" At his nod, she said, "I was an only child. My folks are great, but I know they were a little disappointed when I got pregnant. They wanted to help out, for me to stay at home and go to college, but I really thought I loved Dave and that we'd have a good marriage."

"Didn't work out that way, huh?"

"No. Dave was never very responsible. Oh, he married me, but then I couldn't go to college because we needed me to work to pay his tuition. He said his studies took up too much time for him to hold down a job. Only his grades were never very good, and then he flunked out the first semester of his third year. I hated to admit how badly I'd screwed up in marrying him, so I made excuses for him and told everyone what a great job he'd gotten. But then he lost that for missing too much work."

Mack's eyes had narrowed, but his tone remained calm. "He sounds like a real winner."

"That's just it. Everyone thought so. He was the life of the party, a real charming guy. People met him and they naturally liked him. Especially the women. I always came across as a terrible nag. His relatives complained about how I had dragged him down, because he was saddled with a wife and a kid, and they said that was why he'd failed college, because he had too many responsibilities."

Mack touched her cheek. "I can only imagine how that made you feel."

"It wasn't *fun*, I can tell you that."

"Not for you, but it sounds like he did all right."

Jessica pulled her knees up, making sure her long skirt covered her legs. She crossed her arms over them and rested the side of her face there. She didn't want to look at Mack. She didn't want to see his pity at the stupid girl she'd been. "He did better than all right. He ended up with a nothing part-time job that left him plenty of free time to run around. I worked full time at a restaurant, and my parents watched Trista for me. Dave had a lot of friends, and they all thought I was a bitch if I suggested he should skip hanging out. Then one day Trista got sick and I needed him to get medicine. I called the house where he was supposed to be playing cards with his buddies, but when a woman answered, I could tell it was a huge party. I went to get the medicine myself, and on the way home I stopped by there."

Mack scooted around to sit behind her. He pulled her back to his chest, closed his arms tightly around her, and kissed her temple. "He was cheating on you."

It wasn't a question, so she didn't bother to answer. "Here I was, still wearing my stained, wrinkled waitress uniform, Trista beside me. I looked horrible from working all day, and Trista had a runny nose and red eyes. But Dave looked great. He was laughing and having a good time. When the woman on his lap looked up, I didn't want to admit to being his wife. They all stared at me, and I could tell they felt sorry for Dave. They thought he'd gotten a bum deal with me. I just turned around and walked out."

She could feel the tension coming off Mack, only this time it was anger. She twisted around to see him, but the minute she was turned, he kissed her. His mouth opened on hers, and his tongue stroked her lips, making her gasp. He seemed almost desperate, his hands in her hair, holding her close, devouring her. His urgency alarmed her a bit, overwhelming her. His hands stroked everywhere, down her back to her bottom, over her stomach and up to her breast, and then his fingers found her stiffened nipple, making her shudder and gasp. A thick, low groan erupted from his throat and she felt him tremble.

All her reservations vanished. She wanted him, and there would never be a better time than now.

Mack cursed roughly when Jessica suddenly relaxed, her arms wrapping around his neck, her breast pressing into his palm. "Jesus. I feel like I'm going to explode."

"Mack . . ." Her small, cool hand touched his jaw, bringing his mouth back to hers. He couldn't think of anything he'd ever wanted as much as he wanted her right now. He understood her so much better after all she'd told him, and he wanted—needed—to prove to her that he was different. He wanted to stake a claim. He kissed her, long and deep.

Then he pulled away, struggling for control. "Sweetheart, we need to slow down. I'm sorry. It's just that . . . damn, I'm jealous."

Her slumberous eyes opened to stare at him. Her pupils were dilated, making her eyes look nearly black. She looked dazed and aroused and beautiful, so damn beautiful.

"I don't understand."

How could he tell her everything he felt? Her ex was an idiot, but Mack was glad, because if he hadn't screwed up, Jessica might still be married, when Mack knew in his bones she belonged with him. Even now she clung to him, her breath hot, her body quivering with need. And he'd barely touched her. The thought made him frantic with lust.

Easing her down slowly, he laid her on the quilt. Her chest rose and fell, and she opened her arms to him.

"Shhh. Let's get these clothes off you. I'm all but naked, and you're bundled up from head to toe."

He reached for her sweater, and she turned her head away. Mack stilled. "Jessica?"

Her eyes squeezed tightly closed. He wanted her so bad, his body burned, but damned if he would do anything to make her uncomfortable. "Tell me what's wrong, honey."

He saw her slender white throat tense as she swallowed, saw her hands fist. "You're used to beautiful women."

He stroked her shoulder, keeping the touch feather light. "And you think you're not?"

"I'm . . . I'm thirty years old, not twenty with long legs and no hips. I've had a baby and . . ."

"And because you're a mother, you can't be sexy anymore?"

"That's not what I'm saying and you know it!"

He stroked her cheek, smoothed back her hair. "I'm sorry, babe, but you're being silly. I think you're the sexiest woman I've ever known. Do you think I walk around with an erection for every woman on the street?"

She made a sound that was a cross between a groan and a laugh. "I wouldn't put it past you."

"Well, you'd be wrong." He reached for the hem of her skirt and slowly began dragging it up her legs. She stiffened, but she didn't say anything. Mack stared at her shapely legs and tried not to be affected.

He wanted his tone to remain calm, not rough with lust. But it wasn't easy. She wore some kind of elastic-topped nylons that ended just above her knees and left her pale thighs bare. The elastic was decorated with small cream-colored roses. His breath rasped unevenly as he touched her knee, urging her legs to part just a bit. "Did you buy these stockings from Sophie?"

Her eyes popped open. "What?"

"She told me you shop in her boutique, that that's where she met you. Did you get them there?"

"Yes."

Things were starting to come together, the goofy way Sophie and Allison had acted. The reason *he'd* been picked to model. It was a setup—and he owed them both more than he'd realized.

The bright photography lights were still aimed at them, illuminating the square of quilt and the two people stretched out atop it. Mack smiled. "I can see you, all of you, very well. I like this."

His fingers trailed above the stockings, moving the skirt higher and higher, until the pale sheen of her silky beige panties reflected the light. The material looked damp between her legs, and he groaned. Without even thinking of her reaction, he bent and pressed a heated kiss there.

She nearly leapt off the floor. "Mack!"

He nuzzled closer. "Damn, you smell good." In a rush, he sat up and unbuttoned the skirt, then tugged it down her legs. "I think I'll leave the stockings. They turn me on."

She panted, staring at him in mingled embarrassment and need. He laid a hand over her belly. It wasn't concave, sinking between her hipbones, but it was soft and silky and . . . "How could you think this isn't sexy? Do you have any idea how you feel to me?" He closed his eyes, stroking her, relishing the touch of her warm, satiny skin, then slid his fingers into her panties and tangled them in her feminine curls. Her hips lifted, and he pulled away.

Straddling her upper thighs, he cupped her face and smiled. "I feel like a teenager again, having to pace myself so I can last long enough to get inside you. God, woman, you affect me. Forget any other man you've known. Right now there's just me. Okay?"

She looked him over, then whispered, "Will you take off your shirt so I can see you again?"

"Hell, yes. And then yours." He pulled the undershirt over his head and tossed it aside. Her hands were immediately there, caressing his shoulders, touching his small nipples to make him shudder. He gave her time to look, to touch him, and when he couldn't take it anymore, he jerked her sweater up. He was awkward and trembling and laughed even as he cursed. Jessica lifted her arms so he could pull it free, then rested back on the floor. She watched him anxiously, her soft brown eyes wide and uncertain, her breath held.

The bra she wore was incredible, beige satin to match the panties, but with a lace overlay, looking sexy as sin and making his heart race. He could just see the dark shadows of her erect nipples beneath the sheer fabric. He locked his jaw, fighting for control, and with one finger he circled a nipple and watched her shiver. He looked up and met her eyes. "I want to take you in my mouth. I want to lick you and suck on you."

Her body arched as she moaned.

"Can we take off the rest of our clothes now, babe?" His voice was a rasp, a bare echo of sound.

For an answer, she sat up so he could reach the back closure on the bra. His hands shook as he expertly slipped the bra open, then slowly slid the straps off her shoulders. Her breasts were so full and white, resting softly against her body. He'd never considered himself a breast man, at least not in any sort of preference and not when he loved everything about women's bodies, but with Jessica . . . The sight of her made his insides twist with need.

He cupped both breasts in his palms, closed his eyes as he felt her, and whispered, "You thought you didn't compare to other women?"

"I . . . I breast-fed. And it shows. I'm not as firm as I used to be. Dave used to tell me—"

"Forget Dave." He looked and saw a few faint lines on her breasts and imagined her swollen with milk, mothering her child. *"God."*

He smoothed the lines with his thumbs, then bent and took one nipple into the heat of his mouth. Jessica moaned, and her fingers tangled in his hair. He switched to the other nipple, sucking strongly, making her cry out. She tried to pull away, but he held her securely, greedy, lifting her breast high, continuing to lick and suck until he knew he had to stop or he'd come.

She collapsed back against the quilt, panting, her body warm and rosy, her nipples drawn tight, wet from his mouth.

She gasped at the look in his eyes, then blurted out, "Dave never wanted me much after Trista was born. I had picked up weight, and my body looked different. He said that's why he started going to other women . . ."

"What a goddamn fool." Heat clouded the edges of his vision and he knew he was near the end. "I'm not him, sweetheart. I didn't break your heart, and I never will. You're beautiful, all of you, in so many ways. I can't imagine ever not wanting you."

"Oh, Mack."

He could see the small quivers in her body, the way her lush breasts shimmered with each ragged breath. "Be right back."

Never taking his eyes from her, he stood and then back-stepped to the curtain where he'd left his jeans, blindly reached for them, and came back to her. With the jeans bunched in his fist, he pressed her legs apart and knelt between them. She looked almost pagan lying on the quilt with the bright lights flooding down on her. Her skin appeared translucent, her breasts swollen and rosy, her thighs open. He hadn't known for certain what love was, but now he knew this had to be it, because seeing her total acceptance of him meant more than he'd ever known was possible.

His heart slowed with the realization that despite all her efforts to fend him off, despite her resistance, he'd fallen head over heels, and he liked it. The Winston curse be damned. He felt blessed. After locating a condom in his wallet, he tossed the jeans aside. He laid the condom nearby, knowing he was near the edge of his control.

He touched her chin, down her chest to circle both breasts, pushing them together, gently rasping his beard-rough cheeks against her. He tickled his fingertips down her belly and watched her squirm, then stopped at the edge of her panties.

"I'm sorry, Jessica," he said, forcing the words out around the constriction in his heart, "but I can't wait much longer. Usually I'm pretty good at this, but now . . ."

She choked on a laugh. "Pretty good at what?"

"Waiting. Making the anticipation build. But you make me burn." He dropped the jeans and hooked both hands in the waistband of her panties, then bent to kiss her belly as he slowly tugged them to her knees. Her laughter turned to a ragged moan. "Lift your hips."

She did, but rather than just removing her panties, he slipped both hands beneath her buttocks, raising her, and tasted her again, this time without the barrier of cloth. Jessica twisted on the quilt, making incoherent sounds of pleasure. Her fingers tangled in his hair, tugged.

"Easy," he whispered, then kissed her again, using his tongue to stroke deep. "Damn, you're so wet. You want me, don't you, Jessica?"

Her body bowed, her head thrown back. He could feel the fine quivers running through her, but he wanted to hear her say it, wanted her to admit that what was happening was special. He blew softly against her heated flesh, ruffled the curls with his fingertips. Slowly, watching her face, he worked one long finger into her. Her thighs tensed and her buttocks flexed.

"Tell me, honey. Tell me you want me."

"Mack. *Yes.*"

His finger pressed deeper, and he was shocked at how tight she felt, proof of her long abstinence. She sobbed, straining toward him. He kissed her sweet female flesh, drowning in her scent, and demanded, "Tell me this is special for you too, babe."

"Yes, Mack, please . . ."

He broke. He couldn't wait another minute, and for the first time in his life, he resented the time it took to use the condom. Jessica shook beneath him, squirming, needing him. As he came over her, she gripped his shoulders so tightly her nails stung, then she strained up against him, trying to hurry him along. Mack entered her with one long, even stroke. They both groaned, but Jessica didn't give him a chance to wait any longer, locking her thighs around him and holding him tight. He began moving into her with a hard rhythm, loving the feel of her lush breasts against his chest, her hot breath fanning his throat. She accepted him, wanted him, and the knowledge drove him over the edge. As he gave a stifled groan of release, he felt her internal muscles clamp tight around his erection, intensifying his pleasure and assuring him she'd found her own climax.

He sank onto her, sated, awash in burgeoning emotions, and then he heard her soft sob.

Jessica tried to cover her face, but Mack wouldn't let her. She'd barely made a sound, and she'd assumed he'd be too far into his own pleasure to hear her anyway. But now he was over her, his expression alert, his hands holding hers so he could search her face.

His brows drawn in concern, he asked, "What's wrong? Why are you crying?"

"Mack, I want you to go now." He had to leave before she totally fell apart. God, she'd been so stupid. She'd thought she could make love with him, enjoy him for a time, then get back to her staid, responsible existence. She knew now that that was impossible, and she felt the sharp bite of panic. How could she ever go back to her old ways after having been with him, after knowing what it could be like?

She'd felt so alive while he loved her, so mindless with pleasure, she knew she'd been existing in a void. All she'd managed to do was show herself what she'd missed.

Mack's frown grew ferocious. "Like hell! I'm not going anywhere until you tell me what's wrong."

But she couldn't tell him. That would be like the final indignity, proof of how desperately pathetic she'd become. She shook her head and pleaded, "Please. You need to leave now. Trista will be home soon—"

"Not for at least another two hours. And we haven't finished the shoot." He smoothed her hair in that gentle way he had, making her heart ache. "Did I hurt you?"

Appalled that he could even think such a thing, she shook her head. Her voice was choked, strained, but she said, "It was wonderful. You were wonderful."

With a slight smile, he pulled her braid loose from behind her and played with it. "I love how you feel, the warm silk of your hair, the texture of your skin." His big hand cupped her breast, stroking it possessively. His gaze locked on hers, too intent, too compelling. "Everything about you excites me. You smell too good to describe, and you taste even better."

She blushed slightly, remembering the places where he'd tasted her. Mack smiled. "I love you, Jessica."

Her eyes widened. "Don't be—"

"Ridiculous?" Slowly, he pulled the tie from her hair and dragged his fingers over it, untwining her braid. "I know what you're going to say. That we don't know each other well enough. That nonsense about you being older than me." He laughed. "Do you realize how much influence your ex had on you? He convinced you somehow that you're old and worn out, but when men look at you, they see a young, very sexy woman. Not a housewife. Not a mother. A woman."

"How would you know what other men think?"

"I'm male." He drew a deep breath. "I dreamed about you even after we were out of college. It was like I knew something very important had slipped through my fingers. We hadn't talked a lot, but I'd studied you every chance I got. I knew you were serious and withdrawn and shy and a little wounded. I knew you were so sexy you made my teeth ache, and I saw how all the other guys looked at you. It made me nuts. I knew even then you were the woman I wanted."

Tears gathered in her eyes despite her resolve. She didn't know what to say, except to be honest. "I did the same."

"Yeah?" He looked pleased, then leaned closer to whisper, "Did you ever touch yourself . . . you know, while you were thinking of me?"

Her face went hot, her breath catching. "What kind of question is that?"

He shrugged, looking mischievous. "I did, thinking about you. I wanted you so damn bad, no other woman even interested me. I won't lie to you and tell you I stayed celibate, as you did, but my sexual encounters were few and far between. And I haven't been with anyone for almost six months. I was so disgusted over this teaching business that I haven't been able to think of much else. I guess that's why my meddling family set us up."

She was still embarrassed—and intrigued—over his very private admission, but managed to clear her mind enough to ask, "What are you talking about?"

His hand slipped down her body, stroking her, petting her. "Sophie used to help me study, and I told her all about you. Not your name, but everything else, like about your incredible breasts, your sexy braid, your beautiful brown eyes. She sympathized with me, in between badgering me enough so I'd learn that damned science that I hated so much."

He lifted her hand and kissed her fingers. "Did you ever tell her which college you went to?"

Jessica thought about it, then reluctantly nodded. "And what years, and that there was this annoying, utterly distracting young stud who kept interrupting my concentration. But she was Sophie Sheridan then, not Winston, and after she married I just never put the names together."

Mack barked a sharp laugh and bit her finger. "A stud, huh? Well, I think Sophie put two and two together, with some help from Allison, my other meddling, very adorable sister-in-law, and the result was this cooked-up catalogue of goofy men's lingerie."

Jessica licked her lips, then admitted, "I don't think it's goofy at all. I think you look downright scrumptious in this stuff."

"Is that right?"

She nodded.

"Scrumptious enough to give me a chance? To give us a chance? Because I really do love you, you know. At first I thought it was just an obsession, that eventually I'd get over you. But I didn't. And now, after being inside you, feeling you squeeze me tight, watching you come, I know it's more. I know I don't want to do that with anyone else but you, because it could never be as good."

She bit her lips to keep them from trembling. Could it be true? Could he really love her? He kept touching her and looking at her body, and she could feel him, hard again against her thigh.

He sounded just a tad uncertain as he continued. "I don't have the teaching position nailed down yet, but I'll figure that out one way or another. In the meantime, I work with my brothers at the bar. Cole bought it long ago so he could support us all, give us jobs as we got older. I worked there to pay my way through college, as did Zane. Now that we're getting other jobs, Cole and Chase have expanded and hired a few outside people. You'll love the place. It's incredibly popular, especially with the women, but it also has a nice family atmosphere."

Talking was impossible. Even swallowing was too hard to manage. Jessica launched herself against him, squeezing him tight. "Mack, I'm so sorry. I've been so wrong about you."

He rolled onto his back and held her close. "Ah, babe, don't cry. Please."

"You're the most amazing man and I don't deserve you."

"Now there's where you're wrong. Tell me you won't boot me out, honey. I'm in an agony of suspense here."

She kissed his face, his ear, his throat. Mack moaned, so she continued, and then she moaned too because he tasted so good she wanted to kiss him all over.

"Is this a yes, Jessica?" His voice shook and his hand held her head as she kissed his belly. "Does this mean we can have an honest-to-goodness relationship? You'll quit expecting me to be some kind of bum you can't depend on?"

Her hand wrapped around his throbbing erection and she kissed his navel. "Yes," she whispered. And in the next instant, Mack had her beneath him, kissing her, exciting her. *Loving her*.

Epilogue

Mack barely got in the door before Trista leaped up, waving her report card in front of his face. "I got three A's," she yelled, and Mack, so proud he thought he'd burst, lifted her up for a massive hug. When he set her back down, she stayed glued to his side and walked with him down the hallway as he perused her report card.

"Three A's and three B's." He put an arm around her and smiled. "I sure hope you're proud of yourself, especially since one of those A's is in science."

Her braces shone brightly when she grinned and confided, "I got the highest score on my science project. Higher than Brian's!"

He couldn't help but laugh. Then Jessica was there, her hair loose down her back, swishing around her hips, distracting him. Just the way she knew he liked it.

"Hey, babe." He leaned forward for a kiss, which she freely gave. God, he loved being greeted this way. "You don't have a shoot right now?"

"Nope. I took the rest of the afternoon off."

His brows lifted. "Oh ho. Any special reason?"

"Yes, but first, how did your day go?"

He realized she was anxious, worried about him on his first day back, and his love doubled. He tossed a few papers on the coffee table in the waiting room and dropped into a chair. "It was great—except for the principal poking her nose in every hour to check up on me."

Jessica perched on his lap, affronted on his behalf. "She didn't!"

"She did. Seems that even though she gave in to the parents' demands to have me back, she's still not happy about it. But I also got a visit from the head of the school board, and he told me they're behind me one hundred percent, so I'm not going to let the principal get me down. Especially now that I know the parents won't hesitate to lobby in my defense." He grinned shamefully, still amazed that the parents had taken on the school board to get him back.

Trista leaned forward and in a low tone meant to mimic his own, said, "Well, I hope you're proud of yourself."

"Come here," he growled, and pulled her onto the arm of the chair, close to his side. In the past few weeks, he'd grown to love Trista like she was his own. And she treated him as naturally as if he'd been around forever.

Mack couldn't imagine being any happier than he was now. Since he had been with Jessica, time had gone by like a dream. The parents of his students had organized and appealed to the school board, which had gotten him hired in the position he wanted, despite the principal's continued opposition. Sophie's catalogue, delivered in time for the Valentine's Day sale, had proved a huge hit. The women swamped her boutique every day now, and the main topic was the model. But with Jessica's insistence, all the photos had been cropped, so only Mack's body was visible. She'd gotten very huffy over the idea of other women knowing it was him in the racy loungewear, once she'd staked a claim.

Zane found the whole situation beyond hilarious.

"So what's your good news?" He toyed with a long lock of Jessica's hair, knowing that she'd left it loose for him.

"I'm going to be shooting another catalogue—this one for kids' clothing."

She looked so pleased with herself he kissed her again, making Trista giggle.

She pulled away with a sigh. "I also heard from the church today. Our wedding date is set. June sixth."

"It's official?" He had to hide his excitement. His damn nosy sisters-in-law had been insistent that Jessica deserved a big wedding this time around. He didn't mind that, because he would do anything to make her happy. But every time they'd come up with a date, they'd run into a glitch. He was beginning to think the Winston curse would fail him.

She looped her arms around his neck and said, "*Everything* is official for June sixth—the hall, the flowers, the dress, the guests, everything. Sophie will have the baby around the end of March, and Allison isn't due until November. The only problem, and it's only a tiny one, is Zane."

"What the hell has Zane got to do with this?"

"Well, your brother keeps complaining about a Winston curse, and he says if he comes to the wedding, it's liable to get him. But I know you want him there . . ."

Mack laughed and hugged her close. "Don't worry about my damn brother. He'll be there, probably with bells on. And I have no doubt he's up to tackling any curse there is."

Trista tilted her head at him and leaned close, fascinated by the talk of curses. "Did you tackle the curse, Mack?"

He touched the end of her nose and grinned. "No, honey. I welcomed it with open arms."

Sinderella

Kimberly Raye

Prologue

It was the most sinful thing she'd ever seen.

And if there was one thing Frankie Brannigan knew, it was sin. Thanks to three older brothers, she'd learned early on about the big S, particularly the carnal variety.

She knew what brand of lipsticks tasted best when it came to kissing. She could recite every brand of condom on the market. And she'd seen enough women's lingerie to fill an entire section at Naughty Nighties, the raciest lingerie shop in all of Houston.

That last aspect of her education had started early on, at the tender age of six, when she'd pulled a pink polka-dot pushup bra out of her oldest brother's varsity gym bag, and continued right up until last year when, while visiting her youngest brother at his apartment, she'd had the misfortune of finding a pair of sheer black panties, minus the crotch, hidden in the cookie jar.

She'd never looked at an Oreo in quite the same way since.

The particular piece of silky sin Frankie was now staring at wasn't crotchless, but it was close. It was a teddy, and the skimpiest, sheerest, most daring she'd ever seen. A wisp of lace here. A few inches of strategically placed satin there. It was an ultra-deluxe

Sinderella brand red-light special, complete with matching garter belt. A guaranteed man-pleaser, and not the sort of underwear the owner of Houston's fastest-growing construction company should be spending her hard-earned money on.

She gave in to the smile playing at her lips and snatched the hanger off the rack. Then again, it came with a guarantee, and she wasn't likely to seduce one unsuspecting Connor McBryde wearing hand-me-down sweats and a holey T-shirt.

And she *was* going to seduce him. She'd wasted enough time already. Ten years, to be exact. No more. Tonight Frankie was living out her ultimate fantasy. Before it was too late.

"So what do you think?" Lisa Moore, her best friend and the best electrician in the business, held up a red bra dotted with white hearts and a matching pair of panties that had a giant heart positioned over ground zero. "It's outrageously expensive, but Sarah gets a great discount."

Sarah was Lisa's cousin and the head clerk at Naughty Nighties, the exclusive home of Sinderella lingerie—the hottest, most expensive undies on the market. The erotic lingerie shop was the last place Frankie would have expected to spend her Tuesday afternoon.

Or any afternoon, for that matter. Her mother had died when Frankie had been a toddler. Without any female influence, she'd grown up a tomboy, wearing old jeans, baseball caps, and watching ESPN. As a teenager, she'd never had the desire or the opportunity to wear slinky lingerie and sexy clothes. As an adult, she'd never had the time. Long ago, her brothers had chosen different career paths, which had left only Frankie and her father in charge of the family business. He'd passed away last year from a heart attack, and now she was the sole owner of Brannigan Construction.

And she was tired.

She needed some fun in her life.

Nix that. She needed to *get* a life.

"I really want tonight to be memorable," Lisa went on. "I

thought I'd wear this under my costume and flash Marc a glimpse every now and then. I did the same thing on our first date, but since it was Halloween, I had pumpkins instead of hearts." A dreamy look crept over her expression and a pang of envy shot through Frankie. "Can you believe we're getting married?"

She couldn't. Marc was . . . well, *Marc*. The last single male Brannigan. A self-proclaimed bachelor and Oreo lover, and one of the last men Frankie had ever expected to settle down. Frankie had nearly dropped the phone when Lisa had called her earlier that morning with the news that Marc had proposed at the stroke of midnight—the official start of Valentine's Day. Tonight was another one of his infamous parties, his yearly Valentine's Bash which was now doubling as an impromptu engagement party where he and Lisa would announce the upcoming nuptials, scheduled to take place on Saturday night, in four short days.

Now *that* was typical Marc. Anxious and no-nonsense. When he made up his mind, he went after what he wanted. The thing was, Frankie never would have guessed he would set his sights on just one woman.

The news had come as a great big wake-up call. If Marc could find Miss Right and declare himself out of the game, then Connor McBryde, Marc's best friend and the object of Frankie's most erotic dreams, could do the same.

Connor and Marc had been the best of friends for over fifteen years. They'd always done everything together. They'd played the same high school sports, double-dated, gone to the same college, and even pledged the same fraternity. They shared a love for football, pineapple-jalapeño pizza, and women. Especially women. According to Frankie's calculations, Connor and Marc had dated nearly the entire available female population in Houston.

And now Marc was settling down, which meant Connor might not be too far behind.

Today he was sexy and single. But tomorrow?

Tomorrow he could be married and starting a family before she could recite the list of circular saws pictured on page 95 of her favorite hardware catalogue.

She had to do something now.

"Great choice, Frankie," Sarah said, as she left her post at the cash register to join the two women. "Did you see that it comes with a matching garter and gloves?"

"What about the mask? Is that included, too?" Frankie asked, her gaze shifting to the mannequin displayed in the window who wore the very outfit that Frankie held in her hands, along with a matching black lace mask.

"That's just a Miss Fantasy prop." Miss Fantasy was the poster girl for Sinderella lingerie. No one really knew what she looked like because in every ad she wore the trademark mask that covered the upper portion of her face, leaving only her luscious mouth visible. And, of course, her killer body. A marketing ploy to convince customers that Sinderella lingerie could make even a plain Jane more sexy and desirable. Miss Fantasy, who frequently changed her hair color from fiery red to jet black to strawberry blond, could have been any woman.

Every woman.

A *fantasy*.

The perfect vehicle to enable Frankie to put her plan into motion.

"We don't sell the masks," Sarah stated. "They're made specifically for the displays."

"What about a loan?" Lisa asked, but the clerk was shaking her head before the question was even out.

"Dirk would kill me." Dirk, store manager, and Sarah's live-in boyfriend was, according to Lisa, a first-rate user when it came to women.

"What Dirk doesn't know won't hurt him. He's gone, right?"

Sarah nodded. "A managers' seminar in L.A."

"Then there's nothing to worry about. You lend Frankie the mask, she returns it tomorrow. We women have to stick together."

"But Dirk—"

"Dirk's a jerk," Lisa stated. "How long have you been working here?"

"Eight years."

"What position did you start in?"

"Cashier."

"What position are you still in?"

"Cashier."

"I rest my case. You're an organizational whiz with a degree in business management, and you're ringing up panties for Miss Fantasy wannabes. You practically run this store, Sarah, yet Dirk's the one off at a wild and wicked managers' seminar in L.A. It's not fair."

"I don't know about wild and wicked . . ."

"Anytime you get a bunch of men lingerie managers together, I'm sure it's nothing short of wild and wicked."

"Well," Sarah seemed to ponder. "They did go out for karaoke last night."

"See there? He's having the time of his life and getting paid for it, while you're here doing his job and getting zero recognition."

"And they did go to Rodeo Drive the night before that." Sarah's worry turned to determination. "I guess I could do it. Just a loan, mind you. In the interest of sisterhood."

"That-a girl."

"Here you go," Sarah said, adding the mask to the pile of lace and silk in Frankie's arms. "In this getup, you'll knock your guy flat on his back."

Frankie smiled. A girl could only hope.

One

"Say, baby, how'd you like to make it with Tarzan?"

Frankie Brannigan's gaze shifted to the loincloth-wearing man who'd staggered up to her and clamped a beefy arm around her waist. Black hair covered his barrellike chest and crept up over his shoulders to disappear down his back. The guy had nothing on Tarzan, but Bigfoot was probably calling his agent right about now.

She shook her head. "I'm here with someone."

"I been watching you since you walked in, sweet cheeks." Bushy black eyebrows wiggled. "And I haven't seen you so much as talk to anyone."

"You will," she vowed, disengaging herself from his arm. Her gaze shifted to the man standing on the opposite side of the spacious living room packed with people.

He wore only a pair of loose-fitting white pants and a matching flowing white headdress. His chest was broad and bare, sprinkled with swirls of black silk that made her fingers itch for a touch. A sword dangled from a low-slung black-leather belt, completing his outfit. The Sheikh. The lover of all lovers. Valentino.

And, more important, the one and only Connor McBryde.

The main reason Frankie had traded another nice quiet Valentine's Day evening, complete with *Love Connection* reruns and a great big box of chocolates, to brave the mask and a killer pair of five-inch heels.

She wanted Connor, despite the fact that he was now the object of some major flirting, courtesy of two buxom blondes, one dressed as Mae West, the other as Marilyn Monroe, both in keeping with tonight's party theme—legendary sex symbols.

She watched Marilyn, legs up to here and breasts out to there, press herself against Connor's arm and whisper something with her lush red lips. He grinned, a heart-stopping tilt to his sensuous mouth, and a pang of jealousy stabbed her. The feeling quickly drowned in a wave of uncertainty. Frankie Brannigan was way out of her element.

Which was exactly the point.

In her element—at the construction site, dressed in overalls and handling power tools—she didn't stand a chance of attracting Connor's attention.

She wanted him.

She'd wanted him since she was a wide-eyed ten-year-old following her three older brothers around her father's construction site. Connor, tall and lanky and barely fourteen, had shown up, desperate for an after-school job to help out his single mother and younger sister. One look into his piercing blue eyes, and her stomach had hollowed out.

Fifteen years later, the reaction had only intensified. A truth that hit home when he glanced up.

Blue eyes collided with hers for a long, heart-pounding moment, and he smiled. A flash of white teeth and dimples that stalled the air in her lungs and sent a spiral of heat through her body.

Before she could stop herself, she glanced away. Old habits died hard, as the saying went, and she'd been denying her lust for much too long to lose her inhibitions because of a little disguise.

She needed alcohol for that.

She downed her third cup of champagne punch in as many minutes, but her hands still trembled, her nerves jumped.

Okay, so maybe she needed Valium instead. That, and a great big dose of courage. It wasn't every day that Frankie Brannigan seduced a man. Hell, Frankie had *never* seduced a man before and she was just a wee bit intimidated by Connor's reputation. With her demanding job, she hardly had time to date, and when she did, she usually went out with nice, nonthreatening men. Of course, she couldn't fall for one of them. No, Frankie had to fall for Connor—six feet of walking, talking sex with a capital S.

He was also one of the best architects in Houston, as well as a die-hard bachelor who had yet to get serious with any woman. He treated them all with a teasing charm that made even the shyest woman want to rip off her panties and hop into bed with him.

Frankie included, not that she'd ever admitted as much. She'd come close at the tender age of fifteen when he'd kissed her in the closet during a game of Spin the Bottle.

A game, that's all it had been, she reminded herself. Even though, for a few intense moments she'd thought he might actually have been interested in her

Then he'd walked right out of the closet and straight to Juicy Lucy Jackson, the prettiest cheerleader at Steadley High.

Frankie had known that, with her average-size chest and Plain-Jane jeans and T-shirts, she would never be able to compete with Lucy, or as the years passed, with any of the other women Connor had gone out with, and so she'd contented herself to lust after him from afar.

Besides, things were complicated. She and Connor were business colleagues—he consulted regularly for her various construction projects—and more important, they were friends. He was so much more than the man she lusted after—he was the guy who'd wiped her tears with those strong but gentle hands of his when she'd scraped her knees on a nasty piece of plywood.

But Frankie wanted more than his friendship.

She wanted one night.

One night to stare into his bluer-than-blue eyes and act on all the feelings swirling inside her. To prove to herself that beneath all the sexless overalls and work boots she wore lurked a real woman. To sate a lifetime of lust and get Connor McBryde completely out of her system. Once and for all.

"Say, you're supposed to be that Fantasy chick, aren't you?" Tarzan's voice pushed into her thoughts, and she shifted her attention back to the man at her side. "The lingerie model?"

"The one and only." Otherwise she wouldn't have been standing in a room full of crowded people wearing an outrageous teddy and a garter belt that would have done a Vegas stripper proud. Not that anyone could see the suggestive getup beneath the knee-length black leather coat she'd thrown on at the last minute, thanks to twenty-five years of insecurity.

She felt Tarzan's hand slide from her waist down the slope of her buttocks . . . she was this close to practicing a defense move her oldest brother had taught her when she heard a familiar voice.

"Say, Mort."

Frankie turned to see her brother Marc clap a firm hand on Tarzan's shoulder.

"Glad you and Sheila could make it."

"Sheila? My Sheila?" At Marc's nod, Tarzan's hand abruptly fell away. "But she's supposed to be out of town this weekend." His head whipped around as he scanned the crowd. "Where exactly is she?"

"She's exactly behind you," a female voice growled. Mort's head swiveled toward a very angry-looking Cleopatra. "Can't live without me, huh? Staying home to ring in Valentine's all by your lonesome, huh? Miss me so much it hurts, huh? You'll definitely be missing something when I'm through with you, Mortimer Windburn Carlisle, and I can promise it's going to hurt." She grabbed his ear and started to haul him off. "I didn't ace that sausage-sculpting class last year for nothing . . ."

"She's a chef," Marc explained.

"And he's a two-timing lout, and lucky you saved him before I had a chance to, uh"—Frankie caught her brother's stare and quickly remembered she was supposed to be a sleek, sexy model, not a ball-busting construction boss with three older brothers—"uh, scream," she said, doing her best to disguise her voice. "Yes—I would have screamed for help."

"And here I was dying to see you demonstrate the walnut crunch that nearly emasculated me back in the eighth grade."

"That wasn't my fault. You were tickling me and I had to pee and—" The words tumbled together as she realized what he'd said. "How'd you know it was me?" She turned an accusing stare on him. "Lisa told you, didn't she?"

"You forget we grew up in the same house, shared the same bathroom, ate at the same table, learned the finer points of hammering from the same father. We're flesh and blood, Frankie. Siblings. I'd know you anywhere." He grinned. "Of course, the fact that you're wearing the coat I gave you for your birthday doesn't hurt either." His gaze traveled the length of her, from her free-flowing blond hair, to the toes of her stiletto heels. His teasing expression faded. "So Lisa's responsible for this getup? I should have known."

"I bought it. She just led me into the den of sin—Naughty Nighties, over on Richmond—and that's all I'm saying, so please, please, *please* don't ask any more questions. Just tell me you wouldn't have recognized me without the coat and get lost."

He studied her for a thoughtful moment before pushing a strand of hair back from her lace-covered cheek. "I wouldn't have recognized you without the coat."

"Thank you."

"And by the way, you look great." He frowned. "Whoever the guy is, you make sure he treats you right. Or I'll come after him. While I haven't had any sausage-sculpting classes, I did read *Everything You Ever Wanted to Know about Chain Saws But Were Afraid to Ask*."

"You read Daddy's favorite book?"

He shrugged. "Hey, I tried to follow in the old man's footsteps. Construction just wasn't my thing. But give me a layout board and just watch the master work." A senior advertising executive for one of the largest agencies in Houston, Marc was good at his job, and not too humble to admit it. "That or a luscious redhead." His gaze paused on Lisa, who stood across the room showing off her engagement ring to a group of his colleagues. "You be careful, okay?"

"I've won the Journeyman's safety award for the past five years. Careful I can handle." It was the blasted shoes pinching her feet that she had her doubts about.

Marc left, and Frankie shifted to give her toes some breathing room. If she could just sit down for a few minutes—

The thought disintegrated as her gaze moved to the empty spot where Connor McBryde had been standing not two minutes ago. He was gone. And so was the buxom Marilyn.

Oh, no!

She'd blown her one chance. She'd let him walk away without so much as batting her eyelashes, much less doing half the things she wanted to do. From smiling and flirting, to touching and kissing.

Gone.

She did a quick visual search of every face. Dread built with each passing second, especially when Tarzan, King of the Hairy Apes, caught her looking at him and obviously misinterpreted her interest. Before she could blink, he ditched Sheila and started toward her. Her toes registered a strong protest at the idea of a quick getaway, but she couldn't just stand there.

She pushed through the crowd, working her way toward the

opposite side of the room and the hallway. The area outside the bathroom was crowded, but she finally squeezed through to a dimly lit section of the hallway that appeared unoccupied. She needed to think, to decide what to do next. How to find him.

"I don't think we've met." The deep, familiar voice sent a spurt of heat through her body.

She turned to find Connor standing behind her, an intimidating shadow filling the hallway, his bluer-than-blue eyes twinkling. Relief flooded her. And lust. And longing. And so she did what she should have done the moment she'd walked in.

She kissed him.

Connor McBryde had been kissed by many women, but never quite like this.

Her lips were so hungry, so desperate, so damned *stirring*. That was what made the difference. One touch and *bam!* he wanted more. Just like that. Just like *this*.

It took all of five seconds before his initial shock transformed into a wave of hunger and he took the lead. One arm slid around her waist to pull her close, while the other stroked up her back to cup the back of her head and tilt her just enough to give him better access.

As eager as she was, she had yet to part her luscious lips—a problem he was more than ready to remedy. He swept his tongue against the seam of her closed mouth, stroking, coaxing, and soon she opened up and he tasted the sweetness inside.

Man, was she sweet! Champagne and strawberries flavored with a hint of innocence.

Innocence?

The thought rooted in his mind, spurred by the way her tongue hesitated against his, the way her hands rested against his chest rather than sliding around his neck. The way her body trembled.

Connor had been with enough women to know that this one was different. Sweeter. Softer. Less experienced. A *lot* less experienced, despite the fact that she was dressed for *sex*cess and had come on so strong.

He fought for control and slowed himself down, enough to soothe her trembling, to tease her with his lips until she relaxed against him and opened her mouth wider. Her tongue darted out, flicked against his, and he felt the soft touch in a flash of raw heat that speared through his body. *So sweet.* Tongues tangled, their lips melded, and the air rushed from his lungs for several furious heartbeats.

"I was going to ask you to dance," he murmured against her lips when they both finally came up for air. "But this works too."

"Dance?" Her disoriented gaze met his, and realization seemed to spark. She stiffened, horror dawning in her bright-green eyes. "Oh, my God. I did it. *We* did it."

He gave her a slow, easy grin despite his pounding heart. "Not yet, darlin', but the night's still young."

His meaning didn't go unnoticed. Heat spread up her neck and her face. The bottom portion that wasn't concealed by the mask turned a delicious shade of pink. "I—I didn't mean *it* it." She shook her head, her soft blond hair a wild tumble around her shoulders, and gasped for breath. "I—I really need to get some air. Would you, um, excuse me a second?" Without waiting for an answer, she turned and fled toward the bathroom, leaving him to figure out what the hell had just happened.

The most incredible kiss of his life, that's what.

Oddly enough, he'd known it would be incredible. The instant he'd seen her standing by the punch bowl, he'd known. It wasn't so much the way she'd looked, her voluptuous body clad in a black leather coat that revealed plenty of tantalizing cleavage and stopped just above her knees to reveal long, black-stocking-clad legs. It was the way she'd looked at him, her gaze so warm and stirring, even across a crowded room. That was why he'd sought her out the minute he escaped from the clingy Susanne something or other, an ad assistant with Marc's firm who'd dressed up as Marilyn Monroe.

She'd come on like gangbusters, and he'd done what he always did with strong, pushy women intent on working their way into his bed and his life. He smiled and teased and pulled back, a reaction he'd developed a long time ago.

He'd never had time for a serious relationship. His father had walked out on the family when Connor had been barely fourteen and he had gone to work, after school and on weekends, determined to take care of his mother and younger sister.

But things were different now. All his hard work had finally paid off. He had a successful architectural business. His sister had recently graduated from college and now worked as a CPA for a Dallas firm. And his mother had finally stopped mourning his father's abandonment and started living again. She'd recently remarried and was the happiest he'd seen her in years.

He had the time now, but the one woman he did want, the woman he'd always wanted, didn't have the time for him, and he'd yet to meet anyone else who provoked more than passing interest.

Until now.

The blood rushed through his veins. His chest burned where her fingertips had pressed against him. He licked his lips and tasted her, and his already prominent erection throbbed in response.

Damn.

He'd never been hit this hard before, this fast. Only once, and that had been a mistake. A fluke caused by raging hormones and the artless kiss of a girl who'd wanted desperately to be a woman. She'd been a friend, was still a friend, and therefore was off-limits.

But this woman . . .

As if his wishful thinking had conjured her, she walked out of the bathroom and pushed past several people waiting to go in. Little trickles of moisture dotted her neck and the visible portion of her face, and he knew she'd been splashing cold water onto her flushed skin.

The notion brought a smile to his face, or maybe the smile came from the fact that she wasn't running the other way. She was walking back toward him.

"Did you find some air in there?" At her blank look, he grinned. "You said you needed air." He couldn't help himself. He caught the slow glide of a drop of water as it made its way down her smooth-as-silk neck. She shivered beneath his touch. "That is what you needed, isn't it?"

"Actually," she licked her lips, holding his stare for a long moment while she seemed to work up her courage. "What I really need is standing right in front of me. Can we, um, go someplace?"

The refusal was there on the tip of his tongue. This was crazy. Insane! While he was no saint, he certainly wasn't in the habit of picking up strangers.

The trouble was, she didn't feel like a stranger. She felt soft and warm and so damned eager, and he couldn't help himself.

He reached for her hand. "Come on."

Hell, sanity was overrated anyway.

Two

"Did you bring a coat?" he asked her as they neared the front door.

"You're looking at it."

He grinned. "Actually, I'd like to look under it."

"Really?" Surprise filled the breathless word and set off a chorus of warning bells in his head.

His gaze hooked on her luscious mouth, and he remembered the feel of her trembling lips, the artlessness of her kiss, the overall innocence of her response. He clenched his fingers and fought to control his raging need. "Maybe we should go somewhere first. Have a drink or something."

"Trust me, that won't help. I've had a few already. It's better if we just cut to the chase and get to it before . . ." As if she realized what she was saying, she caught her bottom lip and blushed. "Um, I really don't want a drink."

His gaze lingered on her mouth for a long second before shifting to the bright green eyes, filled with heat and desperation. "So what do you want?"

"I already told you."

"Tell me again. I want to make sure there's no misunderstanding between us. That we're both clear on where we're going and what we're doing. What we're going to do."

"I . . ." A dainty pink tongue darted, and she licked her lips. "I want you."

Her voice whispered through his head, so sweet and sincere and . . . familiar. He eyed her. "I swear I know you from somewhere."

Panic flashed in her eyes before fading into determination. "Sure you do." She licked her lips again, the bottom one quivering so slightly that he might not have noticed. Except that he noticed everything about her. The way the pulse throbbed frantically at the hollow of her throat. The way she clasped her hands together a little too tightly, the way she seemed to gasp for breath every time she stared directly into his eyes. "Everybody knows me. I'm Miss Fantasy."

She certainly looked the part. It was as if she'd stepped off any of the dozen billboards plastered around town. But there was something else as well. Something achingly familiar in the way she nibbled her bottom lip as she waited for his reaction. Despite the mask she wore that concealed the upper half of her face, he could imagine her brows drawn together, her forehead wrinkled, her gaze intent—a look he'd seen before, and not on any billboard. But with his body flushing so hot and his heart hammering so loudly, he just couldn't remember where.

He would. Before the night was over and done with, he would peel away that black lace mask along with everything else and see who she really was, and why she seemed so intent on hiding from him.

"My place is on the third floor," he said as they traded the noise and laughter of Marc's apartment for the quiet hallway outside. He steered her toward the elevator at the far end.

"I know." Her gaze snapped up to meet his, as if she realized she'd just made a mistake. "I mean, I thought it might be."

"Why's that?" Connor guided her into the elevator and punched the button for the third floor.

"Marc, um, mentioned you were a neighbor, and since he's on the second floor and there's nothing on the first floor, I took a guess."

"So how do you know Marc? Personal or business?"

She nibbled that luscious bottom lip a few seconds more, before her mouth hinted at a grin. "I could tell you, but then I'd have to kill you."

"You're already killing me, darlin'" he said in all honesty, because he'd never wanted a woman this much, never ached to taste someone as badly as he wanted to taste her. Again.

"Really?" The innocent question zapped some sense into him, making him stiffen and back up when all he wanted to do was haul her close.

When the doors opened on his floor, he didn't budge. Instead, he pushed the lobby button. "I don't think this is such a good idea—"

"No." She stabbed the emergency stop, and the doors stalled a few feet shy of closing. The light from the elevator spilled out into the dim hallway. "Please. I think this is the best idea I've had in a long time."

"You don't really know me."

"I do." She cleared her throat. "I mean, I know what I need to know."

"And what's that?"

"That I want you," she said again, the words filled with a need that echoed through his body. He stiffened and drew a deep breath.

"Don't make this harder, sweetheart. Don't make me harder. I'm trying to preserve your innocence."

Her mouth formed a thin line. "What makes you think I'm innocent?"

His gaze swept her from head to toe, lingering too long at the most distracting places until a rosy flush crept up her neck. "That's what makes me think you're innocent."

"Because I'm blushing? Maybe it's just hot in here."

"Too hot." And he had the hard-on to prove it. But it wasn't something he intended to act on. Not now. Not with her.

No matter how much he wanted to.

"I'm not innocent."

"Whatever you say." Now he reached for the emergency button, determined to start the elevator on its way and put some much-needed distance between them.

Her hand closed over his. Her fingers trembled only slightly at the first moment of contact, then they drew tight, purposeful, as she urged him away from the control panel.

"I'm *not*." As if she needed to prove it to herself as much as him, she tugged at the belt that held her coat closed, and the leather edges parted. Her arms fell to her sides, and the coat slipped away. She stood before him wearing nothing but a black satin teddy cut high on her hips and a garter belt with thigh-high black stockings.

His gaze traced the endless expanse of her neck to where it dipped into cleavage. The teddy barely covered her full breasts. Her nipples pebbled against the soft fabric and he swallowed. Hard.

But it wasn't the sight of her scantily clad with her nipples so ripe and eager that melted his determination. It was the look glittering in her green eyes when his gaze, after a leisurely trek over her voluptuous body, finally met hers.

Need he could have handled. Women had been needing something from him his entire life. His mother had needed a provider. His sister had needed a father figure. The less-than-discriminating women in his past had needed the sure touch of an experienced lover.

This woman stared back at him with nothing short of pure *longing*. As if she wanted not just his body but his heart as well.

Emotion welled inside him at the thought. Lust and hunger and a strange tenderness that made him think that maybe she wasn't just any woman. Maybe she was *the* woman. The woman he needed, as well as wanted.

Crazy. Connor McBryde didn't believe in love at first sight. Love sprang from compatibility, from similar interests and shared goals that grew over time. Otherwise, there was always the risk that one person would wake up someday and realize that while the sex was great, that was all there was. It had happened to his parents. They'd met and married within two weeks, a whirlwind courtship that had led to a loveless marriage that had finally ended when his father had worked up the courage to walk out.

This . . . *this* was just a healthy dose of lust.

At least that's what he told himself as he gave in to the heat clawing at his gut and stepped toward her. Lust.

Yeah, buddy. And I've got some swampland in the Sahara.

Frankie half feared he would reach past her and punch the elevator back into action, sending them to the first floor and killing her plans. Instead, he planted his hands on either side of her, trapping her against the elevator wall as he leaned toward her. She closed her eyes, feeling the warm rush of his breath against her lips, anticipating the firm press of his mouth, the coaxing of his tongue.

"Touch me." At his deep command, her eyes opened to find him staring down at her, his gaze dark and intense and hot.

"W—what?" It wasn't much of a seductive comeback but all that heat was burning up her common sense.

"Touch me."

This was it. The moment of truth. The kiss earlier had been impulsive, a bold move fed by desperation and sheer relief that he hadn't left before she'd had a chance to put her plan into motion. But this was different. This *was* the plan. The first moment of this one incredible night. Her chance. One she could either take or spend the rest of her dateless life regretting.

She reached out.

Her trembling hand met the solid wall of his chest, and heat scorched her. He was so incredibly hot. So hard. So *real*. His scent—a mingling of musky cologne and warm male—filled her nostrils, calming her fears and provoking a different emotion. Desire.

Her fingers relaxed, her palm flattened, and she felt the frantic thud of his heart for a long moment before her hand trailed down, encountering warm, hard muscle covered with silky hair. The chest hair thinned, funneling into a single line that disappeared beneath the waistband of his white sheikh pants. Her touch followed the delicious path, like a pirate in search of buried treasure. She paused at his waistband before sliding her fingers just a fraction beneath it. His breath caught. A surge of feminine power shot through her. She'd wanted him her entire life, and now, finally, he wanted her. She could see it in his eyes. Feel it in his body's response. Muscles contracted, shivered, boosting her confidence.

She smiled, gathered her courage and trailed a fingertip over the outside of his pants, down the hard ridge of his erection, from tip to root.

His breath caught on a hiss and his hand closed over hers.

"My turn," he growled.

He lifted her arms, holding them out to her side and pinning them in place.

"Don't move," he told her as his hands fell away.

Then he touched her. His fingertip met the frantic beat of her pulse, then slid down, over the slope of one breast. The slow glide of skin against skin made her breath catch. His thumb grazed her nipple, and pleasure rushed through her.

Strong hands skimmed the sides of her breasts, her stomach, her thighs, until her fists clenched against the delicious sensations. And the frustration.

And then he stopped.

"Please." The word burst from her lips before she could stop herself, and her eyes snapped open. She found him staring at her, his gaze hooded as if he were trying very hard to figure something out. To figure her out.

Panic bolted through her, followed by need—the raw, raging need he'd stirred with his hot looks and his even hotter touch—and she kissed him. A blazing, open-mouthed kiss that held nothing back. She had no clue what she was doing, only that she wanted to taste him, and she did. She tasted him, pressed herself against him, rubbed her body against the rock-hard length of him straining against the silky fabric of his pants.

She anticipated his response. Anything from a deep masculine chuckle at her obvious impatience to him prying her arms loose and staring down at her with a sexy grin as he whispered, "We've got all night." If Connor McBryde was anything, it was calm. Cool. Smooth. Especially when it came to women. He laughed and teased and smiled and flirted as if he had all the time in the world.

She had yet to see him anxious or impatient or hungry.

He was all three in that instant as he wrapped strong, purposeful arms around her, his lips eating hers, his tongue plunging deep. The sudden assault rocked her body and her senses until she felt the heat flood between her thighs. It lasted only a few moments and then his muscles seemed to relax. His grip eased as he depressed the emergency button and steered her out of the elevator and down the hall to his apartment, as if he'd recovered from his momentary loss of control. The click of a lock, the creak of a door, and they were inside. He led her into the bedroom with a smile and a wicked wink, straight over to the bed.

He sat down and pulled her between his open legs. Reaching for the straps of her teddy, he skimmed them down her arms and pulled the material to her waist. Suckling one nipple with his eager lips, he licked and nipped and teased until she sagged against his mouth.

A sigh escaped her, followed by a soft moan when his fingers grazed her thighs as he unsnapped her stockings. He peeled the teddy down her body until she stood before him, naked except for the thigh-high stockings, a puddle of expensive Sinderella silk at her feet.

His hands slid around her waist and cupped her buttocks as he dipped his head to kiss her navel and lower . . .

"*Connor.*"

"It's okay, darlin'."

Before she knew what was happening, his wonderful hands had moved between her legs. He turned and eased her onto the bed, leaning over her, pushing her thighs as far apart as he could. She caught his gaze before his head dipped and a wave of embarrassment swept through her, followed by a rush of excitement. No man had ever touched her like this.

"Relax, sweetheart. I just want to see if you taste half as good as you look." He parted her with his thumbs and rasped her with his tongue.

She jumped and he chuckled, before the sound changed to a distinct growl, as if her response brought out something fierce and primal.

Crazy. This was Connor with his teasing smiles and soft, warm hands and . . .

Thought fled as he licked her again, and kept on, plying her soft, swollen tissue, drawing the sensitive heart of her into his mouth and suckling. She arched against him, her hips lifting off the bed, searching for more.

But it was already too much. *He* was too much. The pressure built inside her, like a bowstring being stretched tight. Tighter. When he slid a finger deep inside, a cry burst from her lips and she climaxed.

He continued to lick and suck and drive her wild, his hands firm and strong as he held her, until the last spasm subsided and she lay spent, her legs spread wide and trembling.

"You taste even sweeter, darlin'. Much sweeter," he murmured as he leaned back from her, his gaze never leaving her face. His movements were unhurried and smooth. Only the faint tremor of his hands gave any indication that he was wound as tight as she.

He shoved his pants down. His erection sprang forward, hot and huge and pulsing, and every nerve in her body jumped to attention. Her vision sharpened. Her senses heightened. Her nostrils flared as she drank the delicious scent of aroused male and steamy sex. Her nipples tightened and her blood rushed and need sharpened to a fine point that stabbed through her.

She wanted more.

More kissing.

More touching.

More.

She watched as he took a condom from the nightstand. Large, tanned fingers tore open the packet, and a vision hit her. Those same fingers opening a sugar packet, his grin warming her insides as he slipped the sweetener into her morning coffee on Mondays when they routinely met to go over current projects.

A wave of doubt swept through her, but she fought it back. While this was the man who slipped the sugar into her coffee, she wasn't the same overall-clad, workaholic crew boss who gratefully accepted the mug from him. Tonight she was one hundred percent woman. Feminine and sexy and a little bit wild. Tomorrow she would go back to being plain old, boring Frankie Brannigan, and Connor would never be the wiser.

She felt a niggle of guilt for deceiving him, but then—if he knew her identity, he wouldn't be touching her, tasting her, loving her. He would reject her, and she couldn't bear that. She needed this night with him, this chance to feel all of the things she'd been holding back. Things she'd never felt for any man but him.

She deserved it.

She was twenty-five years old and she'd never indulged her

feminine side. She'd been too busy playing the dutiful daughter, sacrificing dates and fun to prove to her father that she was every bit as competent as her brothers, every bit as capable of following in his footsteps. She'd worked twenty hours a day to bring projects in on time and within budget, determined to keep the business on track, to see her father's dream continue.

But this was *her* dream. This one night.

He came to her, settling himself between her legs, arms braced on either side of her, his hot erection pressed against her damp cleft.

"You're wet for me." So wet and warm and ready, and Connor forgot all about the soft touches and seductive petting he engaged in with most women. He forgot everything except the need to be inside her.

His first thrust was deep and urgent. She stiffened, her body tightening. A small cry burst from her luscious lips, and he froze. It couldn't be. She couldn't be . . .

She was too beautiful. Too sexy. Too stirring.

Too tight.

He'd figured her for naive, despite the show she'd put on. She'd been nervous, her bottom lip trembling when he touched her, kissed her, as if it had been far too long since she'd felt a man. But he'd never expected her to be this snug. She was a grown woman, for Christ's sake.

And he was her first.

The knowledge stirred a tenderness he'd felt only once before. With a sweet, innocent girl who'd never been kissed.

The thought faded as her fingers pressed into his buttocks.

"Don't stop." A slight shimmy of her hips followed the soft plea, and it was all he could do to keep from burying himself as deep as he could go. "Please."

He tightened his body, muscles bunching, coiling as he fought against the heat drawing him forward. "Are you okay?" he managed.

"No," she breathed, her body seeming to relax with every heartbeat. "Not unless you start moving again." Her sweet mouth curved into a grin and warmed him inside even more than her sweet body was heating him from the outside.

"Take this off." He went for the mask, but her hand caught his.

"No."

"I need to see you."

"And I need to feel you." She lifted her hips, drawing him a fraction deeper and the air stalled in his lungs.

His hand fell away, because he sensed her fear and at that moment, he wanted her to feel anything but fear. Desire. Pleasure. *Him.*

Anything but fear.

He thrust into her, deep and strong, checking the depth of his strokes, making sure he brought her as much pleasure as she did him. Soon she wrapped her legs around him, her body arching to meet his, to join him.

The pace increased, his body moving, the sensation rushing through him, until it was too much. He pounded into her one final time. His climax hit him like a runaway freight train, fast and furious and blinding. The air bolted from his lungs and pleasure, so acute and hot, rushed through him. When he finally caught his breath, he eased himself down beside her.

What had just happened . . . the fierceness, the urgency, the *rightness* of it, floored him and choked the soft, tender words he always whispered in his throat. He turned onto his side and pulled her back against him, her bottom nestled against his groin. Without saying a word, he buried his face in the curve of her fragrant neck and closed his eyes.

She'd fallen asleep.

The thought gripped her the moment her eyes opened to the

dim bedroom, the rising sun creeping around the window blinds. Her hands went to her face and panic flooded her. The mask was gone. *Gone.*

Dozens of fears rushed through her mind. Connor had seen her and now her cover was blown and life would never be the same again and—

Get a grip.

She searched her mind for her last conscious thought. The quivering between her legs, the strong arms sliding around her waist and the slow rise and fall of his chest. He'd nodded off before she had, and her mask had been firmly in place at that time. She'd felt it, fallen asleep with one hand touching the edge.

She must have tugged it off in her sleep. That had to be it.

She worried for a second that he'd stirred during the night and seen her, but if Connor McBryde had opened his eyes and found Frankie Brannigan in his bed, he wouldn't likely have rolled over and gone back to sleep. He would have called her out for deceiving him. The way he'd called her out in the closet that time.

"You want to kiss me, don't you?"

As stupid as she'd been, she'd nodded eagerly and he'd kissed her. An act of charity, she now realized.

He'd been perfect and smooth and good-looking, and she'd been just one of many who'd wanted to kiss Connor McBryde.

Never again. She had her pride, after all. She might want him, but he damn well didn't have to know it. He would never know it.

She took a deep breath and forced her panic aside. The mask had come loose and now all she had to do was find it before he woke up—

That plan stumbled to a halt as her gaze fell on the small Chihuahua sitting on the floor next to the bed. Cu-Joe, fulltime weenie addict and now the proud owner of her mask, wagged his tail, the familiar scrap of lace dangling from his mouth.

She put a hand over her eyes, turned her head, parted two fingers, and cautiously peeked at Connor, who slept on his side, facing her. His dark eyelashes cast spiky shadows on his cheeks. He looked so handsome and sexy, even while sleeping that her heart ached.

Her heart?

She forced the thought out of her mind. Of course she ached. After the night she'd had, her entire body ached. But not her heart. This was sex. Lust. One night.

And it was over.

And she had to get that mask.

Slowly she crept out of the bed, her heart jumping into her throat when he sighed and rolled onto his back. But he slept on and after a few breathless moments, she managed to move again.

Once free, she reached toward the dog, who promptly turned and trotted off to the other room, her mask dangling from his mouth.

She cornered Cu-Joe in the living room where she'd spent many a Sunday afternoon watching football with Connor and Marc. She'd also spent more than her fair share of time playing ball with Cu-Joe.

"You owe me for all those games of fetch. Now give it up." A fierce growl erupted, and she snatched her hand back before he made good on the threat.

She had no doubt that he would. Connor hadn't named him Cu-Joe for nothing.

"Ssshhh." She touched a finger to her lips. "Now be a good doggie and give it to Frankie." She reached out and managed to pet him for a few heart-pounding seconds. He seemed to relax. Until she went for the mask. A fierce growl, a show of teeth—and Frankie retreated.

"Okay, if you want to be difficult . . ." She crept into Connor's kitchen and searched his refrigerator until she found a package of Cu-Joe's favorite wieners.

"Here's the deal." She waved a weenie at him. "You give me the mask and I give you the weenie." When Cu-Joe just blinked, she added, "Two weenies."

A few sniffs and he dropped the mask.

Frankie snatched it up and grimaced as her fingers came into contact with the now wet-with-drool lace. Okay, so she couldn't put it on. Not the end of the world. Connor was asleep. She would just get her stuff and get the hell out as fast as she could. She snuck back into the bedroom, pulled on her coat, and simply scooped up the rest of her stuff.

She was halfway through the living room when the first sharp bark behind her made her jump. Her clothing landed in a heap at her feet and she whirled to find Cu-Joe licking his chops, obviously eager for more goodies.

"All right," she muttered, rushing back into the kitchen to grab the pack of wieners from the refrigerator and toss the whole thing to him. Back in the living room, she snatched up her stuff and fled. Halfway down the elevator, her gaze fell on the red-and-black tag stitched inside the teddy. *Sinderella*.

The irony hit her and she almost smiled.

She felt like Cinderella, all right. Like the poor, dowdy, ordinary servant girl fleeing the ball before the Prince realized she wasn't the lady she appeared to be.

But there would be no glass slipper in Frankie's future, no happily ever after, because this was the real world, not some silly, romantic fairy tale. Last night had had nothing to do with romance and everything to do with lust.

With sex.

And now it was over.

"Some watchdog you are." Connor sat on the side of the bed and glared at the dog stretched out on the floor, head on his paws. The smell of wieners filled the air. "You let her get away."

Cu-Joe yawned, his whiskers twitching before he settled his muzzle back down on his paws as if to say, "Who do you think I am? Big Brother?"

Connor traced his finger over the impression that this woman, whoever she was, had left in his bed, and his frown deepened. "You could have barked, whimpered, scratched—*something*."

The dog got up and trotted into the living room.

"Just wait until you need a belly scratch," Connor called after him. "You can forget it."

Connor brushed a hand over his face as images of last night rushed through his mind. So much for peeling away the mask and uncovering the truth. He'd fallen asleep. She'd been so warm and sweet and innocent, despite the show she'd put on, and so he'd closed his eyes, never imagining that she would slip away after the intensity of what had happened between them. Last night had been too incredible. Too special.

A one-night stand.

The trouble was, it had felt like a helluva lot more. Too much. For the first time in his life—make that the second—he'd actually trembled because of a woman. Crazy, because Connor McBryde didn't tremble at a woman's touch. He made women tremble with the slow glide of his hand. Made them pant with his kisses and want with his teasing grins.

But last night, he'd been the one trembling and panting and—

The thought stalled as he felt something brush softly against his skin. He opened his eyes to see Cu-Joe standing beside the bed, tongue lolling, tail wagging, before his attention shifted to the scrap of black lace the dog had dropped beside him.

His fingers closed over it and he flopped back on the bed to examine the intriguing item his mystery woman had left behind. His head hit the pillow and the scent of her—apples and cinnamon—filled his nostrils and sent a burst of heat straight to his groin.

"I'm crazy." He shook his head and eyed the ceiling. "I can't be falling for a woman I just met. No way, no how. There's no such thing as love at first sight."

Next to him, Cu-Joe barked his agreement on the subject.

"Hell, even if there were, last night doesn't qualify because I didn't actually *see* her. I don't know the first thing about this woman. Not her name, where she's from, what she does for a living."

And it didn't matter, he realized.

He knew all he needed to know. She sighed his name softer and sweeter than any woman he'd ever met. And stroked his back with the edge of her fingernails just enough to send shivers up and down his spine. And stared at him in a way no woman ever had, longing bright and vivid in her green eyes.

Familiar eyes.

His fingers tightened on the mask.

He knew her. He didn't know how or where, but he'd met up with Miss Fantasy before, and he didn't intend to rest until she was back in his bed, and he was hilt-deep inside her. This time there would be no barriers between them.

Three

Business as usual.

That was what Frankie told herself the next morning as she drove out to Whittenburg House, a fading Victorian mansion near Buffalo Bayou. Her company was handling renovations to the fine old home.

Once inside, she pulled on her work gloves and picked up a nail gun, much to the surprise of her head carpenter and two apprentices who were busy working on the hand-carved banister. But she needed to *do* something. Doing was much better than thinking.

The next few minutes passed in a noisy blur as she shot the hell out of the new wall studs, relishing the feel of the tool in her hands and the trickle of sweat that ran down her temple. Work for her was cathartic, invigorating. It made her heart pound, her blood pump, and when she finished, she felt a sense of accomplishment about the job she had done. Proud.

She'd trade a nail gun for a NordicTrack any day.

When her father had been alive and running the company, Frankie had been part of the work crew, paying little attention to the business side of things. However, there had been little time for her to do the hands-work after her father had passed away last year. These days it seemed like she never got out of the office. Most of her time was spent on the phone with suppliers and contractors, or doing paperwork and battling it out with the fax machine from hell.

Not for long. She was taking control of her life, both personal and professional. Sick of all the paperwork and day-to-day hassles, a few days ago she had finally called a personnel service and inquired about an assistant. Last night had been a major coup in her sex life. Namely, that she finally had one.

Yes, she was finally taking control.

She'd indulged with the lust of her life, and now she could get on with finding the love of her life—a man who appreciated the finer points of flannel and didn't measure a woman's worth by the size of her chest. A man who would love the real Frankie, no matter whether she paraded around in skimpy lingerie or sweats and a battered T-shirt. A man who would look past the surface and see the woman beneath. Her soul mate.

A man the complete opposite of Connor McBryde.

Over and done with. She'd tasted the forbidden fruit, sated her craving, and now it was time to chuck the core out the window and move on.

"So, Miss Fantasy girl, how did it go last night?"

Then again, maybe not.

Frankie turned to see Lisa poised in the doorway. With long red hair and a body that made Frankie regret the chocolate doughnut she'd had for breakfast, Lisa made even overalls and work boots look good. More than that, however, she had a mind to go with the body, and the ability to splice wires better than anyone Frankie had ever seen.

She'd met Lisa five years ago, when they'd both shown up at the union hall to take the admittance exam for a carpenter's apprenticeship program. Frankie had been fresh out of junior college with an associate degree in business, while Lisa had been recovering from a bad marriage. They'd been the only women to apply, and they had scored higher than any of their male counterparts. A fact that, despite a lot of sexist mumbling and grumbling, had gained them instant admission to the program.

Later, Frankie had added plumbing and basic electrical skills to her repertoire and gone on to get her journeyman certification, while Lisa had built a solid résumé as a top electrician.

The redhead smiled. "So, did you knock the mystery man's socks off or what?"

"He wasn't wearing socks."

"Before or after?"

"Before."

Lisa's eyes twinkled. "Which means there was an after."

"Maybe."

"Come on. Frank. I'm dying here. Have a heart. I'm your best friend. This time next week I'll be family. I can't believe you won't tell me who you got all dressed up for. I didn't see you talking to anyone except—"

"It wasn't Tarzan."

"Then who was it?"

"It's not important."

"Of course it is. C'mon, Frankie, last night was the first time I've seen you wear your hair down in years. Forget important—this man has got to be pretty friggin' fantastic to get you to do that."

"It's just hair."

"Which you always keep pulled back in a ponytail and tucked up under a hard hat. Hell, I'd forgotten you had hair."

"Very funny. For your information, I wear both the ponytail and the hat for safety reasons." She stared pointedly at Lisa until the woman shrugged and plopped her own hard hat on her head, her long hair still flowing free.

"I'm talking after hours," Lisa said. "I bet at any given moment, the hair police could stop at your place and arrest you for carrying concealed."

"I like wearing it up." Usually. But last night, with Connor's fingers running through it, tugging and stroking and feeling, the three hours spent brushing and curling and cursing had almost been worth it.

She put that thought aside and stiffened. "It's definitely easier to manage when it's up, and a lot less time-consuming."

"You're hopeless," Lisa snapped. "Say, this guy of yours isn't married, is he? Omigod, it's not that Bernie Culpepper that works with Marc? He's cute, but his wife works vice for HPD. She's got her very own Glock, and rumor has it she's a crack shot."

"Geez, Lisa, it's good to see how much faith you have in my ability to pick a man. Of course he's not married and so of course it's not Bernie."

Lisa seemed to think for a minute before her expression turned knowing. "Oh, honey. You poor thing. Let me tell you, it's nothing to be ashamed of."

"What are you talking about?"

"Your guy is appearance-challenged and you're uptight about it."

"First of all, he's not *my* guy, and second, what the heck is *appearance-challenged*?"

"You know," Lisa motioned with her hands. "Not so good on the eyes. A *GQ* reject. The opposite of Brad Pitt." At Frankie's puzzled look, she added, "I'm talking ugly, honey. Although, I'm sure your guy isn't *that* bad. Besides, it's what's on the inside that counts. Take my cousin Sarah, the one who works at Naughty Nighties. Her boyfriend, Dirk, is a hunk and a half, but also a complete jerk. He's got Sarah running the shop for him, cooking his dinner, warming his bed, and he does absolutely nothing in return except bat those pretty-boy eyes of his and take credit for all her hard work."

Lisa paused briefly. "Hey, it's not that plumber Jimmy Chase, is it? He's ugly, all right, but I think a little pimple cream and a good haircut would move him up from ugly to passable."

"It's not Jimmy."

"Of course not. You're the boss. You don't date employees. Though that new roofer, Jake Montgomery, would sure be cause to break the rules just once." Her eyes twinkled. "I heard from Sue Ann Delaney that he posed almost totally nude in *Hot Bods* last year and that construction's just his way of staying in shape while he beefs up his modeling portfolio—"

"It's not Jake."

"So who is it? You *have* to tell me. I'm engaged, remember? No more hot nights of wild, mindless sex to tide me over into my old age. My only joy in life is to live vicariously through my single friends."

"You've been engaged for twenty-four hours," Frankie said, shrugging off her flannel shirt and relishing the rush of air over her bare arms. "And from the looks passing between you and my brother last night, I'd say you added at least a few more hours of wild, mindless sex to your résumé after everyone left." She tossed the shirt near her toolbox.

"Oh, we were doing that *before* everyone left. I never realized Marc's linen closet was that roomy." She waved her hands. "Okay, so forget vicarious living. Let's talk debt. You owe me. I turned you on to Naughty Nighties and the perfect opportunity to seduce Mr. Mystery right out of his BVDs. Not to mention that I conned Sarah into letting you borrow the mask off the front window mannequin. Without my help, you would have been wearing a paper bag with cut-out eye holes."

"Okay, so I owe you." She turned back to the wall studs. "I'll buy lunch. Bobo's at noon."

"Forget juicy burgers," Lisa whined. "I want juicy details."

"No."

"Just describe him. Give me five specifics and I'll paint my own mental picture."

"No."

"Four."

"No."

"Three."

"No."

"You really expect me to come up with a nice visual from one stinking detail?"

"I don't want you coming up with any visuals. I appreciate you taking me to the lingerie store and I'm forever grateful for the mask, but last night is over. I'd really like to put the entire evening behind me."

"That bad, huh?" Lisa's gaze fell on Frankie's exposed neck, and a smile curled her lips. "Or that good." Her smile widened. "I can spot razor burn at twenty paces. And, if I'm not mistaken, that's a hickey on your lily-white neck."

"Who's got a hickey?" Marc's deep voice preceded him as he walked into the room and straight over to Lisa.

"No one," Frankie said, pulling a bandanna from her pocket and wrapping it around her neck before her brother could see the aftermath of last night. "What are you doing here?"

"Looking for the future Mrs. Marc Brannigan," he said, turning to Lisa. They stared into each other's eyes, suddenly oblivious to Frankie and the world around them. "The caterer called. She can do angel food with whipped-cream icing," he told Lisa, punctuating the sentence with a lingering kiss on the lips.

Frankie marveled at the sight. She'd seen Marc with many different women, but she'd never seen him look at any of them with the heartwrenching tenderness that he did with Lisa. She never would have thought it possible that he could or would change from a Casanova to a one-woman man.

Then again, maybe he hadn't changed. Maybe this I-only-have-eyes-for-you version of her brother had been there all along, hidden beneath the love-'em-and-leave-em' heartbreaker who had gone through women the way she went through a box of Godiva chocolates.

They said love brought out the best in people.

And the worst, she reminded herself, remembering her stolen kiss in the closet with Connor so many years ago. Shameless. Hungry. Desperate. She'd thrown herself at him, all in the name of love.

Or rather, what she'd thought was love. But as the years had passed and Frankie had matured, she'd realized that what she felt for Connor McBryde was just a good, old-fashioned case of lust. Nothing that one hot night couldn't cure.

Last night.

Now she was cured.

If only she didn't ache in so many tender places, a constant reminder of his hands, his mouth, his slow, lazy touches that had driven her to the brink and beyond.

". . . last night, little sister?" Her brother's voice finally penetrated her thoughts.

She forced the lustful images away and concentrated on Marc. "What did you say?"

"I asked how last night went, but from that blush on your face and that hickey you're trying to hide, I'm thinking pretty damned good."

"They call it a personal life for a reason," Frankie said, pulling the bandanna tighter when Marc angled in for a closer look.

"I'm your best friend," Lisa declared.

"And I'm your brother."

"And I'm really busy." And just to prove her point, Frankie started to reload her nail gun.

"Has she always been this stubborn?" Lisa asked Marc.

"Worse than a pit bull."

Lisa chuckled. "You ever seen a pit bull with a hickey?"

"Can't say that I have, but it sounds interesting."

Frankie turned on them. "Enough, okay? Don't you have a meeting or something?" she asked Marc. "And you're supposed to be rewiring the library downstairs," she told Lisa.

Lisa didn't look as if she was going to let the subject drop, but after a pleading look from Frankie, she shrugged. "You're off the hook, for now. But I'm ordering a double burger at lunch, with large fries, a milk shake, *and* dessert. If you won't dish up the info, you can darn well dish out some cash. And help me pick out a cake, and a dress, and the flowers, and don't forget you're being fitted for the bridesmaid's dress tonight." At that moment Lisa's cell phone rang. She fished the small contraption from her pocket and punched the On button. "This is Lisa. Oh, Mr. Julian. Yes, I've tried to call you several times. It's going to be at the Four Seasons Hotel, and we want the entire ceremony videotaped, including the reception."

"And the honeymoon," Marc added with a wiggle of his eyebrows.

The conversation lasted a few more seconds before Lisa stabbed the Off button and thanked the Powers Up Above for cell phones. "Otherwise I'd never be able to throw together a halfway decent wedding in such a short time *and* finish the library. Lunch," Lisa reminded Frankie before giving Marc another long, deep kiss that stirred a rush of heated memories for Frankie and made her attack the next row of wall studs with renewed vigor.

Over and done with, she reminded herself as she pounded nail after nail into the wall and prepared herself for more questions. She'd been able to fend Lisa off with desperate looks and promises of a free lunch, but she knew she wouldn't be able to get rid of her brother as easily. Marc could be somewhat of a pit bull himself when he set his mind on something.

"She even looks great in overalls," was all he said.

Frankie found him staring after his bride-to-be, and she couldn't help but smile. "You hate overalls."

"Only on my kid sister." He leveled a stare at her. "Because you wear them so much that I'm starting to think they've been surgically attached. Lisa, on the other hand, knows when to let her hair down." He grinned. "Speaking of which, you looked really good with your hair down."

She held up a hand. "I don't want to talk about it. Please, Marc." She went back to the wall and resumed shooting nails, never missing a beat. *Bam, bam, bam.* "I'm not bringing the guy home and marrying him, so what's the big deal? I was just having some fun."

"That's the big deal. You don't have fun."

"I have fun." At his pointed stare, she added, "Okay, so I don't have *fun* fun. But I'm trying. So can we please talk about something else?"

"Vince and Cheryl are flying in tomorrow night."

"That's great." Vince was their oldest brother, a successful lawyer in El Paso, happily married to Cheryl, who was also a successful lawyer. "I think. Tell me they're not bringing the Toilet Bowl Terrors." Otherwise known as Emily, Edward, and Ericaa—four, six, and two, respectively—all of whom shared a fondness for water and porcelain.

"The kids are staying with Cheryl's parents."

Relief swept through her. "Thank God. I love them dearly, but my bathroom still hasn't recovered from the time Vince and Cheryl went to that law conference and I volunteered to babysit the terrors while they were away. Day one, I had to call a plumber to extract Emily's Beanie Baby. Day two, he rescued Erica's waterlogged Barbie doll and two My Little Pony figurines. And day three, Edward actually got his foot stuck in the bowl."

"I think I saw that on a *Rescue 911* episode."

"Very funny. So what about Trey?"

"He's coming, but by himself. The doctor said Elaine couldn't fly because the baby's so close to coming." Her middle brother, Trey, was a reporter for the *Dallas Star*, happily married to Elaine, a portrait photographer. Both were eagerly awaiting the birth of their very own Toilet Bowl Terror.

Her gaze went to Marc, her youngest brother and senior by three years and, up until last week, the poster boy for bachelorhood. He lived for good food, fine wine, and attractive women. Or he had. Until Lisa Moore had flashed him her pumpkin on Halloween.

"Bring him to the wedding," Marc told her.

"Who?"

"That's what I want to know. Say, is it—"

"It's not Bernie Culpepper or Jimmy Chase or Jake Montgomery."

"Actually, I was going to ask if it was—Connor, buddy."

The name echoed through her head and she pulled the trigger twice and shot two nails. Sparks flew. "That's crazy." She turned on her brother. "What makes you think I'm even remotely interested in—" Her words tumbled together as she looked up to see Connor standing in the doorway.

For a long, breathless moment, she drank in the sight of him, from his blue denim shirt to his worn jeans and faded boots. His dark hair was still slightly damp, curling around his collar, his jaw freshly shaven. He looked dark and delicious in the shimmering morning sunlight, and a slow heat swept through her.

One night, she reminded herself. *One night*.

"What's crazy?" Connor's gaze went from Marc to Frankie and back.

Her brother grinned. "Our little Frankie's a big girl now. She finally gave in and—"

"—played Lotto," Frankie cut in, casting a desperate glance at her brother. "I swore I'd never, what with it being such a waste of money and all, but then those little pencils started calling my name and before I knew it, I was frantically bubbling in numbers and now I'm hooked." By the time she'd finished running off at the mouth, a knowing look lit Marc's eyes.

"Hey, honey, everybody's got their vices," Connor told her.

"Yeah, so what are you doing here?" she asked, eager to move the conversation to safer ground rather than the quicksand that was currently sucking her under.

He held up a cylinder. "Designs for the downstairs kitchen. I would have left them at the office, but I needed to talk to Marc and his secretary said he was here." His gaze went to her brother. "It's about last night. There was this woman—"

"Marc was just leaving," she blurted. "Urgent meeting."

"But—" Connor began.

"Desperately urgent. You'll have to talk to him later. Right, Marc?"

"Um, yeah," her brother mumbled as she hooked her arm through his and escorted him to the door, pushed him through it, and slammed the ancient wood shut before he could mutter more than a quick "Later."

Frankie drew a deep breath and tried to slow her pounding heart. "Now, let's take a look at that new kitchen." She snatched the plans from Connor's hands and walked a safe distance away. At least she thought it was safe, but then the musky scent of soap and warm male followed her. Her nostrils flared. Her heart pounded. Her nipples tingled. Her thighs throbbed.

This was *not* good.

Connor watched Frankie spread the plans out over a nearby workbench. She looked her usual self, sexless and professional in her hard hat, work clothes, and heavy boots. A yellow ribbed tank top hid beneath the heavy denim overalls, lending a strange softness to the entire getup. He smiled, remembering a similar yellow T-shirt that had driven him crazy ten years ago.

And then he frowned.

What was he thinking? He'd found the woman of his dreams last night. He shouldn't be standing here thinking about Frankie, wanting to reach out and see if those blond wisps of hair that had worked their way loose from her hard hat felt as soft as they looked. As soft as he remembered.

"Could you hand me that ruler over there?" Frankie pointed to her toolbox. "I just want to check some of these dimensions."

"Sure." He leaned down, grateful for the distraction. His hand brushed the soft flannel shirt draped over her toolbox. He caught the sweet scent of apples and cinnamon, and a strange sensation skittered over his skin. Lifting the material to his nose, he closed his eyes and inhaled. And remembered.

Nah. It couldn't be.

Probably dozens of women wore the same fragrance.

He told himself that as he forced his hand to let go of the soft shirt. Forget dozens. Probably hundreds. Thousands. This was just a freak coincidence.

His gaze went back to her, and he froze. It wasn't the way she smoothed her palm over the drawings, her fingers softly stroking the paper, that shook him so hard. It was the look on her face. The way her brows wrinkled. The way she caught her bottom lip.

Her.

The truth staggered and angered and thrilled him all at the same time. *She wanted him.* And he'd never had a clue because she never so much as looked at him a moment too long. Never flirted or teased or did any of the things women usually did when they wanted a man.

But Frankie was different. She wasn't the flirting, teasing type, and by last night's estimate, not very experienced when it came to men. And damned if those things didn't make her all the more appealing. They always had.

Which was why he'd made a fool of himself that night so long ago when the bottle she'd spun had pointed toward him and they'd walked into the closet together. In the heated darkness, she'd admitted she wanted him, and he'd gladly obliged, kissing her hard before he'd had the good sense to pull away. She'd been a kid, barely fifteen and never been kissed, thanks to three older, watchful brothers and Connor himself, who'd looked out for her like his own sister, though he'd been much more selfishly motivated.

He'd wanted to be her first. Her first touch, her first kiss, her first *everything*. Right then and there. In a closet in a house full of teenagers all saying good-bye and wishing him well. He and Marc had been heading off to the University of Texas the next day, both ready to pursue their dreams. But he hadn't expected that he would be leaving a dream behind.

Seeing her standing there in the shadowy closet, looking up at him, into him, had filled Connor with a sudden desperation. He'd lost it for those few seconds when the door had shut and his mouth had touched hers and he'd felt all those blossoming curves up close and personal. He'd wanted her so badly then.

And he'd never stopped wanting her. But his reasons for not acting on the feeling had changed. At fifteen, she'd been much too young and inexperienced for the lustful thoughts that had raced through his mind, and so he'd pulled back.

And he'd held back all this time, despite the fact that she'd grown up to be one sexy-as-hell woman. He hadn't wanted to mess up the friendships that had come to mean so much to him. Connor had always been too busy working to spend much time developing solid friendships or any type of regular social life. Friends were rare, and the ones he did have, he valued, Frankie included. Especially Frankie.

He hadn't been willing to risk any awkwardness between them by coming on to her again. He'd made his feelings plainly known that night with that one kiss, and so the next move had been hers.

And she'd finally made it. Last night. Ten long years later.

His gaze roved over her, from her hard hat to her work boots. In his mind's eye, he could see all the delicate curves hidden beneath the huge overalls—pert breasts tipped with cotton-candy-pink nipples, the subtle swell of her belly, the roundness of her hips, the smooth line of her pale thighs, the triangle of soft blond curls. Why the hell hadn't he figured it out earlier?

The question rushed through his head, but he didn't feel the expected swell of anger at himself, because deep down, he *had* known. His heart had known it was her, but his head had refused to admit it because then he would have had to put the brakes on, to listen to his damned conscience and put a stop to what he'd wanted so badly.

What he still wanted.

He barely resisted the urge to haul her into his arms, lay her down on the dusty floor, and love her fast and furious. Then slow and long.

He wanted to, but he wouldn't. For whatever reason, Frankie had gone to a helluva lot of trouble to dupe him, and now she wanted to pretend that nothing had happened.

Because she'd wanted only a one-night stand? Maybe, but why him? She was so damned sexy, she could have had any man. Why go to so much trouble?

Because she felt the need as much as he did, wanted him as much as he wanted her. He'd seen it in her eyes last night. She just wasn't ready to admit her feelings for him. Yet.

But she would, because Connor McBryde wasn't going to make resistance easy for her. He wouldn't force a confession, but neither would he sit and wait another ten years while she worked up the nerve to come to him.

She'd seduced him last night, and now it was his turn.

"Where were you last night?" The question rumbled in her ears and she jumped, bumping into Connor, who had walked up directly behind her. Strong, muscular arms came around her as he placed the ruler on the drawings and rested his hands on the sketch, just half an inch from hers.

Her mouth went dry as she watched his fingers trace the edge of the paper. He had the best hands. Large and tanned and strong, yet gentle. She'd always loved his hands. Always.

"So?" His voice pulled her away from her thoughts, and she whirled, coming face-to-face with him, their bodies a scant inch apart.

"What?"

"I asked where you were last night. It was your brother's engagement party, so I figured you'd be there."

Which meant he was asking because he thought she wasn't there. Relief swept through her, but it was short-lived. He was standing much too close, his scent filling her nostrils, his body heat reaching out, drawing her closer.

"So?" he prodded.

"So what?"

"So why weren't you there?"

"Why wasn't I there?"

His gaze narrowed as he eyed her. "Are you okay?"

"Why wouldn't I be?"

"I don't know, you're just acting strange."

"What makes you say that?"

"Because you're answering all of my questions with questions."

"I am?" Her face heated under his knowing gaze and she forced herself to take a deep breath. Okay, so he was standing close. She'd been close to him before. She could handle this. And she would, because she was no longer a slave to her lust for this man. She'd sated it last night. All of it, she reminded herself. "I don't mean to. I'm just a little stressed with this project."

"And you look a little hot." His eyes darkened. "Are you hot?"

"Yeah, it's a little warm in here." Frankie turned and busied herself with unfolding the new scale drawing and doing her damnedest to ignore his presence and the tender aches that whimpered each time she moved. Reminders of last night. Of him.

"So where were you last night?" he persisted, sending a wash of dread through her. "I had a pretty interesting time myself. I met a woman."

"Oh, yeah?"

"Yeah."

"That's nice."

"She was. The trouble is, she was wearing a costume, so I still don't know who she is."

"That's great," she managed. "I mean, great that you met someone, not so great that you don't know who she is."

"I can't stop thinking about her."

A smile spread across her face before she could stop herself. It wasn't as if she cared that he couldn't stop thinking about her. It wasn't really *her* he couldn't stop thinking about. It was Miss Fantasy. An illusion.

That was what had him so mesmerized. The whole charade. The idea of the perfect woman. And Frankie in the bright light of day, in her overalls and work boots, smudges of dust on her hands, was far from his idea of perfect.

"Maybe you could help me figure out who she is. I mean, you know most of Marc's friends."

"I don't think—" Her response faded in the shrill ring of her cell phone. Thankfully. "Sorry. Duty calls," she said, sliding the phone out of her pocket and punching the On button. "Frankie Brannigan."

"Hey," Lisa's voice floated over the line. "I forgot to tell you. Sarah needs the mask back by tomorrow, ASAP. Dirk the Jerk gets back from his seminar in a couple of days and he expects everything to be perfect, for which he'll take complete credit, of course."

The mask. The words echoed in Frankie's head as she closed her eyes and visualized the last place she'd seen the scrap of lace. In the pile she'd dropped when Cu-Joe had started his tattletale barking. The same pile she'd dumped in the back seat of her car, and then in her closet.

"No problem. I'll be right there."

"You don't have to do it right now. Just bring it to lunch."

"I know. Urgent. I'm right on it," she said before tucking the phone back into her pocket and trying to calm her pounding heart. But it was hard to do with Connor standing so close, making her tingle.

Tingle?

"I have to go." She inched past him and started toward her toolbox. "Major disaster with one of the suppliers. You know how it is."

"I know *exactly* how it is." And for a split second, she feared he did.

His gaze was too dark, too assessing. But then the look faded into a teasing light that eased her fears. She was jumping at shadows, letting her guilt get the best of her. After all, she had deceived him, a fact that still nagged slightly at her conscience.

But it had all been for a good cause, she reminded herself. Her sexual education, not to mention her sanity. She'd had to get him out of her system. Otherwise, she would have lusted for him for ten more years and died an old shriveled-up virgin because no man could make her feel even a fourth of what he did.

But now . . . She would tingle with any man. Every man. Because now she knew what she'd been missing all this time. It wasn't that she wanted *him*. She was now a sexually active woman who'd been deprived for far too long.

Or so she hoped as she snatched up her toolbox, and started for the door. "I'll see you later."

His deep voice followed her and sent a strange heat trembling up her spine. "You can bet on it, darlin'."

Four

Where *was* it?

Frankie sat on the floor in her bedroom and stared at the pile of lace and satin she'd shoved into her closet before heading off to work that morning. It had to be here. She'd bribed Cu-Joe herself, grabbed the mask, and headed for the door. So where could it be? Wiping a tired hand across her eyes, Frankie tried to recall the events of that morning hoping that maybe she would remember where she'd put the blasted thing. Except that her mind refused to replay the details of her leaving Connor, lingering instead on all the delicious feeling she had experienced during the night while wrapped in his embrace.

Frankie sighed deeply. It had been a long day and it still wasn't even over. She had spent most of the afternoon attempting to evade Connor McBryde and his endless barrage of questions. He'd shown up everywhere: the job site at the Whittenberg House, her office, even the hardware store where she had been buying some last minute supplies. And all because he was desperate to pick her brain about all the guests at Marc's party last night. Frankie wondered why he didn't just go straight to Marc and demand to see the guest list himself but she wasn't about to risk bringing it up. That's all she needed—Connor asking Marc who the mystery woman in the mask and black leather coat was.

Shaking her head, Frankie dragged her attention back to the task at hand. She had to find the mask and fast. At lunch Lisa had been vehement that she get the mask back to Sarah ASAP. Frankie had mumbled some excuse about being too busy to leave work in the middle of the day to go home but Lisa, true to form, was not about to let her off the hook so easily. She'd made Frankie promise to bring the mask with her to the bridal shop later that night; Sarah and Frankie's bridesmaids dress fittings were at the same time so it would be a perfect opportunity for Frankie to return the mask.

Except that she didn't have it. Frankie willed herself not to panic and started picking through the lingerie, piece by piece, desperately hoping she had just overlooked it the first twenty times she had gone through the pile. Teddy. Garter belt. Stocking. Glove. Stock—

Rrrring!

She reached for her cell phone. "Frankie Brannigan."

"Am I going to have to send Marc to give you an armed escort over here?"

"He doesn't have a gun."

"Oh, yes, he does, honey, and trust me, he knows how to use it."

"You're shameless."

"And you're late."

"I know, Lisa, and I'm so sorry. The wrong tile came in for the Whittenburg House, and I spent an hour on the phone trying to get them to issue the right shipment, and then when they sent the confirmation, the fax from hell chewed it up and spit it back out at me, and then when I was walking out the door, my cell phone rang again, and—" The words stumbled to a halt as she took a deep breath. "I have to get an assistant."

"Amen. But first things first, get over here *now*."

"I'm on my way."

She hung up and spent a few more seconds going through the pile of lingerie. There was no mistake. The mask was missing. *Gone*. She closed her eyes and mentally reviewed her last steps to Connor's front door. Cu-Joe. Weenie bribery. Cu-Joe again. More bribery. That was it! She'd dropped the pile of lingerie when Cu-Joe had started to bark again and scared the bejesus out of her. Which meant the mask was still . . . Oh, no!

In Connor's apartment.

Before she could dwell on that awful thought and what it meant, her doorbell rang.

She shoved the lingerie under the bed and got to her feet, hiked up a sliding overall strap, and headed for the door.

"I told Lisa I was on my—" The words choked in her throat as she hauled open the door and found Connor McBryde standing on her doorstep.

He wore a white T-shirt that stretched across the broad expanse of his chest and faded jeans, the soft denim clinging to his muscular thighs. A fresh mingling of soap and hot male filled the air, teasing her nostrils and before she could stop herself, she inhaled.

And then she panicked.

He was here. Now. *Oh, no*.

"What are you doing here?" she blurted. He couldn't know. Could he? Maybe he could. He'd questioned her all day. Maybe he'd found someone who had actually answered those questions and now he was here to call her out.

"Hello to you, too." His slow grin eased the fear beating in her breast. If he knew the truth, no way would he be standing on her doorstep smiling at her.

He'd be spitting mad. She'd deceived him, after all, and Connor wasn't a man to take such things lying down.

Ugh. Lying down was not a position to be thinking of right now, not with last night still so vivid in her mind.

She tried to ignore his enticing aroma and concentrate on talking without tripping over her tongue.

"I—I'm sorry. You just surprised me. I'm on my way out."

"Bridesmaid's fitting?"

"How did you know?"

"The best man knows everything, darlin'. I thought I'd stop by and give you a ride." Her gaze shot to his black Mustang, sitting in her driveway.

A ride—as in the two of them sitting side by side, inhaling the same oxygen. "I've got my truck."

"I have to get fitted for my tux and you're on the way, so there's no sense in us using two vehicles." His grin widened. "Besides, I won't bite, Frankie. Unless you ask me nicely, that is."

If she didn't know better, she would have sworn he was flirting with her. Wishful thinking. It was a known fact that Connor McBryde flirted with everyone *but* her.

She tried to calm the butterflies fluttering in her stomach. "I guess a ride couldn't hurt."

It was the longest ride of her life. She sat beside him, breathless, nervous, practically jumping every time he said something to her. Worse, she couldn't take her eyes off his hand, resting so lazily on the gearshift, stroking it every now and then with a seductive motion that she felt along the entire length of her spine.

By the time they reached the bridal shop, she was so worked up, her nipples tight and her thighs trembling, that she was close to simply crawling into his lap, taking that beautiful hand, and touching it to all the places now begging for his attention. The minute he shoved the car in Park, she all but jumped out to race inside.

She heard the steady thump of his boots on the pavement behind her, but she didn't glance back. She was too hot, too flushed, too crazed.

What was happening to her?

Biology, she told herself. She was a woman now, with a woman's needs, and Connor had been the one to unlock those needs. Of course she would still be turned on by him. It was a purely physical reaction.

Nothing a big glass of ice water and a few hours with a rack of poufy, frilly dresses wouldn't cure.

But three glasses of ice water and twice as many dresses later, her heart was still pounding.

She eyed her reflection in the wall-to-wall mirror. "You can't really mean to make me wear this?" she asked Lisa, who sat on a nearby sofa surrounded by mountains of shoe boxes.

"What's the big deal? You wore a bridesmaid's dress in Vince's wedding, didn't you?"

"That was different. That dress was more . . ."

"Nauseating?" Lisa quickly supplied.

Frankie pictured the powder-blue Southern belle special, complete with wide-brimmed straw hat and matching powder-blue parasol, and shrugged. "Okay, so Nauseating's my middle name."

"Clueless is your middle name. Not only does this dress show off your figure, but you'll be able to wear it for other things."

"That's the point. This is a wedding. You're supposed to pick something hideous that no one would want to wear for other things. Besides, I don't do *other things* that would warrant a dress like this."

Frankie stared at the strapless blue dress with a neckline that plunged just enough to show off her cleavage. The dress molded itself to her hips and stalled at mid-thigh.

"Don't you think it's a little short?"

"It's fashionable. And speaking of fashionable, I wonder if these come in ivory." Lisa snatched up one of the shoe boxes and left the dressing room in search of the clerk. "Stop stressing. You look sexy," she said before disappearing.

Sexy. Right.

She eyed her reflection. "Okay, so maybe a little sexy."

"*Very* sexy."

Frankie's head snapped up at the sound of Connor's voice, and she met his gaze in the mirror.

He stood in the doorway, clad only in a pair of black tuxedo pants. Dark hair sprinkled the hard muscle of his chest. An enticing line of silk crept down his abdomen and plunged beneath his waistband. As her gaze lingered, she noticed the hard ridge that pressed against his fly.

She snapped to attention, and her eyes collided with his in the mirror. A fierce light gleamed in the blue depths, his look intense before it faded into another teasing grin that made her cheeks burn.

"Um, uh, you, too."

He leaned against the doorway and folded his arms, eyeing her. "You think I'm sexy?"

She busied herself tugging down the hem of her dress, which only succeeded in exposing more of her cleavage and bringing another grin to Connor's handsome face. "I suppose some women might consider you sexy."

"Some women? As in . . . ?"

"As in any woman with eyes."

"Including you?"

"I have eyes, don't I?"

"Among other things." She ignored the heat that his words stirred and concentrated on her aggravation.

"Do you always barge into women's dressing rooms half dressed?"

"Only yours."

"Lucky me."

"Does it bother you?"

"Are you kidding? You don't have anything I haven't seen before."

"Then why are you blushing?"

"I'm not blushing. It's just hot in here."

Silence stretched around them as she tried to avoid his eyes and the image of him half naked, smiling wickedly in the mirror.

"You are," he stated, as if tremendously pleased at the sight. "You're blushing."

"So?"

"So, you're blushing, that's all."

"Who's blushing?" Lisa asked as she walked back in, followed by a female salesclerk and an irate-looking Chinese man carrying a pincushion.

"There you are," the man said when he spotted Connor. "We still have to alter your trousers."

Connor grinned and winked at Frankie before following the man back to the other side of the store.

Frankie took the opportunity to peel off the dress and yank on her jeans and T-shirt while Lisa debated between a pair of closed-toe pumps and strappy sandals with three-inch heels. The bride-to-be had just talked herself into the sandals when Sarah, who was also a bridesmaid, arrived for her fitting

"Sorry I'm late, but I had to close the store and I was five cents off, so I had to comb over the day's receipts to find it."

"For five cents?" Lisa asked.

"It's my job."

"Which you take way too seriously."

"I'm detail-oriented."

"You're obsessed."

"That, too." Sarah took the bridesmaid's dress from Lisa and turned eagerly to Frankie. "Do you have it?"

"Not exactly." Panic flashed in Sarah's eyes and Frankie rushed on. "But I'll get it."

"Before Saturday. Dirk gets back on Saturday."

"Saturday," Frankie reassured the woman, grateful for more time, but still stressed that she hadn't found the blasted piece of lingerie.

Connor's apartment.

She cleared her throat. "Let's um, just say, hypothetically, of course, that for some reason, I misplaced the mask." At Sarah's distraught face, she added, "Not that I did. I'm just wondering how much something like that would cost."

"My job. That's what it would cost."

"Good riddance," Lisa said.

"And Dirk," Sarah added. "No mask would cost me Dirk."

"Hallelujah."

"So sayeth the woman with a good job and a man," Sarah said. "I need my job, and I need Dirk."

"You *think* you need him, only because nothing better has come along. But it will, Sarah. You just have to open yourself up to new options. Put in a few job applications, for heaven's sake."

"But I've never worked anywhere but Naughty Nighties."

"And you've never slept with any man but Dirk. You're in a rut, addicted to the comfort, not to the job or the man. Stop hiding. Take a chance."

"I did. I violated company policy and lent out company property and—"

"—You'll have that property back in no time," Frankie cut in, eager to move on to a safer topic. "Now let's see how this dress looks on you."

Fifteen minutes later, Frankie bummed a ride off Sarah, eager to get gone before Connor emerged from the men's fitting room. She was just following Sarah to the doorway when she heard his voice.

"Are you ready?"

She turned, ignoring the flutter of her heartbeat when her gaze met his. "I have an emergency at the office, and Sarah offered to drop me by on her way home."

"I'll drop you by."

"You've already gone to so much trouble bringing me. I couldn't inconvenience you anymore. Besides, you know my office is way out of your way, and it's right on the road headed for Sarah's."

"It is?" Sarah asked.

"Practically next door to your apartment," Frankie reassured her before turning back to Connor. "Thanks for the ride. It was really sweet of you."

"Not half as sweet as it could be," he whispered as he moved past her. At least that's what she thought he said, but when his gaze caught hers, she saw only the usual playfulness. Not a touch of seriousness to hint that he'd actually meant what he'd said. Or that he'd even said it.

She was jumping at shadows, reading more into his innocent teasing because she felt so guilty about deceiving him.

But he *didn't* know. He would never know, because last night was over and done with, and now Frankie Brannigan was going to keep her distance from Connor McBryde, no matter how good he looked in a pair of tuxedo pants.

Frankie stood on Connor's doorstep the next night and fought back a wave of anxiety that had built up throughout the day as she'd anticipated tonight. She had to do this. Sarah had put herself on the line to lend Frankie the mask. The least Frankie could do was return it, which meant she had to get inside Connor's apartment again.

"Talk about surprises," he said when he opened the door after her third knock.

The sight of him clad only in a pair of worn jeans, his chest chiseled and hard, stalled the air in her lungs for a long second before she managed to give herself a great big mental shake.

"I hope I didn't catch you at a bad time."

He grinned. "Just kicking back."

"Good." Frankie held up a pizza box and a six-pack of beer. "It's game night and you've got the big-screen TV." Thankfully otherwise she would have had a hard time finding an excuse to stop by. But they'd always watched sports together.

"I thought the Rockets were playing B-ball tomorrow night?"

"I'm sure it's tonight." She pushed past him, ignoring the enticing scent of sandalwood soap and freshly scrubbed male that teased her nostrils. Taking discreet whiffs of him when he wasn't looking was not part of tonight's agenda. She was on the wagon where Connor McBryde was concerned.

No matter how good he looked wearing nothing but a faded pair of jeans and a knowing grin.

Knowing? No, he didn't know. That was the only redeeming feature of this entire disaster. Everything had backfired. She'd meant to work him out of her system, but now she wanted him even more. Wanted to throw her arms around him, melt against the inviting wall of his chest. Almost as much as she wanted to run and hide.

She was going to do neither.

She had a mission.

"The Rockets play tomorrow night," he told her as she plopped the pizza box on his coffee table. He indicated the TV guide. "It's Thursday."

"What do you know?" She flipped through the channel listings. "I think you're right." Her gaze caught his, careful not to linger too long—no way was she falling into those dangerously deep blue eyes. She'd never learned how to swim, and she would drown for sure in those depths. "Seems a shame to let a good pizza go to waste, and you do have cable. I'm sure we could find something to watch. You don't have plans, do you?"

"Well—"

"Here it is," she cut in, her gaze falling on a listing. "Whitewater rafting finals live from Canada. I just love rafting."

He eyed her. "Since when?"

"Oh, for a long, long time. And I haven't seen a good rafting competition in months." Try forever. "Why don't you grab some napkins and plates and I'll open us a couple of beers?"

She could have sworn she saw a flash of amusement in his eyes, but then the expression faded to something unreadable and he nodded. "Be right back."

"Take your time."

He disappeared into the kitchen, and Frankie didn't waste a minute. She hit the floor, peering under the sofa, the coffee table, crawling toward the TV, and mentally retracing the route she'd walked that morning from his bedroom when she'd been snatching up clothes. She had to have dropped it—

"Here we go—what are you doing?"

Her head snapped up, and she peered over the back of the sofa at him. "I, um, lost something."

"What?"

"My, um"—her brain scrambled for a plausible explanation—"my contact." She stood up and brushed her hands off.

"I'll help you look."

"That's okay. They're temporary. I've got a whole box of them at home. No big deal. Say, you don't have hot sauce, do you? I love pizza with hot sauce."

He eyed her again. "Are you okay? You're acting a little funny."

"Jittery is more like it." She made a big show of shaking her arms. "I've been off the sauce for days—the hot sauce, that is. It's this new diet Lisa and I are doing to shape up for the wedding. No spicy foods and condiments. You see, the more bland the food, the less you like it, the less likely you are to eat. Anyhow, I'm heavy into withdrawal and if I don't get a fix right now, I'm not responsible for my actions."

"I'll see what I can find."

"Take your time." He disappeared and she rushed toward the dining room.

"I don't have hot sauce, but I've got some cayenne pepper," he called out from the kitchen.

"Perfect. And I'll need salt, too."

She scoured the floor, beneath the large table, the nearby hutch . . . nothing.

"Where is it?" she hissed at Cu-Joe, who lounged beneath a dining room chair, his whiskers twitching as he watched her.

"What did you say?" Connor called from the other room.

"Nothing." She made it back to the couch a heartbeat before he returned from the kitchen, salt and cayenne pepper in hand. "I found these for you." He set a jar of whole jalapeños on the coffee table next to the spices, then plopped down next to her, so close his scent pushed away the enticing smell of cheese and tomato sauce and made her mouth water for something altogether different.

Over and done with, she reminded herself.

"Exactly how hungry are you?"

"Starving," she replied, and she meant it. She needed a kiss, a touch, a taste more than she needed her next breath.

"Here you go." He handed her two slices of pizza, and Frankie tried to stifle her disappointment.

What was wrong with her? She had to get over this . . . this *want*. She didn't want him. She wanted to find the mask and get the hell out of there so she could forget him and the best night of her entire life.

"You know what would really be good?" she asked.

His gaze narrowed as he eyed the pile of jalapeños she'd put on her first slice. "Some sardines and hot fudge? Because I swear if I didn't know better, I'd say you were pregnant."

But he did know better—he'd been careful last night . . . She shook away the thought. That was not what he was talking about. And no way did he know the truth. Even if he was looking at her as if he wanted to . . . kiss her?

She blinked. It was there. Want. Need. Hunger.

The thought faded as he turned his attention to the pizza and she saw just how hungry he was. He finished off half the slice with one bite.

Geez, he had great lips. Strong. Sensuous. She knew firsthand because she'd felt them on every inch of her body—

"Hold on a second." His voice preceded the soft brush of his fingertip at the corner of her mouth. "Sauce," he explained, wiping at the spot again. The feel of his skin on hers sent goose bumps racing down her arm.

". . . you okay?" His deep voice pushed into her head and she realized he was staring at her, inside her, his deep-blue eyes so penetrating that she felt as if she'd been caught with her pants down.

"F—fine. I just need some water."

"I'll get it."

"No." She jumped to her feet. "I'll get it. You just get comfortable and save some pizza for me."

Thirty seconds later, she was crawling around the floor of his kitchen, peeking under chairs and tables and appliances.

"Are you finding everything?" At the sound of his deep voice, her head snapped up, bumping the table.

"Everything," she called out, stifling a groan of pain. *Not*. She climbed to her feet, poured the water, and took several deep, calming breaths. She knew she was acting crazy, but she was a desperate woman, and desperation could drive even the sanest woman over the edge. She had to find that mask, and she had to get out of here before she did something really stupid. Like throw herself into his arms and kiss him.

The next few hours were the longest of Frankie's life. Connor was, to put it mildly, a sports enthusiast. He yelled out advice, threw his hands when some poor Canadian capsized his raft, and cheered vigorously when the same Canadian won his trial, until Frankie thought she could take no more.

His arm brushed against hers, his thigh shifted, bumping and stroking and *reminding*. Every action, from the deep rumble of his voice, to the subtle touches, stirred images and set her entire body on fire. Her nipples tingled, her thighs ached, her stomach fluttered. To make matters worse, there was no escape. She'd been about to go after her second glass of water, when he disappeared, then came back with a full pitcher.

Okay, so maybe that was the one saving grace. By the time the last rafting team reached the finish line she'd finished off the pitcher and two beers and felt very near to exploding.

She excused herself, hightailed it to the bathroom for some much-needed relief and a few splashes of cold water on her flaming cheeks. There. That was better.

She stared at her reflection in the mirror, her bright eyes, the high color in her cheeks. Fear. Panic. Desire. Guilt.

Geez, she was paranoid. And pathetically hopeful. Because truthfully, one night hadn't been nearly enough with him. Not that the realization was changing anything. This visit was strictly business. Find the mask and get the hell out. *Now*.

She slipped out of the bathroom and tiptoed down the hallway toward his bedroom to take a quick peek.

The door was open, a soft light shone from his nightstand. She hadn't had the chance to really study the room the other morning, but she did so now. It was infinitely masculine, decorated throughout in deep blues. The bed took up most of the room; the only other furniture was a chest of drawers and a large bookshelf filled with volumes on architecture and sports.

She ignored the nearly overwhelming urge to throw herself across the bed, bury her nose in his pillow, and simply inhale.

The mask, she reminded herself.

She hit the floor, crawling around, looking under the bed, the chest, in every corner. The search led her into his closet, a huge walk-in lined with shelves. His scent was strong there, making her hands tremble, but she managed to keep her mind focused. Find the mask and get out. Before—

"So this is what's taking you so long." His deep voice sizzled across her nerve endings, and her head snapped up. In the full-length mirror, she caught his reflection.

He stood in the closet doorway, arms overhead, hands grasping the door frame. His large body filled the small space and, worse, blocked her escape.

"I—um," she swallowed, searching for words when the only thing she could seem to think about was how really great he looked without a shirt. How each muscle bulged and shifted as his hands gripped the door frame. "I'm looking for something." She stood and whirled around.

A slow grin spread over his handsome face. "Your contact?"

"Yes," she blurted. "Not the same one I was looking for in the living room. The other one. See, I was coming out of the bathroom and I thought I heard a noise."

"A noise?"

"Cu-Joe. It sounded like he was whimpering, and I thought it was coming from in here, so I came to take a look. I blinked, and what do you know? Out popped my second contact." The whole explanation was lame and farfetched, but it was the best she could do with him so close, staring at her so intently.

She expected him to drill her with more questions. To laugh. To scoff. Instead, he stepped inside, and her heart stopped in her chest.

"Remember the last time we were in a closet together?"

"I, um, can't say that I do."

"I remember." He touched her cheek, just a slow glide of his fingertip, but it set every nerve ending ablaze. "Your brothers had given me and Marc a going-away party and a bunch of us were playing Spin the Bottle. You were supposed to be upstairs in bed."

"That wasn't fair. I was the only fifteen-year-old in the freshman class with a bedtime. Do you know how embarrasing that was?"

"So you do remember."

She turned away from him and found herself staring at his reflection in a full-length mirror attached to the wall at the opposite end of the closet. "I seem to recall a few contraband six-packs of beer, a pretty good cake, and enough Charlie perfume to make my eyes water."

"Marc always did have a thing for sweet-smelling girls."

"So did you."

"Actually," he said, stepping up behind her. He trailed one fingertip up her arm, starting at her wrist, flesh gliding against flesh, his gaze locked with hers in the mirror. "I had more of a thing for a certain stubborn girl who snuck back downstairs after her daddy ordered her up to bed."

His words stirred so many emotions she tried to hide. She couldn't be hearing him right. He'd had a *thing* for her? "I—I couldn't leave when the night was just starting to get good."

"Really good," he went on. His hand lingered on her shoulder, and she thought he might actually lean down and kiss the exposed curve of her neck.

Wishful thinking, she told herself. It was all just wishful thinking.

"I can still see you sitting there on the other side of the circle, wearing those blue-jean shorts and that smiley-face T-shirt without a bra."

"How did you . . ." she started, the words fading at the hot, pointed stare he directed at her chest. Her nipples pebbled.

"That's how I knew."

"I didn't think anyone ever noticed."

"I noticed. I always noticed. I wanted to peel that T-shirt off you and see those pretty breasts and those taut little nipples up close and personal. And kiss you. I really wanted to kiss you."

The admission staggered her. He'd thought about her? Fantasized about her? *Noticed* her? "But you pushed me away after a few seconds."

"I had to. I was afraid I wouldn't be able to stop. I damn near didn't."

"But afterward you left with Juicy Lucy Jackson."

"I needed a ride home."

She gave him a skeptical look in the mirror. "A ride home, or just a ride?"

"After that kiss, darlin', I needed both. But Lucy's car was the only thing I got into that night."

"Why are you telling me this now?"

"Nostalgia maybe." His gaze met hers. "Or maybe I just finally found my courage." He dipped his head, and his lips feathered across her neck. "I wanted you. Just you. I wanted to kiss you and touch you and taste you so bad I hurt, but I couldn't act on any of it. You were my best friend's kid sister. Hell, you were like a sister to me, and I hated myself because the thoughts racing through my mind at the time were anything but brotherly."

"And now?" Again, she caught his gaze in the mirror.

"Now I want to be inside you so bad I can't see straight, and now that I've got you back in the closet, I'm not letting you out until I do everything I wanted to do that night. Until I kiss you." His lips touched her neck. "And touch you." His hands slid around her waist and swept up her rib cage to cup her breasts. "And taste you. Every inch of you." He nibbled at her neck before licking the spot. "How about you? Do you want to kiss me, Frankie?"

His words seduced her senses the way his hands were playing havoc with her body. Her traitorous body arched into him when she ordered it to resist. She wanted to believe him, but it was too unbelievable. Too wondrous. To find out that after all this time, he really did want her. That he always had. That their one night in the closet had been nothing more than poor timing. He hadn't turned away because she hadn't been some drop-dead gorgeous glamour girl who pranced around in full makeup and sexy clothes like Juicy Lucy and the other women who'd always chased after him. He'd turned away, held back, because he'd wanted her too much.

"Do you want me, Frankie? Do you *really* want me?" he asked, turning her in his arms.

"Maybe." She wouldn't say it. Not again. She couldn't. "I—I don't know."

"Then let's see what we can do about making up your mind."

His mouth was hot and wet, his tongue bold as it plunged and stroked. Her knees trembled, and an answering pull echoed between her legs. She would have slid to the carpeted floor if he hadn't been there to hold her up.

A small voice whispered that this couldn't be happening. That after ten years, they couldn't simply push aside their friendship in favor of this heat because they'd landed in a closet together and started reminiscing about the past. But there was more to it than simply a walk down memory lane, a stirring of past feelings. More to the lust brewing in his gaze. The possessiveness in his touch.

But then he deepened the kiss, tilting her head to give himself better access and the *more* took on an altogether different meaning.

He kissed her again. Hard. Fierce. As if he wanted to consume her. She was ready to be consumed. She wanted him so much, a need that surpassed that of two nights ago because it was different now. She wasn't wearing a mask or pretending, yet he still wanted her, and the knowledge made her burn all the more.

"I need to see you again," he gasped, pulling his mouth free to grasp the edge of her T-shirt and pull it over her head.

Again? The word prodded at something inside her, stirring an unease, but then he unclasped her bra, peeled the straps down her shoulders, and caught one pert nipple between his fingers, and she ceased to think.

"Do you want me to kiss you here?" He tugged at the nipple and she moaned raggedly.

As if that were answer enough, he dipped his head and drew the throbbing tip into the moist heat of his mouth. He suckled her, deep and hard, until she cried out and then he nibbled a blazing path to her other breast. His teeth closed over the bud just enough to send a sharp spurt of pleasure through her before he opened his mouth wider, sucking so strongly that her body quivered.

"I think you've made up your mind," he breathed after a few heart-pounding moments.

"Not quite, but if you do that again, I just might."

He chuckled, the deep sound vibrating against her breast. And then it faded into a raw growl. "Christ, you're sweet, Frankie." He savored her for a few more moments before he dropped to his knees in front of her and worked at the button of her jeans. Strong fingertips grazed the sensitive skin of her belly, and she caught her breath. He shoved the denim down her legs, his hands gliding, setting her nerves on fire before he pulled off her boots and tugged her jeans and socks free. His fingertips lingered at her ankles, stroking them softly before making a slow, leisurely trek up the backs of her calves, then her thighs, then tracing the curve of her bottom. The ache between her legs intensified until it was almost unbearable.

His dark gaze held hers for several long seconds before a fierce light fired in his eyes. He slid his hands around and hooked the edge of her panties where they rode high on her thighs. He pushed them down, leaned forward, and pressed a hot kiss to the triangle of blond curls.

Pulling her down in front of him, he urged her back until the plush carpet met her bare skin. He held her wide open, his hands urging her thighs apart until she was completely open and exposed to him.

"I want to taste you again, Frankie. I have to." There was nothing soft and seductive about the words, no hint of teasing in his voice the way there'd been two nights ago. "It's all I've been thinking about. You're all I've been thinking about. Whether you still taste as sweet, as mind-blowing. Do you want me to taste you here? Do you want it as much as I do?"

He didn't give her a chance to answer. Not that she could actually form any words, not with the anticipation coiling inside her, holding her captive. He simply slid his hands beneath her and lifted her to his hot, open mouth. A shiver tingled up her spine, and she grasped the sides of his head as his tongue rasped against her soft, slick folds.

He licked and nipped and sucked until she arched her back, pushing against his mouth, the sensation building and coiling inside her body. It was too much and, at the same time, not enough.

As if he sensed her desperation, he lifted one of her heels to his shoulder and tilted her hips, drawing her more fully against his mouth so he could add to the pressure and the pleasure. His tongue plunged deep, and his lips, his sweet, wonderful lips, kissed and suckled and loved her until her vision blurred and her heart shifted into overdrive.

The climax hit her hard, sending shudder after shudder through her body, making her clamp down and clutch his shoulders and cry out his name until she was hoarse. It wasn't until her voice had quieted to a contented sigh and her legs relaxed that he finally pulled away from her.

He rocked back on his heels, one of her legs still draped over his shoulder, the other spread wide. His gaze locked on hers and she saw such intense pleasure that it shocked her. *Pleasure*, despite the fact that a very prominent erection still stretched his jeans so tight she marveled that the zipper didn't burst. *Pleasure*, because he'd given her pleasure. He'd touched her in a way no other man had, a way he'd wanted to touch her for so long. She knew by the deep hue of his eyes that her reaction had been all he'd hoped for.

She expected him to give her one of those slow, sexy smiles and whisper something wicked like, "You taste even better than you look," the way he had the other night.

He didn't.

He couldn't. He was too desperate, too needy, too intent, He looked fierce, his face flushed, his nostrils flared as he struggled for air. His chest rose and fell with each frantic breath. His taut muscles gleamed with sweat.

"I do want you." The truth tumbled from her lips before she could stop it.

As if the admission was all he'd been waiting for, his hands went to his fly, working at the zipper of his jeans. She caught a glimpse of him, hot and huge and throbbing as he shed his clothes, and then he was over her, pressing her down into the carpet, his hands pushing her wide open. He filled her with one deep, thrilling stroke that wrung a raw, throaty moan from him and made her gasp.

It was as if she'd never come apart in his arms before. The pressure was there again, building as he sank into her, over and over, pumping hard and fierce as if his life depended on it. He was so hot beneath her touch, inside her, so desperate that it frightened her, yet sent a thrill from her head to her toes.

This was the other side of the man. The serious side she'd only glimpsed a few nights before when his hands had trembled in the elevator and he'd surprised her with his urgent kiss. Only a kiss.

But now it was almost as if he wanted her to know her effect on him, to know that she made him this crazy, this desperate.

As if he wanted no secrets between them.

"Connor, I . . ." she began, but her words faded into a low moan as he reached down between them, his fingers catching her swollen clitoris and pressing. She moaned, the moment of truth lost in a wave of pleasure so sharp she couldn't stand it.

But she did. Over and over as his fingers played her and his hips hammered, his erection thrusting hot and deep. Their union was fierce and furious, so different from their first night together. This was wild and wicked and overwhelming, and she loved every moment of it.

Where she'd fallen in total lust with the seductive charm of Connor McBryde, she could fall in love with the fierceness of this man. The raw emotion pulsing through him, glittering hot and vivid in his eyes as he stared down at her, into her for one long, breathless second before the feelings overwhelmed her and she exploded.

His climax quickly followed. His legs locked and his hips jerked forward as he filled her so fully and completely that she felt tears sting her eyes. His entire body went taut, his muscles as hard as stone as he cried out her name.

He collapsed on top of her, his heartbeat in frantic sync with hers. She knew she needed to talk to him, to tell him the truth about the other night. About now. That her feelings for him went beyond sex. That she felt . . .

She didn't want to think about the emotions bubbling inside her, pushing and pulling . . .

"Relax, darlin'," he whispered, as if he felt the fear coursing through her. "Relax."

He kissed her then, slow and deep, before pulling away and scooping her into his arms. He carried her to his bed, where he laid her down and settled in next to her. He turned her away from him, pulling her back into the warm heat of his body, as if he didn't want to face her just yet.

As if the experience just past had rocked him as much as it had her and he was having some serious thoughts of his own.

"Sleep," he whispered, and she couldn't help herself. He was so warm and strong, his arms cradling her possessively, hands stroking her sweetly and gently. She closed her eyes.

Five

It had to be a dream.

The solid mass of warmth at her back, the heavily muscled arm draped around her waist, the gentle hand cupping her bare breast.

A very intense, erotic dream that stirred her senses. Hairy thighs shifted, caressing the backs of her legs and buttocks. Soft breaths whispered against her temple. The musky scent of warm, sleepy male spiraled through her head and made her blood rush faster.

She shifted ever so slightly, her nipple pebbling as it brushed a calloused palm. Need tingled through her, and her eyes drifted open to the darkened bedroom. *His* bedroom.

Memories of the past night rushed at her. From the fierce gleam in his eyes, to his wild seduction and her shameless admission that she wanted him.

Real. Every wild, breath-stealing moment.

Then, and now. She was here. In his bed. His arms.

Connor McBryde had made wild, unrestrained love to her. *Her*. Despite the fact that she wasn't beautiful or seductive or sexy. Crawling around on his floor in a T-shirt and baggy jeans, acting like a complete idiot, she'd been as far removed from Miss Fantasy as a girl could get, yet he'd wanted her anyway.

He'd always wanted her.

The knowledge sent a rush of pure pleasure through her, and she gave herself a few delicious moments to savor the warmth of him before she slowly disengaged herself from his arm. She inched carefully toward the edge of the mattress, moving so slowly that it was several minutes before she finally stood beside the bed.

Her breath hitched as she stared down at him sprawled across the pale sheets. He was so dark and sexy and masculine. The mere sight of him made her chest ache. A lock of dark hair fell lazily across his forehead and a day's growth of stubble darkened his firm jaw.

The insides of her thighs quivered in response. She forced her gaze away before she gave in to her baser urges, threw herself into his arms, and begged him to do everything he'd done to her last night again and again. As happy as she was, the feeling was too new, and she was still too nervous. She'd lied to him. Pretended. How would she ever tell him the truth?

Even more, what would he think of her when she did?

The questions tempered her joy and sent her scrambling for her clothes and some much-needed distance. Inside the closet, she slipped on her shirt and jeans and boots. She needed to get out of here, to sort out her feelings and come up with a plan. But first she had to find the mask. She searched each room as carefully and as quietly as she could, then ended up back in the living room. While she'd checked around the couch the night before, she hadn't been able to really give it a thorough once-over.

"Where the hell *is* it?" she asked Cu-Joe as she crawled around the sofa for the sixth time and peered underneath. "It couldn't have sprouted legs and walked away."

"It didn't."

Her head snapped up. Either Cu-Joe had one heck of a deep, sexy voice or—

The thought scattered as she saw Connor standing in the bedroom doorway, naked and very tempting, a familiar scrap of black lace dangling from his fingertips.

The mask. Suddenly everything that had happened the past few days fell into place. His seductive comments. The intense way he looked at her. His confession of the night before. He'd gone from a family friend to a lover seemingly overnight.

She wanted to think it was just as he'd said, that he'd wanted her for so long and simply hadn't had the courage. But she feared his admission came from the fact that he'd fallen not for her but for the woman she'd pretended to be.

Miss Fantasy.

Beautiful, sexy, seductive Miss Fantasy, who had enticed him into bed in only a few hours. A feat that Frankie Brannigan hadn't been able to accomplish in all the ten years she'd been fantasizing about him.

The joy she'd felt faded in a wave of disappointment and humiliation. Her entire body trembled, and tears rushed to her eyes. "I—I don't know what you're talking about," she blurted, fighting against the emotions battering her control. "I was just looking for my, um, my—"

"—contacts, right?" He shook his head. "Baby, you don't wear contacts." He fingered the lace. "This belongs to you."

"That's crazy."

"It's yours."

"It is not," she said with conviction. It belonged to a naked mannequin at Naughty Nighties.

"You seduced me."

"I—I really have to go." She snatched up her purse and started for the door.

"We need to talk."

"I'm late for work and I have a million things waiting and I'm meeting Lisa at the flower shop and—" Her words stopped short as he caught her arm, his fingers strong, yet oddly gentle.

"It was *you*."

"You're wrong." She shook her head. "I'm nothing like that woman. This is me." She indicated her jeans and oversized T-shirt. "For heaven's sake, do I honestly look like the type to parade around in a black Sinderella teddy?"

He seemed to weigh her words, his gaze roaming from the top of her head to the tips of her work boots and back up again before he let her go. Instead of relief, however, she felt a rush of disappointment.

Crazy, because she wasn't the sexy-lingerie type. She never had been. She had never gone in for all those frivolous things that were a waste of time and money to a woman who spent her days at a construction site. She'd traded soft and frilly for her father's love and trust a long time ago, and she'd never regretted it.

Until now.

His voice was low when he finally spoke. "If it wasn't you, then how did you know it was a Sinderella teddy and not some other brand?"

"Lucky guess," she managed, pulling free. She was this close to the door when she turned and plucked the mask from his fingers. And then she walked away before she did something really stupid, like throw herself into his arms and admit that the feelings pushing and pulling at her went much deeper than lust.

Falling in love with Connor McBryde was *not* part of her plan. While they did share a passion for beer and pizza and sports, they were still all wrong for each other. He was Connor, beautiful and sexy, and she was plain, ordinary Frankie.

She couldn't fall in love with him.

• • •

She'd fallen in love with him.

Frankie finally admitted that truth to herself early Saturday morning as she stood in Naughty Nighties, mask in hand, and waited for Sarah to finish ringing up a customer.

She hadn't wanted to love him. She'd feared loving him, because it would mean putting herself on the line and risking his rejection. As long as she believed he could never be interested in someone like her, there was no need to blurt out her feelings. No risk. No rejection. No pain.

The thing was, the notion of never feeling his arms around her again, of never sitting next to him during a basketball game or soccer match or whitewater rafting rerun, or never again making wild, passionate love to him hurt far worse than him pushing her away in that closet so long ago.

She loved him, all right. She'd always loved him, since she'd been five years old and he'd picked her up off that scaffold and carried her to the office to doctor her scraped knee. And she'd loved him every moment since then, though she'd done her damnedest to pass it off as a bad case of lust, even which hadn't been too difficult, considering her nonexistent sex life.

Connor McBryde *was* sex, with his smoldering bedroom eyes, his teasing grin and seductive mouth. But his appeal went even deeper than a great body or a handsome face, or wicked hands, or the fact that he knew how to use them.

He drew her to him. The gentle, tender boy he'd been who'd worked day after day to support his mother and sister. The grown man he was now, who put up with a weenie-addicted Chihuahua. The man who teased and smiled and wiped tomato sauce off her chin and made her feel every bit a woman no matter what she was wearing.

She loved him.

And he loved Miss Fantasy.

That's what she wanted to think, but she couldn't forget the fierceness in his eyes last night when he'd made love to her in the closet. She hadn't seen the same expression when she'd been Miss Fantasy. Other than the brief loss of control when he'd kissed her in the elevator, he'd been his usual teasing, charming self. But last night, when he'd peeled off her jeans and T-shirt, he'd been different.

He'd been open and honest about his feelings, not hiding his desperation behind a wicked grin or tempering his hunger with a seductive wink, and the least Frankie Brannigan could do was reciprocate.

"Over here," Sarah motioned her forward as she slammed the register drawer shut. A shrill bell erupted, a sound reminiscent of Frankie's most stubborn piece of office equipment when it went on a chewing frenzy. Sarah wasn't the least bit intimidated. She positioned her fist a little to the left and gave the machine a quick, efficient smack. The ringing stopped.

"I was starting to worry," Sarah rushed on, coming around the counter and straightening a few bottles of body lotion in the process. "Dirk got in this morning, and he's coming in an hour to take over for me so I can leave to get ready for the wedding. So do you have it?"

Frankie smiled and stuffed the mask back into her pocket. "Actually, I've got something better. How are you with temperamental fax machines?"

"What did you do to my cousin?" Lisa asked Frankie that night, after the cake had been cut and the pictures taken, and the reception was in full swing. She stared across the dance floor at Sarah, who'd kicked off her shoes and was now getting down and dirty to the macarena with a cute blond guy from Marc's office.

"All I did was hire her as my personal assistant."

"And boost her self-esteem enough for her to break free from Dirk the Jerk's reign of terror." Lisa smiled. "Thanks, Frank."

"I should be thanking you. Sarah's an organizational whiz. She insisted on going by the office before she came here. In little under half an hour, she managed to clear off my desk and get my fax machine to purr like a kitten."

"Speaking of purring." Lisa smiled at her new husband, who was doing his best to keep up with Great-Aunt Felicity, the oldest Brannigan and a Jazzercise instructor at a nearby retirement home. The old woman had already exhausted Frankie's oldest two brothers, Vince and Trey, who were now sitting at a nearby table sipping champagne and recuperating. "Doesn't Marc fill out a tux better than any man you've ever seen?"

"Well—" Her gaze shifted to Connor, who looked downright mouthwatering in his own black tux, his dark hair slicked back. "I can't say that I agree." He stood near the bar, a beer in his hand and a frown on his face, no doubt because she'd been avoiding him since the start of the ceremony. But with more than a hundred guests and her and Connor's duties as members of the wedding party, neither had had the time to talk. Or the privacy. And Frankie wanted both.

"It was him, wasn't it? That night at the Valentine's party?" Lisa asked.

"Marc told you, didn't he?"

"Marc didn't say a word." Lisa's gaze caught hers. "He didn't have to. It's there in your eyes, honey. The way you're looking at him right now. The way you looked at him in the dressing room at the bridal shop a few days ago. Hell, the way you've always looked at him. I just never noticed."

"Neither did I." But she did now. She knew how she felt and, more important, she'd admitted it to herself. Now it was all a matter of finding out how he felt. She knew he wanted her, that he'd always wanted her. But love?

"He doesn't look too happy. What did you do to him?"

"Nothing." She fought back a wave of doubts and smiled. "Yet."

Connor had reached his limit. He'd gone through a sleepless night and bided his time all day, barely resisting the urge to storm over to Frankie's apartment, toss her across his shoulder, and carry her back to his place, his bed, his life, right where she belonged. He would have, but the fear he'd glimpsed in her eyes when he'd confronted her had stayed in his mind. He didn't want to screw this up and scare her off.

He stared across the room to where she stood with her middle brother, Trey, and another man from Marc's firm. She looked sexy as hell in that blue slip of a bridesmaid's dress. The strapless number bared her creamy shoulders and showed off her long legs. She laughed at something Marc's colleague said, and a stab of jealousy hit him.

A man could take only so much.

The beer bottle hit the bar top before he pushed his way through the crowd of people, across the dance floor, temporarily losing sight of her. When he finally reached the spot where he'd last seen the trio, they were gone.

"Shit," he muttered.

"Are you Connor McBryde?" The question came from a waiter carrying a bottle of champagne. When he nodded, the man handed him an empty bottle and a folded slip of paper. "Then these are for you." The waiter disappeared.

Connor tucked the bottle under one arm and opened the note. The frown creasing his face eased into a smile as he read the directions and the scribbled line "If you want to play . . ." He folded the paper, stuffed it into his coat pocket, and headed down the hallway in the direction the note had indicated.

He wanted to play, all right.

But more important, Connor McBryde wanted to win.

"You have a thing for closets, don't you?" he asked as he stood just inside the doorway of a darkened linen closet and watched Frankie step out of the shadows, into the bright shaft of light spilling from the hallway.

The air lodged in his throat, and his groin tightened at the sight of her clad in the familiar black lace teddy and mask.

"I have a thing for you," she said. "I . . ." Her voice trailed off as she licked her lips. "It was me that night. I dressed up like Miss Fantasy because I wasn't brave enough to admit how much I wanted you. Not to you, and especially not to myself. But I *do* want you."

He stepped forward, but she held up her hand. "Wait. There's more. You see, I love you. I've always loved you. So if you don't love me, take the bottle and leave, and let me get dressed before some unsuspecting waiter peeks in here and has me arrested for indecency."

"And if I do love you?"

Relief flooded her beautiful features, and she smiled radiantly. "Then we'll both get arrested for indecency."

He grinned, the expression fading as he pulled her into his arms for a fierce, possessive kiss. "I do love you, and I'm going to marry you."

He expected her to argue. To question his motives. To tell him how wrong they were for each other.

"You're breaking the rules," was all she said.

"What rules?"

"The kissing comes *after* you spin the bottle."

"I can't wait." He kissed her again, slower this time, savoring her taste and the feel of her pressed up against him. She was in his arms, in his heart, and he was never letting her go, rules or no rules.

"Besides," he said when he finally pulled away, "I've got something else in mind for that bottle." He saw the flicker of fear in her eyes, followed by a flash of excitement that made him chuckle. As innocent as she was, there was a hunger inside her every bit as wicked as the lingerie molding to her voluptuous curves, making his groin ache almost as much as the sight of her slightly trembling bottom lip made his chest hurt. She was still afraid. Still uncertain.

He pulled out a candle he'd swiped off one of the tables, stuck it into the mouth of the bottle, lit the wick, and slammed the door shut all the way. A warm glow filled the room, bathing her in a wash of soft light.

"I want to see you," he told her.

"Why?"

"Because you're Miss Fantasy. *My* fantasy. With the lingerie and the mask, and without them." He reached out, and this time she didn't stop him as he pulled the mask from her face the way he'd wanted to that first night. The Sinderella teddy followed, and then she stood naked in his arms. "Especially without them. *You*. You're the woman I dream about. The woman I want." And then he proceeded to show her just how much.

Leather and Lace

Maggie Shayne

One

"Granted, Kayla, I *do* need the money. But there is no way I'd do *that* for it."

"No?"

Hands firmly planted on her hips, Martha Jane Biswell shook her head. "No."

"It pays one thousand dollars. Cash. In your hand, the second you finish."

Martha Jane's mouth was already opening to refuse by the time her roommate's words registered. She snapped it closed so fast she nearly bit her tongue. "Don't be ridiculous, Kayla. I know you don't have that kind of money, and I couldn't take it from you even if you did. I've got almost as much invested in this business as you do, you know. I want to see it succeed."

"Hey, you're the one who helped me set the budget. One thousand is what we set aside to pay the model. It's already earmarked for that. And besides, if this doesn't work . . . well, we're finished. It's all or nothing."

Martha Jane shook her head. "*You're* modeling, and you aren't taking any money for it."

Kayla tossed her head. "Okay, what if I do? Say we split it. Five hundred each. Cash."

Biting her lip and battling a desperate need and a heavy-duty guilt trip, Martha Jane waited for a sign to tell her what to do.

"And you could have it in your hands tonight," Kayla went on. "Before you even put your old-maid clothes back on, if you want."

Lowering her head, pacing the apartment they shared, Martha Jane eyed the headless mannequins and the scandalous scraps they wore. Silken teddies. Lacy bustiers. Leather panties. Each piece of lingerie had one thing in common with all the others—a tag that read "Leather and Lace Designs."

Martha Jane's roommate and best friend, Kayla, *was* Leather and Lace. She'd been working her tail off to design this line of lingerie. She was a creative genius. But she'd needed help on the organizational end of things, and that was where Martha Jane had come in. She'd devoted countless hours and long nights and weekends to the cause. In return, Kayla gave her a one-third ownership of this roomful of lingerie. It could become more, someday—maybe—if they could sell the line.

Tonight was their big chance—maybe their *only* chance—to get this company off the ground. To make Kayla's dream come true.

"You know I'd do anything for Leather and Lace, Kayla," Martha Jane began. "But having me parade around in this stuff isn't going to sell it, and I think you know that. Can't we find a *real* model?"

"Are you kidding me? This is the biggest lingerie show of the season, Martha Jane. They're all booked solid. I hired one girl, because you said she was all we could afford, and now she has the flu."

"Everyone in the city has the flu," Martha Jane protested.

"*You* don't," Kayla shot back.

Martha Jane bit her lower lip, opened her mouth, closed it again.

Kayla jumped on the silence like a wolf on a rabbit. "Look, I'll be there with you. We'll parade down the runway wearing next to nothing *together*." She turned Martha Jane around, positioning her in front of the mirror. "Besides," she said, "you've been dying to play dress-up in some of these things."

"I have not."

"Have so. I watch your eyes, girl. I can see what you're thinking."

"Oh, don't be—"

"You're a knockout, you know. You just hide it."

"I'm as plain as a brown paper bag."

"Bull." Kayla pulled the pins out of Martha Jane's hair and shook it loose, letting it spill around her shoulders. "Your hair is incredible. Oh, what I could do with a little mousse and a blow-dryer."

"It's brown. It's plain, straight, and brown, and you couldn't do anything with it even if you had a *whole* moose."

Kayla scowled at the bad pun. "It's not plain *or* brown. It's *mink*," Kayla said. Then, reaching up, she took off Martha Jane's glasses. "And your eyes are so blue they make the sky jealous."

"But pretty much sightless without my glasses," Martha Jane said.

"Lucky for you the runway is straight and free of obstacles."

"I'm too short to be a model."

"You're petite. That's sexy."

"And not nearly skinny enough."

"What, are you kidding me? You got curves, girl!"

"And I'm not exactly . . . perky." Martha Jane looked down at her chest.

"My Dream Bra will take care of that, sweets. That little number is going to be the most talked-about miracle of the twenty-first century! Every woman in the country will want to own a dozen."

Martha Jane sighed. "I just don't know . . ."

"Look, hon, you've been out of work for almost a month, thanks to Mister Wonderful. They're gonna repossess your car if you don't make a payment pretty soon, and the rent's already late. You *have* to do *something*."

Licking her lips, Martha Jane glanced again at the revealing wardrobe she'd be required to wear. To model. In front of strangers. "And you're sure no one from Gable Brothers will be there?"

"Look, I saw the guest list. I swear, no one from Gable Brothers Department Stores was on it. This thing is exclusive, invitation only."

Martha Jane frowned at her friend. "I can't believe they weren't invited. They're one of the biggest chains in the state."

Kayla shrugged. "Even if someone from Gable Brothers *did* come, it wouldn't be good ol' Clark."

"Richard," Martha Jane said. "My boss's name was Richard, and you know it."

"Hmmph. Couldn't tell it from the way you go on about him." Kayla tipped her head back and fluttered her eyelashes. Then she grinned. "But back to the point. If the Gables did send someone to the show, it would be their lingerie buyer. And she's a female, and besides that, you've never even *met* her." Then Kayla reached out to run her fingertips over the red satin that barely covered a mannequin. "But to tell you the truth, I'd give my right arm to see Richard Gable eating his heart out in the crowd when you took to the runway wearing something like this. The jerk. Firing the best secretary he ever had just so he could hire his latest bimbo of the month."

Martha Jane sighed heavily. She had been devastated when Richard—Mr. Gable—had told her he had to let her go. It had hurt all the more when she'd seen her replacement, a twenty-year-old big-haired blonde with vacant eyes and a D-cup, gravity-resistant chest. The truth was, Martha Jane had been secretly falling head over heels for her boss since her first day on the job. But he would never give a girl like her a second glance. She was smart, efficient, and cool. She didn't bounce or wiggle or giggle, and she supposed it was just as well she was out of there. She'd never had such a foolish, self-destructive urge in her life as when she'd first set eyes on Richard Gable. And she hoped she never would again.

He was something, though. Those dark, smoky eyes, that smile. No wonder women were practically falling at his feet. "He wasn't *completely* heartless about the whole thing," she said softly, automatically defending her former boss, though she knew she shouldn't. "He *did* offer me another position in the company."

"And thank goodness you had enough self-respect to tell him where to stick that offer," Kayla snapped.

It wasn't so much self-respect, Martha Jane thought, as it was wounded pride. Wounded . . . everything. She'd been deeply hurt by Richard's treatment of her. Too hurt to be practical. And now she was suffering for it. She should have taken the offer. Sure, maybe she'd have had to see him fawning over his new secretary every day, but at least she would be able to pay her bills.

Sighing again, she tried not to acknowledge the slight stinging sensation behind her eyes.

"I promise you, no one you know will be at this lingerie show," Kayla was saying. "And the total amount of time you're going to spend on the runway will amount to only minutes when you add it up. It's so simple, Martha Jane. You walk to the end, turn, and walk back. Change your clothes backstage and do it again. You won't even be out there long enough to work up a decent *blush*!"

"If I could be sure of that, then maybe I'd *consider* it," Martha Jane finally said.

"Wait! I have an idea!" Kayla dashed off into the bedroom, and emerged a second later with a scrap of black leather that looked like . . . like a mask. Oh, God, it *was* a mask. She quickly wrapped it around Martha Jane's face, the black silk ties going beneath her hair and then knotting in the back. The two almond-shaped eyeholes fit right over her eyes.

"My God," she whispered, squinting into the mirror. "I look like somebody's bondage fetish come to life."

"I've been working on a few different mask designs just to set off the clothes. Come on, now, give it a chance," Kayla cajoled. "When you put these things on, Martha Jane, you're gonna feel like a different woman. Like a . . . like a love goddess. And with the mask . . . well, that just makes the illusion complete." She fluffed Martha Jane's hair. "You can keep the mask on all night— No, no, wait! I have some others, in different colors, one with a feather. We can pair them up, a mask to go with each outfit!"

"I . . . I couldn't . . ."

"Oh, come on, Martha Jane, you have to! Honey, when I get through with you, there'll be no way anyone could *possibly* recognize you! You won't recognize yourself." She tilted her head. "In fact, it'll be good for you. You'll be surprised how freeing it can be to be totally unrecognizable. You might learn a little something you didn't know about yourself." She shrugged. "Either way, to my way of thinking, this means there's not one single reason left why you should turn up your nose at a quick five hundred bucks."

There was a knock on the apartment door and a shout from the hall beyond. "Martha Jane! Come quick!"

Recognizing the voice of Mrs. Crump from upstairs, Martha Jane tugged free of Kayla, pulled off the silly mask, and yanked the door open.

"Someone appears to be stealing your car, dear!" Mrs. Crump said.

"What?" Whirling, Martha Jane raced to the window, grabbing her glasses on the way. She put them on fast and looked at the street below. Sure enough, a white tow truck with BERNIE'S REPO SERVICE painted on the side in fat 1970s-style lettering was backing up to her car.

Something tickled her hand. She looked down to see five crisp hundred-dollar bills sliding into her palm. "Tell you what," Kayla said, closing Martha Jane's hand around the wad of money and her own hand around Martha Jane's. "Take your share of the pay in advance. Go down there and pay Bernie so he'll leave your car alone."

Licking her lips and feeling backed into a corner, Martha Jane closed her eyes, and nodded. "Deal."

Richard Gable looked across the desk at his brother and shook his head. "No way in hell, bro. It's Valentine's Day weekend. I have two dates with two gorgeous models. Both at the same time, of course, thanks to the secretarial skills of our niece, Babs the airhead. But frankly, despite the effort it's going to take, I plan to find some way to make the most of each of them."

Michael Gable crooked an eyebrow in the disapproving way that only an older brother could manage. "Since when does your secretary's job include managing your social calendar?"

Richard shrugged. "Martha Jane never had a problem with it. Hell, my life ran like clockwork when she was around. Now I've got Babs and I'm swimming in chaos."

Michael gave him a "serves you right" sort of look. "Luckily, the women you date make our Babs look like a female Einstein, so it shouldn't be too difficult to lie your way out of the situation."

"Exactly," Richard said with a grin, not bothering to defend his women to his brother. He knew what they were and what they were not. He wasn't in denial about any of that.

"But now, you see, you don't *have* to lie your way out of it," Michael said quickly. "You have a *legitimate* excuse to cancel both dates, Richard. You have to haul your big brother's butt out of the fire."

"Being happily married, you may not remember it, Mike, but Valentine's Day sex is usually the best sex of the year."

"Oh, I *remember* it, all right. I'm *living* it, most of the time. When you find the right woman, *every* day is Valentine's Day." Michael grinned and gazed at some distant spot in space. Hell, he'd only been married six months, Richard thought. The guy was practically still on his honeymoon. But Michael's dreamy expression turned serious as he spoke again. "Problem is, I won't be getting anything except divorce papers for Valentine's Day this year if I attend the lingerie show as planned."

Richard sighed, shook his head. "How the hell did Cindy find out you were going, anyway? It's not like you went home and told her about it." His brother averted his eyes. "Is it?" Richard asked.

"What, you thought I was going to *lie* to her?" Michael seemed stunned by the very thought.

"Jesus, Michael, you *didn't* go to your wife and *tell* her that you had to attend a lingerie show on Valentine's Day, did you?"

Michael avoided his brother's gaze. "Of course not. Well . . . not exactly. I, um, I asked her."

"You asked her," Richard repeated, his tone flat.

"I thought she'd understand. I mean, with Hannah Mandrake sick with this damn flu bug, someone has to take her place at the show. Do you realize how important it is? She practically had to jump through hoops to get the ticket. She runs the lingerie department almost single-handedly, and she's doing a fabulous job for us, Richard. So it's fairly obvious that one of us has to stand in for her at this thing. It's important to her, to her department, and to Gable Brothers." He shrugged. "I just thought Cindy would understand. It's business."

"Right," Richard said. "You thought Cindy would agree to let you go watch a gaggle of gorgeous models parade around in their underwear for you on Valentine's Day while she stayed home watching videos, alone."

Michael sighed. "I guess it wasn't the best idea I've ever had. But Richard, one of us has to go. And, hey, come on. These are the kind of women you like best here. Models. *Underwear* models, for heaven's sake. I can't believe you're not wrestling me to the floor to get that ticket away from me."

Richard lowered his head. Oh, yeah, they were his type of women all right. Tall, leggy, lean, gorgeous, vain, and well informed on the latest hot colors, fabrics, vacation spots, and advances in laser surgery, even if they couldn't name the capitals of their own states. Frankly, since he'd been forced to let the best secretary he'd ever had go so he could give his bubbleheaded niece a job, he'd had his fill of that kind of woman. Babs was that kind of woman. *She* ought to be modeling underwear.

He wanted his efficient, myopic, conservative Miss Biswell back.

"Uncle Riiii-charrd," came the singsong voice that could set his teeth on edge in a single note.

Richard reached across his desk and pushed the button on the intercom. "You're supposed to call me 'Mr. Gable' at work, Babs."

A high-pitched titter came back. "Sorry. I thought I'd tell you that you just had a message from Fate."

"I did?"

"Mm-hmm."

Richard looked across the office at his brother, who was biting his lip to keep from grinning. "Babs, um, do you think perhaps it might have been . . . Kate?"

There was a long silence. "Well, I guess it might have been."

"Well, now, let's see. Did she call to tell you my reason for living, Babs, or did she just want to say hello?"

He could almost see his sister's youngest child searching her empty head for the answer. "She wanted to know if you were planning anything special for Valentine's Day."

His throat went dry. It was Kate. Would have been better, though, if it had been Fate, calling to say he was going to hell in a handbasket. "And what did you tell her?" he forced himself to ask.

Her voice came back, brighter than ever. "Same thing I told Heidi and Fawn," she chirped. "That you'd be at the Valentine's Day Ball at the Westcott Room at eight o'clock sharp."

She sounded as if she thought she deserved a raise and a promotion for being so efficient. Ending the intercom connection, Richard gave Michael a desperate look. "Make that three dates."

"And one perfect excuse." Michael held up the ticket. "Or do you want them all showing up at the ball at eight and meeting each other?"

Running a hand through his hair, Richard sighed his surrender and pressed the button again. "Babs?"

"Oh!" she squeaked. "You scared me! What?"

He closed his eyes. It was probably not a good idea to have Babs call Heidi and Fawn and Kate with his regrets. "Never mind, hon. I'll take care of it myself." He walked over to his brother, took the ticket. "This is going to cost me a small fortune in flowers, candy, and apologies," he told Michael.

"Don't bother with the candy, Richard. They're models, remember?"

It was, Richard thought, a good point.

Two

"I cannot believe I am doing this."

"Oh, be quiet and suck in!" Kayla slid the zipper up as Martha Jane held her breath. "There!" she said, stepping back. "What do you think?"

Models were running back and forth in various states of undress, all of them at least six inches taller than Martha Jane was, even though she had donned stiletto heels in an effort to appear taller. She felt as insignificant among them as a crow among swans as she lifted her head to the full-length-and-then-some mirror.

Then she widened her eyes. She didn't *look* insignificant or crowlike at all. Her first thought was that she really ought to put on her glasses, but she knew full well she could see up close without them. It was distances that gave her trouble. Kayla had worked wonders on her hair, making it seem fuller and wilder and glossier all at once simply by her clever use of a hairbrush and blow-dryer. It was a big, fluffy, sexy, mink-colored mane now, rather than the straight, lifeless tresses she usually kept captive in a tight bun. "Wow," Martha Jane whispered.

"I told you. You look incredible."

"I look . . . like someone else." Martha Jane eyed herself. Her body was hugged tightly by white leather. The high-cut leg openings and white open-toed spike-heeled shoes made her short legs seem longer, and the white stockings she wore were topped with wide bands of elasticized lace. But the amazing thing was the way the scrap of leather managed to make her waist look so small. And . . . other things look . . . gravity-proof.

"I have *cleavage*," she said, staring at the gentle swells as if they were foreign objects that had suddenly landed on her home planet.

"There's Dream Bra technology built into every piece I create," Kayla announced proudly. She stood beside Martha Jane, wearing a short red baby doll that was almost as transparent as glass. Underneath it were a red-sequinned Dream Bra and matching thong panties. Her stockings were red, as were her shoes, and she wore a little headband with a pair of plastic devil horns.

"Here, get the gloves on." Kayla handed her a pair of long white gloves, then pulled on her own red ones.

Sighing, incredibly uncertain, and feeling a flutter of panic in her chest, Martha Jane put the gloves on and lowered her mask. It was white, like the rest of the outfit, with tipped-up corners accented in white feathers. It was supposed to allude to the wings of an angel. Right now, Martha Jane thought, she felt more like a chicken.

The music Kayla had chosen—Robert Palmer's "Simply Irresistible"—came crashing over the loudspeaker, and the sultry voice of the female emcee drifted in, announcing the first-ever showing from a new designer. Kayla grabbed Martha Jane by the arm. "Come on! This is it!" She left Martha Jane in the curtained area just off stage left, then raced around to the other side, her heels clicking all the way.

Martha Jane looked across the stage and saw the fuzzy red outline of Kayla waiting on the other side. This meant everything to her friend. Everything. It meant a great deal to Martha Jane as well. It was important. She could do this.

"I give you," the emcee said, "Kayla Hart's brand-new line of fantasy lingerie, Leather and Lace!"

The music boomed louder. Martha Jane held Kayla's gaze—or rather, tried to focus on where that gaze would be—and counted off. On three she took a deep breath and stepped forward. She concentrated on remembering everything Kayla had told her about walking onto that runway. Left foot, right foot, legs crossing in front of each other with every carefully placed step. Back straight, chin up. Eyes wide and not squinting in the bright lights. Lips slightly turned up in a mysterious almost-smile, but not a full-blown one. Keep them slightly parted, and moist. Move the hips with every step.

She made it to the center of the stage, where she and Kayla stopped at the same moment, just the way they'd planned it. A soft swell of applause started, then grew. Kayla caught Martha Jane's eye, and Martha Jane took the signal and began her solitary trek forward along the long, narrow runway, between the lights that lined its sides, heels clicking. Cameras flashed, but the lights were too bright to allow her to see any faces in the crowd—not that she could have seen them anyway without her glasses. She tried to focus on what the emcee read from the card Kayla had provided. Something about the butter-soft leather of the "Angel" ensemble. Something about the built-in Dream Bra.

Martha Jane stopped at the end of the runway, one foot in front of the other, pivoted, pivoted again, turned around fully as the applause suddenly swelled, and made her way back. She kept going, right off the stage as Kayla started down the runway in her "Devil" costume.

Once backstage, Martha Jane felt her knees go weak and her stomach clench up a little bit, but beyond that, there was no paralyzing reaction. No horrible sense of shame. In fact, she felt . . . good. Those people had cheered for her. She lifted her gaze, looked into the mirror. A stranger looked back at her. An utterly feminine, utterly desirable, sexy female looked back at her. The kind of woman who could bring a man like Richard Gable to his knees. The kind of woman she'd always secretly wished she could be.

"Damn!" she whispered. "Kayla was right—I do feel different."

But there was no time to give the feeling the substantial amount of thought and analysis it needed. She had two more outfits to model, the most outrageous one saved for last. She swallowed her shyness, her inhibitions, and found it far easier to do than she had expected. She rapidly yanked off her angel getup and pulled on a black-velvet bodysuit with cat ears and a detachable tail. She had to change her gloves and mask as well, and pull on the tall, shiny, spike-heeled thigh-high boots. But she did it in time. She was ready to walk out there again by the time Kayla got back.

Oddly, she didn't have to force herself this time. Instinct told her that if this crowd had liked the first getup she'd worn, they were going to like this one even better. She almost smiled when she stepped out onto the stage. And she didn't have to remind herself to move slowly, to take her time, so Kayla would have enough time to get changed. She walked slowly, a little slinkiness in her step to keep to the feline motif. At center stage, just as planned, she paused, turned to one side, then the other. The applause came louder and louder. She really was doing this, and apparently the crowd was believing the lie—that she *was* this she-cat she was pretending to be. Amazing.

She walked slowly along the runway. At the end, she reached behind her, just as she and Kayla had rehearsed. She removed the detachable "tail" and ran it slowly through her fingers, then snapped it hard on the stage to demonstrate how it doubled as a playful velvet whip. It made a satisfying crack and the audience gasped, then burst into wild applause as Martha Jane wound the tail up, turned, and moved slowly back. They were going wild, shouting for more. A wolf whistle pierced the din, and she almost burst out laughing.

A wolf whistle, aimed at plain Martha Jane Biswell. Imagine that!

One more outfit to go, she thought. Just one more. She'd thought it the worst one of them all, at first. Now she thought maybe it was going to be the best. Certainly it was the most shocking. The most taboo. The most . . . *sinful*.

She stepped backstage, passing Kayla on the way.

"Is that a smile?" Kayla whispered as she passed. "I knew it! You're a closet sex kitten, Biswell! I knew it all along!"

Martha Jane stuck out her tongue and picked up the pace, slipping quickly into the final outfit. It was made almost entirely of leather straps with silver buckles. They crisscrossed her entire torso. There was actually no more of her showing than there would have been had she been wearing a bikini—but it seemed like more. A lot more. Still, black leather cupped her breasts and bottom and covered her where she needed covering, held in place by the straps that ran from top to bottom, crisscrossed her middle, encircled her shoulders, and wove their way down her back.

That wasn't the part of the outfit that made it seem so outrageous, though. The mask that went with this one was made to look just like a blindfold, except that, of course, she could see through it. And the little satin-covered bracelets she wore on both wrists had tiny chains hanging from them, which could be linked together. When Kayla came prancing off stage, she paused long enough to hook the chains behind Martha Jane's back.

"You sure you're okay?" she asked.

Kayla's eyes were gleaming and she was smiling ear to ear. Martha Jane swallowed hard and nodded. "How do you think it's going?"

"Oh, they're loving it! And this will be the clincher! Remember, walk tall, head tipped slightly back, chest out, shoulders back. Okay?"

"I remember. I can't walk any other way in this state, anyway."

"Great! Go!"

The music throbbed, and Martha Jane stepped out onto the stage. The crowd went dead silent. Not a sound came. Not a breath, she thought. Swallowing hard, she moved to the center, and the tapping of her spike heels seemed louder than anything she'd ever heard before. She paused at center stage, turned left, and right, then started along the runway. She'd lost them, she thought, wishing she could hurry. But that wasn't an option. She was afraid to walk fast, because if she lost her balance, she would fall on her face. In fact, she was probably walking slower than she had before.

At any rate, she made it to the very end of the runway, and stopped.

Slowly, the clapping began. Bit by bit. Louder, and then louder still. And then it was thunderous, deafening. Martha Jane was startled, but mostly relieved. Then, as the applause went on and on, that other feeling returned to overwhelm everything else. She felt . . . sexual. She felt desirable and physical and feminine. Earthy. Female. Powerful. They were applauding for Kayla's designs, yes—but *she* was the one making them look this good. She'd never believed herself capable of it. Of being . . . sexy.

Smiling, almost giddy with this newfound sense of herself as a woman, she pivoted and headed back. She almost wished Richard Gable *could* see her this way!

Kayla passed her on the way out, wearing regular clothes again—if you could call them regular. She was gorgeous, and as the emcee introduced her as the designer of this bold new line, she paused and gripped Martha Jane's shoulder. "Omigod," she whispered. "Martha Jane . . . *look*."

Martha Jane's back was to the crowd, as she'd been leaving the stage, but she turned now and squinted toward the audience. When the stage lights dimmed, she could see them—not clearly, but enough. They were getting up, one by one, rising to their feet. A standing ovation for Kayla's line. They loved it! They loved Kayla and they loved Martha Jane. Kayla's dream was coming true. And she was gripping Martha Jane's arm so tightly that Martha Jane had no choice but to step onto the runway once more, as Kayla received her glory.

Halfway out, Kayla stopped and released her grip on Martha Jane's hand to blow a kiss to the crowd, and Martha Jane pivoted, intending to make a quick escape. But she pivoted too fast, and her damned hands were still hooked together behind her back. She wobbled, teetered, flapped her elbows in a useless effort to regain her balance. In that instant she thanked her stars that the spotlight and all eyes were on Kayla, who had continued on to the end of the runway alone—and then Martha Jane went over the side.

There was a thud as her back hit the floor, fortunately only a few feet below her. It knocked the wind out of her, and she couldn't even speak for a heartbeat. Shaking off the impact, Martha Jane managed to work her arms down the backs of her legs, and push her feet through them so they were linked in front of her, rather than behind her. She sat up, and though, clumsy without the use of her hands, she got as far as her knees before she realized there was a man standing in front of her. His hands were on her shoulders, as if he were going to try to help her up, but he had frozen in the middle of it. And no wonder, with her nose about an inch from his zipper. A zipper that seemed to be . . . swelling, she thought, blinking.

She swallowed her embarrassment, ignored the little devil voice inside her that wanted to laugh and shout at this new feminine power, and forced herself to tip her head back and look him in the eye.

Richard Gable stared down at her, too close to be a mistake or a product of her bad eyesight, and he said, "I think I dreamed something like this last night."

She closed her eyes, mortified that he should see her like this.

"Don't be embarrassed," he whispered "You were the hottest

model up there all night. Believe me, I know. What's your name, anyway? I don't think I've seen you before."

She blinked, frowned . . . and realized she was still wearing the mask. He didn't recognize her! The mortification vanished. Something else replaced it. A kind of triumph. He'd said she was the hottest model up there. That was good, right? Her. His efficient little ex-secretary. Miss Biswell, hotter than any of the bimbos he'd preferred over her for so long. Hotter than any of the women he'd fallen all over himself trying to get into bed while ignoring the woman right under his nose who was halfway in love with him.

"My name?"

He nodded, smiling.

"It's, uh, Valentine. Yes—it's Valentine," she lied, trying to keep her voice very soft and slightly deeper than normal so he wouldn't recognize it. The result was a sultry-sounding purr.

"Yeah? Well, you're the nicest Valentine I ever got." His smile deepened. "I'm Richard. Nice to meet you." His hands were still on her shoulders, his crotch still an inch from her face. "I, um, I hate to offer, but can I help you up?"

She looked up, and some demon woman she didn't even recognize said, "If you insist," and sent him a devilish half smile.

He looked as if she'd zapped him with a stun gun. "Damn, woman," he said, sounding a little breathless. "You're deadly, aren't you?" He gripped her outer arms and helped her to her feet, a motion that brought her body very close to his. He remained there, close to her, not speaking.

"Thank you," she said softly.

"No, thank *you*."

A bit of her bravado fled as she felt other eyes on her, but Richard seemed to sense it instantly, because he took off his jacket, and draped it around her shoulders.

Still, people were staring. *Men* were staring. Men who were not Richard, and the looks in their eyes were . . . predatory. She didn't like it. It was fine for him to look at her like that, with that sexual gleam in his eye—God, she'd *dreamed* of him looking at her like that. But not them. Not strangers.

"Anything else I can do for you?" Richard was asking.

"Yes," she said, answering in such a rush that she didn't even think first. "Get me out of here."

He stared at her, his eyes going just a little wider, then gleaming with sexual appreciation. His lips parted in a smile so hot it was indecent, and he said, "Whatever you say, lady." He took her arm, started forward.

Her foot went right out from under her and she almost fell, but he caught her. "Ow . . . oh!"

"What is it?"

"These shoes. I think I broke a heel when I fell," she said.

He smiled again. "Well, I can remedy that easily enough." And before she knew what was happening he scooped her up into his arms and strode through the crowd with her. The next thing she knew, she was being settled into the passenger seat of a low-slung black sports car, and he was climbing into the driver's seat beside her.

He started the engine, turned to face her. "Your place or mine?" he asked, his voice deep and full of innuendo.

She licked her lips, blinked rapidly, told herself to get the hell out of this car and do it *fast*.

The stranger who'd taken over her body whispered, "Yours."

He smiled at her, melting her, and the car lurched forward.

"There's . . . just one thing," she began. He glanced down at her, waiting. "The mask . . . stays on."

Again he smiled. "Now I'm *sure* I dreamed this last night."

She felt herself blush hot and had to avert her eyes.

"I'll tell you what, Valentine. You can keep the mask on, on one condition."

"And what's the condition?" she asked.

He reached down, caught her wrist in his hand, and ran his thumb over the satiny bracelets with their linked chains. “Consider keeping the cuffs on, too?” He grinned, winked at her, and stomped harder on the gas pedal.

Three

Martha Jane didn't know what it was. The two or three drinks she'd had to bolster herself for the show? Her longtime feelings for her boss, combined with the way he'd constantly ignored her as a woman while mooning over brainless twit after brainless twit? The triumph she felt now, that he was finally seeing her the way she'd dreamed of? Or something else?

She only knew that it was Valentine's Day, and she was wearing a mask and taking this chance. She was going to make her most secret fantasy come true. She was going to have wild sex with Richard Gable.

He carried her into his house, which was a stunning creation of adobe and knotty pine. Inside, she caught only fleeting, out-of-focus glimpses of a wide foyer with cathedral ceilings, a forest-green and oak living room with a fireplace, and then he was carrying her up an open metalwork staircase and through a door at the top.

His bedroom.

He set her on her feet and stood facing her. He stared down at her for a long moment, and then, finally, he lowered his head and he kissed her. His hands slid the jacket off her shoulders and let it fall to the floor, and then he stood a little straighter, just looking at her.

She'd never felt more exposed. More vulnerable. And yet . . . she felt powerful too. Because she could see what looking at her was doing to him. He looked as if his dreams were all coming true.

"I . . . I didn't mean what I said before," he told her. "About those, er, bracelet things. You can take them off if you want."

She stared up at him. If she didn't know him so well, she'd be terrified right now. But she did know him. He would never hurt her. She was perfectly safe with him. "I, um, don't have a key."

He closed his eyes. "Then I guess you're . . . at my mercy."

She lifted her head as heat shot through her, met his eyes head on, and knew this was perfect. She didn't have to worry about knowing how—about performing. He'd have to do it all. She didn't even need to feel guilty about it. Or overcome her shyness. Or anything at all. "I guess I am," she whispered.

He smiled a devilish smile and moved her backward, until her back was touching the coolness of a wall. Reaching down, he hooked a finger around the chain between her wrists and slowly lifted it until her hands were above her head. She looked up, saw the little clothes hook on the wall above her, watched him drape the chain over it.

"Oh . . . my . . ."

He paused, waiting, watching her. Giving her time, she knew—but she said no more. He smiled again. Reaching out with both hands, he touched her breasts, running his fingers over them again and again. Then he shook his head. "This leather is sexy, but, uh, too thick. I think it's going to have to go." He slid his palms around behind her as she tried to control her trembling. His hands lifted her hair, slid along her spine, locating the first of the buckles. Slowly, he unfastened it, and then the next, and the next. She shivered when his fingers trailed over the base of her spine.

"You're shaking," he whispered.

"No, I'm not."

"Yes, you are." He kept his hands where they were, fingers tickling her spine. Leaning in, he kissed her neck and her shoulders, and her cheeks. She was breathless and filled with turmoil. He straightened again, and the leather bodice hung loose about to fall down in front. She wanted to clap her hands to it to hold it in place, but she couldn't. Then it did fall, and he just stood there, staring at her.

She stood there, staring back.

He reached out, gripped the leather, pulled it slowly down. His hands slid over her skin as he did so. Her waist. Her hips. Down her thighs. He let it go, let it fall to the floor around her ankles. Stepping out of the leather, she kicked it aside.

"You're beautiful," he whispered.

God, she'd never felt so exposed. Her hands were itching to cross in front of her body, to cover herself, but she couldn't.

He trailed the backs of his hands over her breasts again, knuckles brushing her nipples. She closed her eyes. Turning his hands, he stroked with his fingers. Then he drew thumb and forefingers together . . . a gentle pinch. A soft sound was wrung from her. His smile widened. He pinched again. "Like that?" he asked.

Breathless, she nodded.

"Good." One more pinch, then without warning his hands fell away, and his head swooped down. He caught a breast in his hungry mouth and suckled her hard, scraping with his teeth, flicking with his tongue, biting and nipping. And now his hand was slipping down her belly, diving between her legs. Fingers spread her, opened her, touched her.

He nipped harder at her breast and drove his fingers inside her.

She cried out, moving against his hand, arching against his mouth.

Then suddenly he moved away from her. Stepping back, he stared at her as she opened her eyes. She watched as he slowly unfastened his belt, his zipper. Erotic as some pagan fertility god, he undressed. And she couldn't take her eyes off him as he did. He was big, and dark, and hard. Then he came back to her. Without a word, he slid his hands down her back and cupped her buttocks, squeezed her thighs. Then he lifted her legs, until she wrapped them around his waist, and he plunged himself inside her.

"Richard," she whispered. It was so good. He filled her, stretched her. And when he took his hands away, her weight lowered her further, so that he sank even more deeply into her. Nothing supported her now but the flimsy chain slung round the hook above her head, and the man inside her. It was the most erotic thing in the world. He bent to nurse at her breasts again as he began to move, driving himself inside her harder and harder until her body was pressed to the wall with every thrust. She panted and moaned as he pushed her closer and closer to climax. She couldn't believe the power of it, couldn't believe the tightening, tensing, coiling sensations going on inside her.

And just as she hovered at the very brink, he lifted his head. "Open your eyes," he whispered. "I want to watch you."

She opened her eyes. He kept driving into her, harder, deeper, faster, and his hands came to her breasts, and his eyes never left hers. "Come for me," he whispered, as he closed his fingers on her nipples. Then he pinched harder. "Now."

She screamed aloud as wave upon wave of feeling washed over her, shaking her to the core. By the time she came to herself again, Richard had slipped her little chain off its hook, fumbled with it until he got it to come apart, and was carrying her with him to the bed.

Hours later, Richard lay sated and utterly relaxed, with the woman snuggled close in his arms, when it occurred to him that she hadn't said anything for several moments . . . not since she last screamed his name, in fact. He thought she might be sleeping.

He wasn't too certain how he felt about that. His one-night stands didn't usually stay overnight. Then again, this had been . . . different. He couldn't quite put his finger on why, but there was no denying that it had been just that. Different. Intense, yes. Incredible, yes. He thought, though, that the main difference was the woman.

She wasn't putting on a show. She truly had been a bit shy—at first. Trying to hide it behind her mask and her bold lingerie, but still, it had been obvious in those initial tremulous kisses. In her trembling, and the way she would avert her gaze now and then, or the way her cheeks kept coloring hotly when he looked at her. When her hands had been free to touch him, those touches had been almost hesitant. And her responses had been an odd combination of delight and—and surprise. As if every sensation were new to her somehow.

The difference was even more obvious in the way she'd curled up beside him afterward, the way she nestled still in the crook of his arm, so content and relaxed that she might be sleeping. His kind of women were usually in the shower within minutes of lovemaking and on their way home shortly thereafter.

This one was in no hurry. He wasn't even certain she was awake.

"I . . . don't know about you," he said, keeping his voice low, trailing a finger over her cheek. "But I'm starving."

"I could eat an entire side of beef," she murmured.

He felt his face split in a smile. His first thought was that she was no more an ordinary model than she was an ordinary woman. "I thought you might be sleeping."

She sat up a little, staring down at him in the darkness from behind her mysterious mask. "Not sleeping. Just . . . basking." A shy smile tugged at her lips, and she turned her face away a bit. If he could see in the dark, he thought he'd see her blushing. "It was . . . wonderful, Richard."

"It was pretty wonderful for me, too."

"Really?" She seemed surprised, and maybe relieved, too.

"What, it wasn't obvious?"

Again, she looked away. "I guess I just wanted to be sure."

He nodded, once again getting the feeling she wasn't exactly experienced at these sorts of games. "What do you want to eat, Valentine? You name it, I'll get it. Serve it to you in bed." His words surprised him.

"I told you, a side of beef."

He laughed softly. "You're not like any other model I've ever met," he said.

"That's because I'm not a model," she said in her soft, raspy voice.

A little alarm bell went off in Richard's head. "You're not?"

"Well, I was tonight. But for the first and last time." She smiled at him, making his stomach flip over. "Even though I enjoyed it a lot more than I expected to."

Richard cleared his throat. "What . . . do you do? For a living, I mean?"

She quickly looked away. "I've been helping a friend get a new business off the ground. Creatively, she's a genius, but she has no head for books or budgets or organization."

Richard's throat went dry. She was not what he had thought she was—not at all. "You do that full time, then?"

"For the moment, yes."

"And this modeling gig was what, a walk on the wild side?"

She laughed huskily. A deep, rich sound that stroked his nerve endings like brushed velvet. "A favor for a friend. Her model got sick at the last minute."

"I see."

She drew a breath, sighed, looked at him with something soft and intense in her eyes. "I argued hard against the whole thing. But now I'm very glad I let her talk me into it."

"Oh."

She tilted her head then, her eyes narrowing when they saw his expression. No doubt—it was one of impending panic.

"I'm sorry," she said, her voice going a bit harder. "I'm ruining it for you, aren't I? I should have said I was an aspiring actress, and added a breathless little giggle for good measure."

Richard frowned. Her tone had changed, and he hadn't expected to see such sharpness in those eyes. "What are you talking about?"

She shrugged. "That's the kind of woman you usually date, isn't it? They're safe."

"Safe?" He sat up, leaned back against the headboard. This was fascinating. Chilling, too. This woman seemed to know more about him than he'd realized. And from the look in her eyes a moment ago—she might not know a one-night stand when she saw one.

"Convenient," she said. "No demands, no expectations." She shrugged. "Don't worry, Richard. Smart women can have casual sex, too."

He tilted his head to one side. "But it's a first for you, isn't it, Valentine?"

She shrugged and looked away.

"How do you know so much about me?" he asked. He saw her tongue dart out to moisten her lips. She looked around the room as if in search of a change of subject, and her gaze fell on the tripod in the corner.

"I don't know much about you at all," she answered then. "I didn't know you were an artist, for example." She nodded toward the blank canvas on the tripod.

"I'm no artist. I used to draw some, but—"

"Used to?"

He shrugged. "I haven't worked on anything in months." Because he hadn't felt sufficient passion for anything in months to want to capture it in charcoal.

Until tonight.

And that made him even more uncomfortable. So he changed the subject. "Just who are you really, Valentine?"

She sat up quickly, putting her feet on the floor and her back to him, clutching the sheet to her chest. "I really should go . . ."

"No, don't." He said it too quickly, yes. He knew that. He usually couldn't wait for his dates to leave, usually found talking to them as boring as mud. But not this time. This woman was different. Totally different from the others. And in spite of his self-imposed set of rules, he found himself really wanting her to stay. To *talk*, of all things! "Don't go. If it makes you so uncomfortable, I won't ask again."

She wasn't relaxing, though. Not yet.

"Besides, I haven't fixed us that side of beef yet." He ran the back of his fingers slowly down her spine. She arched in response, and calmed visibly. He saw her lips curve in a slight smile.

"What do you mean, us?" she teased softly. "You don't expect me to share, do you?"

He laughed again, so relieved he was damn near giddy with it. He couldn't remember the last time he'd been out with a woman who'd made him laugh. "Wait here. I'll be back in no time." He got up, reached for a robe, and pulled it on. Then he looked back at her for a long moment. "You intrigue me, Valentine," he heard himself say.

She shook her head. "It's not me," she said, and he thought there was a touch of sadness in her voice. "It's just the mask."

"No. No, it's you."

He turned and headed to the kitchen. As he sliced hunks of left-over roast beef sent home with him by his nurturing sister-in-law, he wondered about his mysterious Valentine. She was disguising her voice, never raising it above that deep whispering tone that told him nothing. She was hiding her face, behind that silly mask—and her personality behind the rest of the costume she wore tonight. Even when that costume was nothing more than her delectable skin. She was a shy woman, normally. A woman who must think he would know her if he saw her face or heard her true voice. A woman he must have known at some point in his life—that much was obvious by how well she seemed to know his dating habits. Several times he'd looked at her and caught a glimpse of the truth. But it had been just out of reach, too far away to grab hold of. Nevertheless, there was something very dear, very familiar about this woman.

He heaped a platter with roast beef sandwiches on kaiser rolls, surrounded them with some healthy raw veggies, cheese, pickles, and a bag of potato chips. Then he grabbed a couple of cans of soda and carried the mess of it back into the bedroom.

But when he got there, she was gone. The only thing on his pillow, where her incredible mass of silken hair had been, was a note.

He set the tray down, and picked the note up, feeling like Prince Charming picking up a lone glass slipper.

> It really was just the mask, Richard. The woman behind it isn't the least bit interesting to you. Believe me, I know this to be true. You've told me yourself . . . without saying a word. Remember this night for what it was: a Valentine from a secret admirer—and a dream come true for a lonely woman. I'll never forget it.
>
> Love,
> Valentine

He blinked down at the signature, the handwriting. It was a scrawl he knew, too familiar to be forgotten.

"Oh my God," he whispered, holding the note against his chest as his heart turned over and his blood rushed to his feet. "Miss Biswell!"

Four

"Where in the name of sin have you *been*?" Kayla had come off the sofa as if she'd been shot out of a cannon the second Martha Jane stepped through the apartment door. "I've been worried sick! I called everywhere. Even the police, but they said you had to be gone for forty-eight hours before they could—" She stopped, her eyes widening as Martha Jane shrugged off the too big jacket she'd *borrowed* from Richard's place. "Omigod, you're still wearing . . . Martha Jane, what *happened* to you last night?"

Martha Jane sighed. She wondered if she looked as shell-shocked as she felt. "I'm not sure. Maybe it was temporary insanity. Or maybe I'm coming down with multiple-personality disorder or something."

"Huh?" Kayla forced the puzzled expression off her face, gripped Martha Jane's shoulders, and dragged her into the nearby bathroom. "Come on, you're a mess. Your makeup is all over your face. Have you been crying? You have, haven't you? God, girl, your hair looks like you just came off a night of wild . . ." She paused there, blinking, leaning closer and peering into Martha Jane's eyes. "No. No way. You didn't . . ."

Martha Jane merely shrugged and looked away.

"You *did*!" Kayla stood there frozen, then shook herself and turned away to start the shower and adjust the water temperature before facing Martha Jane again. "So who was he? You were onstage with me and then you were gone. I went backstage to wait for you, but you never came." Hands on her hips, she stared at Martha Jane accusingly. "You left with some man, didn't you? You walked out of that place, wearing that getup—with some stranger! Are you out of your freaking—"

"No," Martha Jane denied softly. "No, Kayla, not with a stranger. With Richard Gable." Her voice sounded a little dreamy, and when she looked into the mirror she saw that her eyes were rather vacant.

"Richard Gable?" Kayla was behind her now, unbuckling her, stripping the outfit off her the way a big sister would do. She guided Martha Jane into the shower and slid the door closed, and the entire time she never stopped talking. "*Richard Gable?* As in your ex-boss? The guy who fired you so he could hire some bimbo? The guy you've been secretly in love with for almost a year?"

Martha Jane yanked the sliding door open. "I am *not* secretly in love with him!" She slammed it shut again.

"No, you're not, 'cause it's sure as hell no secret now!"

"Yes, actually, it is." Martha Jane sighed and turned her face up to the warm, soothing spray. "Kayla, it was . . . it was so . . . so *exciting*!"

"But . . . but . . . he . . . you . . ."

Martha Jane yanked the stall door open again. "He never knew it was me! It was the mask. And I don't know, I felt . . . freer somehow. Like I could do anything, be anyone I wanted to be—just like you said."

"Yeah?" Kayla tilted her head to one side. "So who *were* you?"

Martha Jane felt her cheeks heat, and she pressed her hands to them as a trill of laughter escaped her lips.

"My God, you *giggled*. I've never heard you giggle in my life. What did that man do to you?"

"Just about everything, I think." Martha Jane slid the doors closed again and ducked her head beneath the rush of water. "It was the most incredible night of my life," she said, water running down her face. She washed her hair and soaped her body, then stood there clean and refreshed, just letting the hot water rush over her.

Suddenly there was an urgent pounding on the apartment door. Martha Jane just continued basking in the afterglow, relaxing in the shower spray. So much to think about. She wondered about this new part of herself—a part she'd never in her wildest dreams expected to find. Kayla sighed and left the bathroom. Martha Jane heard voices, but she didn't let them intrude. She conditioned her hair and rinsed it under the spray. But then the voices got louder and broke into her lovely state of being.

Cranking the water off, she stepped out of the shower and wrapped herself in a big terry robe.

"How did you even find out where I live?" Kayla asked in an overly loud voice, sounding slightly nervous. It was as if she were *deliberately* speaking at high volume. Martha Jane reached for the bathroom doorknob as Kayla went on. "I mean . . . I wasn't expecting company, *Mr. Gable*."

"Omigod," Martha Jane whispered. She jerked her hand away from the doorknob as if it had burned her. "He's here!"

"Um . . . your address was on your business cards," Richard said, sounding a bit confused at Kayla's behavior. "Everyone who attended the show got one. Surely you knew that?"

"Well . . . well, of course I did. But I thought anyone who wanted to order from me would . . . would call, not drop by unannounced." Then she paused. "Wait a minute—is that why you're here? Do you want to . . . order my line?"

Curious, Martha Jane gripped the doorknob again, turned it, and opened the door just a crack to peer through.

"Well, why else would I be here?" Richard asked.

Martha Jane gasped, pressing a hand to her mouth to cover the sound. In the next room, Kayla looked stunned.

"I expected to find an office, not an apartment," Richard was saying. "I am truly sorry if this is an inconvenience, but if you want to be in business, you really shouldn't greet the customers with open hostility."

Martha Jane closed her eyes. That one had to hurt, even though Richard had said it in his charming, teasing tone. Kayla huffed, gaped, and started over. "We're . . . in the process of . . . relocating our . . . er . . . headquarters," she said.

Martha Jane could almost see Richard's reluctant smile. "Just starting out, huh? Well, you've got nothing to worry about. By the end of the day, you'll have more orders than you can handle. Including a hefty one from Gable Brothers."

"I . . . will?"

"Absolutely."

"Well, I . . ." Kayla clasped her hands together. Probably to keep from high-fiving him, Martha Jane thought. "Thank you. Thank you so much!"

"No need to thank me. It's business. Your clothes are going to make my stores a lot of money. But, uh, that's not the *entire* reason I'm here."

It's not? Martha Jane thought.

"It's not?" Kayla asked.

"No. I, um, I'm trying to track down the, uh, the model you used last night. And I thought—"

"Oh, well, um, you know that's strictly against policy. I mean, no designer in the biz would—well, you know that, Mr. Gable. You've worked in this business long enough to know we absolutely have to protect our models' privacy."

"Well, sure, but she *wasn't* a model. Not really."

Martha Jane gripped the doorknob so hard her knuckles turned white.

"I paid her to walk down a runway wearing my clothes," Kayla said, her voice dry. "Or do you have some other definition of what constitutes professional modeling?"

"Look, I need to speak to her. It's important."

"Well, I'm just not sure I . . ."

Martha Jane opened the door and stepped out. "Mr. Gable?" she asked, feigning surprise. "I *thought* that was your voice I heard. How are you?"

He looked at her in surprise—or she thought it was surprise. But then again, there was something utterly false about it. As if he'd been expecting her to pop in long before she had. But then he smiled broadly. "Martha Jane! I didn't know you lived here! You two are . . . roommates, then?"

Martha Jane nodded.

"How are you?" Richard asked. "I can't tell you how much I've missed you at the office."

Kayla snorted and turned her head.

"Oh, I'm sure Buffy is doing a fine job," Martha Jane managed.

"Uh . . . it's Babbette. And no, she's not half the secretary you were." He shook his head. "If I'd had any choice in the matter, you'd still be there. But, you know that."

"Bimbette has that much control over you, does she?" Kayla drawled.

Richard grinned, shaking his head, either not hearing the not-too-subtle slam in Kayla's tone or pretending not to. "It's Babbette, and she has me wrapped around her little finger, I'm afraid." Martha Jane almost winced. God, he might as well poke her with sharp sticks. "But remember my offer, Martha Jane. I can move you into any department you want, and give you a pay raise to boot. Just say the word."

She opened her mouth.

Kayla spoke first. "Oh, you'll just have to fill those slots with more like Boobette," she said brightly.

"Babbette," Richard corrected.

"Whatever." Kayla waved a hand dismissively. "Martha Jane is working with me now. In fact, she's my second in command. She's way too good to be any man's secretary. Especially a man who'd replace her with some little—"

"Kayla." Martha Jane said it firmly but not loudly. "Richard is our first paying *customer*. I'm sure he's not here to discuss his secretary with us."

Kayla fell silent, and even looked a little apologetic.

Richard looked right into Martha Jane's eyes and said, "I had no idea you were a part of this clothing line." Then he held out a hand. "Well, then, let me be the first to say congratulations, Martha Jane."

"But we haven't even—"

"I imagine your venture—Leather and Lace, isn't it?" Kayla nodded fast when he glanced her way, then he went on, "It's going to be as big as Victoria's Secret. I'd bet money on it, and believe me, I know about these things."

Martha Jane looked past him at Kayla, whose eyes got wider.

"Now, back to the subject at hand. This model . . ."

"I'm sorry," Kayla began.

"I can get a message to her," Martha Jane interrupted quickly.

"You can?"

She nodded.

"You know her, then?"

"Yes. But I can't tell you anything about her. I mean, I'd have to ask her first, and . . . so why don't you just give me the message and I'll pass it along?"

He shook his head slowly. "Is there anything you *can't* do, Martha Jane?"

She shrugged and tried not to blush with pleasure. "I don't suppose I'd be very good at modeling lingerie," she said. Meanwhile, she ignored Kayla, who was staring at her over Richard's shoulder as if she'd grown horns.

Instead of saying anything more, she went to the telephone stand and picked up the pad of paper and pen that lay there. "Here you go, Mr. Gable," she said. "Just jot down what you want to say, and I'll see that she gets it."

He smiled brilliantly and took the pad from her. His fingers brushed hers, and for just a second his eyes, sparkling with some unnamed intensity, met hers and held them. She had to look away. He was probably just thinking of his masked lover. Martha Jane Biswell was the furthest thing from his mind. Finally he began writing. He wrote for a long time, paused, licked his lips, and wrote some more. Then he tore the sheet off, folded it, and handed it to Martha Jane. "Now, this is for her eyes only. Okay?"

"You can trust me, Mr. Gable."

"I know I can," he murmured. "Martha Jane, in all the time you worked for me, didn't I ever once tell you to call me Richard?"

Lifting her head, she met his gaze. Still intense, still probing. His eyes this morning seemed to be examining her, over and over again, as if he'd never seen her before. "No," she answered him honestly. "You never did."

"I was an idiot, then." He closed his hand over hers, around the note. "Thank you, Martha Jane. This means a lot to me." Then he leaned closer and pressed his lips to her cheek. It was, she thought, the most intimate cheek kiss she'd ever had. Long, and tender. Then he turned to Kayla. "And again, congratulations on your success. The buyers from Gable Brothers will be calling you later on today to officially place that order."

"Thank you, Mr. Gable."

He nodded, smiling, then turned and left the apartment, but as they pushed the door closed, he put a hand out, holding it open.

"Your morning paper is here," he said, bending to pick it up and hand it in to them. "I've already seen mine. You might want to check out the fashion section."

Then he nodded good-bye and pulled the door closed behind him.

Kayla's wide eyes met Martha Jane's. "Fashion section?" Kayla whispered. Her hands were shaking as she pushed the newspaper at Martha. "You do it! I can't!" Martha Jane took the newspaper, knelt on the floor, and began flipping through it.

She didn't have to look far. A full-color photo of Kayla and Martha Jane, wearing their angel and devil numbers, side by side, center stage, covered the front page. Above it was the banner headline NEWCOMER KAYLA HART, LINGERIE'S HOTTEST NEW STAR!

The two women, squealing with laughter, hugged each other and danced in circles.

Just outside the door, Richard went still as he heard the sound of his mystery lady's laughter. He waited, listening, unable to move away.

"But why did you go and tell him I was working with you?" He heard Martha Jane ask.

"Because you were about to take him up on the job offer! I could see it in your eyes, Martha Jane. And you're too good for a man who'd fire you just to give one of his floozies a job. Way too good."

Martha Jane lowered her voice. "He's not as bad as all that."

"Oh, no? He's bad enough that he doesn't even look at you as a woman. My God, he stood right here and didn't even know you were the same one he spent the night with. The same one he's driving himself crazy trying to find now. He's shallow, Martha Jane. He's a Neanderthal who's convinced himself that a decent, intelligent woman can't be sexy and that a sexy woman can't be decent or intelligent. Besides, you don't need to take his job offer now. If what this fashion editor says turns out to be even close to the truth, we're both gonna end up millionaires, honey. Men like Richard Gable will be looking at you in a whole new way—and you won't have to fall at their feet in your underwear to get them to do it, either."

Martha Jane sighed loudly. "I don't really *want* any other man looking at me that way. But the rest sounds great."

Richard stepped away from the door slowly, feeling more confused than he ever had in his life. More rotten and selfish and shallow, too. Kayla had him nailed. "She's right," he whispered. "I've been the world's biggest, blindest fool. But damned if I know how to make it up to her. Or if I should even try." He shrugged, pushing his hands into his pockets, and walked back down the hall. If he let Martha Jane know how special he thought she was, she might get the wrong idea. She might think he was serious about this thing, that he wanted—he swallowed hard—a *relationship*.

Hell, maybe it was better to pretend he didn't know her identity. But one thing was certain. He *had* to see her again. He had to.

Five

While Kayla took her turn in the shower, Martha Jane slipped into her bedroom, closed the door, put on her glasses, and took Richard's note from her pocket.

> Valentine,
>
> I have to see you again. I've never met anyone like you before, and I want to know you. I'm not talking about sharing secrets here, or even unmasking you. But . . . you fascinate me. And I want to see you again. No more than that. Meet me tonight, at midnight, at the fountain in the park. I'll be there. I'll wait for you.
>
> Richard

Martha Jane stared at the note, striving to read more into it than what was there. What did it mean? Why would he want to meet her outdoors, in the middle of February? She couldn't very well show up in a negligee there. What did he want from her? She swallowed hard, trying with everything in her not to believe she meant any more to him than any of his other one-night stands. She knew her ex-boss. She'd seen him go through women like selections on a dessert tray. A different flavor every time. She was no more to him than a new flavor. If she let herself think she was, she'd be in for a broken heart.

Besides, the note made it pretty clear. It was one more round of sex he wanted. Nothing more. At least he hadn't written "bring the handcuffs."

Kayla was right. He really was a bastard. Martha Jane swallowed hard. She loved the bastard. Had for months now.

The telephone shrilled, breaking into her thoughts. Absently, she reached for it. "Hello?"

"Um, yes, I was trying to reach Leather and Lace?"

Oh, hell! That didn't sound very professional, did it? What was she thinking? "I'm sorry, you must have dialed the wrong number," she lied.

"Oh. Sorry to bother you." Click.

Two seconds later the telephone rang again. She took a deep breath, let it ring twice more, then picked it up and put on her best secretary voice. Crisp and efficient. "Leather and Lace, please hold."

She covered the mouthpiece with her hand, counted slowly to ten, then came back. "I'm sorry for the delay," she said. "How may I direct your call?"

"This is Boudoir Boutique," the female voice replied. "And I'm calling to order your line of lingerie."

"One moment, please."

She reached for something to write on, smiling ear to ear. But as she was in the middle of jotting down the boutique's list, the Call Waiting beeped and she had to put the first caller on hold. It was another chain, placing another order. And Gable Brothers hadn't even called yet.

Martha Jane bit her lip, kept her cool, and took down the information.

Kayla came out of the bathroom wrapped in a big robe, and

Martha Jane put down the phone. "The newspaper and Richard were right," she exclaimed. "We've got to get in gear, Kayla. We need office space, and a secretary, and another computer, just for starters. Then we need to go through the offers from manufacturers, find the best bid, and get this line into mass production."

Kayla was frowning, shaking her head. Not getting it.

"Kayla, hon, we just got orders from two chains, for almost a thousand items, and Gable's hasn't even called yet, and—"

The phone shrilled again.

"Leather and Lace, may I help you?" Martha Jane said. "I'm sorry, can you say that again? Twenty-five sets of the entire collection? Oh, for each store? And how many stores would that be, Mr.—" She bit her lip. "A hundred and one, you say?"

Kayla smacked her palm on her forehead. "I'm not ready for this!" she exclaimed as Martha Jane jotted the order on the back of an overdue electric bill.

"Well, you'd better *get* ready, kid. 'Cause we're in business. Listen, can you man the phones?"

"I guess so, but I—"

"Good. I'm going to get us some help. See you in an hour."

Martha Jane ran back into her room, shaking off the remnants of that other woman she'd briefly become. It wasn't difficult. She tossed on a sensible suit, pinned up her hair, and looked in the mirror to see the logical, dependable Miss Biswell looking back at her. Even if she *did* seem to have a new sparkle in her eyes. Sending herself a secret smile, Martha Jane headed out of the apartment at a brisk pace.

Richard sat in his office, a cup of coffee in his still-shaking hand, and told his brother about his date—minus the more personal details—with the mystery lady who turned out to be his own efficient, prim, and proper Miss Biswell.

Michael sat in a chair across from him, and all he did was shrug.

"So what part of this surprises you, Richard? That Martha Jane is a knockout? That she is an actual woman? You're telling me you never noticed it before?"

"Oh, come on, Michael! She wears blazers and—and *tweed*. And those big glasses. And her hair is always—"

"So she doesn't go around the office in a thong and a bustier," Michael said. "It might surprise you to learn this, little brother, but most women don't."

"I just never . . ."

"Bothered to give her a second glance," Michael said, shaking his head. "I just wish I'd realized she was nursing a crush on you, Richard."

"Why?"

"*Why?* Why do you think? Must have been like a slap in the face when you told her you were letting her go so we could hire our niece."

Richard sighed. "She doesn't even realize Babs *is* our niece. I think she believes she's one of my . . . you know."

"Oh, hell. No wonder she threw your job offer back in your face."

Richard lowered his head. "All this time, she was a few yards away from me, day in and day out. And I never got to know her at all. I mean, there's so much more to the woman than meets the eye."

"What, just because she's fun in bed?"

Richard's head came up sharply, and he fixed his brother with a stern glare. "Don't even— That wasn't what I meant, and you know it. She's . . . she's funny. And sexy. And smart. She's an entrepreneur, for crying out loud. And all this time I thought she was just . . ."

"Just a secretary," Michael finished for him. "So does this mean you're considering . . . an actual relationship?"

Richard frowned at him. "A second date," he said. "Just a second date. I haven't *entirely* lost my mind."

The buzzer on Richard's desk sounded and he heard a familiar titter that set his teeth on edge. "Oh, Riiiicharrd . . ." Babs sang out over the intercom.

He sighed heavily. "What is it, Babs?"

"There's a lady here to see you," she said. Then she whispered, "And she's kinda cute, but not very friendly."

"Does she have a name?"

"Well, of course she does, silly!" Babs giggled again.

Richard clenched his teeth. But then another voice came, one so familiar his heart ached with missing its soothing sound on the other end of an intercom. "Richard, it's Martha Jane, and it's important."

He looked up and met his brother's eyes, his own widening. "You know nothing, you understand? She still thinks I don't know it was her last night, and I want to keep it that way."

"Why, for the love of God?"

He opened his mouth, closed it, shook his head. "Damned if I know. Because I can't think of anything else to do at the moment."

Michael rolled his eyes, and Richard went to the office door, opened it, and saw Martha Jane standing there, looking at Babs with blatant disapproval. He felt lower than pond slime. "Martha Jane," he said. "I didn't expect to see you again so soon. I see you've met Babs."

"Yes."

"She's uh . . . our niece."

Martha Jane looked at him with one eyebrow raised. "Of course she is."

"Hi, Martha Jane," Michael said, coming out of the office. Then he looked at his brother, and Richard tried to send him a plea for help without saying anything out loud.

Michael sighed and glanced at his niece. "Babs, are you and your mom still coming to our place for dinner on Sunday? Cindy's been planning all week."

Babs smiled from ear to ear. "Sure are, Uncle Mike. We still having that special roasted chicken Aunt Cindy makes?"

"Absolutely." He sent a wink at Martha Jane. "My sister's been trying to get that secret recipe out of my wife for months. Maybe she'll succeed this time." Then he sauntered away, and Richard sent a silent thank-you after him.

Martha Jane was blinking, looking from Babs to Richard again and again. "You mean . . . she *really* is your niece?"

Richard bit his lip to keep from saying anything rude in front of Babs. Instead he took Martha Jane's elbow and led her into his office, closing the door before he spoke. "Martha Jane, I had no choice but to give her the job. No one else in the company would have put up with her. And with Michael's secretary six months from retirement, we couldn't very well—"

She held up a hand. "It's okay. I . . . understand."

"It's not okay. It wasn't fair, and believe me I've been suffering for it every minute of every day since you've been gone."

He watched her battle a smile. The smile finally won. "I know. I heard her on the intercom." The smile grew into the soft, sultry laugh he'd become enchanted with last night. "I was thinking it served you right."

He nodded, studying her. Those eyes, dark and mysterious. The makeup had only enhanced what was already there. And the mask had just made her eyes even more noticeable. But when he looked into them now, he saw that she was the same woman . . . the same beautiful, sexy woman he'd spent the night with. It was all there. He'd just never looked deeply enough to see it.

He wanted her so much it hurt!

"I came here to ask for your help, Richard. Kayla's getting swamped with orders already this morning, and we just—well, we weren't ready for it."

He nodded at a chair, and she sat down. He didn't. He hovered close by, not wanting to move too far from her. Why hadn't he noticed before how gracefully she moved? She crossed her legs, nylons whispering as her thighs brushed each other. Richard's blood was running hot, and he had to clear his throat before he could speak again. "So what can I do?"

"Well, we need to get some office space set up, put in a computer, get some phone lines turned on . . . not to mention see the bank, get our line of credit raised, and write a big fat check to a manufacturer so they can start sewing. The problem is, we need someone at the apartment manning the phones while we do all that."

"And?"

"And we don't have time to interview secretaries. I was hoping we could borrow one of yours."

He looked at her and smiled.

She looked right back, her head tilting up to do it, and he could see that she read him loud and clear. "No. Not Babbette."

"Well, it was worth a try," he said, grinning back at her.

And then her smile died and she was frowning at him. "What's going on with you today, Richard?"

He blinked down at her. "What?"

"You're . . . different. Almost . . . playful."

He drew a breath, then took the time to walk back to his desk while formulating a response to that. She was right, he realized. At work, he was usually brusque and businesslike. Not relaxed and teasing, as he was with her today. But then again, she was usually stiff and tense with him. She was different today, too.

He took his seat, folded his hands on his desk. "You seem a bit more relaxed today yourself," he told her.

She smiled, and her cheeks got pinker as she averted her eyes. "Well, I'm no longer your employee. I suppose that makes a difference."

"Was I that tough to work for?"

She shrugged. "Obviously your new secretary agrees with you. She's certainly improved your mood."

"She's driving me insane," he blurted. "The only thing improving my mood is what happened to me last night." He clamped his mouth closed.

Too late. Martha Jane had popped out of her chair so fast you'd have thought he'd electrocuted her. "That's really none of my—"

"This one was . . . different." He wasn't sure why he said it. Maybe just to see how she'd react. But then, it didn't matter, because he couldn't tell how she was reacting. She just went very still, her face frozen and expressionless.

"How was she . . . different?"

He watched her standing there in front of her chair, looking ready to run. "She had a brain, for starters. She . . . made me laugh. I talked to her, you know what I mean? I don't usually talk to the women I date. But this one, this one made me want to talk to her."

"Really?"

He nodded.

"What did she look like, this . . . this woman?" She had turned now, paced softly over to the windows and pretended great interest in the traffic below.

"She was beautiful. But not in the way the others have been. She wasn't tall or reed-thin. In fact, she must have been similar to you, physically speaking."

She didn't reply to that.

"I never saw her face fully, you know. She . . . she wore a mask."

"How mysterious," Martha Jane whispered. "I suppose that's why you're really so intrigued, Richard. Not because of the woman, but because of the mystery she presents."

"Funny, she suggested the same thing. But no. No, I don't think that's it at all." He walked over to where Martha Jane stood in her tweed skirt and white blouse and color-coordinated blazer. Her hair was in a neat bun, and her eyes hid behind big tortoiseshell glasses. He stood very close behind her, and felt her body stiffen, and heat.

"Suppose she wore that mask because she has some horrible scar on her face? Or is missing an eye or something?" Her voice trembled as she spoke.

"I thought of that. And you know what? It didn't matter. In fact, this morning when I woke up and thought back on the night, it hit me that for the first time in my life, what a woman looked like didn't matter in the least to me."

"I don't believe that for a minute, Richard. And I don't think you do either."

"Don't I?"

She turned to face him. "Oh, no. Tell me, what was this mystery woman wearing besides a mask? Something revealing? Something that told you she was the sex-kitten, one-night-stand type of girl you always go for? Would you have noticed her at all if she'd been wearing something else? Something like . . . oh, say, like this?" She spread her hands, palms up, down the front of her, indicating her outfit.

"If I hadn't, it would have been my mistake. My loss."

She held his gaze, her eyes probing. "So how special is she?" she asked flat out. "Special enough to make you want to give up all the others and take her home to the family? Hmm? Or just special enough that you'd like a replay of last night?"

He swallowed hard, feeling as if she'd driven a dagger through his heart to the hilt. "I just want to see her again," he muttered.

"And what makes you think *she* wants to see *you* again?"

He looked up fast, meeting her eyes. "Doesn't she?" he asked, startled at the very thought.

Martha Jane looked away quickly. "I don't know. I haven't . . . spoken to her yet. And I . . . I think we got a bit off the subject here."

"I guess we did." He took a step away from her, just to put

some distance between them. She had him off balance. Confused. Uncertain. And that wasn't good. He didn't like it one bit. He could see that it wasn't going to be easy to convince his prim Miss Biswell to see him again. No. Not when she seemed to think there was something wrong with a casual relationship like the one he had in mind. Sex wasn't going to be the answer to this, either—never mind how unbelievably great it was. He gave his head a shake, having no clue what to do. Best to get back to the subject at hand, give himself time to think, to regroup.

"You wanted to borrow a secretary—but not Babs," he said. "Who did you have in mind?"

"Mrs. Nye," she said, seeming relieved to be back on safer ground.

"Done." He said it without giving it a second thought.

Her brows went up. "Just like that?"

"Just like that." He racked his brain for something to say, because she looked toward the door, and he knew she was thinking about leaving, and he really didn't want her to do that. Not unless he went with her.

What the hell was wrong with him?

"I'll need a few minutes," he heard himself saying. "Then I'll bring her over to your place myself."

Martha Jane blinked, licked her lips. And Richard wondered why he'd never noticed how full and sensual those lips were, until last night. Hell, they were even just the tiniest bit swollen this morning. He could still taste them.

"You don't need to do all that," she said.

"But I want to. In fact, I'm taking the rest of the day off and spending it with you and Kayla. I'm an old hand at business matters. I can be a lot of help to you two."

"But, um, I mean—that's just not . . . What will your brother do without his partner *or* his secretary?"

"Oh, never fear. He can have my secretary for the day." Richard wiggled his eyebrows, relaxing again now that *she* seemed to be the one off balance. "Babs to the rescue."

Martha Jane's smile appeared like sunshine on a cloudy day, and her eyes sparkled up at him. Damn, so much for his ability to relax a little. Surely she was more beautiful this morning than she'd ever been before. She couldn't *possibly* have been this incredible before.

But she had been. She always had been. He'd been stepping over a diamond to pick up bits of glass, and he hadn't even noticed.

Six

Martha Jane was feeling as if she'd stepped out of the ordinary world into some parallel dimension, where nothing was as it should be. By the time she got back to the apartment, Kayla had promoted herself from bathrobe and towel to a sexy red suit and from scribbling on the backs of old bills to keying them in on her laptop computer. She was typing in orders slowly, still not up to speed on the software she'd bought for "someday."

Martha Jane barely had time to explain what was going on, when Richard arrived with Mrs. Nye in tow. The older woman knew the program backward and forward, she assured Kayla, and she sent the three of them on their way.

The first stop they made was the bank. And that was where Martha Jane finally realized that her life was never going to be the same again. Because they didn't get stuck in a hard chair in the lobby, only to be led later to one of the cubicles out there. No. They were taken straight through the doors in the back and into a real office, where a fat man who smelled like cigars smiled at them as if they were his best friends.

He listened to their plans but didn't make any notes. And when they left his office, they had an unlimited line of credit.

Unlimited.

Kayla was smiling all over, and Martha Jane couldn't quite absorb it. She blinked in the sunlight outside the bank, and still couldn't digest it all.

"I have a suggestion, if you want to hear it," Richard said.

"Shoot! You suggest to your heart's content," Kayla said. "I'm too excited even to think straight."

"Well, the top floor of my building is vacant. We've been planning to lease it to local businesses, but the remodeling just wrapped up last week, so no one's even seen it yet. I'll tell you, there are some great suites up there."

Martha Jane shook her head and said automatically, "Richard, we can't afford . . ." But she let the words die as she met Kayla's eyes. "*Can* we?"

Richard smiled at her in a very un-ex-boss-like manner. "Yeah, you can," he said. "Ladies, the orders you've taken this morning alone are . . . well, here. Just off the top of my head"—he yanked a calculator out of his jacket pocket and began punching in numbers, muttering as he went—"let's see, you've got orders for about, what, four thousand pieces?" Click, click, click. "I can make an educated guess what it will cost to produce them, and I know what you're charging for them—it was on the program from the show." Click, click click. Then he turned the little screen to face them. "Here's your profit for this morning's orders. Roughly."

Kayla looked at it, then looked again.

"So—do you think you can afford office space?"

Kayla looked at Martha Jane. Martha Jane looked at Kayla. They both smiled.

For the rest of the morning, Richard helped them get their offices set up on the top floor of the Gable Brothers Building. Martha Jane, despite her lengthy list of things to do, found herself pausing often just to watch him. He was like a different man. Or maybe she was just seeing him as he really was for the first time. Before, he'd been her boss, her dream, a fantasy beyond her reach. Now, he was just . . . a man.

He'd taken off his jacket and his tie. His shirtsleeves were rolled up to the elbows, and she couldn't help staring at his forearms at every opportunity. Strong. Tanned. Dusted with hair. Flexing when he lugged office furniture right along with the deliverymen. She watched him when he crouched behind desks, hooking up computer cables, too. Because she knew the shape and feel of his backside, his thighs, and she couldn't help remembering.

He was amazing.

It wasn't fair, Martha Jane thought, that he should turn out to be even more wonderful than she'd thought. She was eating her heart out. Oh, sure, he'd said all those sweet things about his mystery date. But he hadn't known she was plain old Martha Jane.

"So, this desk is for your office, right?"

Richard's voice was soft and close to her ear, and it startled her so much that she jumped. He just smiled and laid a calming hand on her shoulder. "Sorry. You must have been a million miles away."

"I—yes, I was thinking."

"About what?"

His eyes . . . they were so dark and deep, so knowing as they probed hers. Oh, but that was ridiculous. He couldn't know. She'd die if she thought he knew!

"Why did you stop drawing?" she asked.

He tilted his head to one side, those dark eyes on hers like a touch. "Now, how did you know I ever *did* any drawing?"

"I . . . I guess . . . I must have heard someone mention it around the office. Your brother, maybe." She spoke fast, wishing she could grab the words from the air and shove them back into her mouth. Stupid, stupid, stupid!

But he only shrugged. "I don't know why I stopped. But it's funny you should ask me now that I've started again."

She blinked twice. "You have?"

"Maybe I just hadn't come across anything worth drawing in a while."

They stood in what would be the reception area of the office suite. The door behind them led to the hall and the rest of the building. The one on the left wall led to what would be Kayla's office, and the one on the back wall to her studio, where Kayla was already ensconced and having the time of her life. The double doorway on the right led to the office that would be Martha Jane's. That was the one Richard had been referring to, and the one he was heading into even now.

"Oh, this is going to be great," he said. He stood beside the open doorway until she came in, and then he closed it. "Look at the view."

The entire outer wall was windows, floor to ceiling. "Oh!" she breathed. "My goodness. It's like sitting on a mountaintop throne, with the whole city at my feet," she said. "I'm never going to want curtains in here, or blinds, or anything like that."

Richard smiled at her. "In that case, you're going to want your desk—" He pointed. "Over here, I think, is best." As he spoke he walked to the spot. "You can't really have your back to the door, and if you have the windows behind you, then the glare on the computer screen will make it invisible most of the day. So, here."

"It's perfect."

He smiled, walked back into the reception area, and easily pushed the padding-wrapped desk through the double doors and across the carpet into the proper spot. Then he sat on the floor and began snipping the packing tape and padding away from the sides. With a sigh, Martha Jane began to do the same with the foam and tape covering her chair.

"So what else are you going to put in here?" he asked her.

"I can't believe you'd really want to know," she said.

"Well, believe it. The way you decorate your office says a lot about who you are."

"You think so?"

"Sure."

Martha Jane looked at him quizzically. "Then what does your choice of office decor say about you?" she asked. "You've got all these extreme-type photographs, blown up and framed on every wall. The hang glider, the rock climber, the windsurfer . . ."

"All the things I wanted to do before I got too old," he explained.

She lifted her brows in surprise. "And did you?"

"What is that, some crack about my age?" He grinned at her, and she shook her head. "Yes, I've done them all. Often enough that they bored me. Everything's seemed to bore me for a while now." Then he looked at her. "Well, until lately."

She cleared her throat and changed the subject. "What about that birdcage you have hanging in the corner with the stuffed parrot inside?"

"That? Oh, that's there to remind me never to let myself be caged."

"Like your brother?"

Richard nodded slowly. "That was the idea I had when I put the bird up, yes."

She averted her gaze. She was right—he would never change.

"So, you didn't tell me—what are you going to put in your office?"

She looked around the room, thought about her life. "I want a print behind the desk, there. I saw one last week that I haven't been able to get out of my mind. A woman with three faces, each one representing some different part of her personality."

"I've seen that piece," he said. "So you'll put it here to remind people that there's more to you than what they see?"

She shook her head slowly. "To remind myself. I've been living a one-dimensional life for a long time. I didn't even know there was more to me, until— Anyway, I don't want to forget again."

He muttered something that sounded like, "I don't plan to let you."

She turned quickly, frowning at him. "What?"

"I said, uh, what would you like me to get you? As an office-warming present."

She shrugged. "You don't have to get me anything at all."

"Well, of course I do," he said, as if it bore no argument. "What else do you have in mind?"

"Oh, I don't know. Lots of plants, I suppose. Maybe an aquarium. And by the windows I want a giant rock."

"A rock?"

"Mm-hmm. A pretty one. I saw one in a shop once, amethyst spikes all over one side of it. All pointy and sparkly purple. It would catch the sun in these windows and shine like a diamond."

"And why would you want a rock in your office? Does that have some significance too?"

She nodded. "To remind me that what I want in life is security and stability. Permanence. The occasional walk on the wild side is one thing, but I wouldn't want to lose sight of what I really want."

"Walk on the wild side?" he asked. He looked surprised . . . but the expression seemed contrived somehow. As if he were teasing her. "I never would have guessed."

She shrugged. "Maybe I should borrow some of your extreme prints," she said with a smile. "There are a lot of things I've never done that I intend to try. Rock climbing, hang gliding . . ." She could have sworn he shuddered.

"Those things are dangerous, Martha Jane. Besides, I thought you said you wanted stability and permanence."

"But I don't have them yet," she said, smiling a little bit, thinking again about the night they'd shared. "So why shouldn't I go for the thrills in the meantime?" Then she frowned. "Besides, who's to say a person can't have both?"

Richard stood there looking at her as if she'd just confessed to selling government secrets to China. Finally, he shook his head. "Tell you what. If you really want to try any extreme sports, you just say so. I'll take you myself. At least that way I can make sure you don't break your pretty neck."

She looked at him and tilted her head to one side. One hand flew to her neck automatically, fingers trailing over her pulse point.

"What's wrong?" he asked, an almost smile tugging at his lips, his eyes, once again, holding that gleam that could give her chills. "Haven't I ever told you that you have a pretty neck before, Martha Jane?"

She swallowed the lump in her throat.

"You do, you know."

Was he . . . flirting with her? With plain Martha Jane Biswell? No. This was all in her head. He'd awakened some primal, sex-craving part of her last night, and that was where all these false impressions were coming from. She was being ridiculous. She had known what last night was before it even began. An adventure, like one of his extreme sports. Dangerous, and thrilling, and very, very brief. A one-night stand. Over and done. It meant nothing to him. *She* meant nothing to him, not as Valentine and certainly not as Martha Jane Biswell. He wouldn't give his former secretary a second glance.

And it would really, *really* be a huge mistake to see him again tonight. A huge mistake.

Oh, but dammit, how she wanted to. Stability and permanence were fine. But she didn't have them yet. She'd only been teasing him but now she wondered—what would be so wrong about taking just one more thrill ride?

Seven

He didn't think she was going to show up. He almost hoped she wouldn't. Because she'd scared him today with all her talk of stability and permanence. He knew what she meant. One man, one woman, and one whopper of a commitment. He knew himself too well to think he could be happy with that kind of an arrangement. So it was probably just as well that she wasn't coming tonight. Better not get too used to her.

Then again—when he'd offered to escort her on those . . . thrill rides, as she called them . . . he'd meant it. The things that had become boring to him had taken on a new allure when he thought of doing them with her. And maybe that was what she'd meant about stability *and* excitement. About being able to have both.

No. No, he knew what he wanted and what he didn't want, and it would be best for both of them if he made that clear to her before she got any crazy ideas in her head.

He paced away from the park bench. The fountain was behind him, making so much noise with its incessant splashing that he wouldn't be able to hear her coming if she wore bells on her ankles. Not that she was going to show up, anyway.

"Hello, Richard."

He spun around so fast he almost tipped over.

She kept her voice low, all rough and soft at once, like velvet on tender skin. He knew she did that just so he wouldn't recognize her. But it turned him on nevertheless. Now that he knew her *intimately*, Martha Jane Biswell *always* turned him on. Even in her tweed business suits. Even in the full-length houndstooth-check coat and woolen hat she was bundled in now. Even with her shoulders hunched against the cold and her hands stuffed into her pockets.

He narrowed his eyes on her. It was dark, but . . . oh, God, she was wearing a mask again. A different one this time. Kind of a horn-rimmed number, in black something—velvet, maybe. Another of Kayla's kinky creations, he thought, aching. So she still wasn't ready to let him know who she was. Well, fine. Maybe it was better if he kept up the pretense, just a little longer.

"I didn't think you were coming," he whispered.

"I didn't want to come," she told him. "But I couldn't seem to help myself."

He nodded. "We should talk." He put a hand on her shoulder, walked her back toward the bench, nodded at her to sit down, and she did. He could see her breath, and his own. It was damn cold out here tonight.

She just sat there, waiting.

"I like you," he finally blurted.

She took one hand out of her pocket. A black glove covered it. Her fingertip touched his lapel, trailed slowly down it. "I like you, too."

"Last night was . . . it was incredible. I never . . ."

"Me neither," she whispered.

He closed his hand over hers. Then he stared hard into her eyes. "You aren't . . . all that experienced at this sort of thing."

"So? I thought men liked a bit of innocence in a woman."

"I just want to make sure you know where we stand. I feel bad that we didn't talk about any of this the first time."

She shrugged. "I don't. In fact, I was hoping the second time could be . . . similar."

He looked at her, stared at her, and couldn't believe this was the same woman who'd been discussing office decor with him earlier today. But she was the same. "No," he said. "Look, we're not going to go any further with this until we talk it through. Now I know you probably want different things in life than I do, and so it's only fair that you know up front—"

"I do want different things in life," she said. "But I don't want them from you, Richard. You don't need to worry about that." She smiled at him slowly.

"What the hell is that supposed to mean?"

"Well, you're not exactly the kind of boy a girl would bring home to her mother."

"I'm *not*?"

"Oh, no. But don't take it too hard, Richard. You have your . . . talents."

He stood there, staring, not getting it. What the hell was she doing? Using his own words against him like that?

"I— Look, maybe tonight wasn't such a good idea," he said suddenly. Why not, his mind wanted to know. This was the way he liked it. Wasn't it? One-nighters. No commitment. No expectations.

"Really?" she asked in that sexy whisper. "Well, I can go home, then. If . . . you're sure that's what you want." She got to her feet, and as she did, she let her coat fall open.

He almost fell off the bench onto the ground. She was wearing another of those sinful creations—a tiny scrap of black. He didn't see detail. Just those legs, encased in dark stockings. Those breasts, swelling over the top of the thing.

She smiled softly at him, pulled the coat around her, and tied the sash. "Good-bye, Richard," she said, and she turned and started to walk away.

He lunged after her, caught her shoulders in his hands, and spun her around. "Don't go." His own voice was hoarse, choked.

"Why not?"

He stared down at her, but no words came. He just couldn't think of a damned thing to say—or to do—except . . .

He tugged her against him and covered her mouth with his. And she parted for him, opened to him, arched against him. Hot. The inside of her mouth, her breath, her cheeks. All of her. He scooped her right up off her feet just the way he had before and carried her to the car with his mouth still clamped to hers. And then somehow he managed to open a door and tumble into the vehicle with her. Backseat. Door still open. He didn't give a damn. He landed on top of her, her back across the seat, her legs sticking out the open door, spread, and cradling him in between.

He pushed hard against her, arching his hips. She pushed back, and then she said, "No."

She said it softly, firmly. It hit his brain like ice water. "What?"

"I said no. Not here. Not like this."

He frowned, not quite understanding the woman. What was she trying to do, drive him insane? She pressed against his chest until he sat up, getting slowly off her. "Drive, Richard. Take me to your house."

"Jesus, it's too damn far."

She shrugged. "Then pick someplace closer."

He smiled down at her, liking this bossy new mood. Okay, so maybe she thought he needed a lesson. Whatever. He was going to have her, tonight, soon, wrapped around him hot and tight, and that was really the only thing he could think about right now. He got up and clambered over the front seat, got the car started. He adjusted the mirror so he could see her. Watch her. She sat up and closed the door as he pulled away. She stared back at him in that mirror, never looking away.

He had to look away, of course. He had to watch the traffic or kill them both. But he watched her too. She'd let the coat fall open again . . . just for his viewing pleasure, he was sure.

God, she was hot.

He pulled into the parking garage of the Gable Brothers Building, got out of the car, and yanked open her door. He took her wrist and tugged her out.

"Your office?" she said, sounding scandalized.

He almost quipped, "Or yours," but stopped himself just in time. She still didn't know he knew her. And he had a feeling that was the only reason she felt free enough to play these sexy little games with him. "Yes, baby. My office." He held her hand and ran for the nearest elevator, took it straight up to the ninth floor, and ran almost all the way to his office. He could barely hold his hand still enough to get the key in the lock.

Then he flung the door open, jerked her through it, slammed it closed, and reached for her.

She took a step backward, smiling slowly. "Sit down," she told him.

He was shaking all over, burning and sweating and shivering. He went to the nearest chair, and he sat.

Sweet, innocent little Martha Jane opened the coat and let it fall to the floor. Hell, it was the cat suit. That's what she had on tonight. She reached behind her, snapped off the whiplike tail, and came toward him, sliding it around his neck. She straddled his lap and used the tail to pull his head to her for a kiss. She opened her mouth. She used her tongue.

He damn near exploded.

When she sat back again, she reached down to undo the snaps that held the little suit together between her legs. Then she unfastened his jeans, and freed him, and then she sat down again. And this time, when she did, she took him inside her. Fully, deeply.

Holding him close, she moved over him. She took her time, moving slow, and he was content to hold on and enjoy the ride. She was the best he'd ever had. The best he ever would have.

He kissed her mouth when he exploded inside her.

She screamed his name, tightened around him, convulsed and shuddered, and gripped and finally, slowly, she relaxed. Then she lifted her head lazily, looked him in the eye, and said, "I'm sorry, Richard, but I can't see you anymore."

"What?" He searched her face, panic bubbling up in his chest.

"It's like you said—we want different things out of life. And if I spend all this time with a . . . well, a casual fling, then I'll never find what I *do* want."

"How . . . how do you know *I'm* not what you want?" he asked, amazed he'd even said the words.

She smiled. "I know I'm not what you want. That's enough."

"But what if you are?"

She pressed her lips together, swallowed hard. "You don't even know me."

"No? Well let me take a stab at it, hmm?"

She shrugged as if she could care less.

"I know you were fairly inexperienced until the other night with me. I know you've never done anything like this before in your life. And I know you wouldn't have the guts to let go like this now, if you couldn't hide behind that mask." He studied her. "Am I close?"

She lowered her eyes. "Without the mask, you wouldn't even know me. And if you did, you wouldn't give me a second glance."

She got to her feet, reached for her coat, pulled it on. "This was the last time. I'm the furthest thing from what you want or need. So—"

"So you're saying good-bye."

"I'm afraid so."

He opened his mouth, then closed it, and told himself not to do anything rash. He needed to think. He needed to approach this thing just right. He didn't want to let her go—but she wouldn't be gone. Not really. "I'll find you, you know," he said.

She shook her head.

"I will. Don't be surprised if you find out that . . . that I'm not the man you think I am."

"Of course you are."

"Maybe, maybe not," he told her. "Maybe I'm not even the man I think I am."

Eight

"This is— I don't— I'm stunned."

Martha Jane stood in the reception area, staring through the open door into her office. She and Kayla had come in early Monday morning, eager to get things up and running. Martha Jane had been secretly glad, thinking there would be less chance of running into Richard this way.

He'd said he wanted to see her again. But it wasn't *her* he wanted. It was his sex kitten. His fantasy lover. And part of what he liked about her was that she expected nothing from him.

Well, she had let him know that nothing wasn't quite enough. And she imagined he probably thought he'd had a narrow escape once he'd had time to give it any thought at all.

It had been a mistake to see him again Saturday night, just as she had known it would be. She might have convinced herself that one more night of passion with Richard would be anything less than shattering to her, but she knew better. Had known better all along. It only made her ache more for him than she already had. And as for that mean streak that had driven her to strike back just a little bit—to show him two could play the "let's-not-get-serious" game—well, that had blown up in her face, hadn't it? Because she still wanted him. She'd barely slept all weekend, and she'd done some crying too, which was totally unlike her.

Even more unlike her, she'd been thinking maybe she could stand to keep seeing him, knowing he would never commit to more than a sexual relationship. Maybe it would be worth it.

She'd been kidding herself, though. It would kill her, and she knew it. She was in love with the man.

At any rate, there had been a surprise waiting for her in her office this morning. She stood in the open doorway, blinking at the huge hunk of amethyst sitting near the bank of windows on the far side of the room. The early-morning sun slanted in on the concave stone, and its crystals glittered as if they were artificially lit from within. Or filled with captive fireflies.

"I can't believe this."

Martha Jane walked closer to the stone. It was waist-high shaped like half an egg split lengthwise and standing on end. The inside of it was a crystal cave of sparkling amethyst. The outside was rough and gray.

"That thing is big enough to crawl inside," Kayla observed from the doorway. "But where did it come from?"

She didn't need to, but Martha Jane bent to pick up the folded sheet of notepaper that lay within the amethyst cluster. "It's beautiful, and it's exciting—*and* it's solid. No wonder you liked it so much. It's just like you." The note was signed with an elaborate "R."

"Well?" Kayla asked.

Licking her lips, Martha Jane said, "It's from Richard." Then, seeing the gleam in her best friend's eyes, she rushed on. "But it doesn't mean anything."

"If it doesn't mean anything, then there will be one just like it in my office. But I'm guessing there isn't." Kayla bounded across the room, snatched the note from Martha Jane's hand, and read it. "Well, well, well! Isn't *that* interesting?"

"He's just repeating something I said to him yesterday."

"Sure, and I'm a natural blonde. Honey, are you *sure* he doesn't know it was you behind that mask?"

Martha Jane's head came up. "Of course I'm sure. God, I couldn't look him in the eye if I wasn't!"

"Sure you could! You've obviously got the man tied up in knots, hon. You don't have a thing to feel self-conscious about."

Martha Jane shrugged. "Anyway, it's over. I told him Saturday night—"

"Told who what, Saturday night?" Richard called from behind a huge box in the doorway. Only the bottoms of his legs and the top of his head were visible.

"What in the world? Here, let me help you with that." Martha Jane rushed forward, grabbed the other end of the box, and together she and Richard lowered it to the floor. Then, straightening, she looked at him, the big box between them. "What are you doing here, Richard?"

"Errands." He smiled at her, looking less like himself than he ever had. He had circles under his eyes and whiskers shadowing his cheeks. His shirt was wrinkled and looked as if he'd been wearing it all night. "A ton of errands, actually. This was just the most recent one." He patted the box. "I was hoping to get it all set up before you arrived, but . . . well, it's been a busy weekend."

"It looks it." She wanted to go to him, smooth his tousled hair, and run her palm over his stubbly cheeks. "Are you all right, Richard?"

His grin was lopsided. "Better than I've ever been. You know, I haven't slept in . . ." He glanced at his watch. "Shoot, I don't even remember anymore."

"Why not?" She was growing more concerned by the minute. What was wrong with him?

"Did you like the rock?" he asked, smiling.

She looked at Kayla, who shrugged and shook her head.

"I love it, Richard. It's incredible and stunning and so generous, but I . . . Richard?"

He was bent over now, opening the flaps of the cardboard box and pulling stuff out of it. Long, slender tubing, and a plastic scuba diver, a miniature oyster shell, some plastic seaweed.

"What *is* all that?" Kayla squeaked.

"It's an aquarium," Richard said. "A big one, with all the trimmings. Top of the line. And I've got a whole boxful of filters and pumps and various other paraphernalia. It's still in the trunk of my car, but—"

"Richard, you're not making any sense here. What is this all about?"

He looked up, met Martha Jane's eyes, and his narrowed as they slid down her, making her feel as if he could see right through her sensible suit. "Kayla," he said, without looking away. "Would you excuse us for a second?"

"Whooo-boy," Kayla said, "I'm outta here. In fact, um, I'm going out to breakfast. I'll be back in . . . an hour?"

"Make it two," Richard said, and his eyes were dark, intense.

Martha Jane shivered when Kayla left and closed the door. He looked dangerous this way. Tired, running on no sleep. Unshaven. His shirt wrinkled. "Richard, what is this all about?"

He shrugged. "You're so good, you know that?"

"What do you mean?" She took a step backward.

He took a step forward. "I mean, you've had me jumping through hoops, you've driven me insane, and you stand here pretending to be . . . innocent. But the jig is up, Valentine. No more games. No more masks."

Blinking rapidly, she whispered, "I don't know what you're talking about."

"Don't you?"

She shook her head.

"Prove it, then."

Her throat went dry. "H-how?"

"Take off the suit, Miss Biswell."

"*What?*"

Smiling, he came closer. She backed away until she hit the desk, and still he came on, until his chest was an inch from hers. "Take it off, Martha Jane. I'm curious to know what you're wearing underneath."

He lifted a hand to her jacket, undid the button, and slid it down her shoulders. She would have resisted had she been capable of it. Instead she froze, because he bent so close that his warm breath fanned her mouth and made her go limp.

Her hands braced on the desk behind her, her blazer pooled around her wrists, she could only stand there as Richard unbuttoned her blouse, one button at a time. "A prim, proper woman like the one you pretend to be would have something boring under here," he murmured. "But you're not all that prim and proper, are you, Miss Biswell?"

"I—"

The blouse unbuttoned, he smiled and pushed it open, staring at the lacy black camisole. "See that?"

"Richard, I—"

"Shhh. I know, you see? I know you didn't mean what you said. You still want me. Don't you?"

Holding his gaze, helpless, she nodded.

"So, let's see what you have on for me today, hmm? What about underneath the skirt? What delicious little fantasy do you have for me down there, Valentine? Hmm?"

She couldn't speak. Without her mask, her boldness was gone.

It didn't matter. He closed his hands on her waist, lifted her until she perched on the edge of the desk, and then dropped to his knees. Before she knew what he was doing, he was lifting her skirt, poking his head right up inside it. "Oh, yeah," he whispered. "No panties at all. You read my mind." His hands shoved her thighs apart, and then he kissed her. She shivered, and threw her head back. He just shoved the skirt up higher and licked at her until she was biting her lip to keep from screaming out loud.

When he finally got to his feet again, it was only to ease her back onto the desk and climb on top of her. He pressed himself inside her, slid his hands underneath to grasp her buttocks and hold her to him as he rode her hard. She clung to him, too swept up in passion to worry about not having her mask anymore. And when her nails dug into his shoulders, and they both climaxed at once, she whispered, "I love you, Richard," in a voice gone hoarse with ecstasy.

He held her for a long time. Then slowly, he got off her and gently righted her clothes. "I haven't slept all weekend. I—you made me crazy, Martha Jane."

Maybe, she thought, he hadn't heard that final stupid declaration. If he had, he would be running for the hills by now. "How long have you known?"

He smiled at her, a lopsided, boyish grin. God, he was too damned good-looking to be going around unshaven and sleepy-eyed. It was killing her! "Did I ever tell you?" he asked. "That I always wanted an aquarium?" He finished buttoning her blouse, but left it untucked. The jacket, he tossed aside. Then he took her hand, drew her to her feet, and knelt down to smooth her skirt, sliding both his palms down over her hips, her thighs, until it was just so.

Breathless, she said, "No, I guess you never did."

"I even bought all the stuff, but I never took the time to set it up or actually start collecting fish." He shrugged, got to his feet, looked into her eyes again. "I think maybe I liked the *idea* of having one, but I was a little bit shy of all the work involved. Major commitment, keeping fish, you know." He shook his head slowly. "You know how funny that is? It's like some kind of microcosmic mirror of what's wrong with me."

"What?"

"Never mind. Suffice it to say, I figured since you wanted an aquarium too, we could make it a . . . joint project."

"You did, did you?"

"Yeah. Oh, don't worry. I promise to do my share of the work. I mean, that's sort of the point."

"It is?"

He nodded. Then, studying her face, he sighed. "Look, I haven't lost my mind or had a breakdown, I swear. I'm running on adrenaline and caffeine here. And I'm a little bit worked up." He slipped his arms around her waist, bent closer to press his lips to the line of her jaw. She wanted to touch him. Hold him. Tell him that whatever had him so worked up, it was going to be okay.

Instead she just nodded slowly. "I don't think you're insane or having a breakdown," she told him.

He nodded at the boxful of fish stuff. "Once we get it set up, maybe we can go shopping for some fish. You know . . . together."

She raised her eyebrows. "You want to take me fish shopping?"

He nodded, his eyes serious. "Among other things."

She was starting to feel a hint of panic in her chest. He mustn't go saying things to make her believe he might want her for more than just sex. He mustn't. She couldn't stand the disappointment if he did.

"What . . . other things?"

Richard seemed genuinely . . . nervous. Rubbing his chin, he walked away from her as if thinking very deeply about his answer. She looked around the office, at the rock, the fish stuff. "Why are you doing all this, Richard?"

He whirled, and came back to her, gripped her shoulders gently. "Because I'm a changed man. Saturday night I learned how it felt to be treated like a piece of meat. How it felt to be told that I was only good for a one-night stand, to be left longing for more from a relationship than I was allowed to want. I didn't like it. I didn't like it a bit, Martha Jane."

"I'm . . . sorry. I didn't realize it would upset you this much. I was only trying to show you—"

"How I'd been making you feel. Right, Martha Jane?"

She turned away from him and walked toward the windows. As she did, she saw something she hadn't noticed before. On the far left wall was a charcoal drawing, framed and hanging in the perfect spot. Only—it was different from the one she'd admired. Same idea, but a whole different style. A different artist. Then it hit her, and her eyes widened.

"Do you like it?" Richard asked, coming up behind her. His hands slid upward, over her shoulders, closing on them, warm and strong.

She stared at the drawing. It was a woman with three faces. And she looked like—she looked like—like *her*. Like Martha Jane. The face shown in right profile wore a mask and her hair was big and fluffy. The one shown in left profile had her hair in a tight bun and wore large glasses. But the one facing front was the most striking, because she was so simply drawn. Hair loose, yes, but hanging gently, not "done." She stood there, looking out from the wall, her eyes soft but large, and deep, and filled with love. She held out one hand, as if reaching for someone.

"It's been a long time since I made an attempt at anything artistic," he said. "But I couldn't resist."

"You . . . *you* did this?"

"Do you hate it?"

"My God, Richard, you made me . . . beautiful."

"You are beautiful," he said. "You're beautiful—even when you cover your face with a mask."

She closed her eyes.

"I knew it was you that first night," he said softly, his lips near her ear.

"You didn't!"

"Oh, yes, I did. And now, I think it's time for you to face me without any masks to hide behind. You said you loved me, Martha Jane. Did you mean it?"

"I—" She turned away, knowing that it had been the worst possible thing to say to a man like Richard. The surest way to make him bolt.

He gently turned her around to face him. "You didn't think I was going to let you turn my world upside down and then just walk away, did you?"

"Richard—Richard, I didn't mean—"

He smiled at her. "I hope you did. Because I am in love with you, Martha Jane. Valentine." He slid his arms around her waist and held her close, so her body was pressed to his. "My brother told me once that every day is Valentine's Day when you find the right woman. I didn't believe him then. But I do now."

"You do?"

"It's been running through my mind all weekend. I couldn't stop it, not by trying to forget you, not by drawing you. I didn't think I wanted . . . this. But it's the only thing I want. I just don't know why it took me so long to realize that I've been head over heels for my prim little Miss Biswell for months but was too damned dense to admit it. That's why I've been so depressed and moody and bored since you left, Martha Jane. I was missing you."

"You were?" She blinked up at him, then shook her head, terrified that this was all a mistake. An infatuation. He would change his mind in a week or a month and leave her devastated. "Richard, you're tired and confused and—"

"You going to make me beg? Fine, I'll beg." He dropped to his knees. She closed her eyes, and he took her hand, sat back a little, looked up at her. "I can be what you want," he said softly. "Solid, stable . . . I swear to God I can."

"I don't know if I can be what *you* want," she whispered.

"Martha Jane, you already are. You have been all along. You're what I was looking for in all those other women and not finding."

"I am?"

He nodded, then smiled slightly. "It's not entirely my fault, you know. You were hiding yourself from me awfully well."

She lowered her eyelids. "I didn't think I stood a chance beside the bombshells waiting in line for you."

"There won't be any more bombshells, sweetie. You nuked me for all the rest. I only want you."

Finally, she met his eyes, held them. "Do you mean that, Richard? Because I couldn't take being just one of your flings."

"Then don't be," he said. "Be . . . be my wife instead."

She smiled very slowly. "Richard . . . ?"

But he was already pulling the ring from his pocket, slipping it on her finger, pressing his lips there to seal his promise. "I mean it," he told her. "I want you to marry me. I want to love you every night, whether you're wearing a negligee or flannel pajamas. I mean it. I honestly mean it, Martha Jane."

Blinking back her tears, Martha Jane sank to her knees and into Richard's waiting arms. "I love you," she whispered. "I've loved you all along."

"Is that a yes?"

"Yes, Richard," she said. "Yes."

He sighed as if he'd been holding his breath, clasped her tight to him, and rose to his feet, picking her right up off hers. "I love you, Martha Jane!" he shouted. "You really are the best Valentine I ever got."